P9-DNT-216

THE LIGHTEST OBJECT IN THE UNIVERSE

THE LIGHTEST OBJECT IN THE UNIVERSE

a novel by

Kimi Eisele

ALGONQUIN BOOKS OF CHAPEL HILL 2019

Published by
Algonquin Books of Chapel Hill
Post Office Box 2225
Chapel Hill, North Carolina 27515-2225

a division of
Workman Publishing
225 Varick Street
New York, New York 10014

Printed in the United States of America.
Published simultaneously in Canada by Thomas Allen & Son Limited.
Design by Steve Godwin.

LIBRARY OF CONGRESS CATALOGING-IN-PUBLICATION DATA
Names: Eisele, Kimi, author.
Title: The lightest object in the universe : a novel / by Kimi Eisele.
Description: First edition. | Chapel Hill, North Carolina :
Algonquin Books of Chapel Hill, 2019.
Identifiers: LCCN 2018038000 | ISBN 9781616207939 (hardcover : alk. paper)
Classification: LCC PS3605.I8255 L54 2019 | DDC 813/.6—dc23
LC record available at https://lccn.loc.gov/2018038000

10 9 8 7 6 5 4 3 2 1
First Edition

For my parents, Tura and Fred,
and for all the hearts that mourn and yearn

Everybody woke up the next morning and everything was different. . . . There was no electricity, all the stores were closed, no one had access to media. The consequence was that everyone poured out into the street to bear witness. Not quite a street party, but everyone out at once—it was a sense of happiness to see everybody even though we didn't know each other.

—Resident of Halifax, Nova Scotia, after an October 2003 hurricane, from Rebecca Solnit's *A Paradise Built in Hell*

If the mental environment we live in has a single distinctive feature, the way that oxygen defines our atmosphere, it is self-absorption. . . . Some years ago, working on a book, I watched every word and image that came across the largest cable system in the world in a 24-hour period—more than 2,000 hours of ads and infomercials, music videos and sitcoms. If you boiled this stew down to its basic ingredient, this is what you found, repeated ad infinitum: You are the most important thing on earth, the heaviest object in the universe.

—Bill McKibben, "The Mental Environment," *Adbusters* 38, November/December 2001

THE LIGHTEST OBJECT IN THE UNIVERSE

PROLOGUE

THIRTEEN DAYS INTO the second month of the year, the lights began to go out. Which is to say that the power grid died. In some places, the darkness came suddenly, an abrupt and violent nightfall. Elsewhere, it pulsed intermittently—like the wings of an injured bird—until finally landing for good. Everyone pressed the buttons and switches they were accustomed to pressing, but nothing happened. No light beams radiated across the room, no sound surged through the speakers, no hum or whir or tick emerged from the hard drives. The switches simply did not switch anything.

Though no network television or internet news could report the blackout, the word "cyberattack" started making its way across the landscape. But no one could say with certainty who its perpetrators were. Many assumed it was the work of the crescendoing jihad in one of the misunderstood countries to the east. Some presumed a coalition of domestic anarchists had done it, a final act of liberation. Others believed those "anarchists" had been hired as professional agitators by the government. Some said it was a superworm gone rogue.

The darkness was the final stroke in a series of blows that had pushed the world to its knees. In a system of uneven distribution, where "debt" was a word without consequence, only so much teetering was possible before the party ended. The companies that were too big to fail failed. The oil supply chain broke after a series of terrorist attacks halted extraction. Fuel costs rose by 200 percent. In the United States, young people who'd been sold a future they couldn't afford defaulted on student loans. All these events precipitated the October Shocks, when the dollar fell by more than 40 percent, forcing the government to print more bills—so many bills that kids needed backpacks to haul around their lunch money. Then the rest of the public utilities went. Then the companies that had scrambled to stand in for the public utilities went. The government shut down, and no one could bail it out.

Meanwhile, the flu swept across the globe like a wind, extinguishing hundreds of thousands of people. A potent strain, it came on like a cold but burned up its victims with fever and drowned their lungs. Those who'd caught earlier, milder strains were fortunate in their resistance but were left to deal with the dead.

Nature continued to exact her own revenge. Torrential rains led to floods that swallowed bayous and bog towns. Forest fires, now unstoppable, swept across the West.

Onto the topography of change and despair came the darkness. There were neither prescriptions nor predictions. Grief and pain could make you either cruel or generous; the only common denominator was loss.

While changes circumnavigated the globe, they were noticed particularly in the country that had for so long perceived itself as the center of the universe, due to its wealth and style and the ever-burning beacon it offered for those living in places arguably darker and poorer and seemingly more precarious. It wasn't just electrical power that they'd lost, but purchasing power. No more caffe lattes with scones. No more handheld i-thingies. No more tanks full of gas. And no more personal power: the bold bravado, the unwavering invincibility, the belief that they would always be on top, delivered from despair—because delivery was what they knew and delivery was what they believed they were entitled to.

People stood wide-eyed, surprised by sounds that suddenly seemed to fill the silence: birdsong, wind, heartbeats, their own breath. Amidst their fear that everything they knew was ending, they saw that some things remained constant. One such thing was the sun, which continued its arc over the edge of the world, marking the days one by one, oblivious to their particulars but illuminating them all the same.

PART ONE

Darkness

CHAPTER 1

At the end of a long and narrow street not far from the sea, right around the time of the spring equinox, the sun rose as a sliver between two skyscrapers. Carson Waller could see it if he stepped out onto the tiny balcony of his apartment at precisely the right time. One morning in mid-March, he woke just as the light was shifting, the beige color of his bedroom walls warming to yellow. Time to rise. To admire the light and to tend to the tasks of this strange new life: fill water buckets, forage for food, track down supplies. In a few days, he'd leave this apartment—this whole city—behind.

He rolled onto his back and exhaled. The inhale came of its own accord and, with it, a surprising and fragrant tang. Sweetness. The smell was unmistakable. Citrus. Oranges. How was that possible here, right now, near the end of winter? He breathed in again. There it was.

He thought immediately of Beatrix. Her smile, her auburn hair, her hands, the sound of her voice. Closing his eyes, he inhaled again and imagined her next to him, the weight and warmth of her almost real.

He lay still. The cold morning fell over him. When he opened his eyes, the light had shifted and the smell of oranges was gone. All that remained was a cavern inside his chest.

Shivering from the cold, he dressed and went to the bathroom sink, where he scooped enough water from a bucket into his hands to rinse them. Since the rooftop cisterns had emptied, he'd been hauling water up from the street.

He toasted two pieces of stale bread over the gas flame of the stove. Another temporary luxury. It would probably go soon as well. He sprinkled some salt over the dry toast, cut up a mushy apple, and carried his breakfast into the living room.

From the window, he could see the vendors below setting out their goods on the sidewalk. This was part of the adaptation: you could simplify and run to the country, or you could buy and trade and sell. The marketplace was immortal, but it, too, had changed. Now the collections were random and personal, spread across blankets on the ground. Coffee makers, monogrammed towels, heirloom tea sets, little motors that no longer turned, tangles of useless electrical cords. Even a good find carried a certain bitter aftertaste. And yet there was no telling what might become suddenly useful. An extension cord made for a fine clothesline. Large Tupperware storage bins could hold gallons of water.

He held binoculars to his eyes. One of the vendors was on all fours, reaching across the blanket to arrange pots and dishes and utensils into tidy rows. She was portly and blond and encumbered by a long, heavy coat. A small dog curled up near her feet. She placed clothing into piles and arranged books by color. At the far corner of the blanket, she'd put the things not easy to categorize—a game of Trivial Pursuit, a stack of file folders, a computer keyboard.

A bulky man in a leather jacket moved swiftly along the sidewalk, and Carson tracked him through the binoculars. It was Ayo, one of his building's doormen, before the layoffs six months ago.

Ayo, a Nigerian, had immigrated to the States with his wife nearly a decade ago. He was an educated man, once a student activist. "It is not always a good idea to advertise one's political ideas, but sometimes it is necessary," he once said.

Carson had crossed paths with Ayo a few weeks ago on the street—the first time he'd seen him since the layoffs.

"Mr. Principal!" Ayo had called out from half a block away. "It's you! I thought maybe you had dissolved in a solution of vinegar. You are holed up in your apartment like a mouse?"

"I have not dissolved, no," Carson had said, smiling. "It is nice to see you, Ayo."

"Every day is a blessing, yes," Ayo had said.

Ayo was a hustler now, with access to the new black market, where he could get soap, butter, coffee, meat, flour, batteries, fuel, and almost anything else. "Run by Africans," he had explained that day. "That is why they call it the '*black* market,' sir. We Africans are quite adept at adversity. Or maybe, sir, because we are such good con artists." He had laughed and jabbed an elbow into Carson's ribs.

With the supermarkets stripped and dark, it was a lucky and necessary thing to have a supply man. The shipping containers had become bloated whales stuck up on the sand. It was vendors like Ayo who kept people fed, rolling shopping carts up and down the streets, selling canned beans and stale rice they'd hoarded, or vegetables they'd somehow grown or gleaned from farms outside the city.

Carson tracked Ayo from the window, watching him flow down the sidewalk.

On the other side of the country, in the back of a wagon, Beatrix Banks felt as if she were on a choppy sea, as if all she had to do was yield to circumstance. But what circumstance was this? No metro rail to shuttle her through the city and over the bay; instead, horses. When she'd left the US nearly two months earlier, no one had yet thought to attach a horse to a cart and haul passengers around. At this moment, despite the bumpy ride, she was grateful someone had.

Exhausted and disoriented, Beatrix dug in her backpack for her cell phone. She should call her housemates, Hank and Dolores, tell them she was on her way. But the phone, of course, had been dead for weeks. She held it in both hands, like a fragile, lifeless bird.

Across from her in the wagon, a woman, about fifty, wrapped in a purple shawl, gave Beatrix a sympathetic frown.

"You can kiss that phone goodbye," said a man next to her. He coughed once, and Beatrix stiffened. Was there still flu here?

"No phone service at all? Landlines?" she asked, inching away from the man.

"Only if you're willing to saw off an arm and a leg," the woman in purple said.

There was some murmuring among the other passengers about radio communication and solar power. "What about the almighty generator that preacher uses?" someone said.

Beatrix put her phone back.

She watched the sun inch higher into the sky. Things here had unraveled quickly. No more phone service. Intermittent power. Horses on the highway. She felt panic rise inside. Just get me to my people, she thought.

The wagon dropped Beatrix a few blocks from home, and as the sound of the horse hooves receded into the distance, she felt herself relax a little. Despite her fatigue, she walked quickly. Her house glimmered like a beacon, sunlight bouncing off the windows and warming the front porch. Beatrix headed up the walkway just as a tall man with shaggy hair came out the front door carrying a bicycle. Her downstairs neighbor—Joe, was it?

It took a moment before he recognized her. "You're back. Where were you?"

"Mexico City," she told him. "A fair-trade convention. Or what was supposed to be a fair-trade convention." It dawned on her that what she'd maneuvered—flying south across the border in the midst of a global meltdown—was more of a miracle than she'd realized.

"That was brave of you," he said.

"Or just dumb."

He looked up from the bicycle and held out his hand. "Beatrice, right? I'm Dragon."

"Beatrix, with an *x*," she said.

"So how did you get home?"

"A complicated hitchhike," she said, explaining how the airlines had folded, and then the bus lines, and how what was supposed to be a ten-day trip had turned into six weeks, until she'd finally found a cargo trucker with enough room, fuel, and business smarts to transport her, along with a tired diplomat and a handful of US soldiers, to Tijuana. "As soon as we crossed the border, they all knelt to kiss the fucking pavement."

"Well, that was lucky," he said.

Beatrix nodded, feeling grateful. "Isn't your name Joe?"

"Yeah, formally. I go by Dragon now. A resurrected nickname. Fiercer, I guess," he said, lifting one of his eyebrows and making it disappear behind a dark curl on his head.

She had the urge to pull him into a hug. But they barely knew each other. "It is good to be home," she conceded, picking up her backpack.

"You know they're gone, right?" he said as she started up the stairs. "Your roommates."

"Hank and Dolores? What do you mean?"

"Yeah. They went north."

"North?" Beatrix said, feeling like she'd just been punched in the stomach.

"A whole group went together," Dragon said. "They loaded all their stuff into a wagon and headed toward wine country. More fertile, I guess." He scoffed a little as he said this, then shrugged.

"What? You don't think it's safe?" Beatrix asked. "I mean, if everyone's going."

"If everyone were jumping off a bridge, would you?"

"So you don't think it's a good idea. To go north."

"I just told you what I thought," he said, and turned back to his bicycle.

Beatrix went upstairs, the punch to her stomach now a grip in her chest.

Maybe everything had been a bad idea. The going away and the coming home. All of it. Everyone had advised against the trip in the first place, but the convention had been the perfect opportunity to strengthen the chocolate market in Ecuador, which she'd been working on for the last three years, a time for coalition building with cooperatives in Mexico and Central America. She hadn't even considered that the other twenty delegates might not be able to get there.

She'd felt a clinging obligation to keep up the fight, even though clearly the fight for fair trade had dramatically shifted by then, if not altogether dissolved. The walls Beatrix and her colleagues had worked so desperately for years to tear down had toppled under their own weight.

But there were larger lessons to be learned from their friends in the Southern Hemisphere. They knew what it was like when the cost of milk and corn and movies and everything else skyrocketed, when all the gold flew out of the country and into a secure Swiss bank, when you had to live off very little. "At the very least, they can show us how to prepare for the worst," Beatrix had said.

Now, she felt a sense of relief entering the apartment. Home. Her belongings gave her a measure of comfort. The artifacts from her travels: The balsa wood toucan from Ecuador. Some pre-Columbian pottery replicas. A contemporary mask from Guinea, West Africa. The photographs: Beatrix at a protest in São Paulo. Hank and Dolores in Chapultepec Park. Beatrix on the Fourth of July in a T-shirt that said INDEPENDENCE, MY ASS!

Beatrix found a note from Dolores on the kitchen counter:

Beatrix, love, if you are reading this, then you're finally home. We've been so worried. We're closing down the office and getting out of here before something even more terrible happens. We've waited for word from you, but nothing. We found a place. Brightbrook Farms. 150 miles northeast of the capital. I don't have directions. You're good at that. Come as soon as you can. Please come, B. We'll be waiting for you. We love you.

—Dolores and Hank

Beatrix had met Hank in a college course on modern Latin American history. Beatrix and Hank had believed that the world, particularly America, needed a new revolution. Something to cauterize consumer greed, expose the true cost of goods, even out global trade imbalances. After class, at a bar, they had planned their first action—a zombie parade.

"But there already is a zombie parade," Beatrix had said, remembering the red paint smeared across mouths and hands, the stiff-legged walk, the raggedy clothes she'd seen the previous Halloween.

"This is different. These will be zombie shoppers, zombie consumers, zombie numb-heads," Hank said. "Just in time for the Christmas season. We'll get a bunch of TVs and line them up all along the campus mall. Then we'll sit there and stare at them, just like real people do."

Students from all across campus had joined the parade. They'd made the front page of the student newspaper, the clearest mark of success back then. The year after they graduated, they met Dolores, an activist who led "reality tours" along the US-Mexico border, where she set up interviews with factory workers, then pointed to the shacks on the hillside, the chemical sludge running in the wash. "Free trade hasn't meant frijoles in these parts," she'd said. In Dolores, Beatrix had found a friend, and Hank had found a lover, and the three of them had taken on the world.

Now, Beatrix stood alone in the middle of their apartment, her heart beating too fast. She read the note three more times before dropping it on the counter. *What the fuck, people?* They'd abandoned her for some hippie farm? She wished she'd never come back.

Trembling, she opened the fridge, and a warm and horrific odor wafted out. Nothing was salvageable. In the pantry, she found two cans of beans, a half-emptied bag of rice, a jar of lentils, and—thank the Lord—a healthy stash of *yerba mate*, her favorite morning beverage, courtesy of some Argentine friends. She tried the stove, but there was no hiss of gas.

She went to her bedroom, which looked different somehow—out of proportion or as if someone had come in and redecorated in her absence. But nothing had changed. Her bed hadn't moved, nor the framed photo on her dresser of her and Hank in their senior year of college, each raising a beer bottle and a fist. The desk was in the corner, her laptop where she'd left it.

Her heart jumped. There must be email from Carson. They'd been calling and texting and emailing for nearly a year. She ached to hear from him.

When his school had closed after the government shutdown, he'd written: *I'm concerned for King High. For all the schools actually. Mostly for the students. I feel like Victor Jara, with his broken hands.*

Yes, Beatrix had thought. Like Víctor Jara.

In the last email, Carson had said, *If for some reason everything implodes and the shit really hits the fan and we can no longer send words or speak to each other, I'll come find you.*

Had he meant it?

She opened the laptop. Its dead gray screen stared back at her.

From the closet, Carson unearthed his old camping gear, pleased with himself for having kept it all these years. He packed sleeping gear in the backpack, a few items of clothing, a tent, a water filter, a small axe, a cook pot, matches. In the top pouch, he put a pocketknife, three notebooks, a bundle of pencils, and the *Field Guide to the*

Edible Plants of North America. A few more things from Ayo, and he'd be ready.

Carson thought about the word "ready" and how far from it he felt, even with a small axe in his pack. Nothing was predictable. Who could ever be ready? And ready for what?

He thought about how it might be explained one day. He thought of the corncobs in Chaco Canyon. The purple robes of the Phoenicians. The Egyptian tombs. The Mayan pyramids. The moai of Easter Island. Athens and Rome and Pompeii. The Reichstag. Britain and Spain. Potsherds and buried churches, catacombs and notched bones. Here, too, there would be a history to interpret, an arc of demise to be charted.

He had begun to record his observations.

Buckets of water on the roof, peddlers with megaphones in the streets, candlelight. The city returns to its origins.

MacGyverize: to fix a thing with whatever you have, after that late-'80s television show.

What happens when the last of the canned beans is eaten?

He did not know if the notes would amount to anything. Maybe decades in the future, they'd find his words, and history teachers would assign it as reading to their students.

During Carson's early teaching years, his students had flashed gang signs and symbols at one another, instantly reinterpreting the histories he taught them. At twenty-five, residually adolescent himself, he studied their codes. He was hungry to learn, and they offered him plenty. Later, as principal, he tried to impart this kind of curiosity to other teachers; so many of them just hauled around a textbook, regurgitated the same lessons year after year, presented themselves as the exclusive holders of knowledge. No wonder so many kids didn't give a shit.

His final moments at King High School haunted him. The afternoon light angling through the windows of the west-wing classrooms, the empty hallways, the flutter of discarded papers across the floor.

In a perfect world, the public schools would have been the priority, Carson believed, not the sacrificial lambs. Closing them hadn't done a thing to save government expenditures. And what did any of it matter? Three months later, they'd been plunged into darkness.

Ever since then, protesters had gathered at the city water plant and the phone companies, outraged about the lack of access, the deadness of the internet and cell phones. Just the other day, a teenager had hurled a concrete block and hit a fellow protester. Someone threw a rock back in retaliation, and the protest turned on itself. Six people were killed; thirty or more, injured. People seemed unwilling to accept that the companies had gone belly-up and the executives had fled. There was no one left to protest against.

Beatrix would have disagreed with him on this. "Protests matter," she would have said. "People need to act." But maybe she'd be irritated, too, by what it had taken to make people pay attention. In any case, protesting was preferable to hopelessness.

He opened a window, and the smell of smoke infused the room. Outside, the new homeless—the transient—lit fires on sidewalks and in parks, to keep warm, to cook. It was hard to believe life in the city could be any more public than it had once been. But it seemed every act imaginable now played out on the streets. A woman in pajamas sat on the curb and brushed her hair. A man knelt down on the sidewalk to wipe his baby's bottom with a newspaper. Another man propped a mirror on a park bench and shaved, a small cup of water his sink.

Carson watched a man standing at the blond woman's blanket, pointing to something round and red, with patches of yellow. Some kind of toy. Maybe a gift for a child? The woman held it up like a question, but the man shook his head and moved on. The woman tucked the object under her elbow and watched the man walk away. Carson could not see her face, but from the way she held her body, he could read this woman's sorrow. Her grief reached thirteen stories up.

BEATRIX TURNED ON the bathroom faucet, and a trickle of rust-red water sputtered into the sink. Unmoved, she splashed some of it onto her face, then tried the bathtub faucet. More sputtering. Not wanting to waste one drop, she plugged the drain and let the tap run. She rushed to the kitchen and put a pot in the sink to catch more there. Was this really happening? Of course, she knew this dance well from Ecuador, where water would come and go all the time. But here?

Anxious, she made her way downstairs. Maybe Dragon would know more.

She found his door open and him sitting on the floor cross-legged, eyes closed. How was it possible that he could be so calm?

"It's okay," he said, obviously sensing her there. He pressed his palms together, bowed forward, and opened his eyes. "I'm done."

She looked around his apartment, mostly empty but for an upended bicycle in the middle of the floor and tools scattered around it. More bicycles leaned against the far wall. "You fix bikes?" she asked.

"Make 'em, fix 'em, sell 'em."

"Good skill to have at the end of the world," she said.

"While the rubber lasts, at least."

Beatrix asked about the water, and he told her about the water trucks. "We're lucky. Some of them don't cross the bay because of thugs. There are buckets and jugs under the stairs, but if you come across any more, nab them."

Beatrix nodded. She'd taken her share of bucket baths.

"Oh, we've rigged up a solar shower in the backyard, which you're welcome to use if you help haul water."

"Thanks. I was also wondering about the flu," Beatrix said, nervous about his response.

"Hasn't been any since the first spell. But you never know."

"No, you don't." She pulled Dolores's note out of her pocket. "Brightbrook Farms. Does that ring a bell?"

Dragon held one edge of the paper, his hands black with bike grease. “Nope. But a hundred and fifty miles is really far.”

Voices came from the front hallway. An older woman wearing a cardigan and sneakers appeared, followed by a teenaged girl in a short denim skirt.

“Maria del Carmen and Rosie, grandmother and granddaughter,” Dragon said quietly. “They live there.” He pointed to the door across the hall. Beatrix remembered that a hefty man who always wore too-tight suits had lived there. Did he still?

The girl stopped in the doorway. “Hi,” she said. A fleet of brass bracelets around her arm jingled as she placed her hand on her hip. She looked about seventeen.

Behind her in the hallway, the grandmother called, “Rosie, come help me.”

The girl turned, and they disappeared inside.

“Maria del Carmen cleaned for the guy who lived there,” Dragon explained. “He left right before your friends did. She and Rosie were living in their car, so I told them they could stay there.”

“That was nice of you,” Beatrix said.

“My dad owns this place, but I haven’t heard from him in a long time. No big loss. My friend Flash lives here, too.”

“Flash? Dragon? What is this, a superhero headquarters?”

Dragon chuckled. “I’m only thirty-three. Never too old for superheroes,” he said.

The girl, Rosie, returned holding something wrapped in a towel. “My abuela’s not feeling well. She’s all out of her anxiety tincture.” She put a finger on the side of her forehead. To Beatrix, she said, “Who are you? I’ve never seen you before.”

The girl had one brown eye and one blue eye, and Beatrix wasn’t sure which one to look at. “I’m away a lot,” she said.

“What about the couple that lived there before?”

“They left, apparently,” Beatrix said.

"Rosie!" the grandmother called.

Rosie shook her arm, making the bracelets chime, and turned her head slowly toward the door, as if in defiance. "I gotta go," she said. She handed the towel package to Dragon. "These are for you."

"Thank you," he called after her. He unwrapped it to reveal a stack of flour tortillas. He peeled off half and handed the rest to Beatrix.

"Seriously?" Beatrix said, equally astounded by Dragon's generosity and the reality of the tortillas now in her hand. "She makes these?"

Dragon folded one into his mouth and nodded. "The grandmother does. She worked at a bakery, and when it went under, her boss paid her retirement package in flour. Bags of it," Dragon said. He explained that recently a butcher had been coming into the neighborhood on horseback selling packets of lard, which meant she could make tortillas, by the dozens. "She's a little nervous, but she'll warm up to you. And Rosie only has attitude around her grandma. She's a softie, and pretty naive. She looks older than she is. She just turned fifteen."

Dragon wiped his hands on his jeans. "Here, follow me." He led her down the common hallway and out to the backyard, where there was a picnic table, a beat-up countertop with a faucetless stainless-steel sink, and a set of wire shelves that held a mishmash of pots and dishes. Nearby was a fire pit.

"We've been cooking here," Dragon said. "We share food. Mostly I find it, and Maria del Carmen cooks it. Protein is hard to come by, though we caught a pigeon last week. At the moment, we have firewood, but please be sparing with it. You're welcome to share with us, if you contribute."

"Great," Beatrix said, thinking for a moment of the rabbits and guinea pigs people raised in the Andes. Surely that was doable here, too. But she wouldn't be staying long. "Thank you, but—"

"You have a bike? You'll need one. Let's find one that fits you." Dragon gestured to a small fleet of bicycles parked under a ramada, then undid a combination lock and freed a long cable from the stack. He pulled out a red bike with a large wire basket at the handlebars. Beatrix sat on the seat and rang the bell. A lightness came over her.

"Looks like a fit. Just be sure to always keep it locked up," Dragon said. "And I wouldn't do anything crazy like cross the bay. It's not safe. Just stick around here. And try not to go out alone."

Beatrix nodded. Right. Shit. How was she going to get out of Dodge?

"So, I gotta run," Dragon said. "But I'll see you later, yes?"

"Yes," Beatrix said, wishing he wouldn't go anywhere just yet. She returned the bike to its place, locked it up, and went back upstairs. She ate a tortilla and tacked the note from Hank and Dolores onto the fridge next to a photo of Carson—a snapshot he'd sent her of him on a trail in the Grand Canyon under a purple-orange sky, taken long before she knew him. She paused at his wide smile, then went to her bedroom.

She opened the drawer of her nightstand and pulled out a small velvet pouch. Inside was a coin. *I mutilated a quarter for you*, Carson had written when he'd sent it to her. They'd thought they were so clever: a small puncture into the madness of consumption, a little "fuck you" to the system. It was also a reference to that funny restaurant they'd gone to together—Diner/Bar, either a diner or a bar, depending on where you sat. They ate waffles on one side, then drank beer on the other, where there was an old-fashioned photo booth. They'd squeezed into it together, but they'd been short a quarter and had to beg one off a guy at the bar.

Beatrix shook two photos out of the pouch. In one, she pretended to pick her nose while Carson held his hand over his eyes. In the other, both of them stared deadpan into the camera. She held the photo up close. His physicality enchanted her. His round gray-green eyes, his large hands, his rosy cheeks. The way his tall body moved with an adept and virile grace.

Also in the pouch was a thin leather cord. Beatrix threaded it through the hole in the quarter and strung it around her neck. She lay back on her bed, the pendant resting perfectly in the space in the middle of her collarbone. She tried to empty her head of thoughts, but there was too much swirl. Alone. No water. The power's gone for good. What am I going to do?

March 15

Dear Carson,

For all practical purposes, you have disappeared. I am a wayward Dorothy. The speed of this collapse astounds me. I guess I, too, believed in some kind of American exceptionalism, though I resented it enough to think I could destroy it. Now look. Maybe we did.

Someone knocked at the door. The girl from downstairs, Rosie. Her two-colored eyes showed worry.

"It's my abuela!" Rosie said. "She can't breathe."

SPILLING DOWN THE stairwell of Carson's apartment building were fruit pits and peels, shriveled tea bags, empty cat-food cans, and a small pile of bones (chicken? squirrel?). He'd been stepping over the trash for weeks, but today he gathered up a bagful. Amidst the refuse, he found a small plastic bottle of hand lotion. He opened it, sniffed, and coughed at the overpowering chemical scent. But he tucked the bottle into his pocket anyway, then picked up the bag of trash and made his way out of the building.

He dropped the trash bag on the corner next to others and questioned for a moment the benevolence of his service. Then he walked half a block away to where the air smelled cleaner. Like spring. His wife, June, used to call it a "delicious nonsmell smell" when the snow began to melt. It matched the sound of falling snow, she said, a kind of whisper within the silence. And the sound of snow melting? June said that within it, you could hear the tinny sound of a miniature orchestra.

"Come on, motherfucker!" A man in a bomber jacket shouted at a large Buick town car. He and three other men were rocking the car violently in attempt to move it from the thoroughfare.

"That's it, that's it," the man said. Metal clanged against the chassis, and each time the car landed, Carson thought it might simply break in half.

"Give a hand?" one of the men called out.

Carson approached, and they made room for him at the back bumper.

"Like a seesaw," one of them instructed.

Carson could feel the muscles working in his shoulders and back; his solid legs held the ground. He felt strong and useful. At the end of the world, men could still move cars.

Carson wiped the sweat from his forehead onto his pants as a sand-colored dog with wiry fur yipped at him. The blond vendor with the long, heavy coat whistled, and the dog pranced back to her. Carson followed and stood at the edge of her blanket, still trying to understand the logic in her spread of items.

"I got everything you need but a car," the woman said.

"Not sure I'd get very far," Carson said, gesturing to the one he had just helped move. He perused her items, looking for candles, batteries, anything useful. There was the red-and-yellow toy, which he now saw was a piggy bank.

"What's the story with that?"

The woman stood up, and he noticed her hefty boots—rubber-toed and fur-lined, the kind June used to wear on walks in the field. "Why is everyone interested in this thing?" she said. "It's my piggy bank from when I was a little girl. And then it was my kid's after that. My son. He got the flu." She looked away then.

"I'm so sorry," Carson said.

The woman looked back to him blankly. "There's a Kennedy coin in there. From my grandfather. I can't get it out. Got all the other coins out, but not that one. Dunno how I even got it in."

A man at the next blanket called out, "Lady, get your dog!" The dog had wandered over and was sniffing the man's lunch.

"Lola, get back here!" She turned to Carson. "You want this or not?"

"Okay," he said, not exactly sure why.

He put his hand in his pocket and found the bottle of lotion. "Would this do it?" he said.

"Hand lotion? Dear God, yes." She took the bottle, opened it, and lathered up her hands. Carson held back a cough.

"Take the piggy bank," she said. The dog barked. "Lola says, 'Thank you.'"

June would have approved, Carson thought. June. She would have liked this kitschy vintage thing.

He held up the piggy bank, noticed its exaggerated snout, the painted black circles for nostrils, the bulging yellow eyes. *Chump*, it seemed to say.

Carson shook it, and the coin rattled. A mourning landed in his chest. He found a bench and sat down. After June's death, he thought he might simply disintegrate, shatter into fine particles and blow away over the fields behind their house, blurring the sky. But it had been June who became fine dust, who floated up over the fields.

A voice rolled over him, melodious. "Good afternoon, sir. Are you contemplating the fall of the Benin Empire? And what is that in your hand?" Ayo was standing next to him, pointing to the piggy bank.

"She needed a sale," Carson said, gesturing down the street toward the vendor.

Ayo laughed. "Americans are crazy. Why do you buy such unnecessary things?" He took the piggy bank and shook it. "Ahh, yes. It contains money. You are smarter than you look. Or maybe this is your Eshu," he said, handing back the bank. He let out a loud laugh. "Maybe you can rub that three times and disappear."

When he was a doorman, sometimes Ayo would open the door and say, "Eshu is with you." They hadn't discussed it, but Carson had looked up the meaning of the Yoruba word: "god of the crossroads."

"I'm surprised you are still here, my friend," Ayo said. "Things are developing quickly. You know history. You know what happens." He leaned in close and took Carson by the arm. His grip was firm and earnest. "You do know, don't you, sir?"

Carson nodded. Hunger, a rising level of desperation, fires, riots, raids, guns.

"You just tell me what you need," Ayo said.

"A windup flashlight, iodine tablets, duct tape," Carson said. "That's what I need."

"You got it. Tomorrow," Ayo said, nodding goodbye.

Carson sat alone a little longer. Someone shouted. Then again. The vendors scrambled to wrap up their items, then scattered. A blur of a body rushed past him. Carson crouched behind a concrete planter.

"No! Please!" a voice cried. The vendor who'd sold him the piggy bank was clutching her dog in one arm, a stack of dishes in the other. A man inched toward her holding up a knife.

"Hey!" Carson shouted in his deepest, loudest voice. The dishes slipped out of the woman's grip, hit the sidewalk, and shattered. Startled, the man ran away.

Carson hurried toward home. A boy on a bicycle passed by, swerving slalom-like between the stalled-out cars. He was more than a boy—a teenager, delighting in his speed.

The boy hopped off the bicycle near the entrance to Carson's building. "Can you help me out with something?" the boy said, wiping his forehead. "A delivery." He'd forgotten his lock, he said, and couldn't leave the bike or it would be stolen.

"What, pizza?" Carson said.

The boy pulled an envelope out of a canvas bag. "A letter. Miss Deepika Mukherjee. Apartment six-oh-two," he said, reading the address.

"Oh, are you the new mailman?"

"Can you do it or not?" the boy said, impatient.

Carson looked at the kid, who easily could have been a King High student: the baseball cap, the fidgeting, the slight attitude. Maybe Salvadoran or Guatemalan, given the shiny black hair and wide cheekbones.

Carson took the envelope. On the back were several inked thumbprints. No return address was on the front. "Where else do you deliver? How far away?"

"Just in the city. But there are other riders. Coast to coast, supposedly. No guarantees, of course. This is a new day."

Carson paused, thinking. "If I had a letter to send, where would I find you?"

"Around. This is my circuit." The boy was maneuvering the bike away now, standing on the pedals. "You know Rocco's Café? On Trinity Avenue? I'm on the second floor, but there's a bell at street level. Ring it." He pedaled, and the bike rolled away. "I'm Jairo," he shouted, speeding off.

The sixth floor smelled like curry, and the door to 602 was open, which meant Carson could not just slip the letter underneath it. Inside were women. Indian women. Mothers and daughters, a grandmother, maybe a great-grandmother. Saris hung about the room, and the smell of laundry detergent mingled with the curry.

Carson held up the letter, and a woman with a baby on her hip came to him. She turned to the others and, showing them the letter, began to cry. The women erupted, laughing and hugging. One of the women brought Carson a bowl of rice covered with thick orange sauce. He backed away, but the women made insistent gestures: "Stay. Eat."

It was tangy and creamy. He had not tasted such spices in months. Behind the sound of the women, a man's voice came from a small windup radio. It was a voice too promising for news, too persuasive. Carson caught something about holy sites.

He returned to his apartment feeling lighter. The women had reminded him a little of his sister and her friends when they were younger. The way they had laughed. His sister lived upstate now, with her husband and children, closer to Dad. After Mom died, Dad had gone downhill fast. They'd moved him to assisted living—was he there still? What would he possibly make of this? Nothing. He need not make anything of it. His mind was already gone, his brain addled with perforations. History erased. Carson had not spoken to his sister since the phones went out. Should he go there?

His mind went then to Beatrix—the slight crack of her voice, her unruly hair, her earthy, citrus smell. Had they really spent only thirty hours together?

He sat in the living room and opened his notebook. He imagined the paper in front of him in an envelope in the kid's courier bag, then in someone else's bag, and again, until eventually it landed in Beatrix's hands.

March 15

B.,

Remember when I'd type and hear back from you within moments? Our words flew through cyberspace, landing perfectly on the screen in front of us.

I still write to you all the time. I am making hard choices.

The sky darkened, but every now and then, light flashed, shadows moved. On a rooftop across the street, pigeons wandered and pecked, until eventually they merged with the gray dusk.

When the night arrived, Carson looked from the window up toward the sky. So many stars. And the Milky Way, a thick, bright band of dust, clear as ever, now that the power was out.

Inside, the piggy bank mocked him from the dining room table, its oversized yellow eyes catching the flickering candlelight. He retrieved it and shook it. The single coin made a dull clink inside. He tossed the bank on the floor, where it rolled but did not break. He picked it up again, this time slamming it to the floor. The shattering satisfied him.

He sifted through the pieces to find the Kennedy coin: 1976. He remembered the last message he'd sent to Beatrix, saying if it came to this, he'd go find her.

Heads, west. Tails, south. He tossed the coin into the air. Tails. He stared at the coin. No.

He flipped again. Heads. Yes. Yes.

CHAPTER 2

Rosie sat at the dining room table and fiddled with the seven bracelets around her arm. She was trying to do the special trick she'd invented, which required balancing all of the bracelets upright on the table and moving her forearm through them without knocking them over. A caterpillar wriggling inside a brass cocoon. And then her hand opening and closing—the butterfly emerging!

She felt momentarily elated by her feat and looked around, ready to boast. But no one was watching. Her abuela had her eyes closed, and the woman from upstairs—Beatrix with an *x*—was pouring another round of hot water into the funny little cup. So far, the tea she'd brought seemed to be calming Abuela down.

"Yerba maté," Beatrix said. It was from South America, where apparently she'd spent a lot of time.

A match made in heaven, Rosie thought. A new herb for Abuela's collection. How could her witchy grandmother not love this?

"It's a stimulant, but it doesn't give the jitters like coffee," Beatrix said. She held up the little cup. "This little gourd is called a *mate*. And this—" She pointed to the metal straw in the cup. "This is called a *bombilla*."

Rosie liked the sound of the words but flinched a little. She watched her abuela sip another round of the tea, her facial expression softening. "Better?" Rosie asked.

Abuela took a few more sips and nodded.

"You try it, Rosie," Beatrix said, refilling the gourd with hot water.

Rosie sipped the bitter tea from the straw. She wanted to spit it out, but out of politeness and because her abuela was sitting there, she didn't.

"It's not for everyone," Beatrix said. "*Menos mal*, more for us, *verdad*, Maria del Carmen?"

Rosie bit her lip. She knew what was coming.

"You should speak in English," her abuela said. "This is America."

Rosie rolled her eyes. No wonder Abuela was so anxious. Always policing. Rosie had even kept her own Spanish classes at school a secret. It was so stupid. If you were from Mexico, what was wrong with keeping a little bit of your identity? It wasn't like they were going to get deported now. Who'd waste whatever precious gasoline was left trucking a bunch of brown people back across the border?

"You don't speak Spanish?" Beatrix said. "How long have you been in the US?"

"She hasn't been back to Mexico in, like, forever," Rosie said. "I've never been at all."

Beatrix looked surprised. "Well, someday you'll go," she said. "It's a beautiful place."

"You've been there a lot?" Rosie asked, impressed.

Beatrix nodded. "First, when I was twelve, with my aunt Vera, to see the Mayan pyramids in the Yucatán. We climbed up all one hundred two steps of that huge pyramid and posed next to Chac Mool, the reclining god at the top."

Beatrix looked like a kid telling a story, all animated. Rosie tried to imagine what a reclining god looked like.

"I went back in college to do work against sweatshop labor. And I just spent a few months there. I love Mexico. It's such a beautiful country."

Abuela took a few more sips of the tea and set it on the table. "Come, Rosie, sit," she said, pulling a hairbrush out of a tote bag.

"Abuela," Rosie whined. Why did she have to do braids *now*? Reluctantly, she positioned herself on the floor. Brushing her hair may have had a calming effect on her grandmother, but it made Rosie feel like a five-year-old.

"Why are you tourists never satisfied with just seeing the pretty things?" Abuela said, starting to brush Rosie's hair.

"Excuse me?" Beatrix said.

"You go to Mexico and you want to see things: ruins, Indians, birds," Abuela said. "It's all there for you. But then you want to steal it and take it out of Mexico and keep it for yourself."

Rosie sighed loudly. She could have smacked her abuela. This nice woman, their new *neighbor*, had just brought her some special anti-anxiety tea, and here she was treating her like a turd.

"Head up, Rosie," her abuela said.

Beatrix cleared her throat. "Actually, most of my visits to Mexico and South America have been for work. Helping people sell their products for a fair price, for instance."

"So you tell people what to do," Abuela said. She tugged Rosie's hair.

"Ouch! Abuela!"

"Mmm, not exactly," Beatrix said. "I just haven't been that happy with how the United States has treated Mexico—or many other countries. So I guess I've tried to offer an alternative to that."

"Can you pass that tea, Beatrix?" Rosie said. Her grandmother needed to chill out. "Abuela, have some more."

"Beatrix, are you married?" Rosie asked, hoping to change the subject.

"Rosie," Abuela said.

"I'm not," Beatrix said.

Abuela wrapped an elastic band around the end of the first braid, then started the other.

"But I have a person," Beatrix said. "Maybe. He's on the other side of the country."

Rosie bit her lip. "Oh, that sucks." She thought of Diego, the boy in the neighborhood. He had long dark hair and skin like hers. When she was standing in front of him, she had to bite her tongue to keep from telling him he was beautiful. Just thinking about him fluttered her stomach.

"It does suck," Beatrix said.

Abuela wove the second braid quickly and quietly. When she finished, she stood and went to the altar: a table topped with candles, a rosary, several saint cards, and the Virgin of Guadalupe. Abuela always had to have an altar. Even when they were living out of their car, she'd set up a rosary and a little statue of the Virgin on the dashboard.

"You can say a prayer to Guadalupe if you like," Abuela said to Beatrix, gesturing to the Virgin. She pulled out a candle and handed Beatrix some matches.

Rosie stayed at the dining room table, watching. Beatrix didn't bless herself the way Abuela did. She just sat and stared into the flame.

The glow of the candlelight still in her eyes, Rosie suddenly saw the flickering image of a man walking. He was walking along train tracks. Was he in danger? She couldn't tell. She heard the sound of a whistle, a tune coming from the man's mouth, and then he vanished.

"Rosie, come make a fire, please," her abuela called, now from outside.

Out in the back courtyard, watching the twigs take fire, Rosie wondered about the man in her vision, unfamiliar but not strange.

"Bigger, Rosie. Please. No one likes cold beans."

Rosie added more wood and blew on the flames and wondered if she'd ever get to go to Mexico. When the fire was stronger, she set the grate they used as a grill over it. Abuela handed her the pot. Rosie also set the comal on the grate, and once it was hot, she arranged three tortillas there to warm.

"Go get the lady, now, *mi'ja*," her abuela said, and Rosie called to Beatrix.

"Wow," Beatrix said as she came outside, beholding the food on the table. "Thank you."

"My grandmother really does make the best tortillas," Rosie said, glad that Beatrix seemed happier. "Corn tortillas are her specialty. But flour is what we've got now. Good thing she's adaptable." Abuela might be anxious and Spanish language–phobic, but she liked to cook and feed people.

"I don't think I've ever seen eyes like yours, Rosie," Beatrix said. "They are amazing."

Rosie felt her face blush a little. She liked hearing this. It was true. One blue and one brown, and sometimes they showed her different things. Out of her right eye, the brown one, she could see the past. She saw one scene often, as if on repeat: A road through a tangle of green. Her mother's sandals. A bus bumping down the road. The sandaled feet stepping up onto the bus. The whir of green out the window. Where had she gone?

Out of her left eye, the blue one, she had seen the future. A few times, at least. The first time it happened, she saw in her mind an image of her abuela falling. The picture came and went so quickly: a smudge of berry pink, the same color as her abuela's cardigan sweater. Then it felt like someone had slid a feather down Rosie's throat and jiggled it. She coughed but could not get rid of the tickle. That same day, her abuela tripped on the curb and fell flat on her face. There wasn't any blood, but her face turned pink, flushed from *verguenza*, embarrassment.

Rosie got the tickle right before the October Shocks. The vision had come to her at school—a chemistry worksheet transformed into an eviction notice. A week later, she and Abuela moved whatever they could fit of their belongings into the car and left the rest on the curb. They didn't have the money to fill the gas tank and leave the neighborhood, so they'd drive around the block just to change their parking spot.

"Come back tomorrow if you want," Rosie said, once they'd finished the beans and tortillas.

Beatrix gathered up her thermos and tea. "Thank you," she said. "Your braids look nice, by the way."

Rosie grinned. "Thanks."

MIDMORNING IN THE city, and it was warm already, too warm for the end of winter. A humidity descended over the concrete like a woolly fog. Ayo lit a cigarette, then offered it to Carson.

"Nope," Carson said.

"Here." He tossed Carson a lighter and exhaled smoke. Then he reached into his jacket and pulled out a roll of duct tape and a windup flashlight. "Here you are, sir. As promised."

"Damn, you're good, Ayo. Thank you," he said, reaching for his cash. "No water tablets?"

"Ah," Ayo said, biting his lip. "Yes, yes. I got those. They aren't there? They are not. Dammit. I'm so sorry. They must be at my home. I don't know how. Come with me? We will retrieve them."

How could he refuse a window into Ayo's world? They walked east, and Ayo waved to vendors and pedestrians heading toward the marketplace.

A water cart approached, its soundtrack—a single loud whistle, on repeat—filling the urban canyon. Two men and a woman hastened to keep up with the tank, stripping off their clothes. A man riding the back of the cart reached for their money, then hosed them down as they tossed a bar of soap back and forth. It was a shower of necessity. Who could afford modesty?

"I am grateful to my wife for rigging up the buckets on the roof. We take rain showers," Ayo said.

"And if it doesn't rain?"

"Then I fill the buckets and take them to the roof. I can clean my whole body with just half a bucketful," Ayo said. "I am practiced. I lived in a refugee camp, after all."

They came to a man hunched over a computer keyboard, typing. "That is very funny, " Ayo said, stopping to watch him. "You are drumming, not typing, yes?"

The man tapped out a familiar rhythm, then looked up. "Recognize it?"

Ayo bobbed his head, and Carson listened closely. When the chorus came, Carson spoke-sang along. "You say it's your birthday."

Ayo laughed loudly. "You know the words! Of course, Mr. Principal."

Ayo leaned over the typist drummer. "They say raiders are in the vicinity and coming," he said. "You should take care."

"I've heard that before," the man said.

"These raiders are ruthless, they say. Terrorists."

The man shrugged and tapped out a new tune on the keyboard.

"He does not believe me," Ayo said as they continued on. "Maybe there is no reason to believe me."

They turned a corner. Ayo unlocked a gate to an unmarked door, and they climbed three flights of stairs. He tapped out a special knock, and a woman opened the door. She looked tired, Carson thought, but radiance came through, her body slim and sturdy in a salmon-colored dress.

"Ayodeji, my dear," she said, smiling.

"Sadie, my wife," Ayo said to Carson. He put his hands on the woman's cheeks and kissed her mouth. "It's Mr. Principal. He is a good man. Remember, he is the one who gave us books for the children."

Carson remembered the first time he'd brought Ayo books, all extras from various classrooms—*Othello*, *To Kill a Mockingbird*, a geography textbook. Ayo had lit up and thanked Carson over and over.

Sadie gave Carson a shy smile, running her hand self-consciously over her hair to smooth it. "We have nothing to offer him," she said quietly.

"It's quite alright," Carson said, sorry that Ayo had brought him unannounced.

A toddler in an adult-sized T-shirt wrapped her arms around Ayo's leg and held on as he made his way into the room. "My girl," he said, depositing her on the sofa next to a boy amidst a pile of Legos.

The apartment smelled like cooking oil and dirty feet. It was small and sparse, only the sofa, a folding chair, and a tall empty bookshelf in the living room. "We recently inherited the place," Ayo said, poking Carson with his elbow and laughing.

"Good location," Carson said, smiling. Beyond the Legos, he spotted a cat carrier, two supersized bags of Pampers (where had they found those?), and a rolled-up carpet.

"Father," an older boy said. He was maybe fifteen. He knelt down to the Legos with the younger boy. They were constructing some kind of city. Small plastic buildings rose up from the rug, forming narrow streets and boulevards. As the city sprawled, the Legos became sparse, and in their place were other objects—an old tin can, some knives and a fork, wooden beads.

"Here you are, sir," Ayo said, handing Carson the tablets.

Carson thanked him, then gestured to the Legos. "A utopia, do you think?"

"Yes, I think so, Mr. Toe," Ayo said.

"Mr. Toe?" Carson said.

Ayo slapped his forehead. "Not Mr. Toe, no. I meant Mr. Principal."

"Mr. Toe? What kind of name is that?" said the youngest boy, starting to laugh.

The little girl laughed, too. Carson looked at Sadie, who put her hand over her mouth, as if to hold in a chuckle. "Is he married to Ms. Finger?" she said, then let out an unreserved hoot, which made everyone else laugh more.

Ayo held out his hands to make them stop. "Listen, Mr. Toe was a real person. He came to our village when I was a boy. My brother Adeyemo and I—" He looked at Carson. "We are twins," he said. "We were twins. He is no longer here." He paused. "But Ade and I, we almost ran over Mr. Toe the first time we saw him. With tires! This was a game we played. We used to roll tires and race with them. Someone had distributed a pile of auto tires in our village. We had not ordered them, but they arrived. We never knew who sent them. We played with the tires. I was fast—faster than Ade most of the time."

"And Mr. Toe?" the little girl said.

"Mr. Toe came from England or Australia, I don't remember. His full name was Edward Toe, but we just called him Mr. Toe. He had pink skin and brown hair that fell straight over his forehead. My mother said he was soft like a cloth. He was not like the others, who came always trying to convince us of things. Father would say, 'If they have to convince us it is a good idea, it is not a good idea.'

"Mr. Toe became our teacher, and every day we met him under the guava tree. My children, you have never tasted a guava, have you? Such a sweet fruit. We would have our lessons under that tree because we did not have a schoolhouse. Mr. Toe taught me how to do mathematics and the proper way to hold my mouth to form words in English. If it weren't for Mr. Toe, I would not be where I am today"—he looked at Carson—"a businessman in America."

"Come," he said, calling Carson to the table, where he unfurled a map of the country, stitched together on two pieces of paper and hand-drawn by someone with a good grasp of geography.

Ayo traced a line all the way to the West. "The railroads are the safest way to travel," he said.

Carson studied the map, noticing a legend of symbols in the corner. They were simple line drawings, like hobo markers from the 1930s. He read the words aloud. "Water, shelter, food."

"Yes, a key to signposts, I believe," Ayo said. "Very useful for a traveler." He slid the map toward Carson. "Take it," he said. "You will need it."

Carson rolled up the map and tucked it under his arm and said goodbye to Sadie and the children. Ayo walked him out, and Carson paid him for the water tablets. "And the map, how much?"

"The map is on me," Ayo said, smiling. "And before you go, we will procure you a gun, okay?"

A gun? Carson thought, mildly stunned. But Ayo was nodding, full of assurance.

"Yes, sir. You will need that, too. But that, my friend, you will pay for." Ayo held his gaze on Carson. "You know, Mr. Principal, it is true. You remind me of Mr. Toe. Maybe that is why I am helping you. Payback."

Carson felt grateful. "Or paying it forward, as they say."

"Yes, yes," Ayo said. "Paying it forward."

Beatrix liked the way Carson said her name. The first time he'd called, he'd said it as soon as she'd answered. "Beatrix. Hello."

Her heart was pounding. "I'm making soup," she'd said. "Even though it's hot as hell here. I'm ready for autumn. So I'm making soup, and the kitchen is broiling and so am I. But damn it, it's my night to cook, and my housemates and I are going to eat hot soup for dinner even if it kills me." She heard him laugh through the phone.

"You sound determined, Beatrix," he had said.

He could not see her nodding, but she felt seen and heard.

She'd noticed how he'd said her name the day they'd met, too. It had been a fluke. She had traveled to the East Coast for a climate change rally. As a favor to a friend whose brother had just started teaching high school, she'd agreed to speak to a global studies class. Not the usual sort of thing she did, but why not? She'd been a little nervous, knowing teenagers could tear you to pieces, but she'd found two dozen oranges at a corner market and lugged them into the classroom. Everyone always loved the orange lesson.

The idea was to illustrate how flat maps often distort world geography. Orange peels as the gateway into uneven development and American imperialism.

Carson had slipped into the classroom just as some of the students began lobbing oranges back and forth. She'd noticed him—tall, with dark hair. Easy, confident.

"Hey, hey, people," Beatrix said. "Don't be chucking your world around—that's half the problem right there. Hold it tight. Take care."

She instructed the students to draw a map of the world on the orange. "It doesn't have to be perfect. Just the basic geography as you know it. I'm sure you know where South America is. But did you know that Africa is actually much larger in area than North America?"

Carson had taken a seat in the back of the room. "Hey," she called out, tossing him an orange. "No spectators."

He smiled, held up the orange, then pulled a pen from his breast pocket.

Once their maps were drawn, she had everyone peel their oranges—in one piece, if they could—and then press the peel to the table. "See how the continents split apart? To avoid that, you have to fill in the gaps," she explained. "All flat maps distort the world, either by size or shape or area. So the map you're used to seeing puts North America front and center, and distorts the South. Why does this matter?"

She managed to lead them into a discussion about global economics and trade and offshore markets and manufacturing and who won and who didn't. Some of the students crowded around her, wanting to know more and how to get involved in fair-trade causes. She handed out pamphlets and wrote web links on the white board and told them to start a high school action group. "You all have so much power! Use it."

As she left the classroom, Beatrix raised a fist, and the students echoed the gesture.

She was hurrying down the hallway, looking for an exit, when Carson came toward her.

"Oh, hi. How do I get out of here? All these barricades!" she said.

He had laughed. A pleasing laugh. "Down the hall and through the double doors," he said, gesturing to the left. "Great lesson, by the way."

The compliment flustered her. He introduced himself as the principal, and she'd apologized for having complained about the hallways. He made a joke about trapping students inside and they'd both laughed, and he kept asking questions of her and she had to go catch a train, and somehow he asked for her card and she gave it to him.

"Beatrix with an *x*," he'd said, reading her name out loud. "From the other side of the country."

Some weeks later, he'd emailed her, commenting again on her lesson—he hadn't looked at oranges the same since. She responded and then he wrote again, and their messages grew long and revelatory. Beatrix learned that Carson's political leanings were to the left (phew), that he'd never gotten over his teenaged love of Kurt Vonnegut, that his favorite color was yellow but that he did not own any yellow clothing, that he'd been a history teacher for four years before "moving up" to administration, and that most days at least once he regretted that choice. She learned about June, his late wife, an artist, a painter, about her death two years earlier. Beatrix imagined June as kind, thin woman with straight hair and small features. She knew they'd lived together in an old remodeled country farmhouse near a river and that now he lived in the city. He liked grilled-cheese sandwiches with ham and banana. One of his favorite things to look at was a hawk hovering on a thermal.

After three weeks of writing, he had called. They spoke when she was "stateside," as he liked to say. When she traveled, they sent emails and texts, and sometimes Skyped.

Carson had a concise way of speaking. He often paused between sentences to ruminate, to listen. And then there was his laugh, a kind of chuckle that made Beatrix think of a pond and someone tossing in small stones one at a time.

From the quiet of her lonely apartment, Beatrix tried to summon Carson's laugh now, but she couldn't.

CARSON PAID ATTENTION to small things. Moisture in the air. The way someone's eyes followed him down the street. Birds migrating along the Atlantic Flyway, as they did every spring—even now, in the blackout, warblers to bald eagles. The warblers were so small, but their movements were unmistakable. His father had taught him that, to look at a bird's movements in order to identify it.

On the other side of a chain-link fence, he spotted a magnolia warbler. He recognized it right away—the yellow on its breast, the white patches on its fanned tail.

Watching the bird, he stepped into the street as a taxicab careened toward him. It skidded to a stop, and Carson leapt back onto the curb.

The cabdriver was shouting and getting out of the car. "You!" he said. "It's you!"

Carson backed away, confused. The man was stocky, with dark skin, dark hair, and thick arms. A dark strip of mustache stretched across his face, and beneath it, he was smiling. "Are you okay? I can't believe it's you," the man said, holding out his hand. "Fernando Gomez," he said.

The face was familiar to Carson. Someone's father. A student's. He pictured the girl—long dark hair, smiling eyes, bubbly. Then he remembered: this father had stood up at a school meeting last fall and given a rousing speech about education, how it was why he had come to this country and was all his children had.

"We're getting out of the city," Fernando said. "My cousin has a small farm in Pennsylvania. Everyone is already there—*tíos*, *primos*, *sobrinos*, *abuelos*. They were all farmers in Mexico, so they know how already. You are getting out, too, *sí*?"

Carson nodded, thinking of the map.

"Come with us," Fernando said. "It would be an honor, after all you've done for Yadira, and all the kids. Really, an honor."

Yadira. The girl. A senior who had not been able to graduate because the school had closed. An honor? What had he done for Yadira? For any of them?

Fernando wrote down his address on a piece of paper. "Find me here a week from Wednesday. We can take you."

Heading home, Carson passed the old carriage house, a block-long building, vacant for decades. He slowed now to look at the brick canvas covered with street art. A giant spray-painted rat rose up in silhouette from the base of the building to chase small men in suits. The word "dope" stretched above an archway in bulging yellow letters. Inside the archway, a reproduction of one of the Italian masters' Madonnas had been wheat-pasted, the child in her lap, a young polar bear suckling her breast.

Ahead, someone was leaving the building with a bicycle. Were people living in there? It was Jairo the bike messenger, a headlamp strapped to his forehead. This isn't where he'd said he lived.

"Mail delivery?" Carson asked, confused.

The boy took a moment to remember him. "Nah, got a flat." He removed the headlamp. "Better to take shelter when that happens, if I can. Plus, it's rad in there. You've never been inside?"

Carson shook his head. Jairo put the headlamp back on and led him in.

The building smelled of moisture and chemicals, and Jairo's light spilled over the walls, revealing giant head shapes filled with cogs, machines, and digital numbers; a sky of bulbous dark-gray clouds; and an army of indigenous fighters cut from an enlarged historical photograph. Geronimo and crew, Carson was pretty sure. One of the figures had been transformed with paint into an eagle, cartoonish and angry, a shredded scroll in its talons.

How many times had Carson walked by never knowing this was here, never thinking to look? "Are you one of the artists?" he asked.

Jairo lit up a patch of floor where a bicycle was stenciled in pink paint, its rider in a cape scrawled with the word "power." "Kinda, yeah," he said. "My friends did stuff here, too. But we didn't know a lot of the other artists. Never even saw them. We'd just come in and look for their stuff. It was so lit. There'd be something new almost every day."

Carson's interest quickened. "Like a newspaper," he said. "Or a wiki."

"Exactly," Jairo said, lighting up what looked like a bed with a paper collage of people piled on it, asleep. "The calm before the storm," he said.

In the next room, the same paper people were sitting or standing, holding laptops and cell phones. A broad swath of gold covered some of them, creating the letters *SHTF* painted from floor to ceiling.

"Shit hit the fan," Carson said.

"Yeah. That's Seek," Jairo said, pointing to a tag below the *F*. "Always does big letters like that."

As the light bounced over the walls, the images flashed like a flipbook. Jairo's voice began to fill the space. "If you know what you're looking at, you get the whole history."

The light fell on an array of TV screens wheat-pasted over a stylized forest, then to a painted Popeye, tilting back a can of oil instead of spinach. "Our addiction to our screens, to cheap oil," Jairo said. "Until the supply dwindles. Prices get too high for you and me. The debt bubble expands. Banks have no liquidity when the people come for their money. Debt bubble pops. Check out those bubbles. That's Lady K, she's highkey good." He swung the light to a giant pair of dice. "Energy executives roll the dice on the backs of their customers, and all the wells go dry. The cars line up at the pumps.

"Over there," Jairo said, his light flashing on another wall, "those are the hackers worming into the internet. Worms, viruses, ransomware—off the charts. Facebook explodes with fake news, everyone facing off against everyone. Look, CeeMo was here." Jairo held the light on a jumble of letters. "He's the fuckin' goat, IMHO."

Jairo's words came quickly, full of breath and melody. This kid seemed smart beyond his years—a teenager who had paid attention. Though he was unsure of some of the slang, Carson could pick up the gist of it all.

In the next room, the image of a woman in a hospital gown holding on to her IV rack was cut out and wheat-pasted on a pillar. Carson recognized the photograph from the early days of the flu, when the hospitals began to be overrun. Looking at the woman's glassy eyes, their gigantic desperation, he remembered how haunting that time had been, how lucky he'd been.

"So many dead," Jairo said, as if reading Carson's thoughts.

The light shined on a polar bear standing atop a tiny ice cube. Above the image were names: Katrina, Sandy, Maria. All hurricanes. Carson thought of the moldy sofas on the sidewalk less than a mile south of where they stood. Who knew what storm season would bring this year? Nearby was a tumble of concrete and the word "quake" repeated like an echo. That chain of seismic shifts its own Armageddon, Carson recalled.

"A crippled government exposed in its decadence," Jairo said, illuminating dinner tables clogged with food; a chandelier; a solid-gold toilet on a vast and green White House lawn; stacks of textbooks and the words "Forgive our loans!"; stick figures and skeletons; a flock of vultures; stacks of dollar bills; OCTOBER $HOCKS in green block letters.

"Though it wasn't much of a shock, was it?" Jairo said. "The insiders dodged the bullet. The rest of us—flat broke."

Carson remembered the day. He kept checking online, watching the numbers fall. His retirement fund had dwindled to nothing. He'd let school out early so that students and teachers could get home safely. The riots had already started.

They stood in the darkness. Carson could hear Jairo breathing next to him in this modern Lascaux.

After a while, he heard Jairo's footsteps on the concrete floor. He followed the sound through the dark. The light came on long enough for Carson to see an explosion of orange paint. Then it went dark. On and off. On and off, as Jairo created a dramatic effect. Then on. The entire room was splattered with orange—thick splashes of it across walls, ceiling, and floor, covering everything beneath it. At the center of one of the walls was a large black circle, maybe seven feet in diameter, untainted by orange.

Carson let his eyes absorb the color, then eventually settled his focus on the void. It was like the big bang in reverse, he thought. Staring into the black, he felt a weight in his chest. The last decade compressed into a fifteen-minute art tour.

"Genius cyberhack," Jairo said, "whoever it was."

Carson nodded. "After a perfect storm."

Jairo made a clicking sound, then said, "Hey, man, I gotta get going now."

"That's it?" Carson said.

"That's it. The end."

Her backpack as full as she could manage, Beatrix slipped the note from Dolores into her back pocket and locked the door behind her. Her heart was pounding, but this seemed the best choice. There was nothing here for her.

Just down the front walkway, she heard, "Where to?" She whirled around and saw Dragon standing on the porch.

"I'm off to go find Hank and Dolores," she said. "Wish me luck."

"Oh," he said, raising his eyebrows.

Beatrix waited for him to say something more, but he didn't. "Yeah, I need to find them," she said.

"I see. Well, be careful. There's a lot of bad shit on the roads. You have some kind of protection?"

"What do you mean?"

"I just mean it's kind of horrible out there, and if you haven't thought it through really well, you might just be on a suicide mission."

Beatrix felt her stomach lift into her throat. "I just want to find my friends."

"Do you know where you're going?"

Beatrix nodded, just a half lie. She had Dolores's map.

A singsong whistle came from down the block. Dragon whistled back, and within seconds a man as tall and lanky as Dragon, but a little younger, appeared on a bicycle. He had short and shiny dark hair and wore cutoff shorts and a flannel shirt.

"Flash!" Dragon said. "Beatrix, meet Flash. He's my good friend and roommate."

"Ah, the famous Beatrix, queen of the"—he paused to find a rhyme—"beatniks?" Flash hopped off the bicycle. "I'll think on that one. Just back in town, right? Does that mean you missed the big fall? And the flu, too?"

"I left in January and got stuck in Mexico for a few months. But I was here before that."

"You must have had the early strain, like me?"

Beatrix nodded. Hank and Dolores had called it the "Knock-Knock Flu," a reference to the Bob Dylan song "Knockin' on Heaven's Door." It was so bad they'd really thought they might die. Their tongue-in-cheek title was prescient. When the next flu came around, it was stronger and deadlier, but left alone those who'd had earlier strains.

"I'm praying we don't get another round," Flash said.

"Flash is with the PBB, too," Dragon said.

"The what?"

"The People's Bicycle Brigade," Flash said. He flexed his biceps and pointed to the tattoo on his forearm—a bicyclist in a cape emblazoned with an *F* and a lightning bolt.

"What's the People's Bicycle Brigade?"

"We're kind of like the internet," Flash said.

"On bikes," Dragon said.

"People who stop to help you change a flat," Flash said. "People who, like, keep things going, you know? An information network *and* a help service. No paychecks, no cash. Trade only. We do basic mechanics, carpentry, gardening, heavy lifting. Whatever. We're bike messengers, really," Flash said.

"Speaking of goods, how are you on food, Beatrix?" Dragon said. "Any cash or things to barter along the way?"

Beatrix considered the small wad of bills in her pack and her meager savings, now evaporated from the bank. "What would I barter?"

"Inventory your skills," he said. "Then trade them for what you need."

"Right," Beatrix said, feeling in that moment completely impoverished.

"Wait, I thought you just got home," Flash said. "Now you're off again?"

"She's off to find her friends. North, to a farm somewhere," Dragon said.

Flash made a face. "By yourself?" He shook his head. "Stay put here for a while." He rolled up his sleeves and looked at Dragon. "At least long enough to help us dig a second hole for the compost toilet."

"At least that long," Dragon said. "Then you'll have a skill to trade. Come around back, and we'll show you."

Beatrix followed them to the backyard, feeling suddenly foolish. They wanted her to dig her way out? She set down her pack and watched them take turns with a shovel. She had been using this compost toilet for a few days now but hadn't really understood how it worked.

"Once it's cooked long enough in the ground, it essentially cleans itself. Apparently, we'll have usable compost within a year," Dragon said, tossing a shovelful of dirt into a wheelbarrow.

"I guess you have to see it to believe it," Beatrix said.

"Oh, come on now, where's your faith, Miss Activist?" Flash said. "Surely you believe in things you can't see. Isn't that what change is all about? Isn't that what protest is for?" He looked at Dragon. "I mean, you said she used to help organize protests. Right?"

"I did," Beatrix said, helping Flash move a heavy rock from the soil.

"Cool. I get that. There was plenty I wasn't thrilled about, too," Flash said. "But I'm not really the protesting type."

"You're more of a get-down-and-dirty kind of guy," Dragon said. "Like me."

"I'm not opposed to dirt," Beatrix said, tossing another rock. "But I've never understood how people could not speak out."

"And shouting, er, protesting in the street made you feel like you were doing something?" Dragon said.

"We weren't just shouting. We were proposing alternatives. That seems obvious enough now, doesn't it?" She felt annoyed. "Silence," she said, then paused. "I think silence is a very dangerous thing."

Dragon and Flash looked at each other. Beatrix expected one of them to change the subject, turned off by her tone, but then they looked back at her with interest, so she continued.

"My friends and I spent years being really pissed at the complacency—the crappy decisions that people seemed to accept by virtue of being silent. You know, you get a good deal on a new T-shirt, but never mind that some mother of five sat in a hot factory sewing it for three dollars a week. And, yeah, a Hershey's bar cost you a dollar, but who gets the dollar? Not the farmer who picked the cacao beans. We couldn't handle the disconnect." She stopped herself. There was so much more to say.

"Right," Dragon said, nodding.

"Eventually, though, I kind of settled on fair trade as a way to change things," Beatrix said. She took the shovel from Dragon, stepped up on the edge of it, and let it sink slowly into the dirt. She told them about the work she'd been doing in Ecuador, organizing cacao farmers, promoting

Fair Share chocolate bars. "They're at all the health food stores. The food co-op, too," she said. "Well, they *were*. And they were making a difference. Kids got to go to school. I mean, kids had a school to go to, and a teacher, which they hadn't had before. We eliminated the middleman and got farmers to agree to pool their products and negotiate a fairer price with people who hadn't ever listened to them before."

"That's really cool," Dragon said, taking the shovel back.

"It was cool," Beatrix said.

Beatrix recalled her recent weeks in Mexico: The utter mayhem in the streets, the realization that everything was crumbling, the countless trips to the airport, the pleading with the airline personnel, the growing recognition that a global market for fair chocolate now probably meant nothing. And inside her, a fear taking hold that she might never see Carson again.

Dragon handed Flash the shovel, and Beatrix watched him scoop up the dirt. She thought of Hank and Dolores doing the same thing at the mystery farm. She looked at her overstuffed backpack. It seemed to stare at her scornfully.

THE AFTERNOON WAS warm, and the sky looked like it might rain. Carson took off his jacket and waited for Ayo on the corner as planned. Ayo waved to him as he approached, and Carson noticed a bandage wrapped around his index finger.

"What happened?" Carson asked.

"Silly, stupid cut."

"Be careful of infection."

"Do not be concerned, my friend. There are bigger things to die from than a slice in the hand."

They started walking and soon passed a young woman standing with a grocery cart. Midtwenties, with clear white skin and red lips that looked like a small ripe strawberry. Ayo backed up and looked into the cart. "What do you have to sell?"

"Fiddleheads and mushrooms," the woman said. Her mouth pressed shut like a mail slot.

Ayo's face lit up as the woman peeled back a towel to expose a box full of oblong flesh-colored mushrooms. "They look like thumbs," Carson said.

"Miracles," she said. "Or 'merkels,' depending on where you come from. They grow wild. You think the mushrooms are funny-looking, how about these?" she said, and peeled back another towel. "Fiddleheads. They're baby ferns, but they make me think of pinwheels." She handed one to him. "They're better cooked."

"It looks like that small horse that swims in the sea," Ayo said.

"A seahorse!" the woman said, smiling. "Yes, they do look like seahorses."

Ayo popped the fiddlehead into his mouth and chewed, then made a face. "Bitter. Bitter seahorse."

The woman laughed, her white molars visible, eyes squinting small. Carson wished he could buy a bagful of the seahorses for Ayo to take home to his kids.

"Listen to me," Ayo said, moving closer to the woman. "Do not come out tomorrow. It would not be wise to be out, you, a young pretty girl. They say the raiders are coming."

"The raiders?" The woman frowned.

"I just share with you what they tell me. Please be careful."

Carson and Ayo turned east. They found an alley and ducked down it. Carson pulled out a wad of cash. "I am very grateful to you," he said, and when Ayo handed him the gun, he was surprised by its weight.

"It's not a dead fish," Ayo said, chuckling at how Carson held it. He pulled his own gun from his jacket and explained how to load and store the weapon. He dragged an overflowing garbage bin into the center of the alley. "That's your target," he said. "Strong stance. You are not a seahorse. Look at my hands. High grasp. Tight. Now squeeze it. You don't want your other fingers to move when you pull the trigger. Only one." Ayo's eyes were focused on the garbage bin. Without blinking, he said to Carson, "Have you ever milked a cow?"

Carson laughed nervously.

"Of course you haven't," Ayo said. "Good Lord. You are a smart man, but you don't know what you need to know. But it's okay, because you don't want to milk a *gun* either."

Carson copied Ayo's stance: arms stiff, hands locked on the gun, eyes focused.

"Just hold it tight. Look forward. Keep your eyes fastened. All the way. Loose finger."

Carson looked at Ayo. "Loose finger?"

"Yes. Keep your index finger loose. Not stiff. Do it."

But Carson could not relax his finger, could not pull the trigger. He felt like a small, weak boy.

"Mr. Principal, the only way to do it is to do it."

Carson stood still, aiming. "Right. The only way to do it is to do it," he said. He pulled the trigger and hit the trash, sending a plastic bag into flight.

"Yes!" Ayo cried. "Good. Again. We have bullets, my friend."

Carson shot five more times, then lowered the gun. He was breathing heavily, as if he'd just been running. "Eshu," he said, finally, "thank you."

Ayo let out a laugh. "Eshu, yes!" He put his hand on Carson's shoulder. "Good work."

Carson tucked the gun into his jacket and felt stronger. The feeling unsettled him. He watched Ayo tuck away his own gun. No big deal. Okay. Right.

Ayo handed him a small box. "You'll need this, too," he said. "One magazine, fifteen rounds."

Carson cleared his throat and took the box. He pointed to Ayo's hand. "Take care of that finger, okay?"

Ayo smiled, nodding. "Sadie worries about me. But I am the first of the twins, the only brother in my family still standing. I will not fall."

He looked at Carson in the eye. "Don't forget: every day is another blessing."

"I won't forget."

They hugged quickly, and Carson took his leave. At the end of the block, he turned around. Ayo was standing there still, watching him. Carson waved, and Ayo waved back.

CHAPTER 3

Beatrix rode the red bicycle rode through the neighborhood and passed a park full of camping tents. An SUV was parked on the grass, and next to it a man in a dark wool coat was shoveling dirt.

"What's the ditch for?" Beatrix asked, getting off her bike. Nearby, a woman sat on the ground, holding a small, bundled infant to her chest.

"The car," the man said. "I'll keep digging, and eventually it'll drop in, except for the windows. I saw homeless folks make a house like this back home in Ireland years ago. Remove the seats and the engine, and you end up with a perfectly insulated living space. Wondrous thing, if you don't mind little places. Carchitecture," he said, winking. "Couldn't build fires for food and warmth in a small apartment. And the shit kept piling up, literally. If this doesn't work, we'll join the rest of them and head to the country."

The woman—his wife?—lifted her shirt and tucked the baby

underneath to nurse. Beatrix tried to imagine holding a baby on her own lap, up to her breast to suckle. The task seemed both Herculean and mundane all at once.

"We'll be harder to oust this way," the man said, starting to dig again. "Because you know they'll be comin'. They'll come and kick everybody out eventually."

Beatrix wondered who "they" were and what kind of authority they had. She remembered how residents of a community in Ecuador had once protected their homes from wealthy landowners. When the bulldozers arrived, they'd stood stoically in front of their bamboo houses, their arms locked together in a human chain. Sometimes the simplest gestures were the strongest.

"If they come," she said now, "you'll stand up to them."

The man lifted the shovel, but she couldn't tell if he agreed or not.

She got back on her bike and rode to the business district, where shops and restaurants and the Fair Share office had once operated. She and Hank had found the place after jumping ship from Global Cause, a larger organization that had lost sight of its original mission of putting people over profits. Beatrix and Hank had stayed small, directly supporting Latin American producers. Before everything went dark, Fair Share had become a respected, effective, and solvent operation.

But now the neighborhood was changed. Most store windows were boarded up. Others announced AVAILABLE on sun-faded signs. Beatrix rode past the frozen yogurt place, the head shop, and the food co-op—all closed down. She idly wondered what had become of all the products in the beauty section of the co-op. Back when their causes seemed to be slowly improving the world, when they were relaxed enough to play, she and Dolores would try the testers. Beatrix always chose a citrus-scented essential oil. "Juicy," Dolores would say when Beatrix held it out for her approval. The whole memory seemed so frivolous now.

Three teenaged girls wearing baseball caps and flip-flops rode by on bicycles, and then a bearded man hauling a trailer full of chopped wood.

A boy in overalls stood on the sidewalk selling wilted lettuce from a grocery cart. On the curb, a man in a tie held a sign: WANTED: SHELTER FOR TWO. WILL COOK AND MAKE JOKES.

The Fair Share headquarters occupied a small office above Rigo's Mexican Lonchería, a favorite lunch spot until Rigo had closed up and returned to Mexico. Beatrix cupped her hands to the window and peered in: nothing but a glimmer of chrome counter where they'd ordered veggie tacos and sipped horchata.

She locked the bike to a signpost and made her way up a narrow staircase. Inside the office, she opened the blinds. She had somehow hoped to find an intern, at least one. No such luck.

Posters on the walls proclaimed their latest campaigns: ONE SQUARE = FAIR SHARE and KISS HERSHEY GOODBYE. A photo of a thick bar of dark chocolate and a group of children in one of the Ecuadorian Amazon villages playing basketball on a new court. It read: YOU GET YOUR DREAMS. THEY GET THEIRS.

She flipped through the calendar on the wall to April, just a few days away. On the fifteenth, they were scheduled to host the "Free to Fair to Where? Summit," a meeting of twenty-five international delegates to discuss what the economic downfall would mean for trade. So much for that.

She sat down in one of the chairs and rotated it toward the back of the room, where a map of the world hung, annotated with Post-its and scribbles. A thick hand-drawn arrow pointed to South America: *There's power DOWN THERE.* A page from a notebook taped over the Arctic read: *And then we all drown* . . . That map, with all its stories, had always reminded her of the scope of things. There was a whole world to consider, and every single part of it mattered, not just the pretty purple United States of America.

She remembered Quebec City and the rally to oppose the Free Trade Agreement of the Americas. As the protesters made their way through the streets, Beatrix had felt like they'd become a single organism. Its heartbeat came from the cluster of drummers a few yards in front of her, and its limbs stretched across the city into other cities, across borders into other countries. *Down with exploitation, down with greed! Goodbye, evil system! We are the seeds!* the organism chanted.

"Goodbye, evil system," Beatrix said now, out loud. How prescient. Down with everything, for everyone: the investment bankers; the CEOs; the lobbyists; the farmers, factory workers, and custodians; and their yearning and yelling activist selves, too.

She rummaged through the top drawer of her office desk and pulled out an old phone list. Someone would know about the farm where Hank and Dolores had gone. Someone would know what to do. She scanned the list and sighed. No actual addresses, just cell phone numbers, email addresses, Instagram and Twitter usernames.

She sagged into the office chair and pushed it back, inadvertently knocking into the filing cabinet, which teetered, sending a box toppling to the floor. Beatrix stared at the box for a second, then leapt from her seat. Chocolate. The box was full of chocolate bars! She did a quick count. Six boxes, all full but one. All told, over five hundred chocolate bars.

The chocolate was a little waxy with age, but the flavor instantly reminded her of the rain forest: the almond-shaped leaves of the cacao trees, an orchestra of birdsong, the squish-clomp of the burros as they made their way over damp trails, burlap bundles strapped to their sides. The earthy sweetness lit her up with joy.

Currency, she thought. This chocolate was valuable.

THE RAIDERS ARRIVED in the city mostly by bicycle. They were kids, scrawny and pimpled, though some had mustaches already. They lit torches and hurled them into parks. The trees and trash went up in flames, along with cardboard shanties and whole families asleep inside them. They took food wherever they found it. They knifed and chained and struck those who tried to stop or slow them.

When the loud pops woke Carson up in the middle of the night, he first thought they were fireworks. More cracks and pops. Then shouts and screams from the stairwell, and footsteps down the hallway. First one set, running, then many. He stood motionless in the dark, the gun in his hands, his heart racing.

Disoriented, he went to the window. Giant flowers of orange flame bloomed across the city. He put one hand on the glass and stood watching the burning.

He slept fitfully, fears of flames engulfing his thoughts. Several times, he imagined the building was on fire and he sat up to look out the window at the darkness. His only sense of assurance came from his packed bag.

Morning sun came through the window with a pewter-like cast, and Carson thought the room looked odd, both utterly familiar and completely foreign—the way a place looked when you knew you were seeing it for the last time. He gathered up the rest of his food—bread, pasta, some random cans of vegetables, a few spices—and tucked the gun in the side pocket of the backpack. Out of habit, he locked the door behind him when he went.

The street was quiet and smelled strange. A large black trash bag had been tossed on the sidewalk ahead of him, likely the source of the smell. As he approached, he saw that the bag was not a bag but a body, twisted and charred, burned black, except for a bit of clothing that remained. Carson gasped and turned away, incredulous, his stomach churning. Dear God. Was it someone he knew?

He went quickly to Rocco's Café, which was tucked between a Chinese restaurant and a vintage bookstore, neither one in service. Next to the café's fading yellow sign, a bell hung from a long cord. Carson reached up and rang.

When Jairo appeared, Carson held out two envelopes, one for his sister, one for Beatrix.

Jairo looked closely at the addresses, then slapped the envelope for Beatrix. "Shit, mister. I don't know if the network goes that far."

Carson held out a thick stack of bills. "Is a hundred enough?"

Jairo nodded and shoved the bills into his pocket. His eyes met Carson's. "And prayers never hurt." Before returning inside, Jairo said, "You take care, mister, alright?"

"You too," Carson said, calling after him. Then he pulled from his pocket the piece of paper on which the cabdriver had written his address. He hurried toward it, hoping he wasn't too late.

THE CHOCOLATE IN her backpack, Beatrix left the office and biked back through the neighborhood. Just a few blocks from home, she came upon a man sitting in a folding chair, a red bandana on his head. A man with a rifle slung across his shoulder paced the sidewalk a few feet away.

"You a resident?" the first one said. He was stocky, with a toned chest and biceps that pushed out from his short shirtsleeves like large apples.

What was this? Were they here before, on her way to the office, or had they just materialized? Beatrix felt a trickle of sweat slide down the inside of her T-shirt.

"You can approach. No need to be afraid, ma'am." The man's light-green eyes were striking, but his cop-like manner put Beatrix off.

"Who are you?" she asked.

"Neighborhood checkpoint," he said. "Just state your address and you can go on through."

Beatrix grimaced. "So you decide who gets in and who doesn't?"

The man smiled, the green eyes narrowing. "That's right. If you live here, you'll be glad for that."

A burst of static and a muffled voice came from the direction of the other guard, who was fiddling with a walkie-talkie or a radio.

"We live in the neighborhood. We ask everyone to declare themselves. We're just protecting the place."

Beatrix looked around nervously. What if he searched her backpack? The precious chocolate.

"Look," he said, seeming to noticing her discomfort, "we're just trying to keep people in line. There's a lot of confusion, and that makes people do crazy things. Things you wouldn't expect. We've got word of some kids who are particularly dangerous. They ride bikes, as a matter of fact. You could be one of them, for all I know."

Oh, so she'd gone from "ma'am" to a dangerous hoodlum kid in two minutes? "I live that way," Beatrix said, pointing west. "On Halcyon."

More hissing static came from the radio, then a voice: *"Water coming down the hill. Should be there by tomorrow, no problem."*

"What is that?" Beatrix asked, gesturing to the sound.

"Local radio. Whatever we can get. Usually ham radio."

"Bandits have been cleared from Highway Eighty-Four now, along with the barricades. It is now passable. Highway Eighty-Four is now passable."

"That's KH47," he said. "He's up north. About a hundred seventy-five miles away. Earlier, he reported that the grid went out. As in, there will be no more intermittent power here. All the way black."

"Really?" Beatrix said.

He nodded. "The last domino."

Beatrix thought of Carson, all the miles between them. A light inside her went out.

The radio spewed static. Her mind went then to Hank and Dolores. Maybe there was a way to communicate. "Can you talk back?" she asked the green-eyed guard.

"Not from here, but in my garage I can." He squinted at her and stiffened. "Wait a minute, where did you say you lived?"

"Halcyon," Beatrix repeated.

More static on the radio, and then another voice came, this one clear and absorbing. *". . . the floods would come, and they came. We said the flu would come, and it came. We said darkness would come, and it came. Look around, what do you see through the darkness: desperation, illness, starvation. Who do you turn to? Who can you trust when your neighbor is the one trying to steal your food?"*

What was all this? Beatrix wondered. Was the right wing back at it, instilling fear again?

"You can walk away from all that. You can come to an abundant world. Our coffers are full. Nothing missing here but you. We are waiting for you. We will rise."

The green-eyed guard raised his eyebrows. Beatrix couldn't read him. Did he believe all that?

"That's Jonathan Blue," the guard said. "Aside from us ham operators, he's the only thing of substance. We can't quite figure—"

"Substance?" Beatrix said.

"Meaning his signal comes through clear as day, all the time, on AM." He stiffened. "Miss, what's your name, please?"

"Beatrix," she said.

"Bee-tricks," he said. "Don't be so quick to judge." He then swept his hand out grandly, as if holding open a curtain. "Go ahead."

Pushing her bike, Beatrix peered at the radio. She wanted to know more, but right then she was simply glad for passage. She looked back at the guards, skeptical. What was it about bandanas? She thought back to the activists she knew, the sense of communal identity they'd had when wearing them. Had they just been guises of self-importance back then, too?

She rode a few blocks and came to a chain-link fence around a green lot, where a fair-skinned, redheaded man crouched over a row of lettuce, looking like a strange praying mantis. Nearby, a muscled man shoveled dirt into a wheelbarrow.

"Hey," Beatrix called out. "Who are those men in red bandanas? With rifles."

"Our protectors," the redhead said, with a southern accent. He put one hand on his hip. "Place your trust in them, child."

When Beatrix didn't respond, he said, "I'm joking!"—without the accent this time. "They mean perfectly well. They're neighbors here. They probably have rescuer syndrome, which can be attractive in its own way."

"And annoying as hell," said the other gardener.

"Oh, Finn," the redhead said. "Don't be difficult. Be thankful. Our food is precious here, and they do protect it from those who want to steal it. And some of those men keep us all well-informed with their radios."

"Yeah, they had a radio," Beatrix said. She was about to say more, but Finn rested his massive head on the redhead's bony shoulder.

"So this is your garden?" Beatrix asked.

"Everyone's garden, really. Just gotta put in the work. Food for labor. We can always use help," Finn said. "This is Rog. And I'm Finn. You want some oranges? Someone brought a cartload the other day." He gestured to the gate, and Beatrix wheeled her bike in.

"They gutted a grove somewhere south of here, I guess," Rog said, showing her three cardboard boxes full of glowing navel oranges. "Just when you think the world had run out of kindness."

"Will you sell them?" Beatrix asked.

"We'll eat them," Rog said, tossing one to her. "And trade them."

Beatrix studied the orange in her hands for a moment, savored its color. She peeled it slowly, the way her aunt Vera always did, spiraling the peel off in one single piece. Afterward, Vera would gently re-form the peel into a sphere. As a kid, Beatrix had loved this act of ordinary magic, the transformation of something into nothing, then back into something again. Everything with Vera was like that, it seemed. She'd been gone for over ten years, but Beatrix still missed her magic.

It was Dolores who'd inspired the idea for the global geography lesson. "A little Earth," she'd said one time when Beatrix held up a hollow peel.

She looked at the peel in her hand now and thought of Carson, how he'd smiled and pulled out his pen right away after she'd tossed him the orange that day in the classroom.

A white-haired man in a faded sports jacket pedaled by on a bike, announcing through a megaphone: "Neighborhood meeting tomorrow at three o'clock. Be a part of the solution!"

Just like in Ecuador, Argentina, Mexico, El Salvador, Beatrix thought, the roving vendors and politicians announcing their wares and positions via prerecorded looping messages. She told the gardeners about having just returned from Mexico, about Hank and Dolores and their map to the farm.

"There are hundreds of farms up there," Rog said.

"And there's this farm right here," Finn said, opening his arms to the garden. "It's about to get bigger. Why don't you tell your friends to come on back here and farm with us?"

Beatrix felt a tightening in her stomach, the sense of lostness returning.

"It's hard, I know," Rog said. "No other family around here?"

Beatrix shook her head. "Dad died a long time ago. Mom remarried—the guy's an alt-right nut. They drink in Southern California." She paused, hoping her mother, despite her politics, was okay. There was no way to know. She sighed. "Hank and Dolores were family."

"Oh, honey. I'm sorry. I understand that perfectly," Finn said. He handed her a big sack of oranges. "For what it's worth, we could use you here."

"Thank you. That's very kind," she said. "Oh!" She reached into her backpack and pulled out a bar of chocolate.

"Oh, help me, Jesus," Rog said. "Is that what I think it is?"

"Honey, if you have more of this, you are one lucky gal," Finn said.

Beatrix's anxiety dissipated. Her bike basket full of citrus, she rode away feeling good for the first time since boarding the cargo trucker.

At home, she stopped in the front hallway, took a few oranges out of the bag, and left the rest, along with two chocolate bars, on the bottom step for Dragon, Flash, Maria del Carmen, and Rosie.

BECAUSE HE COULD, Jairo rode at breakneck speed down the carless city streets, darting around campfires and pedestrians and parked cars, all of which blurred like film on either side of him. It was freedom, riding without traffic and just a small bundle of letters on his back.

He slowed as he neared the tunnel, the end of his city-bound route. He circled the intersection until another rider cycled into view: a woman, longhaired and lean, wearing an orange jacket. Sweat beaded her upper lip. She raised her chin to acknowledge him. Without speaking, he reached down and rubbed his thumb on his bike chain, then pressed a greasy print into the back of the envelope. Then they made the trade, one bundle for another. The woman turned around slowly and picked up speed down the hill.

He watched her for a moment, then called out, "Godspeed!"

"Velocipede!" she answered, the last syllable stretching into silence as she disappeared into the tunnel.

THE CABDRIVER FERNANDO had traded his family's basement apartment for a full tank of gas and three five-gallon containers of reserve. Carson packed into the cab with Fernando's wife, daughter, two young sons, and eighty-five-year-old mother.

Leaving the city, they passed throngs of others on foot, rolling suitcases, pushing shopping carts, pulling wagons. The few cars that moved through the streets were crammed with people.

The highway was littered with abandoned vehicles, stripped of doors, hoods, motors, mirrors, bumpers, and tires. *"Los bandidos,"* Fernando said, and Carson remembered Ayo's warnings. Under the pretense of needing help, these bandits would flag down cars, hold a gun to the driver's head, and steal the car and everything in it. Fernando didn't stop for anyone, and they drove all day, out of the city and along the interstate to Fernando's cousin's farm.

It took them half a day to travel 150 miles. By the end of the trip, Carson had learned to sing "Las Mañanitas," the Mexican birthday song, and to say "Erongarícuaro" three times fast. Erongarícuaro was a town at the edge of a lake in Michoacán that Fernando had left behind thirty years earlier when he'd come to the United States. Carson wondered if Beatrix had ever been there.

Fernando invited him to stay on at the farm, said they could use another hand and a teacher, too. Carson considered it, grateful. But he wanted to stay in the river of momentum.

Alone now, Carson stood at railroad tracks, which reached west into an apparent infinity. The morning grass in Pennsylvania was damp, and buds appeared on the expectant branches of maple, birch, and oak trees. Even with the trees, the sky above looked wider without skyscrapers.

He looped his wrists through the straps of his pack and lifted it a few feet off the ground, testing its weight. Easily sixty pounds. He'd been an avid backpacker in his twenties, and back then the push of the pack against his body gave him a strange comfort and a sense of freedom. It had always signaled his entrance into the wild, where all priorities reordered themselves. That was before the job and the farmhouse upstate took up all his time, back when he'd believed in John Muir's adage that the hope of the world lay in wilderness. Maybe it still did. He patted his pocket to feel the map from Ayo, and then hoisted the pack onto his back and stepped onto the tracks.

By early afternoon, he arrived at a tunnel. Likely no passenger train had passed through in more than a year, after the government ended subsidies to Amtrak and all the commuter services—part of its futile attempt to right the economy. His crossing would be safe. Nonetheless, he found himself trembling. Carson took a few steps into the darkness and smelled something stronger than the decomposition of rotting leaves. The noises were amplified, too—dripping water, wind at either end.

He focused on the ground, trying to keep his eyes on the railway ties, as the light from his headlamp bounced off small puddles and bits of broken glass. Every few feet, he glanced over his shoulder. Soon, the tracks curved and the tunnel opening behind him disappeared. He was completely inside the earth, rock wall on all sides. His headlamp created microshadows on the textured surfaces, and in places, water seeped down and made the walls shine. He heard a loud splash, like a large rock falling into a stream. He clicked off his light and stood in the pitch-blackness, holding his breath to listen. Nothing but the thin trickle of water. His mind went to Ayo's stories of bandits. He turned on the light again, shining it in all directions onto nothing. Maybe he had imagined the sound.

When the opening at other side of the tunnel appeared—a white circle of light—he began to run, slipping on the ties but managing to stay on his feet. A small group of travelers was silhouetted against the daylight. He stepped out of the tunnel, debating whether to make himself known.

He remembered Ayo's advice: *Read people's eyes. Notice their movements. Avoid the skittish ones.* Carson questioned whether or not he possessed these special skills, unless reading teenagers for the past fifteen years qualified as any kind of training. He heard Ayo's laugh in his mind.

"Hello," he called out, catching his breath. There were four adults and a young girl. The men wore overcoats, and the women and the girl, skirts down to their ankles.

A hefty man with a dark beard and weathered skin stepped forward.

"Where are you headed?" Carson asked.

"Not much farther and we'll bed down," the man said. "Been walking about a few weeks, all said."

"Where to?" Carson asked again, noting an accent. Canadian?

"We follow God," the man said. "We look for signs."

Cult Christians, Carson realized. He had heard about them, their renouncement of the cities, the amassing congregations in the heartland. "Signs?"

"They're everywhere if you know how to look," the man said, pronouncing the word "look" as "Luke." "There's one now." He pointed upward, to the west, toward a stand of hemlocks down the tracks.

"The trees?" Carson asked.

"The cloud," the man said. Sure enough, sitting low in the sky was a large downy cloud. "Just have to know what you're lookin' for," the man said again. "Well then, be good to you." He tipped his hat and retreated to the group.

Carson nodded, relieved but confused. Wouldn't they want to tell him about God? Invite him to follow God, too? He turned toward the cloud and started walking, feeling strangely snubbed.

Moments later, the little girl came running. With her ashen pallor, she reminded Carson of a Dust Bowl photograph. But then there was the plastic bag dangling from her hand. "Mister," she said. "For you."

The girl's hair seemed to glow, halolike, around her forehead. "Sandwich?" she asked, holding out the plastic bag. "Cabbage and onion."

Carson hesitated, then took the sandwich. "Thank you very much."

"My dad also said to warn you about the demons."

"Ah, yes, the demons," he said. "I know them well."

"You do?" she said. "That's why we're going to the Center."

One of the men hollered out for her. She made a quick smile and ran back to the group.

"The Center?" Carson called after her. The group nodded in unison. Carson held up the sandwich. "Thank you."

ROSIE SAT ALONE in the dim living room with a chocolate bar on her lap. Chocolate from Ecuador, here in her very own hands, thanks to Beatrix, who seemed to have traveled everywhere in the world.

She unwrapped the chocolate bar and found it coated with a white film. She smelled it. Chocolate all the way. Who could complain? She bit into a tiny corner and held the piece on her tongue. The chalky film melted away to sweetness.

Outside, the buds on the tree had expanded into leaves. Dragon had said that by the beginning of September they'd have little golden apples. Too many months away, it seemed. She stared past the tree to the empty street and willed Diego and his friend Charlie to come. Or better, just Diego.

When Diego had finally kissed her, Rosie felt like she'd swallowed a beehive, her stomach churning. Diego said, "I like you." And before Rosie could respond, his dry dark lips were right up against hers, his breath warm and smelling of walnuts. She felt it between her ribs and then in the lowest part of her belly, like water was being sprinkled there. "I'll see you soon, Rosielicious," he said.

"Rosielicious," she said aloud now. Maybe today was "soon."

She browsed the bookshelf of the man who'd lived there before and pulled out a book at random. On the cover was a black-and-white drawing of a young woman who looked a little bit like a man. *The Selected Poems of Emily Dickinson.*

She flipped through the pages. *I held a jewel in my fingers. And went to sleep.* She smiled at the image.

After a little while, she set the book down and bit off another piece of the chocolate. This time, she tasted berries, sweet and tart at the same time. She wrapped up the rest of the bar and placed it on Abuela's altar. Why not? Maybe if she gave the spirits a little something, they'd give her something back.

AT DUSK, CARSON stopped walking and dropped his pack. The night was clear and cold, and already the first stars had appeared. He stood in a clearing, the damp grass and weeds up to his ankles. Exhausted, his body chilled quickly in the stillness.

From a nearby stand of pine, he gathered needles, twigs, and thick branches. He set a match to the kindling, and the sparks made tiny mesmerizing fireworks. He added more wood and warmed his hands. He felt like the last man on Earth.

His shoulders ached, and a blister had formed on the bottom of his heel. He'd made it through his first day. No ambush. No weapons. No compound fracture. No fall from a cliff. No dangling by a hand. Lucky.

He listened to the hiss of flame and the silence beyond it. The problem with fire was that it made the darkness darker. If anyone else was out there, they could see him, but he was blind beyond the fire line. A part of him wished someone friendly would emerge from the darkness, someone in the know, with smart words to offer. Someone like Ayo.

He opened a can of beans and ate them cold. Soon, he'd be foraging. Mice and squirrels. Berries and weeds. Dumpsters.

You know things, he used to tell his students. *Use what you know. The resources are inside of you.*

Where were his students now? Had they fled the city, too? Were they holed up in the suburbs? Did they know enough? He felt a twinge of guilt. He'd given them books to read. He'd made them think about cause and effect, how one event leads to another, how the course of history could be swayed by a single person or a collective theory. He'd honed their critical thinking skills. He'd made them explain themselves, articulate their ideas. They had learned about the rise and fall of so many other civilizations: Sumer, Mesopotamia, Egypt, Chaco Canyon, Tikal, Greece, Rome, Spain, Germany. But not their own. How could he have prepared them for this?

He scraped the last of the beans from the can and wished for more salt.

The morning brought dampness and more aches. Carson didn't want to move. He opened his eyes as a large crow flew overhead. The birds were so fortunate. They could see the sprawl and order of cities. They could take in a long strand of coastline, the blur of white waves crashing. They could drift over the green-gold quilt of farmland. If only he could have that view of the landscape, a more coherent geography, to see clearly where he was going, where he had been.

A crow landed a few feet away, its blue-black feathers shiny like metal. Behind the house where he and June had lived, he used to watch the crows as they flocked to the fields to scavenge for seeds and insects. They'd gather there, a jittery oil slick.

A shadow passed now, and another crow arrived. The two birds stood in the grass pecking, moving with purposeful and sturdy hops. Watching them, Carson had a momentary sense that nothing of any significance had taken place. The world was exactly as it had always been. Earth circled the sun, bringing darkness and light to its surface. Crows searched for breakfast in open fields, devouring grain and insects in the natural order of the food chain. A man could wake up at dawn after sleeping in a field and be covered with dew. As always.

He thought again of John Muir, how he returned home from his wanderings to a wife and child. Carson wanted to go home to that. He wanted to roll over and put his arm around Beatrix.

April 4

> B., I am like a crow looking for the shortest route. I survived day one. I am green and damp. Even my bones have emotions. I hope I have not made a mistake.
>
> Love, Carson

THE SECOND TIME Beatrix met Carson, her stomach went into a spin. He was standing next to the shoeshine kiosk, right where he'd said he'd be. She had traveled east for a meeting of chocolatiers.

A man was shining shoes, and Beatrix made a nervous comment about her scuffed boots. Carson spoke her name and held open his arms.

"I'm hungry," she said. "You?"

The day went by so quickly—coffee, lunch at the Diner/Bar, a walk along an old rail line that had been converted to a park. When evening came, they were not finished with each other.

At his building, he introduced her to the doorman, Ayo. "I have heard about you," Ayo said, smiling. He bowed slightly to her. He looked at Carson. "This is a fine man. You take it from me."

The elevator had brass railings, shiny wood, and mirrors. Beatrix and Carson stood side by side, in the flesh. In all the reflective surfaces, she could practically see the desire there between them, like a third person, large and billowy.

She reached out and hovered her hand over the mirror. "Someone cleans this every day," she said, nervously diverting attention to something else. There was always a menial narrative to accompany polished brass and sparkling mirrors.

"Flora," he said. "She's from El Salvador."

When the elevator stopped, Beatrix looked at Carson's hand as he gestured for her to exit. She'd been noticing his body all day, the long bones that held him upright, the lean muscles of his arms, the gray of his eyes, and now, the strong tendons in his hands.

Once inside the apartment, as he folded his jacket over a chair, she reached for his arm.

Carson turned and brushed her hair off her face and tapped her forehead gently. "Just making sure you're really here."

"Yes," she said. "I am here."

He was taller than she had remembered. She wondered, briefly, if June was there, somewhere, in his mind. He pulled her closer. He smelled like soap and wool. He reached beneath her hair to the back of her neck and pressed his other hand to her heart. He kissed her ears, temples, forehead, cheeks, nose. When he got to her mouth, he pulled away.

"I am here," she said again, and reached her mouth to his.

Carson pulled her shirt up over her head. She pushed her head against his chest. He said her name slowly at first: "Bee-ah," then a quick "tricks."

CHAPTER 4

The neighborhood meeting was held in the elementary school, a beige brick building surrounded by a chain-link fence. Beatrix and Dragon locked their bikes to the fence.

"Schools always look like prisons," Dragon said.

"Or factories," Beatrix said. Carson once had questioned whether schools educated students or just regimented them into routines.

They followed cardboard signs to the side of the building and entered a dim hallway where class schedules still covered the bulletin boards. Beatrix stopped to admire a collection of fourth-grade drawings called "Inventive Species." A bear's head on the body of a giraffe with duck feet. The head and neck of a swan on a pig's body with deer hooves. Beatrix lingered on a cartoonish crow-like bird with large human feet. She liked the deep red of its body, the too-small wings protruding from its shoulders, the tawny flesh of its big human toes. "Is this a crow or a raven?" she said.

"I don't know," Dragon said.

"Me neither, but I like it," she said.

"You should have it," he said, reaching for the thumbtack. He looked up and down the hallway, then fixed his gaze on Beatrix, who gave a small nod. He pulled out the tack, and Beatrix folded up the drawing and tucked it into her back pocket.

"We simply liberated it," she said.

The classroom still smelled like grade-school kids, a mixture of sweat and artificial strawberry. The dozen adults already in the room looked like oversized children at the student desks. Rog and Finn from the garden waved hello.

A woman in a yellow skirt stood at the front of the room and wrote a list on the chalkboard in a perfect swirl of cursive: *Community Garden, Water, Food, Neighborhood Watch, Tool Library, Evictions, Leadership.* Each topic ended with a question mark.

The woman introduced herself as a former teacher in the school, then called up Rog to speak about the garden. He encouraged people to give seeds to and take seeds from the seed library and shared information about an upcoming workshop on harvesting rainwater.

"To keep us from depending so much on Dorn's water," someone said, referring to the horse-drawn tanks. "He's got a monopoly, that guy."

"What choice do we have?" asked a woman in a hijab.

Others nodded. A man in the corner spoke up. It was the green-eyed man who had stopped Beatrix at the checkpoint. "We monitor the water situation pretty closely on the radio. It is a monopoly, yes, but it seems to be a stable supply for now."

"We also have rain," Rog said.

A man in a denim shirt started talking about the neighborhood border, where Beatrix had met the men in bandanas. "We could use a few more guards," he said. "And we've been looking to acquire more arms."

"Arms?" someone asked. "For the guards?"

"For the guards, and anyone else who wants them," the man said. "If you protect yourselves, we are all stronger."

"That's awfully dangerous," someone said. "We can't have every mother, father, and child walking around with guns. This is not Washington, DC."

Several in the room laughed, and Beatrix felt her face get hot. She cleared her throat. "Some protection is in order, yes, but an armed barricade?" she said. "Who do we need to protect ourselves *from*?"

"Yeah, isn't that what the US military is for?" said the woman with the hijab.

"Pshaw. What military?" someone said. "You seen any military around here lately?" He started talking about the Second Amendment and how lucky they were to have it.

"Oh hell, what good is the Constitution now?" shouted a man in the corner.

"We can uphold it," Rog said. "Just because they screwed it up doesn't mean we should throw it all out the window. 'We the People,' remember?"

"We are hearing more and more reports of violence," said the guard Beatrix had met. "Communities with armed perimeters and armed citizens are safer, it seems to me."

"So we'll have a bunch of scared people running around with guns they can't operate," Beatrix said. "And why is it that we're only protecting this neighborhood? What about everyone else? What happens past 'the Perimeter'? Are we keeping people out? Or keeping ourselves in?" It felt like such an old argument, one she'd had so many times with her mother and the ridiculous man her mother had married. She sighed. She hoped they were faring okay.

"I don't know where you've been for the past six months," said the guard. "We can take things into our own hands, or we can stand on the corner and rattle cans that our incompetent government entity will never hear. Which would you choose?"

Beatrix stared at him, stung by his depiction of protesters.

"Listen," the guard said, "the government isn't equipped to do anything right now. We have lives to protect here."

"You're right, Gary," said the man in the denim shirt.

At the front of the classroom, the teacher waved her hands in the air. "Please, everyone. Calm down! I think we need to discuss this carefully. There are children to consider."

"Precisely why we're advocating this. The reports we're hearing are about violent children," the man in denim said.

"Violent children?" the teacher said. "Goodness. We need to get them back to school."

"We haven't seen them here yet, but Gary has heard reports on the two-way, right?"

Gary nodded. "We're asking everyone to keep an eye out and report any suspicious activity."

"Report it to where?" Beatrix asked.

"There's a bulletin board in front of the school. That's one place for sharing information," the teacher said.

"Speaking of information," Rog said, holding up a packet of paper. "We're updating the neighborhood assets survey. Many of you know how this has brought us together in the past. The best way to secure your community is to know your community. In the days to come, we'll be coming around and asking you about your skills and what you can offer. Think of it as an inventory of what we can share."

As the meeting adjourned, Rog tapped Beatrix's arm. "I could use your help with this. It's easy. What do you say?"

Beatrix focused on the red curls atop Rog's head, stalling. She wasn't even sure she was sticking around.

Dragon elbowed her. "C'mon, do it for the team."

"What team?" she said.

Dragon swept his hand out over the empty room.

How was this guy she barely knew so persuasive? She took the packet from Rog.

They rode back to Halcyon and found two teenaged boys on bikes circling in front of the house. "You need something?" Dragon asked brusquely.

"We're looking for Rosie," one of them said. He had shoulder-length black hair, and his face was speckled with a few pimples.

"Hi, guys!" Rosie said from the door. "They're my friends, Diego and Charlie. It's cool."

Maria del Carmen stood in the front hallway. "Those boys keep coming here," she said, huffing, once Dragon and Beatrix were inside.

"Of course they do, Maria del Carmen," Beatrix said. "They're teenagers. They need to be social. They can't text anymore." She understood the longing perfectly.

She thought sadly of Carson's texts.

Good day today? he'd write.

Good enough. Aside from poverty and corruption.

Detention and fire alarms here. I saw a falcon this morning.

Lovely. Lucky. You. The falcon.

"It'll be okay," Beatrix said. "She needs to have friends."

Beatrix went upstairs then and wrote to Carson, adding to a long letter she had no way to send.

April 5

Dear C.,

The principal of the elementary school here wants to re-open the school, despite the lack of lights and water. It's a good idea. They need volunteer teachers. I also have to say, I feel lucky to be in this neighborhood. There's already a lot of cohesion. I've been recruited to survey neighbors. I'll be asking a lot of questions.

I keep thinking about a story Subcomandante Marcos used to tell. A story of two gods connected like Siamese twins. One operated by day, the other by night. One was dark, the other light. They couldn't get anything done because of their differences. Finally, one of them said, "Let's walk." The other said, "How?" And then in this way, by asking questions, they started to move. One step at a time. Soon they were dancing. They came to a long road. "Where does it go?" they asked. To find out, they kept going.

Love, B. (Pressing send)

CARSON WALKED FULL days. By midafternoon, he wanted desperately to lie down. But there were three more hours of daylight, easily eight more miles. The ground beneath him blurred—gravel, railway ties, the dried-blood color of his boots. Fitting. Each step felt like a nail through his flesh.

The tracks sliced through a clearing of grass—wide, green, the sort of place that used to hum with bees. Ahead was a figure, immobile, looking like a lone tree planted in the wrong place. Carson reached for the side of his pack and unzipped the pocket where he'd stored the gun. Just in case. As he approached, the figure came into focus as a gawky man tossing a green apple from one hand to the other.

He remembered how Beatrix had told him about the dogs in Ecuador. Just because its tail wagged didn't mean it was friendly. If it came for you, best to find a stone quick, pick it up, and be ready to hurl it. If there weren't any stones, you could just pretend to pick one up and the dog would slink away. Worked nearly every time, Beatrix had said.

The point, Carson told himself, wasn't to hurl stones at a stranger but to be on guard, ready for anything.

The man was his age, maybe older. Tucked into his armpit was a baseball cap, which he had likely just removed. His thinning hair was damp, and his pale, expansive forehead glistened with sweat. He wore loose jeans and a thin white T-shirt. His narrow eyes darted around as if unable to focus. He tossed Carson the apple. "Save the seeds, please," he said.

Carson rolled the dull, waxy apple around in his palm, wondering whether it was safe to eat. "You live around here?" he asked.

"Don't live around here, no," the man said. "Traveling through. You?"

"Going west," Carson said. "Getting the lay of the land. Chronicling."

"You're a journalist? Wait, are there even any newspapers anymore?"

"I'm a schoolteacher," he said.

"You gonna eat that?" the man asked, glancing at the apple in Carson's hand. "I'm saving the seeds." He reached into the pocket of his jeans and held some out. They looked like shiny little eyes in his pink palm. "Future trees," he said, sifting the seeds back into his pocket. "I'm Jimmy. Jimmy Weed."

Carson felt relief. The encounter could have easily gone another way. An apple wasn't exactly something you'd throw a punch at. Carson had never been a fighter anyway. Out here, he might need another strategy, but so far, so good: a strange cabbage sandwich and an apple.

"And where are you headed?" Carson said.

"Also west," Jimmy said.

Carson gave a nod. "After you," he said politely. That's when he noticed the limp.

"Maybe you've heard of me. WeedRivers Inc. Our company. Rodrigo Ríos was my partner. 'Ríos' is 'rivers' in Spanish. We made video games." Jimmy Weed was panting, struggling to keep up with Carson. "We had a new one in the works called *Colapso*. There were a few similar games out there, but ours would have put them all to shame. The graphics alone. I mean, it was hyperreal. We were just about to launch. We had to—things were already so iffy, but we were gonna do it. We figured if we still had the internet, people would play. And then, well, you know."

Carson stood still for a minute, disbelieving. "You developed a game about"—he held out his hands—"this?"

"Pretty much, yeah. Ríos had family in Puerto Rico. He knew up close what disaster could look like."

"Prescient," Carson said.

"Yeah, but you knew it was coming, too, didn't you? We all knew."

"Art imitates life," Carson said.

"Life imitates art," Jimmy said. "But what good is a video game now? No console. No power."

Carson nodded, wondering if such a video game would have prepared anyone for this. Could anything have prepared them for this?

He recalled his dark apartment. Were any of his things still there? Or had the looters come to take it all? Not that there was much to take. Most of his possessions were stacked in a storage unit outside the city, where they'd been since he sold the farmhouse. All the items of his life with June: dinner party plates, tablecloths, subscription magazines, flower vases, a few antiques. None of it fit in the city apartment, and besides, without her, it had lost its luster. The only things he'd brought to the city were his books, box after box of them. But he hadn't been able to read—the words tangled across the pages, indecipherable in his grief and exhaustion. And now? What kind of nomad needed a personal library? As far as he was concerned, the thugs could plunder everything.

Jimmy and Carson followed the rail line through a small woods and out again, to the edge of a town, where the tracks mirrored a road. Along it were defunct businesses: Pizza Kitchen. PartyLand. Western Union. Kram's Deli. A nameless gift shop still offered weathered postcards on a rack out front, and they wandered over to look.

Jimmy held up a postcard of a lion with a full mane spread out in the grass, and the words "I like LION around." Carson pulled out one depicting Horseshoe Curve, a place where the railroad tracks made a 180-degree turn around the edge of a lake. "I'd like to spend some time 'lion around' *this*," he said, pocketing the postcard.

They walked on, Jimmy limping like a cheerful drunk. "You said you're a teacher?"

"History and world civilizations," Carson said. "High school."

"Like ancient Egypt and stuff? I used to love pyramids as a kid. The architecture, those tombs. I was so fascinated by King Tut. I used to make lists of all the things I'd want with me in my tomb," Jimmy said.

Carson felt a lightness in his step, pleased when anyone was interested in history. It made him feel useful.

"My favorite is the early Southwest," Carson said. "The Ancestral Puebloans, or Anasazi people."

"Oh yeah, the cliff dwellers?"

"Pretty remarkable people. Made life in the middle of the desert. Figured out how to grow food with little rain. Archaeologists found macaw feathers and seashells in Chaco Canyon, which means they traded with the Maya in Mexico. Their structures were incredible, the highest in America until Chicago built steel skyscrapers."

"But they disappeared, right?"

"Population got too big, probably. They cut down a lot of trees. Erosion happened. Then years and years of drought. That finally did them in."

"Damn. I guess they weren't all that advanced, or they would have seen it coming."

"Perhaps," Carson said, a little annoyed at Jimmy's insinuation.

"Seems to me that someone took them down," Jimmy said. "I mean, how can you just outgrow your society? Wouldn't they have seen all the damage they were causing? Seems more likely that an enemy tribe came in and slaughtered them."

"There are theories about that. But there's no evidence of it in the archaeological record."

"Well, I'm sticking to it—the enemy ambush. I just don't buy that they would have missed all the signs. My guess is that we just haven't found that evidence yet."

Carson frowned. He didn't have the energy to argue. "My guess is, no one's going to be looking for that evidence now," he said.

As they walked, Carson turned it over in his head. For a time, he'd believed it was about writing. Without written culture, the Ancestral Puebloans couldn't track their history. They'd lived through drought before. But because those droughts were spread across time, they didn't have continuous living memory of it. But he also knew that the writing of history didn't always mean the reading of it. So what did that mean for this enterprise of his? Another record no one would read?

"Maybe it was about conflict," he said after a while. "Societies fail because they are unwilling or unable to adapt their cultural values to environmental realities. We humans can't reconcile *how* we live with *where* we live."

Their shoes crunched against gravel. To accompany his irregular gait, Jimmy made a little wheeze on each exhale, and their walking took on a kind of jazz rhythm. Carson's own legs were fatigued, and he was pretty sure a blister had formed on the ball of his right foot. The road alongside them meandered southward and disappeared. The sky shifted, grew lighter.

"Or maybe some bad humans just come in and wreck everything we've built," Jimmy said.

AT THE FAR end of Halcyon Street, Beatrix started in on the neighborhood survey Rog had asked her to do. How hard could it be? You just knocked on doors, talked to people, and catalogued their skills. She'd done similar work in Ecuador, when she'd started organizing farmers. The best way to win people's trust was simply to listen. That's what her friend Angel had told her. He'd grown up in one of the local communities and knew the people well. The day they started working together, they drank Nescafé at a wobbly table at a roadside café tucked into the gangly tropical vegetation. "Small talk first," Angel said. "The weather, the children, the crops. Then you listen. Everyone has a voice. Everyone has a wish. Your job is to hear theirs."

On Halcyon, the first woman Beatrix met, Anita, wore a long blue knit scarf, bright against the black coils of her dreadlocks. A midwife, Anita had delivered nearly two hundred babies. She'd also worked at the public library. "I've been meaning to sneak in and take out some books to read," she told Beatrix. "I still have my key."

A couple in their late twenties had more skills than they should have for their age, Beatrix thought. "We went DIY a long time ago," the woman said as Beatrix checked off knitting, sewing, canning, and curing.

"I used to make good money selling beard oil," her husband said, laughing. "It was kind of a luxury, I guess. But I can do practical stuff, too."

"He's the fastest wood chopper in the crew. We used to have contests," his wife said. They gave Beatrix a jar of plum preserves on her way out.

The next house seemed abandoned: a broken window, and leaves and papers strewn across the front porch. But then a curtain moved and an old woman with sunken eyes appeared at the door. No, she didn't have a moment. No, she couldn't answer any questions. "Do you have food?" she asked plaintively. "We're hungry." She opened the door wider and pointed to a cat on the floor, skinny and barely moving.

Next door, a stout middle-aged man told Beatrix, "We've given her plenty of food already. Is it for her or for her cat?"

"Both?"

The man sighed and returned with some dry biscuits. "I can't keep doing this. I've got my own to feed."

"She just seems so desperate," Beatrix said.

"Who isn't?" he said.

Back at the other house, the old woman grabbed the biscuits Beatrix offered and disappeared inside the house. Beatrix made a note in her packet and moved on.

At the next house, no one came to the door. Then three in a row refused to participate in the survey. Just when she was about to call it quits, a block from home, a man opened his door readily, filling the entire doorframe. Gary, the perimeter guard.

"Finally. Someone willing to talk to me," Beatrix said, telling him about the resistant neighbors.

"They're all just afraid," he said.

Beatrix started the survey, checking off his many skills. Construction and repair? Yes. Maintenance? Yes. Managing budgets? Yes. Musical instrument?

"Harmonica," he said, moving close enough so that she could smell a hint of toothpaste, his sun-drenched shirt.

"You're versatile," she asked.

"I was a Boy Scout," he said. "I joined the army and became a general, and then I worked as a defense contractor."

Beatrix flinched. "In Iraq?" she asked.

"And Iran."

"Like Blackwater?"

He nodded, taking the list from her. "Under 'Trade Skills,' you can check off 'Electronics' and 'Radio.' I was really into ham radio as a kid, first, and then later in the service. So I have all the equipment. You'd be surprised. You don't need much power at all to communicate."

Beatrix remembered the preacher she'd heard the other day, but before she could ask about it, Gary said, "It's mostly ham guys like me trading practical information. Water sources. Crime reports. That kind of thing. Two-way talk. Not a lot of long, meaningful conversations."

Beatrix laughed. "About your feelings?"

Gary listed off more skills. "Primitive skills. Survival skills. Orienteering, check," he said. "Firearms."

"That's not on there," Beatrix said.

"No, but it should be. Why would you deny people the right to protect themselves?"

"I don't want to deny anyone anything," she said, feeling her face get hot. "I just—"

"Well, you seem pretty smart, kiddo," he said, "but when someone has a gun pointed at you, you're gonna want to protect yourself."

Kiddo? Did he just call her kiddo? She stared at him without blinking. *Guns don't stop guns*, she wanted to say, but she didn't have the energy to get into it. "Okay then. Thank you for your time," she said, taking the packet and backing onto the porch. Too bad. What a waste of handsome, she thought.

The last house on the block looked like an old farmhouse, set far back from the sidewalk, camouflaged by a large magnolia tree. A stooped old man introduced himself as Mr. Greeb. "You've come for eggs?" he said, inviting her in.

"Eggs?"

Inside, the house smelled of magnolia blooms and something fermented. In the corner of the living room was an ocher-colored reclining chair, its velour upholstery worn through at the arms and headrest. A single strand of red yarn traveled up and over its arm from a basket on the floor.

Beatrix followed Mr. Greeb through the dining room. Covering the table was a collection of brightly colored squares, each made from yarn woven around two perpendicular sticks. "God's eyes," Beatrix said. She remembered making them as a child.

"It's my little hobby. Keeps my eyes working. Summons the view of God," Mr. Greeb said. He led her to the backyard, where a dozen or more chickens were pecking or bathing in the dust. He pointed to one of them. "She's got some eggs under her, for sure. She's hoping they'll become chicks. Sometimes, a hen will do that, even if there's no rooster around. Just need to be gentle when you reach for the eggs so she doesn't take it too hard. No chicks in there, even if she doesn't know it."

Mr. Greeb reached slowly underneath the hen, pulled out an egg, and handed it to Beatrix.

"I'm listing you as 'the resident chicken master,' okay?" Beatrix said, cradling the smooth, warm egg.

"Sounds good to me. Nothing in this yard is secret. Just gotta keep the dogs out is all. And hawks." He led her back through the house. "You want to take some home?"

"They are beautiful," Beatrix said, looking again at the God's eyes. She picked out one for Rosie. Light-blue yarn interrupted with a thin stripe of brown. The colors of her eyes.

"Oh, take as many of those as you want. I meant the hens. You want some? I got so many I can't keep 'em straight. Consider it a barter for all this work you're doing."

"Really?" she said, startled by his generosity.

"Just need to build a coop. Make sure they have a place to roost. Unless you don't mind 'em in your trees," he said. "Go home, build a coop, then come back."

LATE IN THE afternoon, Carson saw a drawing scratched with chalk into a cement post next to the tracks: a square with an *X* in the upper right-hand corner, and a line of *W*s across the bottom, the same symbols someone had drawn on the map Ayo had given him.

"I'm guessing that means water?" Jimmy said.

"That'd be my guess," Carson said, reaching for the map in his pocket. He let out a small gasp. It was gone.

Jimmy pointed to the sky, where dark clouds were assembling in the distance. "Maybe sooner than we think."

Just ahead, they saw a station house, a long room with wooden benches lining the walls. What little light was left in the sky reached through the windows and reflected off the floor.

"We could bed down here, Professor," said Jimmy, collapsing onto one of the outdoor benches.

Actually, it's "Principal," Carson thought, remembering how Ayo always greeted him—*Mr. Principal!* "Let's get a fire started before it rains," Carson said. He gathered up some twigs and began to arrange them on the cement platform.

Jimmy added some larger sticks to the pile. "Maybe my nickname should be Fire Starter." He struck a match and lit the twigs, blowing on them to augment the fire.

"Not Gamer?" Carson said.

"Those days are over. I'm thinking about trees these days. I'm planning to start a nursery at my uncle Frank's in Iowa. I actually have a pretty good green thumb. Kept a hundred houseplants alive. Not just snake plants or spider plants either. I like getting my hands dirty. Maybe I'll even pull off an orchard. But a nursery for starters. Everyone's gonna want saplings."

"Sounds like a smart plan," Carson said, scanning for any larger pieces of wood. "So that's where you're going then—Iowa."

Jimmy nodded. "So for dinner I've got apples and part of a sausage. You?"

"Macaroni," Carson said. "Still some peanut butter, too. Maybe a can or so of tuna. Beans are gone. A few protein bars left. I'm going to have to kill an animal eventually. And plants, of course." He spotted a shipping pallet tucked behind a dumpster and hopped off the platform to retrieve it.

"Yeah, thank God for plants," Jimmy said, then disappeared.

Carson took off his boots. Sure enough, there was the beginning of a blister on the ball of his right foot. He found moleskin in his pack and tended to it. Then he built a fire and cooked noodles with salt and powdered milk, his best approximation of the mac-and-cheese backpacking meal he had made so often. He was halfway through the macaroni when Jimmy appeared again, a mischievous grin on his face.

"I got a surprise for you. Come look."

Carson followed Jimmy behind the station to a boarded-up house. In the backyard was a kidney-shaped swimming pool full of murky water. "Good Lord! You're getting in that water? Sheesh—"

"You better believe it!" Jimmy had already pulled off his clothes. He pounced into the water like a child and let out a high-pitched squeal. "Just a tad swampy. But worth it. C'mon, Professor! Gotta make time for fun."

Carson undressed and lowered himself slowly in. The cold stole his breath, and the water stung his sore feet. He forced himself under and felt the ache in his brain. He got out quickly, trembling, but sensed every cell in his body awake.

Maybe this is what the end of the world felt like, he thought. Like waking up. He recalled those first few weeks after the power went out, the stunned quality of his days. How he'd sunk into a kind of somnambulism: staring out the window, foraging, wandering the streets looking for Ayo, that buoy who'd kept him afloat. Thank God for Ayo. And now Carson was halfway across the state of Pennsylvania with an unlikely companion. Who was his buoy now?

He shivered and looked up at the tree beside the pool. Red maple, probably, as he could see small buds silhouetted against the dusk. In a few weeks, this tree would be a scarlet blaze in the sun. He had no idea what came next for him, but he'd just had a bath, and his body was close to clean, and that was its own kind of miracle.

Later, they revived the fire. Carson gave Jimmy the last of the macaroni. Jimmy split the sausage between them.

Afterward, Jimmy pushed the hot coals around with a stick. "Got any marshmallows?" he said. Jimmy let the stick catch on fire for a moment, then scratched it against the concrete, making marks. He held a flashlight over the markings. "My hobo nickname," he said. He'd drawn a smooth-edged cube with legs and a baseball cap, and two short lines as eyes. He'd labeled it *Marshmallow Man.* He held out the stick for Carson. "Do yours."

Carson studied the charcoal tip, his mind blank. He felt a familiar burden. To mark one's name was a request to be remembered, was it not? A notation of one's presence. *Kilroy was here.* He understood the impulse, but in this moment he wasn't sure he had anything to prove.

A low thunder rumbled, and the sky began to sprinkle rain. They watched it fall for a while, then went inside.

Carson unrolled his sleeping bag and stretched out, listening to the gentle tap of raindrops on the roof. His feet, awakened by the pool water, throbbed from the miles.

Jimmy arranged a blanket on one of the benches. "I had this other idea for a game once. *Secrets.* The objective was to figure out everyone's secrets. There'd be a lot of danger: You'd be stumbling into affairs, murders, thefts. You'd have to maneuver into seedy motel rooms and basements and through other people's heads, trying to decipher the secrets."

Carson stared at the ceiling. "Maybe your avatar could lead people to a room that would enable you to hear all their secrets, really loud."

"You mean like, 'No one knows it, but I still suck my thumb!' or 'I eat my boogers and actually like them!'"

Carson laughed out loud. "But not *all* jokes. How about, 'I stole my colleague's work and published it as my own.'"

"That's harsh," Jimmy said. "Or 'I'm really in love with my wife's sister.'"

"Aw," Carson said. "Sounds like an awful place."

"Yeah, that could be a tough room to go in," Jimmy said.

Carson was silent for a little while and then aired his own secret. "I never liked being an administrator. I stayed because our livelihood depended on it, or the livelihood we somehow convinced ourselves we wanted. And then my wife died. She had told me many times to leave the job. But I was too afraid to." Carson felt the itchy sting of regret beneath his Adam's apple. He heard Jimmy breathing and felt grateful for silence.

But after a few minutes, Jimmy spoke. "My ma died in the Olympia earthquake. We weren't all that near the epicenter, but her building was old. I was at the store when it happened. She got pinned beneath a steel support beam. We waited five hours before any help came, but they couldn't get her out. She was just stuck there, and there was so much blood. Somehow, I managed to reach around the steel beam to touch her. I could touch her, at least. I took off my jacket and tried to cover her with it to keep her warm. And I watched her face change—her eyes just got dim. She didn't have anything left. I reached over, and I just pressed my jacket against her mouth until she stopped . . . until she stopped suffering."

Carson made a sound that wasn't exactly a word. Then he sat up and looked out at the darkness. "An act of love," he said. He pictured June's mouth, her thin pink lips at the rim of the teacup she drank from, both so fragile and delicate. He peeled off his sleeping bag and went outside.

The rain had stopped, and the night was filled with cricket-song. A distant frog repeated itself. How could anyone judge when a life was complete? He looked up at a patch of clear sky, a dozen or more stars there, many of them dead. When there was a lull in the symphony of frogs and crickets, he returned inside.

Sometime later, as Carson was settling into sleep, he heard Jimmy say, "I wish I had an orange."

Carson thought of Beatrix, her love of them. "The fruit of hope," he said.

"A very happy color."

Carson's mind flashed to the walls of orange in the abandoned building that Jairo had shown him, that loud chaos before the darkness. "Once upon a time," he said.

"What's that?" Jimmy said.

"Just plant some orange trees, will you?" Carson said.

At dawn, Carson woke to the chatter of birds. He crawled out of his bag and went outside. Jimmy's drawing appeared clear and dark. *Marshmallow Man.* There really was a resemblance.

Carson picked up the stick and dabbed it into the cooled coals. He scratched a horizon line on the concrete, and the crisscross of train tracks reaching into it. Where the tracks ended, he colored in a half hemisphere of sun, four rays bursting from it. In the best grade-school cursive he could muster, he wrote *Professor* below the drawing.

He quietly packed up his things, then wrote a note for Jimmy.

Marshmallow Man,

Spilled secrets = forgiveness. The world needs your orchards.

Best of luck. Be safe.

—Professor

He retrieved a protein bar from his pack and left it with the note under Jimmy's ball cap.

Carson peered down the stretch of railroad, looking east, then west. He conjured a train: the approaching rumble, the shift in the rails, the crescendo of metal on metal. He longed for speed, to get lost in the blur, to become the train itself and plunge himself into the future. He stepped onto the tracks and began to walk.

ROSIE TURNED OVER the square of woven yarn Beatrix had given her and tried to find the loose end.

"Un ojo de dios," her abuela said, dividing up a batch of tortillas and wrapping each stack in a towel. "They're Huichol."

"Wee-*what*?" Rosie said.

"Wee-choal. Huichol. Your father was Huichol—indigenous, from Jalisco."

"Oh," Rosie said, rolling her eyes. "I didn't know him."

"When a child is born, the father begins the eye at the center, and for each year of the child's life, he adds more yarn. It is said to protect the child." Abuela pointed to the God's eye. "He made you one like that when you were a baby."

Rosie held the God's eye up close to her face and examined it. "He did? Where is it now?"

"Oh, mi'ja, I don't know."

Mi'ja. Her abuela called her this, but it wasn't really accurate. Rosie was her *nieta*, not her *hija*. Rosie was hija only to her mother, whom she hadn't seen since she was eight, because that's when her mother had died. A car accident. The body in the coffin didn't look anything like her mother. The cheekbones were crooked, and she was too pale, except for the bruise coming through the bad makeup. Who could afford to dress up the dead?

It occurred to her then that her father, whom she had never met, had probably been dead for a long time. So that even if the so-called God's eye he'd made for her existed somewhere, it would be skimpy—not because he just didn't bother to wind the yard around but because who could make a God's eye when they were dead?

Her abuela patted one of the bundles of tortillas. "Take these up to Beatrix, okay?"

Rosie tossed the God's eye on her bed and went upstairs.

Beatrix was sitting on the couch. She had a ruler out and was drawing something on a notepad. She lit up when she saw Rosie. "Tortillas, what a treat. Thank you."

She held up the notepad. "Pretty soon, we'll have eggs. I'm trying to draw up a plan for the chicken coop now."

"Cool," Rosie said, sitting in the rocking chair. Outside, a breeze swayed the plum tree. "Do you know what 'prosy' means? As in, the 'winds were prosy.'"

"The winds were prosy?"

"It's from a poem. Emily Dickinson."

"Oh," Beatrix said. "'Prosy.' I think like dull or common."

"The winds were common," Rosie said. That worked.

She stood up and went to look at the dozen or more posters that hung on the wall. "Where did you get all these?" Rosie asked.

"Hank liked to keep them and put them up," Beatrix said. "'A record of the resistance,' he used to say."

Some of the posters announced specific marches and rallies. Others were just images or proclamations. Planets and doves and stylized crops and clenched fists—lots of red and big bold lettering. With her index finger, Rosie traced the wing of one of the monarch butterflies in a poster calling for the protection of immigrants and asked, "How did you get into all of that?"

"Activism?"

"Yeah," Rosie said.

Beatrix set down the notepad. "My aunt Vera. She lived near some orange groves in Southern Cal. There were lots of migrant workers there, mostly all from Mexico. Anytime we ate an orange, aunt Vera always said, 'Thank you, Guadalupe,' or 'Thank you, Julio.' Or Marisol or Diego or Fernanda or Juan Carlos. Many names, many workers. She didn't really know them, but she used to make a point of driving by where they lived so I could see their trailers, their families, their lives."

"Cool," Rosie said. She meant it, but she also felt a little strange. Maybe if her mom had lived, they would have been picking oranges, too.

"There were some kids that lived next door to Vera that I sometimes played with," Beatrix continued. "The Butlers. One day the boy, Lenny, showed me a flattened penny and said we could go make more of them. I wasn't allowed to cross the street that separated the neighborhood from the orange groves, but we went anyway, me and Lenny and Lenny's little sister. I can still remember the smell of the groves—soil and irrigation water and a sweetness. We got to the train tracks and laid out our pennies, and then this other boy came from the other side. He was about our age. He said something to us in Spanish, but I didn't know Spanish back then. He saw our pennies and was nodding like he knew what we were doing. But we couldn't really communicate with him."

Rosie bit her lip, hoping the story wasn't about to turn tragic.

"After a while, someone called out to him," Beatrix said. "I saw the pickers in the groves, and he had to go back to work."

"What about the train?" Rosie said, holding her breath. "No one got hit, did they?"

"Oh God, no," Beatrix said. "The train just came and flattened our pennies. But no—no one got hit."

"Phew," Rosie said, wondering what the big deal was. She took Beatrix's notebook from the table and, looking at her design, started in on a new sketch.

"So that was the catalyst," Beatrix said.

Rosie was confused. "You got pennies, and that Mexican kid didn't?"

Beatrix nodded. "Yeah, that. Exactly. He had to go work. We got to play."

"Oh," Rosie said.

"I was on one side of the tracks, and that kid was on the other," Beatrix said. Her face got sad. "I saw that so clearly."

Rosie nodded. It made sense then, and she realized at that point which side of the tracks she'd have been on, most likely, and that caused a weird gripping feeling in her throat.

"Afterwards, when I told my aunt Vera about it, she said, 'That boy has dreams just like you. Maybe they're different dreams, but no matter—they're dreams.' I always remembered that."

Rosie nodded but didn't say anything. She kept working on the drawing. What good was a dream now? she wondered.

After a little while, she turned the notebook around and set it back on the table. "How about this?"

Beatrix leaned over and looked at the drawing. "Oh my God," she said. "I didn't know you could draw, Rosie. It's perfect. It's a perfect chicken coop."

CHAPTER 5

Carson followed the rails through a town—Altoona, was it?—past brick Italianate buildings with rows of long windows, a white domed roof, a bell tower. People were out selling food, hauling buckets of water, making trades. Women sat knitting on a park bench. One man dragged a dead deer across the road. Full of morning motivation, Carson didn't want to stop.

He headed for a ridge in the distance, pulled by the evergreens. The moleskin had taken care of the blister for now, and his gait was steady and strong. Making good time, he continued along the ridgeline, thick with the dark of pine, fir, and hemlock, and the brightness of new maple and oak. Below, a series of reservoirs reflected the gray-blue sky. Ahead, the ridge made a dramatic curve, and soon he noticed a parallel set of tracks a few hundred feet across the valley. From his jacket, he pulled out the postcard he'd taken from the gift-shop rack. "Horseshoe

Curve," he said, thrilled by the match and by the feat itself: how men could cut into the side of a mountain, turn track into sinews, mirror a landscape.

At the apex, he stopped and looked back over the land. Soon he would leave the Northeast, the terrain he knew so well: fireflies, hemlocks, the singsong call of the eastern towhee: *Drink your tea!* How lucky he was to see this, he reminded himself. How lucky he was to be alive.

Late in the afternoon, his path cut through hilly terrain. In places, the earth butted up against a high cement wall that paralleled the tracks. Large, loose letters painted purple and gold seemed to pop from its surface. *HOw dO yOU mAkE lOvE lAst?* Painted near the letters were bubbles, the same bubbles—or so it seemed—as those he'd seen on the walls in the carriage house, that scroll of history. The same artist?

He wondered about Jairo, if he was cycling through the streets, if he was surviving, if he had delivered the letters. He remembered the resiliency of youth.

He found a rock on the ground and used it to scratch his moniker into the wall. Not as good as spray paint, but something. The Professor was here. Proof. He read again the swirling words nearby: How *do* you make love last?

The first time June asked him to help her die, he ignored her. He was bathing her, and he continued the sponge bath without speaking, circling the washcloth around her neck, underneath her arms, over her belly. He focused on the creases of her joints, smoothed the cloth over the curve of her back. At first, he had not liked those baths. They signaled her debility, her decline, the coming truth. But he began to accept them as one small act he could perform to make her comfortable. An intimacy in movement. Dipping the cloth in fresh warm water, gently pushing June forward, running the cloth over her back, up to her neck, behind the spiral of her ears. It became a meditation on her body, on love.

"You're Mary Magdalene. I'm Jesus," she had said once, when he had reached her feet.

"So I'm the whore and you're the saint?" he'd said, and they'd laughed.

But during that other sponge bath, there were no jokes. Just his own relentless monologue, blatantly ignoring what she'd just asked him to do.

"So today, Martín gets sent to me again," he said. "He started a skateboarding movement through the hallways. I wish I'd seen it. He slammed into Mrs. Chase. Took her out, all the way down. She was furious. The counselors have had it with him. The vice principal can't stand him. So they send him to me."

He rinsed the cloth and made one final steady circle around her neck. "Don't you feel a million times better?" he asked, helping her out of the tub. He wrapped a dry towel around her and pulled a gown over her head. It fell, like water, over her frail body. She looked old, too old. She looked like she was dying. She was dying.

"So he shuffles in. He's got that smirk that he always does. Kind of like this," he said. He pressed his lips together and pushed them to the right side of his face for just a moment.

"Carson," June interrupted.

"Are you cold? Here, let's get you into the bed."

"Just sit with me," June said, squeezing his hand.

Carson sat and stroked her hair. He almost had to clamp his mouth shut. He wanted to fill the room with words, spill them across the floor, the bed, her pillow, to black out what she had asked.

A few days later, she asked again.

"How can you ask me to do that? I cannot."

"Carson," she said. "I am dying. What difference does it make?"

He looked at her thin, sick body, the translucent flesh over her bones, the darkness around her eyes. "What difference does it make?" he said, sternly. "Are you kidding me? How can you even ask that?" He turned away from her, angry. When he turned back, she looked small and terrified, like a wet cat.

Beatrix held a plank of wood steady as Finn pounded in the final nail. "That should do it," he said. They'd spent the morning putting together the chicken coop from old doors Beatrix had found in the shed and some chicken wire Finn had donated from the garden. It wasn't an exact model of Rosie's drawing, but suitable and sturdy enough to keep the hens safe.

"This is perfect," Beatrix said. "When we have more materials, we can add an egg house."

"You know where to find me," Finn said, holding up the hammer. He smiled. "So I guess that means you're sticking around, Beatrix?"

"I guess so, yeah," she said. It hadn't really been a decision she'd made as much as fallen into. She missed Hank and Dolores, but more and more it seemed that Dragon was right, that heading off to look for them might be a suicide mission, that it was safer just to stay put here, where she had shelter, food, community.

"Good," Finn said. "We like you here."

Beatrix smiled. It felt good to be wanted.

She followed Finn out front, where Dragon and Flash were hunched over an old boom box. As Finn hurried off, late for a meeting, Beatrix crouched to get a better look.

"Our very own radio!" Flash said, over the loud static.

Hooked to the boom box was a solar panel the size of a slice of bread. Dragon turned a dial, and the static gave way to the sound of a voice.

"—where people just like you are gathering, ready to embark upon their journey to the Center."

The voice was the same one Beatrix had heard before, a deep male voice.

"People like Myrna Matthews from Houston, Texas. She has her eyes to a better world. She wants to upgrade. Can you tell our listeners why you've come to the Center?"

"I believe in a new world," she said. *"I believe it's possible. I believe all*

this has happened for a reason. So many of the signs have already come, just as prophesized. The flu, the flood, the financial fall."

"The darkness," the familiar male voice said. *"But we don't have to fear the darkness. And here, there is light. Literal light."*

Flash turned the dial and came to the same voice, the same broadcast, every time there was a signal. "This guy is on every station. Jonathan Blue and his bluebell disciples! I can't believe that's all that comes through. I don't get it."

"Jonathan Blue? Where is he broadcasting from?" Beatrix asked. "Where exactly is the Center?"

"Supposedly, the geographic center of the country. But I heard it's actually somewhere in Wyoming," Dragon said.

"So left of center?" Beatrix said, amused. "Is this for real?"

"People believe it's real, and that's all you need, really," Flash said. "Supposedly, they have generators, some mysterious stash of fuel. That's how they tempt people: 'All the amenities.'"

"That's what you need to lure people away from their communities for some so-called 'Ascension.' That's what he calls it," Dragon said. "Says that what we've been waiting for is this kind of unity, and now that the filters are gone, we can finally join it. If we go there, that is. No doubt, this is a new world. But most of what he says sounds like claptrap to me."

"Everybody always wants to be saved," Beatrix said. In Latin America, the idea of waiting for the Messiah seemed to be programmed into people's DNA. First, they'd been waiting for the mythical gods, then for the conquerors, then for Jesus Christ, then Simón Bolívar, then Che Guevara, then the International Monetary Fund, then Hugo Chávez. In the US, well, the US had long believed *itself* to be the Messiah, a model for all other nations, the shining beacon on the hill. Look how that ended up, she thought.

"Right. Where I come from, you don't get saved for doing nothing," Flash said.

"Where do you come from?" Beatrix said.

"California, born and raised. First-generation. My Vietnamese parents immigrated to the States before I happened."

"And how *do* you get saved?" Dragon said.

Flash shrugged, then said, "Good deeds and humility."

"Well, where I come from you only get saved by making money," Dragon said. "It's the only way my dad could measure success, at least."

"A lot of good that did anyone," Flash said. "The new currency is clearly measured in bike smarts."

Gary, minus his red bandana, came up the walkway, carrying a cardboard box. "Nice setup," he said, pointing to the radio.

"Oh, hi," Beatrix said flatly.

"Hey, Gary," Flash said. "Yeah, check this out." He held up the back of the solar panel and explained how they'd configured it. It all sounded like gibberish to Beatrix, but Gary nodded vigorously, seeming to understand everything.

"I can show you how to do a crystal radio set," Gary said. "They take no power at all. Just picks up radio waves."

"You can all make your radios, but all you get to listen to is this Jonathan Blue guy," Beatrix said.

"That seems to be true. He's got some kind of strong power to be able to broadcast so far," Gary said. He turned to Beatrix and held up the box in his hands. "I brought these for you."

She opened the box to find three silver cans, punctured with holes that made patterned designs. Inside each can was a candle. "Lanterns," Gary said.

"Oh, cool," Beatrix said, genuinely impressed. "Where'd you get them?"

"I made them. My dad taught me how when I was a kid."

The gesture surprised her more than she let on. She pictured Gary as a boy with small, determined hands. "That's very thoughtful. Thank you."

Maybe he wasn't just an arrogant army dude. But did he want something from her? God forbid. When he walked away, she noticed the stiffness of his back, the unyielding square shape of his shoulders.

"Well, that was nice of him," Flash said, peering into the box. "Lemme see."

"Peace offering, I guess," Beatrix said.

Dragon elbowed Flash, who made an okay sign with his fingers and winked. "Right. Peace offering."

"No," Beatrix said. "Not interested."

The sound of ringing bells came from a distance. Flash bellowed out an announcement in a booming voice, "Big trucks, trucks, trucks . . . are here, here, here!"

At the water cart, half a dozen other neighbors were already in line. The air smelled of animal sweat and manure. Eight draft horses stood at the front of the water cart, shifting from hoof to hoof and batting flies with their tails. On the cart were three large water tanks that proclaimed, in blue cursive lettering, *H2o from Dorn: Keeping you and yours alive!* Coiled hoses hung on the sides of the cart, and spigots at the back opened the tanks to fill the buckets. A sign listed prices for everything from empty two-liter soda bottles to five-hundred-gallon tanks.

After a ten-minute wait, a man wearing blue overalls took their money.

"Can you tell me where this water is from, exactly?" Beatrix asked.

"Same place it was always from. The mountains," he said. "Comes down the aqueduct."

"Is it safe?" she said.

He widened his eyes and, making sure she was watching, retrieved a cup from the cart and held it under the spigot, then tilted it back and chugged the water straight down.

A woman behind them started huffing for them to hurry up. She pointed to the side of the tank, where *Clean and Potable* was written. "Says so right there, lady. I have three boys waiting on me at home. Can you move on?"

Beatrix turned to Flash and Dragon. "Do you guys trust this?"

"It's what we've got," Flash said, lifting up his full buckets and moving away from the tanks.

Beatrix picked up her buckets and followed, wary and unsatisfied.

Nearly six weeks after he left the city, Carson reached western Ohio. The sun steepened its arc overhead, and the May days turned warmer. Fallow fields filled Carson's view—miles of dirt with cornstalk carcasses. Along the tracks, tiny yellow flowers sprouted from purple stems.

Carson welcomed these luscious specks of color, interruptions to the fatigue in his feet, the monotonous smear of gray gravel. As the days warmed, the tracks pushed through exquisite snarls of green—weeds, ivy, grasses, even fresh dandelions and mustards, which he collected and nibbled as he walked. The greens felt like miracle salads to accompany the venison jerky he'd been gifted some days ago and a can of mystery beans he'd found in an abandoned pickup truck. His pants were loose on him already, his belt notched tighter.

One afternoon, he followed a hunting hawk along a spur of track. The raptor circled and swooped, then rose with a mouse. Hawkeyed.

Carson came to a white building with two open bay doors, along a road flanking the tracks. A body shop. He was hungry. Might there be a forgotten vending machine to break into? As he entered one of the bays, two cats darted past. A third, Siamese, slinked out from behind a barrel and stared at him, its eyes like glacial ponds.

He called out, "Hello!" The cats appeared to be well-fed, but the place seemed long abandoned. Perhaps there were armies of mice here, thinning each day. Stray bolts, dirty rags, and inventory lists lay scattered across the floor, along with a stain of oil shaped like a thick-shouldered bull. A car was suspended on one of the lifts. Its underbelly made Carson feel suddenly out of scale, as if he were looking at a tiny Matchbox model.

Inside, he found the vending machine he'd imagined. He peered into the plexiglass, but it was completely empty. The coffee maker, too, had nothing to offer. He made his way past a stack of red plastic chairs and through the next garage, where a silver Dodge Neon was parked over the pit, as if awaiting an oil change. Surely, the gas had been siphoned out. He opened the door and sat down. He put his hands on the steering wheel for a moment, then reached under the seat and felt around for a key. Fat chance. He turned on the radio and was startled when a man's voice, very deep and clear, came through the speakers.

"Chin up, rise above it. The sprit is resilient. What does it ultimately want? To rise, rise, rise!"

That this was a preaching voice didn't surprise Carson. If anyone could get on the airways, it would be the religious fanatics. He turned the dial and searched for something else, but all he found was the man's voice.

"I, too, was once addicted to my image. My ego wanted only to be massaged. I sought approval and wanted to be liked. But then I tapped into the larger web, the real web. You see, we can break free from the trappings of ego and plug into the higher power. This collapse has created a path for you. I can show you."

Carson turned off the radio. He leaned his head back and relaxed into the seat. He woke with a start to tapping. "Get out! Move it!" A man held a rifle to the windshield.

Carson willed himself to stay calm. I can talk my way out of this. Yes, I can. He reached slowly for his pack.

The man, unshaven and with matted hair, leaned into the window. "What the hell are you doing here?"

"I'm just traveling through," Carson said, trying to sound calm. "The doors were open, so I came in. I didn't know anyone was here."

"Shame on you, trespassing like that," the man said. "This is private property." The rifle danced around in front of his face.

"This is an auto body shop," Carson said, keeping his eyes on the rifle.

"It's *my* place now," the man said. A Siamese cat skulked behind a metal tool cabinet. The man crouched and beckoned, and the cat trotted over to him. He scooped up the animal with one arm, his other arm still wrapped around the rifle.

"You seen my other cats?" the man shouted. "Where are my other cats? D'you go runnin' them off? Dammit."

Carson stepped out of the car, easing his backpack out behind him. He was thinking about how to access his gun.

"You watch yourself!" the man said to Carson. "Go on, git," he shouted. "Next time, stay in the woods. That's public space. This here is *private*."

Carson sprinted across the parking lot to a stand of trees. When he stopped, he could barely breathe. It started to rain, but he kept going, letting the rain soak him.

The rain lightened to a drizzle, then tapered off. The sun unburied itself from the clouds, steam rose from the rails, and everywhere water droplets caught the sunlight. Carson thought of how the man had spoken to his cat, so gentle, so unlike the way he'd spoken to Carson. June used to say men with cats longed for women but hadn't the slightest idea how to talk to them, so they substituted feline for female. June was catlike herself, her petite, sinuous body, her delicate hands.

Something moved ahead of him on the trail, a four-legged blur with pointed ears. A coyote turned around and looked at him, its gray-brown fur dampened from the rain. After a long stare, it turned and trotted away.

Carson stopped to rest on a fallen log. He stretched out his legs and, after a while, pulled out his notebook.

May 21

B.,

I miss you. Still so far away. The other day, I thought I saw one of my students. Kind of an unremarkable kid until he won a national science competition none of us even knew he'd entered. His project was a device that let you power your own cell phone just by walking. Where is that device now? I'd have endless battery! In a different world, you could have fueled my walk with your voice.

Anyway, the kid I saw was carrying a string of dead squirrels. I said hey, and he looked up, but it wasn't the same kid.

I'd give anything for that human-powered battery. I'd give anything for a string of squirrels. I'd give anything for a coyote's cunning sensibility.

Love, C.

ROSIE WASN'T SURE how, but somehow Beatrix had convinced her abuela to let Rosie join the other housemates on a trip to the Gold Mine, some kind of old dump where people scavenged and recycled old trash and made it reusable.

"It's not just a junkyard," Flash explained. "It's a community. They pool all their earnings and divvy them. They eat from the gardens and sleep in bunkhouses built from scrap materials."

"Just like in Latin America," Beatrix said. "Whole communities of pickers live off the dumps. It's a hard life, but not undignified."

The idea of living in a dump didn't seem very dignified at all to Rosie. But it made living in a car seem downright luxurious.

They were in search of building materials for the egg house, bike parts, and—what had helped win over Abuela—jars for storing herbs and tinctures. Abuela now was making her own anti-anxiety solution, a blend of chamomile and poppy. Even though Rosie wasn't anxious, Abuela sometimes added a few drops of it to the health formula she made Rosie take every day.

They rode beyond the Perimeter to the other side of the highway past the rail yards. It was farther than Rosie had ever been on her bike, and she felt a giddy sense of freedom with the movement. She pedaled hard and steady, making sure to keep up with the others.

On the other side of a chain-link fence, up a dry hill, the pickers moved in and out of view. They carried shovels and bags and moved slowly, digging and sorting the trash. Gulls, ravens, and vultures swooped down with finds of their own—a desiccated decades-old TV dinner, perhaps, or a scared mouse. Refuse had been stacked and sorted under hand-painted signs: AUTO, APPLIANCES, MISCELLANEOUS METALS.

There was a gate, and just beyond it a green van painted with the words TRASH TO TREASURES. SUNRISE TO SUNSET. Flash shook a tambourine hanging on the fence, and a brawny rottweiler careened out from behind the van.

"Be right there," a woman called out. "And, yes, she bites!"

The woman was tall, with short dark hair, and she wore a nose ring. A tattoo of a yin-yang symbol rounded over one arm.

"I know her," Beatrix said, lighting up. "Frida, an old friend from immigration activism days."

"Beatrix," Frida said. "Long time no see." She called the dog over and patted her head. "She doesn't bite actually. I just say that to scare people. Good to see you. You've come to the right place. It really is a gold mine here. You wouldn't believe what we find."

"Treasures?" Rosie said, surprised by the sound of her own voice.

"Lots of treasures. And we organize it all for you. Go have a look. Everyone who comes here finds—"

A familiar voice interrupted them: ". . . *where you'll find all your needs, all the amenities you're missing. Bountiful food, clean water, safe shelter. In this place, you'll find the true you, without interference."*

"*Ay, mi amor*, turn that off, will you?" Frida yelled.

A man with a shaved head stepped out from behind the van. "I was just seeing if there was anything else."

"There's never anything else," Dragon said.

"To make it sweeter, we have cold milk, my friends. Fresh cold milk. You thought those days were over, didn't you? Ice cream for the kids. That's right, you heard me: ice cream."

"First it was running water," Frida said. "Now it's ice cream. What'll he come up with next?"

Rosie tried to remember the last time she'd had ice cream.

". . . acres of gardens. This is the land of abundance . . ."

Frida rolled her eyes. "Notice, too, how he's always talking about darkness and light. So dualistic. I bet there's not one black or brown person in that Center place," she said.

"I bet not," Beatrix said.

Rosie nodded. They were probably right.

"This is the land of abundance right here," Frida said, looking right into Rosie's eyes. "Go find it."

Dragon made a beeline for a pile of used rubber. "Hey, people, bike tires! Right here."

Rosie followed Beatrix up the hill toward the mounds of other junk, still thinking about ice cream.

"Jars," Beatrix said. "Keep your eyes peeled for jars." They stood next to a truck bed piled with broken glass. Rosie felt forlorn. This really was just a junkyard.

They moved through heaps of scrap wood, wire, and cloth. Beatrix stepped into one of the piles and pulled up a scroll of chicken-wire fence. "Perfect."

They wandered into a home-goods section, past a bed with a cast-iron headboard, a hope chest, flowerpots, a collection of sports trophies, a remarkably well-preserved stack of *Life* magazines, and a fake Christmas tree strung with gaudy jewelry.

Then Rosie spotted a pile of shoes. She rummaged through misshapen sneakers and scuffed wingtips, and found a single wedge sandal, still blue, with tiny embroidered dragonflies across the strap. She tried it on. "It fits!"

"That looks good on you," Beatrix said, sounding like she meant it. "But can you walk? We used to say if you can't run from the cops or climb a fence—"

"Please let the other one be here," Rosie said, digging through the mound. A strip of blue! There it was. She freed the other sandal and held it up.

"Nice work," Beatrix said. "Hey, look over there." She pointed to an assortment of jars on a rickety shelf.

Rosie put the other sandal on and walked cautiously to fetch the jars. "Abuela will be happy now," she said, feeling relieved.

They returned to the van, where Dragon and Flash waited with a collection of scrap rubber, shipping pallets, and what Flash called "a few fun finds." He held up a large thin cloth painted to look like a fish. "I'm going to turn this into a kite. With a little snipping and some string, I'm sure I can get it aloft."

Rosie smiled. She liked how Flash was always so creative and optimistic.

"I like to think of this place as the great equalizer," Frida said. "Everything returns to its origin. Car becomes metal again. Clothing becomes fabric. Cans of gourmet organic soup or cans of cheap pinto beans—they're all just steel cans again. Ready for repurposing."

She looked at Rosie's feet. "Case in point," she said. "Great shoes."

Rosie smiled, feeling seen. She hoped Diego would think the same.

They settled their barter with one of Abuela's herbal remedies, a few dozen tortillas, and some jars of tomatoes and peaches Flash had earned the week before. Then they loaded up the bike trailers, and Rosie put her sneakers back on, tucking the sandals into a small tote bag on her back.

Before reaching the Perimeter, they rounded a corner and came upon four bright lights, one flashing quickly, five times. "Oh shit," Dragon said. "Turn around, everyone. Now!"

Something whistled past Rosie's ear and shattered on the asphalt.

"Bottles! They've got bottles," Flash said. "T-Rize. Gotta be T-Rize. Those light flashes. It's a code."

T-Rize? What was T-Rize? A bottle bounced off Flash's trailer. Another hit the road ahead, spraying glass in front of them. Rosie tried to go faster, but as they turned down an alley, her foot slipped off the pedal and she stopped to avoid a fall.

"Rosie!" Beatrix called out.

A bike was coming at Rosie fast. She reached into the tote bag, pulled out one of the sandals, and hurled it toward the cyclist, hitting him right on his helmetless head.

Stunned, she jumped back on her bike, just as Flash and Dragon came circling back, and then the four of them sped through the neighborhood to Halcyon.

CARSON WOKE WITH a deep hunger. He'd eaten the last of his protein bars and had only thistle root and half a dozen small apples he'd pilfered from an orchard. He left his sleeping bag to dry in the sun and retraced his steps through a dew-covered field to the deadfall trap he'd set the night before. It had taken him a good two hours to make it. He closed his eyes and made a wish for a squirrel, a raccoon. Anything.

The bait was gone, but the trap appeared untouched. Clearly, he didn't remember how to set a deadfall trap.

Later that morning, the apples gone, Carson veered from the tracks into a small town. He craved grilled ham, cheese, and banana. Fat chance. His mouth watered. He heard people chanting. He followed the sound through a stand of trees to a large white tent. He ducked inside, where over a hundred people were on their feet, hands in the air, voices ringing. "God wants you to have new life! God wants you to have new life!" A young preacher with long, tousled hair led them, pumping his heavily tattooed fist upward like a rock star. The air was thick with human sweat and breath.

Carson spotted a table against one of the tent walls, full of fruit, bread, some bowls, a stainless-steel pot.

"God wants you to have new life!" the preacher shouted. The crowd thundered its response.

They are hungry for salvation, Carson thought. I am just plain hungry.

A line formed in the center aisle, and as the initiates stepped forward, the preacher touched them one by one. Their responses ranged from trembling to hopping up and down to dropping to the ground in convulsions. Carson hurried to the table and loaded up a bandana with rolls, two (hard-boiled?) eggs, a handful of carrots, and a drumstick that looked too big to be from a chicken. He hurried out and ate voraciously, nearly choking as he swallowed. "Bless you," he whispered to the sky.

He headed back the way he'd come, sated and only a touch guilty. Near the tracks, he came upon a man carrying a sack stained with blood. Carson slowed, feeling cautious, but the man turned and said, "Don't recognize you. Where are you coming from?"

The man looked about Carson's age, with brown hair grown past his ears and a sweat-stained cloth tied around his neck. "Just now, from a revival," Carson said. "But I'm just passing through. It's not really my thing."

The man smiled. "Seems we're few and far between."

Two women approached on bicycles, and the man waved them over. One wore a baseball cap, and the other, a green rain poncho that fanned out like a short dress. Both had dust masks covering their faces.

"Dinner later, after the burial," said the woman in the poncho. She looked at the man's pillowcase. "What'd you get, hunter?"

"Raccoon."

"Raccoon stew then. And plenty of venison left for the immediate," she said. She turned to Carson. "You staying, too?" She rummaged in a bag and threw him a mask. "You'll need this. We got flu here," she said.

"We buried someone today," said the other woman. She had removed her cap to reveal a shock of white hair on the front of what was otherwise a frizzy dark mane.

"I'm sorry to hear it," Carson said, putting on the mask. "No one at the revival wore masks." When the woman in the rain poncho rolled her eyes, he clarified. "Just stopped in to hear the chanting."

"Going on all the time. Like amplified mosquitoes," said the woman with the gray streak. She handed him some dried venison from her bag. "You staying for dinner?"

Carson weighed the invitation. Why were they being so nice to him? He would be hungry again soon, yes. But flu? He didn't want to risk it. "Thank you," he said, holding up the venison. "I'm going to push on for another hour of light."

"Can't say I blame you," the hunter said. "There's a house a few miles up. No one lives there. Probably a dry porch."

"What's your destination?" asked the poncho woman.

"Heading west."

"What's west of Ohio?" the hunter said, smirking.

"Gold?" said the woman with the gray streak, who had put her cap back on.

Carson smiled and could see in her eyes that she was smiling. "I'm recording history, I guess," he said.

"Write about us," she said. "Fulton County, Ohio, where some searched for God and some survived the flu."

"And some planted trees," the man said.

The women looked at him. "It's true," he said. "We're known for our trees. The whole state of Ohio is."

"Then, there you have it: flu, God, and trees," the woman in the baseball cap said. "Write that."

Carson nodded and bid them well. He walked for another hour and found the house. Indeed, the porch was dry, but he found no dry wood for a fire. He unrolled his sleeping bag and bedded down.

When he woke in the morning, there was a plate on the porch with a biscuit and some gamey meat he guessed was raccoon. "Bless you," he said again.

B.,

Ghosts everywhere. But I don't feel afraid. The wind nudges me west.

CHAPTER 6

In a thin patch of woods not far from the Wabash River, a giant blue tarp was strung up in the trees. At first, Carson mistook the fraying canopy for the sky. Below it, a handful of people circled a fire pit, but no fire was burning, the summer afternoon warm and humid. Nearby was a picnic table, a bookshelf full of kitchenware, and three metal barrels.

A woman moved around the picnic table in a gold-colored party dress, a funny thing to wear in the middle of the woods, but she was smooth in her movements, like a dancer, and slow, like a mountain lion. As he entered the camp, the faces at the fire pit turned toward him, looking almost unreal, as if cast in wax.

"Who goes there?" asked a man.

Carson introduced himself and mentioned how far he'd come. "I'm traveling through. I'm a teacher, by trade." Miles ago, he'd decided identifying himself that way was the safest bet. What was more innocuous than schoolteacher?

"Well, you've come a long way just to arrive in paradise," the man said. "But come on closer! Give us a lesson. We'll plant seeds in Dixie cups, if you've got seeds." He cackled at his own joke.

Carson laughed, too. *Not that kind of teacher,* he wanted to say, although sometimes teenagers and kindergartners shared traits.

"Welcome to the Jungle," the man said. "I'm Franklin. Where you headed?"

"West," Carson said.

"Well, you got as far as Illinois. That's something," Franklin said.

"Kudos to you," said a woman in a pink knit hat. "Teaching is hard stuff."

"Schools are closed out west, you know," Franklin said. "But you could teach along the way. Lord knows, kids still need the lessons."

"He's right," said a small-faced man in a red parka. "Kids are so lost now they're just sniffing and snorting whatever they can find."

The woman in the pink hat gestured to a pot on the picnic table. "Slop's on the stove. You got your own bowl?"

Carson set down his pack, pleasantly surprised by the hospitality. He pulled out a water bottle, half-full, the last of his supply. "Any water around here, by chance?" he asked.

"In the barrels, sir," Franklin said. "You can refill what you take from the spring that way. A few hundred yards in." He pointed into the woods. "We're blessed around here."

"Which is why we stay," said the woman in the party dress, who walked over and smiled. She looked about sixty, and the muscles in her arms were sculpted and strong. "If you bathe, and we hope you will, do it downstream, please," she said, still smiling.

"That's my Nora," Franklin said, putting his hand atop hers.

Carson walked to the stream, where he filled his water bottles, then sat and took off his boots. The cold water stung the sores on his feet, but he kept them submerged in the current until they went numb.

When he returned to the fire circle, the others were in the midst of a conversation.

"Don't know why they let it get so out of hand," said a man in flannel. "I mean, shit, I didn't mind the critique of big government, but fuckin' A, that doesn't mean they can just wash their hands of everything."

"You were one of those stupid asses who thought government was too big for its britches?" Franklin said. "That's why we're in this mess, because the government deregulated everything, gave up all its power to corporations." He turned to Carson, lifted off his hat for a moment, and grinned. "Have yourself a seat, man. We were just discussing the fall. Joy to the world."

His eyes scanning the group, Carson sat down at the end of a long log. He was glad to listen, but he stayed on guard.

The man in the red parka passed him a bottle. "Care for some whiskey? Traded a raccoon for it."

Carson accepted but poured a swig's worth into the cap of his water bottle so as to avoid any flu germs. The liquid warmed his throat, his stomach, his mood.

A woman holding a baby joined them, sitting down next to the man in flannel.

"We lost our home to the bank," the man said.

His wife jiggled the baby and said, "And our jobs, our car, and our community."

She held the child out to Carson. "Will you take him for a minute?" she said. "Mother Nature calls." Carson took the baby and set him lengthwise on his lap, tucking his hands just under the baby's head and gently bouncing his knees. The baby stirred, a small muscle moving near his upper lip, another near the eyebrow.

Carson and June had wanted a child, but they'd wanted everything to be in order first. You couldn't just be haphazard about these things, they'd thought. You had to have a plan. You had to be established. They'd had it all wrong. Or maybe not. He shuddered to think of making this journey with a small child.

Franklin leaned forward in his lawn chair, making it creak. "You got your dropouts and escapees," he said. The conversation had moved to the taxonomy of travelers. "Then you got the probos, the professional hobos, who started wandering long before all this happened. They never intend to stop."

"Is that what you are?" a woman in glasses asked Franklin. "A probo?"

Franklin smiled. "Maybe. But most of you all are the destined," he said. "You've left behind what you know, but you have a new plan, and you're destined to get there come hell or high water."

That's me, Carson thought, but he kept quiet.

Beatrix stood at the edge of the garden and poked at the wilting lettuce. Where the hell was the rain? The sun beat down on her neck, and sweat dripped into her eyes.

They were down to rationing the last of the yerba mate. How spoiled she'd been, she thought. She pinched the back of her neck, trying to relieve her headache.

But it was the least of her worries. Now the T-Rize were here. That's what the youth gang called itself, short for "Terrorize," people said. Supposedly the first cell had formed in some small rural town in Nevada, right after the blackouts started, and made its way into major western cities, wreaking havoc along the way.

"These are unhappy kids," Flash had said after they'd been ambushed. "They're young and aimless. Given that everything is falling apart anyway, they just wreck whatever they can. They travel by bicycle, in cells. And they've multiplied like crazy."

Flash and Dragon were most nervous about the fleet of bikes in the yard. There was one for everyone in the household, plus half a dozen more they'd fixed up and were ready to sell or trade, or lend out to riders on PBB missions. Not to mention all the random parts. The bikes were locked and covered with a big tarp, but just having them made them a target.

The Perimeter guards were on high alert, apparently, which made sense but also unsettled Beatrix. These T-Rize, they were *kids*, after all. How bad could they be? "Maybe they're just hungry," she kept saying.

Into the backyard came the resonant voice of Jonathan Blue, from the radio inside the house. *"You're weary, you're hungry. You long for what you no longer have. But now there is something more fulfilling for you. It is here."*

Maria del Carmen had been listening for a few days now. Beatrix heard the volume go up.

". . . my story reveals a common one. I, too, once placed my faith in technology. It was my drug, but I thought I was its master. Constantly seeking the next upgrade. Always chasing the newest version. Until I realized there was no other version. There is only one version. Listen, my friends, listen to the truth. What is it that you've lost? What more do you have to lose?"

A breeze carried the stench of the neighbor's pit toilet into the yard. Beatrix tossed a handful of weeds into the compost bin and cursed. Hearing Mr. Blue's voice pissed her off. What was it that she'd lost? What hadn't she lost? And just how would going to this Center help her find it again?

She heard the bells from the water cart down the street. It was her turn to fetch. She looked for the small wagon but couldn't find it, so she carried as many empty jugs as she could and headed for the cart.

But Dragon and Flash were already coming down the sidewalk, the small wagon in tow, full of water. "You beat me," Beatrix said.

"No sweat," Flash said. "It was quick. Not much of a line today."

"More people leaving, maybe," Dragon said.

"Going where, the Center?" She shook her head and helped them unload the jugs.

"This is a new world, this is *the upgrade. We can help you see it here, at the Center."* Jonathan Blue's voice continued inside the house. *"You can*

leave the filth of your cities and neighborhoods and come here, where we are creating a new technology. A simple technology. There is food and water and shelter. There is community. We come together to ascend. The choice is yours."

"He's still at it, I see," Flash said, sitting on the top step of the porch to rest.

"'The filth of your cities and neighborhoods'?" Beatrix said.

"He makes it sound pretty nice, doesn't he?" Dragon said, winking.

"What the fuck?" Beatrix said. She swatted a fly off her arm and sat down next to Flash.

"I'm just saying it's easy to see why folks are tuning in. All those promises," Dragon said.

"Are you kidding? Who really believes that shit?" Beatrix said. "I mean, I get the appeal and utility of communal living, but I thought you couldn't really run from your problems. That running was a sure way to keep them with you. Isn't that what they say? So why not just stay home, face your issues, and build a community here?"

Dragon squinted at her. "Yeah, why not, Beatrix?"

Beatrix opened her mouth to respond but then stopped.

A breeze shook the cypress tree in the front yard, and it sounded like someone was saying, *Shhhh*. Beatrix closed her eyes and heard the water bells on some other block now, and a muffled conversation somewhere. Flash drummed his hands against the floorboards of the porch. It was true what Dragon had said, that sounds got louder when you closed your eyes. That's why radio was sometimes more powerful than television. The idea took hold in her chest as a burst of purple.

"We need to give them something else to listen to," she said. In other places in the world, rural communities used radio for popular education. Soap operas shared messages about birth control, good nutrition, conservation. Why couldn't they do the same thing here? An alternative to Jonathan Blue.

"Real broadcasts," she said.

"I'm not following you," Dragon said.

Beatrix stood up. "Think about it. What is Jonathan Blue doing?"

"Preaching," Flash said.

"He's trying get everyone to jump ship, to leave their communities and get to some mythical 'Center.' He's appealing to their desire for comforts. But it's the same old story. Like false advertising," Beatrix said.

"Fake news," Flash said.

"Where you are sucks, so come here where it's better," Dragon said. "Beatrix is right. Blue is all about 'the grass is greener.'"

"And everyone is so desperate and scared, they just want to be saved," Flash said.

"And he promises to uplift you once you arrive," Dragon said.

"Which is bullshit. It's like all that heaven talk or waiting for the Messiah," Beatrix said. "It absolves you of your responsibility to make change right here. We should be sharing stories about how to live right here in our new world."

Rosie came up the walkway, looking guilty.

"Where've you been?" said Dragon.

"Just at the end of the block," Rosie said.

"With whom?" Dragon said, his gaze fixed on her.

"What are you, her father?" Beatrix said.

"God." Rosie sighed. "I swear, if I go one inch past this block, everyone yells at me," she said. "I might as well wear a leash. Seriously, I was a block away, not a foot off Halcyon."

"Halcyon," Beatrix said. "Halcyon Radio."

"Oh my God, right," Dragon said. "That's perfect."

"What are you guys talking about?" Rosie said. "What's Halcyon Radio? And who is Halcyon anyway? Some historical figure?"

"Halcyon days," Flash said. "Peaceful and easy, right?"

"Yeah," Dragon said. "From Greek mythology, actually. Alcyone was a Greek goddess who threw herself into an ocean in grief after Zeus killed her husband. She got turned into a bird—I forget what kind. When it was time for her to lay eggs, she did it in a floating nest at sea, kept calm and safe by the god of the winds."

"Dude, how do you know all that?" Flash said.

Dragon shrugged. "I looked it up once."

"You're alright, man," Flash said.

"Thank God for the wind god," Beatrix said. "Some compassion for a grief-stricken bird-woman." Some calm and safety is what they all needed now, she thought, wishing she could ask Carson about this mythical bird.

CARSON STAYED THREE nights in the blue tarp camp called "the Jungle," an old hobo term. "A refuge in the wild for the weary travelers," Franklin had explained. "There'll be many more as you go." On his final morning, the rain finally let up. Carson woke to the smell of summer and a thick floor of mud.

"Stick-to-your-ribs mud," Nora said. "Just like this cornmeal." She scooped up a gray lump from a pot and let it plop down again.

"Hey, it's food," Carson said, shaking out his sleeping bag and looking for a place to hang it out to dry. "I'm grateful for it."

"Me too," Franklin said, eating a big spoonful. "Yummy grubworms, too," he said.

"Another thing to live for," Nora said.

"That and the Ascension," said the father of the baby. The man joined them, sitting next to Carson on the log.

"Right," Franklin said. "That's what happens to you if you pray hard enough."

"Surely you've heard of this place, the Center, where the man who preaches the Ascension is gathering his disciples?" the father said to Carson. "They have all kinds of things up there—food, drink, electricity. It's somewhere near the center of the country—on the Plains, I think."

"I heard Wyoming," Franklin said.

"Jonathan Blue," the father said. "He's the one who runs the place. He's monopolizing the airwaves."

"Some of his followers have come through here," Nora said. "You know them from the skirts. The women all wear skirts."

"Not all of them," Franklin said. "All kinds of people going now."

"I get wanting to believe in redemption," Nora said. "But I don't get having to walk to a specific place to get there."

"Gives them something to do," Franklin said, then laughed loudly. "It's tempting if he's got all he says he's got. But what's the cost? I think there are other ways to make do." He opened his arms. "I mean—this isn't such a bad spread."

The father cleared his throat. "I'm not sure I buy his promises. But this is no holiday. We're eating squirrels and mush. There's no power, no jobs, no reliable way to communicate with anyone. We've lost everything, and we're supposed to be celebrating? My wife and I have a baby to feed. What kind of world is this for a child?"

Nora looked startled at first. Then her eyes softened. "We have learned to make do. We find crumbs. And there is a whole pot of cornmeal over there, which you are welcome to. And when that runs out, we'll grind more corn and berries. Or mice. We'll keep going. And every now and then, we'll find something shiny and pick it up and put it in our pockets and keep it as a reminder of what's good and what's bright."

The rest of them stared into the nonfire. No one said a word. The woman in the pink hat came to sit down, her hands wrapped around a mug of tea. "What? Did someone die?" she said.

"We're just contemplating the so-called Ascension," Franklin said. "Or decline, as it were."

Nora turned to the father. "Open your hand," she said. She placed something in his palm.

She asked the same of Carson, then handed him a small glass marble—opaque white, with swirling stripes of orange. It made him think of an orange Creamsicle, and he conjured the taste of one.

They sat in silence for a few minutes. Then the father stood up, tossed his marble into the fire pit, and walked away.

That afternoon, Carson followed Franklin into the woods to check a deadfall trap.

"You don't use a skill, the knowledge of it dries up, doesn't it?" Franklin said. He moved the collapsed sticks and squatted down next to a large rock. "Something's in there." He lifted the rock and found a small mouse, crushed dead and flattened. "Puny little thing," he said, sounding disappointed.

Franklin retrieved the sticks and showed Carson how to set them up in the shape of the number 4. "You put notches in the wood like so," Franklin said, pointing to small wedges in each of the sticks. "Then there's where you set your bait." He motioned to the end of the innermost stick. "When the animal tries to get at that, the sticks move and the rock falls. You need a heavy rock. You want that animal dead." He stabbed the dead mouse with a stick and lifted it.

"Never touch a mouse," Franklin said. "Hantavirus. Will kill you quicker than the flu. Gotta dunk it in running water right away or put it in the fire to burn away the fleas."

They found some wood dry enough to burn and started a small fire. "Just hold 'im in there, good and hot." Franklin handed Carson the mouse-on-a-stick. "There's your Fourth of July barbecue," he said. "Happy Independence Day."

The flame singed off the mouse's fur and shriveled its body. Carson pulled it from the fire and extracted the meat from the tiny bones with his teeth.

PART TWO

The Center

CHAPTER 7

BEATRIX LOATHED THE idea of giving Gary any more reasons to be proud of himself, but if anyone knew how to start a radio station, he would. She walked the block to his house. "I'm here with questions," she said when he opened the door.

"Nice to see you," he said. "Come in."

She followed him up a short staircase, her flip-flops sinking into the thick carpet, to a tidy living room, where a blue-brown plaid sofa faced a giant unusable television on the wall.

"Tell me about your ham radio," she said, cutting to the chase. "Could it do more than what it does now?"

"More?"

"Yeah, like broadcast. Real radio. Something else to listen to."

"With a few equipment changes, yes. You have something in mind?"

"I want to broadcast stories and interviews, let people share their stories about the good, creative things they're doing. Give people real information."

"Like NPR?" he said, sounding somewhat suspicious.

Beatrix nodded. "Kind of."

"A news show? With reporters?"

"How long would it take to set up?" Beatrix said, ignoring his questions.

"Well, we'd need a different kind of transmitter, and a better antenna." He held her gaze. "I could work on it. Maybe you get the People's Bicycle Brigade to search out a few things."

"The PBB—they can find anything," Beatrix said, turning to go.

"I heard about the T-Rize ambush. Sorry that happened."

"Me too. But Rosie saved the day."

"Lucky. We've been hearing about them on the ham," he said. "They're everywhere."

She sighed. "Like a new flu. What do we do?"

"We stop them from coming in."

"And then?" Beatrix asked.

"We find a place for them."

"Lock them up?" she asked, relieved he hadn't suggested killing them off.

"Honestly, I don't know," Gary said. "Reform them somehow. But in the meantime, we need to protect ourselves."

"You mean imprison ourselves," Beatrix said, annoyed.

"Beatrix, these kids are beyond pissed. They no longer have Xboxes and Game Boys and iPhones and iPads and all the things kids had before. They aren't going to have anything we had."

"Xboxes? What are Xboxes?"

"Something you'd want really badly if you were twelve."

"I doubt it," Beatrix said. "When I was twelve, all I wanted was for the school cafeteria to stop serving hamburgers made from beef bought in Brazil, where they were chopping down rain forests to—"

"Yeah, yeah, Beatrix, I get it." Gary held his hands in the air. "But you weren't like normal twelve-year-olds."

No, she wasn't. She turned again to go, and saw on one of his walls a painting of a night sky, a distant city beneath it, all lit up with white lights. "Pretty," she said, trying to be nice.

"Thanks. I painted that. The Iraqi sky."

This surprised her. "What else did you see over there?"

"A lot of blood, explosions of lights in the desert."

His candor took her off guard.

"Men are forced to make difficult decisions," he said, then paused and looked directly at her. "Historically, I have disliked protesters."

She stared back at him, silent.

"Have you ever done anything you later regretted?" he said.

She considered the question. She could lie and say no. She was good at convincing people. There had been a time when she was quite sure of herself. "Yeah," she said. "In Miami. At a protest against the Free Trade Agreement of the Americas. My friend Hank and I got separated in the crowd. I stopped to try to find him. Suddenly, there was this girl, her face all smeared with war paint. For some reason, I was holding a rock. I don't know why. The girl looked at me and said, 'Do it. Break it.' I don't know if I picked the rock off the ground or if she handed it to me. But there I was with the rock, and this girl, telling me to throw it."

Beatrix noticed Gary was leaning forward slightly, listening with interest. She continued. "We were next to a Vietnamese restaurant, and I looked in the window and saw this man, small and thin, glasses. A young boy was in there, too. Maybe his grandson—I don't know. When they saw me, the man pulled the boy behind him, started shaking his head. I remember the look on his face. And his baggy khaki slacks. He was so thin, that man. But the girl next to me said, 'Do it!'

"So I threw the rock. The glass shattered, and I ran away, pushing through the crowd. For a second, I felt exhilaration, and then I just felt shame. We thought the only way to wake people up was to do something big and dramatic."

Gary widened his eyes.

"I never did anything like that again."

"Courage," Gary said.

"Courage? I don't see it like that."

"In the moment, you did what you believed was right. You had the larger view. Right or not, you followed through."

Beatrix shrugged. "I guess so." She opened the front door. "Let me know when you have a list of supplies ready, and I'll get the riders on it." She paused for a moment, then turned back and said, "Thank you, Gary."

CARSON STAYED SOUTH, following country roads at Franklin's advice, to avoid the rails in and out of Chicago. Lead in the water supply had upended the city even before the grid went, and now there was nothing but mayhem, he'd said. He followed Route 24 for many miles, passing signs for Peoria, a town he maybe had heard of once. The sun was merciless, but a wind pushed at his back, cooling his sweat. An arc of birds flew over the treetops, a mini migration.

On the side of the road, chairs from a Ferris wheel hovered in the air, the centerpiece of an abandoned carnival, its traveling days long over. Ivy crawled over the rides and kiosks, its plentiful green leaves obscuring the dulled colors. Thick electric cords snaked along the pavement, and Carson had a sudden hankering for a Coca-Cola. He heard a shout and turned to see a group of kids hiding on the other side of a rickety carousel. When he called out, they scattered.

A plywood clown grinned menacingly at the foot of the ramp to the Tilt-a-Whirl. NO ONE UNDER MY HEIGHT GETS ON THIS RIDE read the sign. Carson walked up the ramp, his footsteps echoing against the metal. He remembered the swing of the ride, its quick successive loops, the tilting and whirling of his stomach.

He wandered past empty food kiosks and came to a freestanding mirror. Not quite a fun-house mirror—he wasn't squashed or elongated—but something was strange about his reflection, which he hadn't seen in months. He'd grown thin, his hair longer and maybe grayer, and he had a full beard now. His face seemed crooked. The mole on the lower side of his cheek was on the wrong side. He lifted his right arm, and the reflection lifted its right arm also. No mirror mimicry. He noted tiny words etched into the top of the glass: TRUE MIRROR.

This man looked nothing like the man Carson had once been: the school principal who'd worn a jacket and tie and made uncomfortable compromises, who had risen up the ladder rapidly, without even trying, as if he'd tricked the system. Tapping young male teachers for leadership roles early in their careers was a common practice. Carson had been in the classroom for just four years. He loved it there. But the offer to move up made him feel singled out, competent. And the salary meant he and June could start on their future. This future?

He raised an eyebrow, giving himself a dubious look. Then he smiled, aiming for authenticity. A flicker of wisdom showed behind all the hair, a certain conviction. He did not know who he was anymore, but he no longer felt like a fraud.

Something darted behind him in the mirror. One of the kids? His backpack! He spun around, then realized he was still wearing it. Thank God. Then he saw the kids: five boys and a girl. The oldest couldn't have been more than thirteen; the youngest, about six or seven. They stood there looking steely, holding metal bars, tree branches. One had a brick.

Carson's heart quickened. His gun was in the top of his pack. If he had to, he could reach for it. He put up his hands. "What do you want?" he said.

"Food," the girl said. She was wearing an oversized sweater and pants ripped at one of the thighs. Her hair was a tangled mess.

No, he thought. He'd just foraged that morning. Jesus Christ, no. He considered running, but what if there were more kids? Or armed adults? The girl's brown eyes bored into him. He could forage again.

He dropped his pack and pulled out a clump of dandelion greens, a few wild onions, a handful of roots, and some blackberries he'd tucked delicately into a sock and placed at the top. There was also a ziplock bag half-full of peanut butter he'd traded for a week ago and a few hard chunks of bread. He laid it all out on the ground. "That's it, kiddos," he said. "All my fucking food."

The oldest boy, in black Converse high-tops, dirty jeans, and a ragged black T-shirt, nodded to the girl, who scuttled forward and swept up the food. "Nothing else?" he said. He inspected the bundle of whitish carrot-like roots. "What are these?"

"Thistle roots," Carson said. "Boil them or eat them raw. They taste like dirt, but they'll fill the belly." He kept his cool. They had weapons, but they were weak with hunger.

The boy bit off the end of one of the roots, then gestured for the girl to pass the rest around.

"That's all I have," Carson said, wondering how they had managed for this long. He considered pulling out his field guide to edible plants but couldn't risk losing that, too.

The oldest boy was watching him now, holding the metal bar steady in the air. "Water? You got water?" he said.

He did. He had just filled his bottles in a stream that morning. He pulled one out and set it on the ground. He reached for his notebook, and the boy let out a whistle. The others firmed their hold on their weapons. Two of them inched closer to him. Carson opened his notebook. Draw for your life, he told himself.

With a ballpoint pen, he drew small leaves, and tiny flowers with square petals, and, since he didn't have color, he labeled the petals *white*, the flower center *light green or yellow*. He looked up, "You can read, right?"

The boy nodded. Another boy, younger, with red hair, said, "So can I."

"Me too," the girl said.

Below the first drawing he wrote, *Common chickweed, crop and ground cover.* Then he got to work on the next drawing: lamb's-quarter, an elongated oak-like leaf. "You can eat the seeds of this one, too," he said, drawing his best rendition of a stalk of seeds. The oldest boy began parsing out the rest of the food, divvying up the berries, breaking the thistle roots in half, and squeezing peanut butter thinly on the stale chunks of bread.

Carson drew wild carrot, wild asparagus, burdock, sorrel, and sumac. The children came closer. One little boy leaned a hand on Carson's shoulder, his breath quick and warm in Carson's ear.

The girl pointed to berries Carson had darkened in with black ink and said, "Those are red. I've seen them."

"Sumac," Carson said, nodding. He wrote the word "red" next to them. "They are indeed red. And some red berries are poisonous, so you have to pay attention. These are edible. But don't overdo it. They'll make you vomit."

The boy who'd been leaning on Carson took a bite of thistle root. He broke off the rest and offered it to Carson.

Carson was moved by the generosity, but he declined, then began a list of the plants they were likely to know already: dandelion, thistle, mint, raspberry, blackberry, strawberry, and stinging nettle.

"You know dandelions, yes?" Carson asked.

"You can make wishes with them," said the girl.

The oldest boy held up the greens Carson had given him. "These, right?"

"Exactly. And thistle is what you just ate. You now know what it looks like and how it tastes."

"Bitter," the boy at his thigh said. "Like dirt."

Carson handed the drawings to the oldest boy. "If you're not sure, try a tiny bit and wait."

"Wait?"

"For a reaction. Make sure it agrees with you. If you're really not sure, leave it. It's the best you can do. Whatever you do, don't eat that one," he said pointing to an oak tree a few feet away.

The boy with the brown eyes looked up, curious. "Why not?"

"It'll turn you to stone," Carson said, smiling.

The boy made a small O with his mouth, then froze, his knee bent, his arms stiff, his eyes wide.

"That's right," Carson said, gathering up his things. "You do that well. But stay away from the oak. You make a better boy than a statue."

"BOUNTY COMIN' IN. It's July, and we are flush." Flash wheeled his bike into the yard, his trailer full of mason jars. Rosie closed her notebook and smiled. How was it that he could be so cheerful all the fricking time?

Flash placed a jar on the picnic table right where Rosie was sitting. Inside were fleshy red tomatoes, like smooth hearts. On the bottom of the jar was a label. "Who's Helen McDonald?" Rosie said, reading it.

"The woman who canned those. So she gets her jar back," Flash said. "The new currency. Barter, barter, barter." He held up another jar. "Green beans." Then another. "Pears. Peaches."

"Yum," Rosie said, reaching for a slippery peach.

"We have high-ticket items here, thanks to Mama Maria Señora Tortilla and Miss Beatrix the Queen of Cacao."

"Don't forget Abuela's tinctures," Rosie said.

"Those too."

Beatrix came out to the yard and sifted through the jars. "Can I take two of these? There's that lady down the street with her cat. They're both starving."

That was Beatrix, Rosie thought. Always saving the neighbors.

Jonathan Blue's voice drifted into the yard. *"Where you are, you look around and all you see is violence, scarcity, darkness. None of that is here. Here, there is kindness, abundance, and light. Trust in the power of the holy. That power can lift us out of the darkness. Look up. You can be lifted."*

Rosie glanced at Beatrix, knowing what was coming.

"Brainwash alert," Beatrix said.

"Abuela says it makes her happy," Rosie said.

"Rosie, listen to me," Flash said. He sat on the bench and patted the seat next to him.

"Okay, but I'm not five," she said.

"I know. You're a beautiful woman with a good head on her shoulders."

Rosie felt her face warm. A beautiful woman? She sat down and tried to hide her smile.

Flash draped his arm around her, and the caped superhero tattooed on his forearm looked like it was flying straight for her heart. "When I was your age, my grandma was really important to me. She was like your grandmother, an immigrant to America. My parents brought her here after I was born. Her faith was really important to her. She went to church every Sunday. She prayed every night. We said grace before every dinner. That's what kept her alive. That faith, it was everything to her."

"Um, Flash," Dragon said, "I hate to break it to you, but that faith is a little different than what Jonathan Blue is asking for."

"Kind of," Flash said. "And kind of not."

"What are you talking about?" Rosie said. Flash and Dragon always seemed to speak in some boy code she couldn't decipher.

"So I used to get irritated with how religious my grandma was. Her prayers, her church gatherings, her community service, blah-blah-blah. But she just kept resting her hand on my forehead and blessing me," Flash said. "When I started doing my own good in the world, it didn't seem all that different than the good she did, only mine didn't have some specific God attached to it, per se."

"What was your good?" Rosie asked.

"Little things. Like I helped to get a bike path built through the neighborhood. Not just me, but a group of us. We petitioned the neighborhood association, held some fundraisers, spoke at city council meetings. I'm not saying this to brag—I'm just saying we all need some good deeds."

"What I really need is permission to leave the house," Rosie said. "My abuela is terrified of everything. And she hates my boyfriend."

"'Hate' is a strong word," Beatrix said. "But yeah, Diego is not her favorite guy."

"I don't think she hates him," Dragon said. "I think she's just protecting you."

Flash rubbed his chin. "Maybe we need to get Maria del Carmen on a bike. Let her see the world a little bit."

Rosie laughed, picturing it. But she knew Flash could do it. Maybe it would lighten Abuela up. Or better, help her loosen the leash a little.

Carson squinted at the landscape—a long stretch of rolling plains patched with lifeless croplands cut off from their irrigation hoses. There had to be water nearby, though, because that morning a great blue heron had soared over him, its wings wide brooms sweeping the sky. Maybe a wetland somewhere?

Late afternoon, he came to a structure shining in the low sun. First, he willed it into a wide, cool lake, then he wished simply for a diner. An old-school diner, with gleaming retro chrome, spinning stools at the counter, and a milkshake with the extra on the side, in one of those chilled stainless-steel cups. A mile back, he'd seen a symbol of a skirted stick figure holding a fork. Not all hope was lost.

The shine came from the solar panels on the roof of a small house. Potted plants lined a path to a wrought-iron security door. He called out, "Hello?" and then peered in to see a tattered sofa, a table for two, a fireplace, and a wall of family photographs.

A woman cracked open the door. "Unload your weapons first," she said.

Carson stepped back, startled by the greeting.

"Just our policy, you understand," she said, stepping into the light. She was in her sixties. A bold-patterned scarf—yellows, blues, and greens—covered her hair, and a strand of seedlike brown beads hung around her neck.

Carson figured this woman could see his gun in her crystal ball, but that didn't mean he wanted to surrender it.

"If you hand over your weapons, you can stay. Work for trade. We need help with the beehives and the blackberry harvest. You look hungry. You decide."

He sized her up. Her eyes softened. Was he a fool? But food and bed. He unzipped the top pouch off his pack and handed her the gun.

"You'll get it back," she said. "I'm Naomi."

"Carson," he said.

She gestured to a bench near the door. "Have a seat."

She disappeared inside and returned with a bowl of cold soup and a hunk of bread. Carson tried to eat slowly, but he gulped the soup like a starving dog. When he finished, she brought him a serving of peach cobbler. He exhaled, finally relaxing. "I've landed in heaven?" he asked.

"Nope," she said. "It's all real. Peaches are a little early this year. Apples coming this fall. Right now, it's blackberries. I hope you don't mind thorns."

Carson was tempted to lick the bowl.

"We had to chase off thieves a few days ago." She pointed to the roof. "They came for our solar panels. Daniel sent a shot up and scared 'em off the roof. Daniel's my son. Being in prison somehow made a man of him." She looked at Carson, as if anticipating a comment. "My boy was locked up, but you won't believe that when you meet him."

She poured hot water from a thermos into a mug and placed it in front of him. "Spearmint," she said.

Carson sipped the tea. More heaven.

"You can bunk here a few days in the extra room. Work starts early. Milking goats. Tending hens. Beehives. Picking."

The room was more of a closet than a bedroom. But there was a mattress, clean sheets, a window, and, outside, a solar shower and a compost toilet. "The shower should be good and hot," Naomi said.

It was indeed good and hot, and once clean, Carson lay on the bed and slept deeply.

When he woke, it was evening, and Naomi served him more tea. Daniel, the son, had not yet appeared, and Carson started to think he might just be a decoy, a way for Naomi to protect herself against strangers.

"My husband always drank tea in the evenings. Don was Irish, so tea mattered. He steeped it in a little pot and drank it with milk. Our place was right off the highway. One night, we were out of milk. Don went out to get some on his bike, at dusk. Witnesses said the truck hit him from behind. The driver never even stopped."

Carson gasped, taken aback by her frankness. "I'm so sorry."

"Once they took his body away, I went out to where it happened. I found a little button on the road—pewter, vintage. Not Don's, at least not that I recognized. Just a little button the color of the sky in a storm, rough and with a little imprint of a horse's head on its surface, nearly worn away. Don loved horses, always watched those silly races. So it seemed like a special sign. A little piece of him. Or something to keep us fastened together, at least."

Everyone has a button, Carson thought. The detail that lodges itself in the brain at the moment of loss. An object or two that can anchor the feelings or contain them somehow. His were the oil slick of crows in the field behind the farmhouse and a whale-shaped cloud in the sky.

"After that, I moved here and started fending for myself," Naomi said. "Homesteading, I guess you could say. Just wanted to feel prepared and safe. Some days, I still miss him freshly." Naomi stared at Carson for a moment, then swept her hands across the counter and started putting things away. She moved swiftly, efficiently, like a waitress.

"My wife died three years ago," Carson said.

"Oh, you poor soul," Naomi said. "Grief slices you down the middle. It takes a good long while before any sweetness returns. And even then, the hurt still comes, like heavy clouds."

Carson's grief was more like a prickling sensation that burned up from his feet through his veins, as if he'd been injected with something not meant to enter the bloodstream. In the first few months when it came on like that, he'd have to lie down immediately.

"Did you ever see that bird video?" Naomi asked. "That parrot bopping up and down in tune to the music."

Carson nodded. He remembered the video. It was a cockatoo, not a parrot.

"At one point, I thought if a bird could dance, why couldn't I?" Naomi said. She started moving, swaying her body to an imaginary beat. Carson watched, hoping she wouldn't ask him to join her.

"Sometimes when you dance, joy slips in. Even when you think it's not possible," she said. "Doesn't erase anything, but makes space somehow." She stopped and looked at him. "Try a little jig sometime. Just to see."

Carson wasn't so sure, but just before sleep, well-fed and clean and alone in the small room, he held his elbows at his sides and wiggled his hips. He stepped to the side a few times, back and forth, then loosened his torso and shook it. Just a tiny moment, long enough for a little laugh to come out.

Along one interior wall of Gary's garage was a table covered with broadcasting equipment. A cord stretched out the door up to the roof, where it connected to the solar panels. Beatrix didn't quite know what she was looking at, but she knew what it could do, and that pleased her.

"As always, the PBB delivers," Flash said.

"No small price, though," Dragon said. "Three bikes for those solar panels."

"And a few hours of labor," Gary said.

"Thank you. Thank you again," Beatrix said. "Today feels like Christmas."

"Christmas in July!" Flash said.

They could broadcast locally for now, Gary explained, and with the wire antenna he'd mounted above the garage, they had pretty good range. AM could travel via ground waves, he said, with a better and farther range at night. An old cassette recorder and some blank tapes could help them get to stations in other towns, provided those stations had solar power and cassette players. "You can have a whole network," Gary said.

"Like Blue?" Beatrix said.

"Sort of," Gary said. "But he's probably got access to more power. Big solar arrays or powerful generators, I'm guessing. This will be more old-school, but effective. You can have folks gather to listen, too. Like FDR's fireside chats."

"I like it," Beatrix said.

To advertise, they'd spread the word through the PBB, made announcements at neighborhood meetings, and chalked handwritten messages on streets and sidewalks.

On the evening of the first broadcast, Gary leaned over the table and turned a knob. "AM ten-eighty," he said. "Whenever you're ready."

Flash flipped a switch, and a small red button lit up. "On the air," Del said.

Beatrix and Gary went outside to listen on the speakers Gary had set up in his yard.

"Greetings from the end of the sidewalk," Dragon said. *"You're listening to Halcyon Radio, the station of the People's Bicycle Brigade, PBB, western chapter. You know us, or you know of us: we bring you good deeds on the ground and good ideas on the airwaves. And we know you: you make your neighborhood strong and beautiful."*

Beatrix thought about how dozens of strategies and solutions would soon be revealed via low-power radio. Why believe one man's false promises when instead you could live in the truth of everything and everyone around you? It was about listening to the people. That was all. Just like her friend Angel in Ecuador had said. Listen first. For the first time in a long while, Beatrix felt something close to optimism.

"Hey, kid, do you have a bike?" Flash said, using his deep sports-announcer voice.

Dragon, in a childlike voice: *"Yes."*

"Tell me about your bike. Do you like your bike?"

"I do. Very much."

"What do you like about it?"

"It takes me places. I can get around. I can go faster."

"And what do you do if something happens to your bike?"

"I fix it."

"You know how to fix your bike? Where'd you learn?"

"From the People's Bicycle Brigade."

They shared information about basic bike mechanics, where to find spare parts, and the bicycle fix-in schedule. After fifteen minutes, Flash closed the show with a short riff on the guitar.

Beatrix was up next. Her hands were sweating. She sat in front of the microphone and took several deep breaths. "Good evening, everyone. I'm BBX for the PBB and Halcyon Radio, the people's station."

Now giddy, she read off a list called "Necessary Neighborhood News," announced the upcoming garden workshops, the composting toilet cooperative ("Like an Amish barn raising: you help them, they help you"), and the call for more Perimeter volunteers. "Also, this Saturday morning at Squat Park, you can learn to make soap. And at four o'clock at Fifth Street and Sparrow, a small orchestra will play a mix of classic rock and Beethoven—don't miss it.

"This is your station. People-powered radio. Have something to share? Start a program or join us for an interview. Everyone has a voice. Everyone has a wish. Share yours. We're listening."

Feeling more confident in her voice than she had in a long time, Beatrix warned listeners of the T-Rize, urging them to tell the Perimeter guards about any sightings, damage, or violence. "Please do not confuse all cyclists for T-Rize. The People's Bicycle Brigade, or PBB—which also has some young members on bicycles—provides you with information and resources. Note that PBB helmets and armbands are marked with the red-and-yellow PBB logo. Stay alert.

"And please, friends, do not use the T-Rize as your justification for joining Jonathan Blue's exodus. This so-called Center is fabled to be a land of milk and honey. But we know little about it. The exodus itself is dangerous: anything could happen along the way. Go if you must. But weigh your decision carefully. There is milk and there is honey right here in the neighborhood. I'm not kidding. Tune in. AM ten-eighty. Halcyon Radio. Your source for survival. A safe nest on the shore. A respite from the storm."

CHAPTER 8

In the morning, Carson woke to the sound of a hissing kettle. Sunlight poured through the small window. Outside, the leaves on the fruit trees were full and green. Naomi stirred something in a pot. Beyond her, a man, partially bald, stacked empty cardboard boxes against the side of the barn. Naomi's son wasn't a myth after all.

Carson dressed and went outside to introduce himself. Daniel's eyes were the same color as Naomi's, blue like bottle glass. The skin of his arms was inked with designs. On his left biceps was a serpent and an apple; on the other, a fish with a sinewy tail.

"You came from the East," Daniel said. "What did you leave there?"

"No job and a city that was about to erupt," Carson said.

"Nothing's erupting around here," Daniel said. "Not yet, at least."

Carson followed Daniel into a dark and dusty barn. Upon entering,

Carson inadvertently kicked something, nudging it across the floor, and nearly lost his balance. "Ouch."

"What on earth?" Naomi said. Behind them, she slid open the door, letting light flood the space. She quickly picked up what Carson had kicked—an assault rifle.

"Danny, please put this thing away!" She shook her head and looked at Carson. "Are you okay?" She hung the rifle on a rack on the wall, where it joined a small arsenal of others. "Really, this is for protection only. It's supposed to go here."

Carson thought of his handgun, stowed in Naomi's kitchen cupboard. Were these other travelers' guns, never returned?

"Sorry, Ma," Daniel said. "Thought I heard someone last night. Probably just kids, those glue sniffers."

Glue sniffers? The kids Carson had met a few days before hadn't seemed high on anything but the vapors of potential food. Rumors. He kept his eyes on the gun and gauged the distance between where he stood and the door. *Listen with your whole body*, Ayo had said.

"The barn doubles as my shop," Daniel said, gesturing to a table saw and an assortment of hammers and other tools hanging on the wall. A high, stuttering wail came from the side yard. Carson jumped.

"Tabitha," Daniel said. They went outside to a small pen, where a goat stood, baying. Nearby, a dozen or more chickens scuttled about. "Milk and eggs," Daniel said. "And over there, honey." He pointed to a stack of bee boxes.

Two large cisterns flanked the house. "For rainwater?" Carson asked.

Daniel nodded. "Plenty to live off around here."

The rest of the morning, Carson worked with Naomi, picking blackberries from the bushes around the perimeter of the property. In the afternoon, he worked with Daniel to tend the bee boxes. He donned a mesh mask and gloves, and Daniel handed him a small bellows for smoking the hive.

"When they smell smoke, they think there's a fire, so they get busy gorging on honey and ignore me," Daniel said. "You have to stay calm, too. One false move, and they'll swarm."

Carson felt his heart pick up its pace. He watched as Daniel opened the hives, scraped wax from the frames, inspected for parasites, searched for the queen. He noticed how carefully and methodically Daniel worked.

"Want to see the lovely lady?" Daniel said, holding up a frame. "The queen has a long body—slender, without stripes."

Carson leaned toward the honeycomb where Daniel's gloved finger pointed.

"See where all those drones are, circling her?"

Carson saw the drones, but wasn't sure he'd seen the queen. By then, other bees were flying toward his veil, so he bellowed smoke and mumbled a yes.

"She can lay fifteen hundred eggs a day," Daniel said. "And her scent keeps the whole hive together. That's some pheromone action right there."

The bees came at Carson's veil, and he ducked, feeling sweat now at his upper lip and temples. Maybe he was allergic to bees. Was he?

"Easy there, partner," Daniel said. "Calm down, or they'll swarm. Blow some smoke, would you?"

By the time Daniel finally closed up the boxes, Carson was drenched with sweat.

"Gotta trust me, man," Daniel said. "It's a delicate process."

Relieved it was over, Carson retreated to the front of the house. In his notebook, he started in on a list: *How to be self-sufficient after the apocalypse.* He'd already known vaguely about these strategies; he could have implemented them years ago when he and June lived in the country. Why hadn't he?

"What are you writing about us?" Daniel asked, appearing suddenly at Carson's side.

Carson dropped his pen, startled. “Nothing incriminating,” he said. “Just about what you’re doing here. How you’re surviving.”

“A ‘going green without machines’ kinda thing?” Daniel retrieved the pen and plopped into a squeaky lawn chair. “Write down that honeybees are a good blueprint. No drone, worker, or queen bee can survive without the support of the colony. Everyone’s got a necessary task. Plus, they dance.”

Carson knew that. “Their way of making maps, right?”

“Worker bees telling each other where the pollen is, or water, or new sites for nests. Ma loves that. Just don’t ask her about it, or she’ll do the waggle dance for you ad nauseam.” Daniel picked up a small stone from the ground and threw it across the yard, hitting a wheelbarrow.

“And what are you gonna do with all the info?” he asked. “Put it in the history books?”

“Something like that,” Carson said.

Daniel picked up another stone. “What’s out west?”

Carson gathered a few stones himself. He jiggled them around in his palm, feeling little confidence in his throw. “Someone I’m hoping to see there.” He imagined Beatrix’s face and lit up at the image.

Daniel hit the wheelbarrow again, making it reverberate.

“Dang,” Carson said. He threw a stone, and it bounced against the chain-link fence at the edge of the property. “Maybe I’m a fool,” he said.

“Women are great, so long as they don’t suck out all your blood and distract you from your higher purpose,” Daniel said.

Carson waited for more, but no more came. His higher purpose? He looked at the tattoo on Daniel’s forearm: the sharp fangs of the inked serpent’s open mouth looked surprisingly realistic. “If you don’t mind my asking, what were you in for?”

“Oh, you want that story for your notebook?” Clang! Another hit to the wheelbarrow. “It’s not all that mysterious. Just drugs. Sold a little green for some green, mostly to help out Ma. But the fuckers caught me. Twelve fucking years, if you can believe that. I only served eight, though." He picked up another stone and squinted.

"That place was so gray," he said. "I would lie there for days just trying to imagine the color yellow." He tossed and hit a tree, dead on. "Then one day, all this light floods in, and all the doors open up. It's like in *The Wizard of Oz* when Dorothy opens the door and everything turns to color. My cellmate, Harvey, is standing over me, saying, 'Come on, you fuckin' cracker. Let's get the hell out of here. They're gone.' The guards, he meant. They were gone. We ran and ran till we hit this big green field. I just dropped to my knees. I wanted to drink up that color."

"What happened to the guards?" Carson asked.

"Someone set off a bomb. And it set us free. I still don't know if it was an inside job or an outside job. Gifts come in strange packages. Mine came dipped in fertilizer and nail-polish remover, or whatever it was they used to make that bomb. I only walked for half a day before a truck driver stopped for me. He brought me all the way here, without a scratch."

"That's luck," Carson said. He aimed for the wheelbarrow again and threw the stone, this time nailing it.

The People's Bicycle Brigade fix-ins were held every Saturday morning at the high school soccer field. A few dozen bicycles and their owners were already there by the time Flash, Dragon, Beatrix, and two other PBB riders arrived.

Penny, a rider in a yellow cap, set up a folding table and began unloading tools and snacks from her bike trailer. Beatrix pulled out the clipboard for gathering names, ages, and addresses, along with a stack of the homemade flyers she'd made to advertise Halcyon Radio. She'd raided the Fair Share office for paper and pencils and pens to make them.

All morning, the PBB riders moved from bicycle to bicycle showing people how to fix flats, tighten brakes, adjust derailleurs. It was like a teach-in, Beatrix thought, learning the essential skills for the resistance, or in this case "the persistence." Each rider was a spoke in the wheel, essential to a larger purpose, which on this day was a way of staying put, of working together to get three dozen tuned-up bicycles.

Power to the people, she thought. It was clichéd, but it mattered. It was a kind of love.

"Penny, I heard you're joining the service," Flash said.

"True story," Penny said.

"That makes sense," Flash said. "You're the fastest rider in the fleet."

"What service?" Beatrix asked.

"Velocipede," Flash said. "The mail service."

"Like the Pony Express," Flash said. "Coast to coast."

"Really?" Beatrix said. "Mail?"

She thought of the pages she'd written to Carson but hadn't been able to send. She could write to her mother, too—at least let her know she was okay. "Maybe bicycles *will* save the world," she said. "Along with radio! Penny, what did you think of the first broadcast?"

"Um," Penny said. "I didn't hear it. I don't have a radio."

Beatrix's heart sank a little. She looked at Flash. "Problem."

Flash nodded. "Definite problem. We'll get the team on it." He held up a fist, and Penny knocked it with her own.

"I'll add it to the list of a million things a bike is good for," Penny said.

"Yes," Beatrix said, feeling hopeful.

But the feeling was short-lived. Arriving home, she discovered that several bicycles had been stolen from the backyard fleet.

"I tried to stop them," Maria del Carmen said, visibly shaken. She pointed to a cast-iron frying pan lying in the dirt. "I threw that into the yard, and they ran."

"Did you get a good look at them?" Flash said.

"They had their faces covered," Maria del Carmen said, her brow furrowed.

Dragon held his hands to his forehead and sighed.

"Everyone knows we have bikes," Beatrix said. "Even when locked up, they're a liability."

"What about Rosie—did she see anyone?"

"No. As soon as I saw them, I ran out and threw the pan." Maria del Carmen made a fist with one hand and said, "Jonathan Blue is right. This is what he means. Violence, scarcity, darkness. It's only getting worse. He's right."

Beatrix looked at Dragon and then at Flash, who raised his eyebrows. Blue's scare tactics. But what could they say to appease her right now?

"It's only part of the story, Maria del Carmen," Dragon said. "But you did good. Thanks for running them off."

THE DAY WAS muggy, and a sweet scent hovered in the air. Rosie held up a single Matchbox car, yellow with black stripes along each side, one of several she and Beatrix had found in the back shed when they were building the chicken coop. Every time Diego reached for it, she pulled it away.

"Come on, girl," Diego said. "Just give it up."

She ran the car along his arm, then moved it up his neck toward his face. He pulled away. "Wait," she said. "Come here." A black-and-blue bruise circled his eye, and she traced its outline with her finger.

"Man walks into a bar," was how he'd explained the black eye. "Seriously. I walked into a crossbar," he'd said. "We were ducking down a stairwell."

Rosie made a circle with her thumb and index finger and held it just over Diego's bruise. It looked like bad makeup. A vision of Diego holding a metal bar over an older man with glasses flashed in front of her, then evaporated.

Beatrix came out of the house. Rosie moved her hand away from Diego's face.

"Smell that deliciousness?" Beatrix said, breathing in. "Jasmine in bloom."

Diego didn't look at Beatrix, but Rosie inhaled and tried to smell what Beatrix smelled. All she caught was Diego's pungent, manly scent. She didn't mind it.

"Oh, great," Beatrix said, her enthusiasm dropping. "There go more."

Half a dozen people walked down the street—women, men, and two children. Beatrix called out to them. She knew everyone, it seemed.

One of the men stopped, hushing the rattle of his shopping cart full of luggage. A woman next to him waved. She looked familiar. Rosie had seen her riding her bike down the street.

"You're off?" Beatrix said.

"We're hungry," the man said. "And we keep getting robbed. It's fucking ridiculous."

"We don't have a yard," the woman said. "So we can't have a garden. Also, the little idiots stole our bikes. Fucking T-Rize."

They continued down the block, the wheels of their carts and luggage like a distant storm.

Fucking T-Rize is right, Rosie thought. They had sequestered her in the house, those stupid kids and their weapons. She hated them. She squeezed Diego's hand. He looked at her, blankly at first, then softened and squeezed back.

Beatrix sighed. "Everyone is leaving."

"You're leaving, too, aren't you?" Rosie said.

"No, I'm not."

"You look like you're going somewhere right now," Rosie said.

"Oh, well, yeah. Just down the block to Anita's," Beatrix said, heading down the stairs.

"Who's Anita?"

"One of our neighbors. The one who delivers babies and used to work at the library. We're launching a mobile library."

"What's a mobile library?" Diego said, once Beatrix was gone.

"A bike that carries books for people to borrow," Rosie said.

"Duh," Diego said, making Rosie laugh.

A horse trotted down the street, a girl about Rosie's age riding it. The horse was black and shiny, and the girl was blond, with long, thin blue-jeaned legs. She looked so confident and independent. Rosie wished she could trade places with her, even for just an hour.

Another horse followed, brown with a white patch on its nose. The man riding it was bald and wore sunglasses. Probably the girl's father.

"Take it easy on the turns, honey," he called out.

Yeah, most definitely her father. "I so wish I had a horse," Rosie said.

"Not as fast as a bike," Diego said.

Rosie watched the second horse's tail flicker out of sight. In its place came a vision of a girl walking alone, horseless, under a gray sky, the sound of her footsteps muffled, as if wrapped in a blanket. Rosie realized the girl was her, and she felt heavy, tears forming in her eyes. She blinked, and the vision vanished.

She heard then the voice of the preacher. *"It's simple, folks. The darkness is a gift. If you want to reconnect, you just get on the path and come. We are here for you. Here, there is light."* The voice came from inside the house, where her abuela was listening.

Jonathan Blue's voice made Rosie think of laundry detergent—at first, it seemed pleasant enough, but then it oversaturated you. Abuela said Blue's voice sounded like hope itself. Abuela wanted to go there, to the Center, away from all the darkness, toward all that hope.

Beatrix was right when she said that sometimes your real family doesn't understand you in the same way your chosen family does. She said her own mother never understood her; only her Aunt Vera did. She said you have to love your blood anyway, but that you also have to thank the stars for the nonblood.

"Good things await you, my friends. Come join us." Blue's voice droned on.

Rosie didn't want to leave this home. She didn't want to leave Diego.

She felt the tickle in the back of her throat. She closed her eyes, and behind her eyelids she saw someone lying on a wooden floor, looking up at her. Dragon? There was a bicycle there, too. She opened her eyes, feeling a little panicked. She'd never had so many visions this close together.

"'I measure every Grief I meet,'" she muttered.

"What's that, *mi linda*?" Diego asked.

"Nothing." She loved that Diego called her this. Mi linda. My pretty. Diego's grandmother spoke Spanish, and his family was from Mexico, too, from Jalisco, where they made tequila. He once told Rosie maybe they'd go there together sometime, after all this.

"After all what?" Rosie had said.

"This mess," he had said, moving his hands in circles.

"And what will come after this mess?" Rosie had asked.

"Something better."

"How will we have time to go to Mexico? We'll be the ones cleaning 'this mess' up," Rosie had said, mimicking Diego's hand motions.

Diego had shaken his head in disagreement, but after watching her grandmother clean up other people's messes her whole life, Rosie knew it was true.

But, when Rosie said the same to Beatrix, Beatrix had also disagreed. She'd said that young people would be the ones to invent new things and lead people in the right direction. "Rosie, you'll be one of the leaders," she'd said.

No one had ever said anything like that to Rosie before. She didn't see herself that way.

"I see it," Beatrix had said. "You just have to pay a lot of attention to things."

"Pay attention to what?" Rosie had asked.

"Everything. People. Places. Keep your eyes open. Take note."

"'Before I got my eye put out – I liked as well to see,'" Rosie said now.

"What?" Diego said, leaning into Rosie. He reached for the Matchbox car in her hand.

Rosie pulled it away and laughed. "Nothing, just lines of poetry."

"Say them to me," he said.

The tickle was still there in her throat, but she ignored it, because there was Diego's friend Charlie pulling up on a bicycle. "Hey, guys, wanna play Crazy Eights?" he said.

CARSON ROSE EARLY to help Naomi milk the goats. After breakfast, Daniel called him over to the back side of the barn, where he unlocked a padlocked door. With a small flashlight, he shined light on a room full of boxes. "DVD players. Coffee makers. Coffee. Sheets. Pillows. Garbage bags. Brand-new shit." He slapped one of the boxes. "That trucker I told you about? He was driving a Walmart shipment through the heartland. All this shit." He pulled down a small box full of unopened packages of AA batteries.

"Oh my God," Carson said. He felt a rush of sensation to his chest, a damp clamminess in his hands. He took a step backward toward the door. All this from a hitchhike ride? He didn't buy it.

"Most of this shit is useless now, but there are some prizes," Daniel said, dropping four batteries into Carson's hand.

"Incredible," Carson said, playing along. "What happened—he just never dropped off the stuff?"

"Nope. Walmart closed its doors. He was still on the road. By the time he picked me up, he was a bit unsteady in the head, if you know what I mean. Too many NoDoz? When I hopped in, he asked, 'Where to?' So I directed him here."

Carson couldn't quite shake the feeling something wasn't right. He glanced over his shoulder. He could slip out quickly if he had to. "Why are you showing all of this to me?"

"'Cause you're a goner, man."

A brick dropped in Carson's stomach. Daniel probably had a weapon in here, too; the supposed Walmart bonanza had just been bait to lure him into this dark room. Walmart sold guns, for heaven's sake.

"And you sure can't carry much with you where you're going." Daniel grinned.

A shallow grave, Carson thought. People were like dogs—they could sense your fear. Spin it, he told himself. Refocus. "Hey, so what about those chickens?" he said. "Ever cook any of them up?"

"Funny you should mention that," Daniel said. "One of them hasn't been laying. And you know what that means."

Carson stared blankly.

"Aw, c'mon bro." Daniel pushed the box back onto the shelf and dragged his finger across his throat. "It means someone's gonna get to kill something."

"Kill?" Carson said, his voice tight.

"When they stop laying, we stop feeding them. So now she'll feed us."

It took Carson a moment to register what he was hearing. He wrung his hands, which were still sweating. Better a hen than him.

"You only feel bad about the first one," Daniel said as they left the shed.

Carson sighed, still not sure what Daniel's show-and-tell was really about.

In the chicken yard, the birds squawked, scattering to the edges. Daniel walked over to one of them, and the hen immediately sank to the ground, surrendering. Daniel wrapped his hand around the bird's head, muffling her frantic clucks. "Hold here," he said. "Like this." He handed the chicken to Carson, folding Carson's fingers around her head.

The bird was warm in Carson's hand. Its beak pressed hard and sharp into his palm.

"Now, whip it around, firm and fast."

Carson hesitated.

"You break its neck," Daniel said. "It's bloodless." With his smooth, balding head, his biceps bulging, Daniel looked like he could kill the hen with his thumb alone.

Carson could feel his forehead beading with sweat. The bird couldn't weigh more than ten pounds. How hard could it be? He tightened his grip, counted to three silently, then whirled the bird around. The hen hung limp in his grip. That fast? He felt mildly nauseated.

"Now bleed it," Daniel said, pulling out a knife from his pocket that looked a little too large for the job. Had that knife been there all along?

They gutted and stripped the bird until it was smooth and pink. "Just like a supermarket bird," Daniel said, scraping the guts off the table.

Naomi cooked up the bird in a pot, and they ate it for dinner with greens and corn.

"Good to eat from your own hands, isn't it?" Daniel said.

"It is," Carson said. He focused on the meat, trying to chew slowly despite a strange knot in his throat. These people were competent survivors, and generous. But something unsettled him. Did they not trust him? Or did he just not trust them?

After the plates were cleared, Naomi placed a small windup radio on the table. "Cute little thing, isn't it?" She turned it on. "We listen every night. Or we aim to, hoping there'll be something other than this preacher. Someone left it here," she said. "A traveler, like you. They're always leaving things."

Carson forced a smile, wondering who would leave such a thing.

"Some fool left this knife, for instance," Daniel said, pulling out the big knife again and stabbing it into the table.

"Daniel, please," Naomi said.

She turned the dial. Static cracked, then a woman's voice came from the radio.

"We came from Chicago. Walked for miles, hitched a ride. We are not hungry anymore. Farms, meat, milk. Like Blue said, abundance. We use our hands. We are plugging into the divine. We will rise."

Naomi sighed. "I keep hoping for music."

"Only one kind of music on the radio now," Daniel said. "The 'Blues.'" He looked at Carson. "You're going there, aren't you? To do research?"

"The Center?" Carson said. Right, he thought. "Yes. Yes, I am."

In the morning, Carson woke to an already-humid day. He raked the goat yard and chopped some wood, then gathered up his belongings. He gave the living room a once-over: cut flowers in a vase, three half-burned candles, a basket of eggs, goat's milk in a bowl. The windup radio sat at the edge of the kitchen counter. He glanced out the windows and saw Naomi and Daniel conversing near the barn. Hastily, he grabbed the radio and slipped it into his pack.

"Come back anytime," Naomi said, once he joined them outside. She handed him back his gun then wrapped him in a big hug.

"Or don't," Daniel said, winking.

"Thank you," Carson said, a strange clump forming in his throat. Was it remorse? Relief? He packed the gun, hoisted his pack, then headed for the tracks, westward.

July 27

C.,

You used to write to me about knowledge. You wondered what kind would serve your students—your kids, as you called them. What did they need to know? I had quick answers back then. Get them beyond our borders, I said. They need to know how big things are. They are not the center of the universe. They need to learn other cultures and other languages, and how to discern between right and wrong, and how to stand up and not be afraid.

> Now what should they learn? How to be good neighbors? How to not trash everything? How to trust? The kids have turned violent is what I'm telling you. Back then, what did you do with the violent ones?

Beatrix closed her notebook. On its cover, she had taped the drawing from the school bulletin board—that strange red crow with its tiny wings and funny human feet. Or was it a raven? A walking raven? She felt a heaviness in her stomach. Sadness? Dread? She wasn't entirely sure.

When she had traveled east to see Carson, they'd visited an art gallery in what had once been the meatpacking district, by then an ailing arts district. As they passed the empty galleries, Beatrix wondered out loud if the paintings had gone to the same place as the cow carcasses—some avant-garde slaughterhouse somewhere. Carson had laughed.

She'd been overly chatty all morning. Since that initial meeting in the school hallway, she had learned so much about him. As they toured the galleries, she was close enough again to smell his woodsy scent, to notice more closely his hands, his mouth, his breath, his body.

One gallery showed large photographs chronicling the photographer's experience of a difficult romantic breakup. On large panels accompanying each image was the story of the breakup, the writing stitched in thread. Again and again, the story, slightly different in each telling. Each image showed a specific detail from the artist's memory—a red telephone, the carpet pattern in the hotel room where she'd received her lover's call telling her it was over. The visual details that had fixed in the artist's mind at the moment of undoing.

"Self-absorbed," Carson had said, looking at the first panel. Beatrix had agreed.

She moved along the wall behind Carson, glancing over the work. Nothing about the images particularly moved her. She stole glances at Carson, saw his eyebrows rise, his head nod on occasion.

"She's kinda stuck, isn't she?" Carson said, shuffling to the next wall.

But in the next room, a new series of panels began. The same format: an image accompanied by words stitched with a rust-colored thread. But here, each story was different, no longer the artist's story, but others' stories: A man whose brother committed suicide. A woman whose child was killed by a car bomb. A family whose house had burned down. The photographs captured these incidental details, the images that had lodged themselves in memory, forever attached to tragedy. A circle of pigeons in a cloudless sky, church bells ringing, a parade passing on the street. The icons of grief.

Beatrix looked at each image closely, read each story. She felt a chill move through her. "The crows in the field the day June died," Carson said. "They were still for a long time, like spilled oil. And then, all at once they flew away."

"They carried her, maybe," Beatrix said. Carson nodded.

Near the end of the exhibit, Carson and Beatrix stood in front of a single photograph, no story attached. A perfect boulder, the size of a small house, in the middle of a road at the foot of a mountain. Had it rolled down the slope? Or been placed there by a team of men?

"The heaviest object in the universe," Carson said, reaching for Beatrix's hand.

His hand was warm and solid and soft all at once, and Beatrix suddenly felt buoyant, as if inside a quiet ascending elevator or hovering over the city in a hot air balloon.

Carson lifted her hand to his mouth and kissed the back of her fingers, his words finally landing in her ears.

"What?" she said, letting go and stepping closer to the frame.

"Grief," Carson said.

They both stood looking at the photograph but also not looking at it.

Beatrix noticed something in the upper corner of the photo: an irregular dark mass above the boulder. Leaning in, she saw the shape was made of singular things, each with its own curve and arc. Birds.

"Good thing for the lightest then," she said.

"What's that?"

Beatrix felt her face flush. Warmth rushed into her chest. Love. Love was the lightest object, the thing that elevated you and kept you aloft. She fluttered a hand at the image and said, "Birds."

CHAPTER 9

The August heat meant Carson carried more and sweated more. A few days west of Naomi and Daniel, he thanked God for a small lake and weighed down his pack with as much water as he could carry. With weary feet and sore shoulders, he repeated his mantra: Keep going. Keep going.

When he thought of Beatrix—often—he sometimes indulged the longing. Other times, he scoffed at it. Surely she'd forgotten him by now.

One afternoon, he came upon a cluster of people on the tracks. It was some kind of brawl, with a circle of onlookers shouting, cheering. One man had his boot on a younger man's neck, calling out, "He's a thief! He's a thief!" A woman clawed at the man's shirt and yelled, "Let him go."

Two other men were locked in a hold. Carson considered trying to tackle one of them, or pulling out his gun and shooting it into the air to make everything stop. He wanted to have this kind of courage. But he also remembered Ayo's warning about bandits and their staged events. *You watch out for you*, Ayo had said. *Only you*. Carson hurried past the group quietly.

"Where you gettin' off to?" said one of the men, lunging toward him. Another man joined in, and Carson took off running.

He tripped on a clump of weeds, and in seconds, the men were on him, their bodies wild and heavy. There would be no reasoning here. Carson swung quickly and hit one, knocking him to the ground. Another man pounced, and Carson managed to block the punch while kicking hard at the man's shins. The man buckled forward and sliced at Carson's biceps with a blade.

The pain came instantly, as air hit the gash. He kept running then, adrenaline propelling him away from the group.

"We'll kill you, motherfucker!" one of men shouted after Carson, but none of them followed him.

When he stopped to look back, the men were far behind, small toy-like figures on the tracks. He assessed the wound on his arm—his shirt was sliced open, but there was too much blood to see how deep the cut was.

His adrenaline now turning to exhaustion, he came to a fallow field and turned down a long road toward a white farmhouse, its black shutters tired and peeling. He peered in one of the broken windows to an empty darkness.

He dropped his pack on the porch, tore off his sleeve, and poured water on the wound. The gash wasn't as deep as he'd feared. He rested his forearm on top of his head to elevate the wound, then sat on the ground against his pack. He wished for a human sound: a song being hummed, a kitchen cabinet closing, the clip of shears on a hedge.

He picked up a fist-sized rock and hurled it at the window. The glass shattered.

He pulled out the windup radio he'd taken from Naomi and Daniel, and stared at it until he felt a burn inside his chest. *We'll kill you, motherfucker!*

He wound the crank on the radio and turned the dial slowly—no weather report, no music, no voices. Just static. He turned it off and heard only silence.

Carson camped there for the night and woke early to walk again. At midday, he met a young farmer pulling carrots. "You a Pilgrim?" the farmer asked. "Goin' to the Center?"

"Not a Pilgrim, no," Carson said. "Is it nearby, the Center?"

"Depends on your definition of 'near.' Cross the Plains and go north, so I'm told. Eastern Wyoming. Where are you headed?"

"West."

"You'll pass the silo then," the farmer said. "Big cement bunker behind chain link. A billionaire took it over a few years before the collapse as a safe house for him and his family. I heard other billionaires did the same thing elsewhere. Rumor has it, they still have caviar. But no one's seen a sign of them in months. My guess is, they went mad from isolation." He handed Carson the carrots he'd pulled. "Good luck to you."

Carson thanked the farmer and continued on. Billionaire bunkers. A strange new world.

That evening, he added the carrots to a salad of dandelion, amaranth, and clover, all more abundant now. He set a deadfall trap and later was euphoric to find he'd caught a squirrel. Until he realized the animal was still alive. Injured, but alive, its limbs and tail twitching, a flutter in its eyes. Definitely alive. Shit. He needed this meat. He lifted the rock and brought it down hard on the squirrel's head. It had to be done. His hand trembling, he touched the squirrel's fur, a small cloak covering a form. No life inside. The squirrel was gone, empty.

Carson sighed. He had not asked for this power.

His stomach growled. He got to work skinning and cleaning. Then he built a fire, cooked the squirrel, and ate it.

• • •

Beatrix went outside, where Rosie was lying on her belly at the edge of the garden. She joined her there, and together they stared at the small, wispy beet greens.

"How much longer until we can pull them out?" Rosie said.

"Just have to keep the soil damp, and in forty to seventy days, Rog said, we'll have beets," Beatrix said.

"That's, like, forever far away," Rosie said, pushing herself up to her knees.

"I don't know why we never planted a garden here before," Beatrix said.

"Because you were gone all the time," Rosie said.

Beatrix nodded. She thought of Hank and Dolores. They were probably pulling full-grown vegetables out of the ground on whatever land they were farming. She pictured Hank, his tall, thin body stooped over thick bunches of greens, Dolores with her hands full of squash. They'd be singing, probably, making up some song about what they were doing.

"Beets schmeets," Rosie said. She made a snowball of dirt in her hands, then tossed it across the yard. "Abuela says we're going to Jonathan Blue's place, the Center."

"What?" Beatrix said. She felt like she'd been socked in the stomach. "No. No, you're not," she said. "We will not let that happen." She offered Rosie a hand and pulled her up.

The front bell rang, and they found Anita at the door. She'd come to help chalk sidewalk advertisements for Halcyon Radio. "I have gifts," she said, handing each of them a small container, a contact lens case cut in half.

"Open it," Anita said. "Remember those resourceful young DIY neighbors? We've been working on some lip balm. While supplies last, at least."

"Oh my God," Rosie said. She had already opened the case and was streaking the red-violet balm across her lips. "This is amazing."

Beatrix did the same. Although it was the least of her worries, her lips had been painfully chapped for months now. "The color—how'd you do that?"

"Berries," Anita said.

"Incredible," Beatrix said as they headed out. On Maria del Carmen's orders, they would stay within the Perimeter.

"And we're sure people have radios now?" Rosie asked.

"Well, more people do, thanks to what the PBB found. And Gary and his ham radio buddies built some radio receivers, apparently."

"Built radios?" Rosie asked.

"Yeah, with wires and old telephone cord," Beatrix said. "I don't get it, but I'm glad they do."

On a brick wall, Beatrix scrawled out a list of upcoming shows—Anita's program on DIY women's health care, Rog's gardening segment, a short show on beekeeping, another on canning and preserving. Rosie made simple drawings of bees, rainwater, and mason jars to accompany them, stopping every now and then to put on more lip balm.

"I'm thinking this lip balm is the official sponsor of Halcyon Radio," Beatrix joked. "Today's programming brought to you by"—she thought for a moment—"apocalyp-stick!"

Anita let out a loud laugh, which made Beatrix and Rosie laugh, too.

"Are these all news shows?" Rosie asked, reading over the list they wrote up at their next stop.

"Music doesn't transmit that well over AM radio, sadly," Beatrix said, as Gary had explained early on.

"When we had a TV," Rosie said, "Abuela would watch evening soap operas on the Mexican station. I watched them, too. They were dumb but addicting. Maybe you could do something like that?"

Beatrix set down the piece of chalk and looked at Rosie. "A radionovela?"

She remembered one radio drama, *El Caballero*, that everyone listened to in Ecuador. Beatrix had first heard it in one of the cacao farmers' homes. All the family members crowded into the dark house, and someone set out dried plantains for snacking. When a man's voice came through a backdrop of syrupy violins, the youngest child bounced on the sofa, squealing. The room filled with the sound of horse hooves and the show's signature introduction: *"Desde el pueblo más lejano, sobre las montañas más altas y nevadas . . ."*

Beatrix did her own rendition of the intro, then stopped to translate, and continued in English. "From the farthest pueblo, over the steepest snow-capped mountains, brandishing his handsome smile, his thick mustache, his yellow wool poncho, and his leather chaps, comes . . . El Caballero."

"The perfect superhero," Anita said, after Beatrix had explained the show.

"Exactly," Beatrix said. "El Caballero did it all. He restored fish to the ocean and saved factory workers from burning buses. That last one was actually a nonsmoking message."

"Sounds kinda educational," Rosie said, smirking.

"Totally. But it was great, and everyone listened to it—kids, adults, rich people, poor people."

"Sounds like what this neighborhood needs," Anita said. "People could learn things from the characters. Isn't it easier sometimes to learn things from make-believe? Like with fairy tales."

"We can hope," Beatrix said. It was a long shot. Maybe it wouldn't do a thing. But at the very least, it could offer a distraction, which Rosie needed, which they all sorely needed. And maybe it was a way to get everyone to think about more than the Center. "We'd need a writer. Anita, do you know any writers?"

Anita's face brightened, and she led them a few blocks down to Thelma Rosen, a woman in her midsixties with graying flyaway hair. Thelma had published short-story collections and written plays. She knew a few things about directing, too.

Thelma twisted her hair around her index finger as she listened to Beatrix talk about *El Caballero*. She pointed to Beatrix's notebook. "Can

I see that for a minute?" She studied the drawing of the red bird on the front. "Curious feet. What about him?"

Beatrix felt a tinge of shame as she began to explain to Thelma where she'd gotten the drawing.

"No," Thelma said, interrupting. "I mean, what about him? The superhero."

"Oh? Him? The crow?"

"Raven. The Red Raven," Thelma said. "That's got a nice ring to it."

Beatrix nodded. "Whatever you say."

Beatrix and Rosie walked home excited, but arrived to find a note from Flash on the chalkboard that immediately dimmed their spirits:

> Dragon sick. Maria del Carmen and I went for herbs. Please check on him. Back soon.

Dragon was shivering in bed, his skin pale like a dawn sky. He opened an eye. "Hey."

On the bedside table was a bowl of water, a washcloth resting on its rim. Beatrix dipped the cloth in the water, then placed it over his forehead. "Do you want a drink?" she said. Then she paused and looked at Rosie. "Do you think it could be the water?"

"But *we're* not sick," Rosie said.

Dragon moved his eyes around in a small circle and blinked. He opened his mouth to speak, but only a small grunt escaped.

"True. But"—Beatrix sighed—"what if it *is* the water?"

Dragon's eyes were closed now. Rosie leaned over him and listened for his breathing. She looked at Beatrix. "What should we do now?"

"Take precautions." Beatrix got up, pulled a bottle of water from their storage area under the stairs, and poured some into a cup to inspect it. There was nothing to see. Of course, you never *saw* a parasite, you just *had* them. It wasn't worth the risk. On a piece of cardboard, she wrote, *Boil all water before drinking,* and propped it against the water jugs.

When he was walking, Carson often forgot that there was ever anything else but walking. As if he had been walking his entire life and would continue to walk forever, and that all there was to life was walking. The placing of one foot in front of the other, the steady glide of the world on either side.

Was he really making his way to Beatrix? Had he completely lost his mind? He wasn't even halfway to her yet. Maybe none of the way. Maybe Beatrix didn't even exist anymore.

He was in flat country now, the sky a perfect half dome over him. The Iowa landscape was green and gold. The breadbasket—hallelujah. He was fucking hungry.

He heard barking and followed the sound to a shade-covered road, where a dog stood alone, as if waiting for him. He crouched, and the dog trotted forward. Female, mottled gray-black, with brown eyes. She nudged her head into his palm, and he felt her matted fur and ribs.

Together, they continued along the road to where the trees cleared and a town began. The afternoon sunlight reflected off parked cars and slanted off houses and buildings. Something about the light was odd; its angle seemed too steep, the shadows too crisp, as if cast by a winter sun. It was the kind of town where folks should be sitting on the porch, waving to neighbors and drinking tea or cocktails, ice clinking in the glasses. Carson stayed alert for any movement. There had to be food here somewhere.

The dog was no longer beside him, but when he sounded a long whistle, she came happily, two twigs sticking out from the side of her mouth. "Play fetch, huh?" he said, reaching for the twigs. But they weren't twigs; they were the two skinny legs of a bird, a common robin. The dog positioned her kill between her paws and ate.

On the porch of a modest house stood a woman in a once-white terry-cloth robe. Her hair was messy, as if she had just woken up. She waved him over. "Can you help?" she said, barely audibly. "Please. My daughter."

Carson approached the house. Maybe she would give him food.

"Have you come with medicine?" the woman said. "Please tell me you've come with medicine."

Inside, the house smelled of mint and rotten meat. On the sofa was a small, pale girl. In the dim light, she resembled a fish, silvery and damp, her mouth open and hollow. Each gurgle of breath shook her.

"Tea," Carson said, imagining a lemon and a sharp knife. He would slice up a lemon. "Give her tea. With lemon."

There was the sound of coughing. The fish flopped onto its side, and a thick yellow liquid spilled from her mouth. Carson backed up to the door and let himself out.

He knocked at the next house, where two wooden ducks in the yard held up a welcome sign. When no one came, he risked it and went in, heading for the kitchen. A weak voice called out, "David, is that you?"

Carson followed the sound to a bedroom, where a thin, ashen woman lay beneath the covers, her head like a prune against the pillowcase. He heard the liquid in her lungs.

"Are you the doctor?" she said.

"I'm not a doctor," Carson said, and the woman's body seemed to shrink. She brought her hand to her mouth, bony fingers failing to cover the cough. Jesus, everyone in this town was sick. Carson stepped out of the room and hoped David, whoever he was, would return soon.

In the kitchen, he opened a pantry door onto more food than he'd seen in six months.

The woman made a noise, and Carson stood very still, his heart racing. Then he moved back to the doorway to her room.

"Take whatever you want. Stay alive," the woman said softly.

Carson knew she would not last long. He went into an adjacent room and looked around. He grabbed a small ceramic duck from the top of a dresser and returned to the woman, placing the duck on the nightstand next to her. "I wish there was something more I could do," he said.

He stuffed his backpack with all he could fit—canned beans, soup, pasta, Tabasco sauce, two mason jars full of fine cornmeal. He moved down the hall to a bathroom. Below the sink, he found toothpaste, soap, and gauze bandages. A windfall. In a closet in the hallway, he found a pair of men's boots.

Before leaving he called out, "Thank you. Bless you."

Outside, he whistled for the dog, but she did not come. A man shuffled by, his head damp with sweat. On his face was a look of resignation.

Carson walked with his hand over his heart. Bless these poor, sick souls.

He continued out of the town and dropped his pack. With the soap, and water from one of his bottles, he scrubbed his hands and washed out his mouth, nose, and eyes. He tended the wound on his arm, cleaning it and wrapping it with a gauze bandage.

He rested against a tree. He'd been foolish to go inside those houses, to expose himself like that. None of those people were going to survive. Was he?

He took off his boots and rubbed his feet, wishing for an icy-cold stream. He tried on the new boots, which were slightly too big. Good enough, he thought, tying the old ones to his pack as backup.

He pulled the radio from his pack and wound it up. The voice was deep and familiar. *"So many are still tethered to the material world. But there is something beyond that, magnificent and magical. If you listen, you can hear it. Right now, I hear the sound of birds. Crows. Listen, my friends."*

There was a distant caw in the background. But it was a raven, not a crow. A raven had a deeper cry, slightly more guttural. It cawed again, and Carson imagined a devoted disciple squawking in the background—the whole thing a sham.

He turned the radio off and looked at the sky, half expecting to see a bird careening toward him, mocking him. That would be a crow. If any bird could mock a human, it was a crow. They were smart, fierce birds. They used to perch on the telephone wires outside King High, calling out as the kids straggled into the building, teasing whoever passed below as if playing a version of the dozens: *You're so late you missed graduation.*

And then, of course, there were the crows in the field behind his and June's farmhouse. In October of the year June died, they were like a sign. The last time she had asked him to help her end her life, he had looked at her ravaged and brittle body, and then he had gone outside and walked around the field. The sky was a pure gray but for a single cloud in the shape of a whale, large enough to swallow everything—the field, the house, June's sickness, his sorrow. He had wanted to rouse the crows, startle them, drive them up into the whale, but he could not move his arms.

He had wanted so badly to find June curled up in the reading chair, a book fallen into her lap, eyes closed in a little catnap. At the sound of the door closing behind him, she'd sigh, set the book aside, and stand, stretching her arms above her head and arching her back.

But that day, like so many days before it, June lay frail and pallid, on a bed in the middle of the living room. They'd moved it there so she could see out the windows, so she could be a part of the living room. The living. But that bed had made the whole room feel sick.

June had stirred as he approached her. There was no book to take from her hands—she held not even the smallest sliver of desire to continue. He placed his hand over hers. When he went to move it away, she turned her palm upward, as if to hold him there. She looked into his eyes, pleading.

Finally, he had nodded, almost imperceptibly.

She blinked. "Thank you," she'd said without a sound.

He hated this single, pivotal decision. Of course they should have planted peonies along the back deck as she wanted, not the geraniums he had bought. Why had he always insisted they have red wine, leaving her to add a cube of ice? (*I prefer cold wine*, she'd say.) Why couldn't they have gone to Mexico instead of rainy Portland? All those decisions. He would have given them all over to her if he could have just persuaded her out of this one.

He had placed his hand on her forehead. He bent over her chest and rested his head there. Minutes passed. Possibly hours. When he was sure that the afternoon was over—the cawing of the crows had begun and they had lifted into the darkening sky—he stood and carried the container of pills to the kitchen. One by one, he emptied the capsules into the lightest cup they had, a thin bone-china teacup with flowers painted inside. Then he boiled the water and steeped the tea.

He propped pillows behind her back, placed the cup in her hands, and put his hands around hers to help her hold it. With effort, she drank. Afterward, he placed the cup on the table and sank to his knees. There was nothing inside him. No blood, no bones, no nerves. No sound, no smell. He closed his eyes.

Technically, she had done it herself. She had sipped the tea. He had not forced her to swallow. It could have been Earl Grey or chamomile. He could have spooned in honey. All she had said was, "Add lemon."

And so he had.

August 20

C.,

Are the angry kids circling your neighborhood, too? Have they infiltrated all the cities? I am afraid of their weapons but cannot bring myself to carry one.

Would it be wrong to put a lock on the gate and not give the key to Maria del Carmen? To keep her here, I mean. To keep her from going off to this mythical Center and taking Rosie with her. They'll have to walk. There are no trains.

At this point, the only train I'd consider boarding is one that would take me to you. It's not that you fade from me, but I can't always hear you anymore. Is this what they talk about when they talk about faith?

Tell me about ravens, please.

Love, B.

After five days, Dragon was still sick. His skin was more pallid, and his eyes were darker, more sunken. Anything he ate came right out again.

"Just give it time, Beatrix," Maria del Carmen said, pouring a jar of dried herbs into a pot. "These herbs are for the stomach. Eventually, it will be able to hold the food we give him."

Beatrix went to the fire and leaned over the pot. "But when?" she asked.

Maria del Carmen kept stirring. "Patience, Beatrix."

She seemed so sure of her medicine, Beatrix noticed. So sure of Jonathan Blue. How could that be?

She tried an appeal to Maria del Carmen's confidence. "What about a radio segment on herbs?"

"I'm no good at talking like that," Maria del Carmen said.

"It could be an interview. Me asking, you answering. Talking like we are now."

Maria del Carmen shook her head and handed Beatrix two hot mitts and gestured to the pot. "Can you set it here, please? It needs to cool and infuse now."

Beatrix did as she was told. "I think you'd be great at it," she said.

Maria del Carmen scooped a cupful of water from a bucket and tossed it into the pot.

Beatrix sighed. What was the way through? Did only Jonathan Blue matter? How was he promising so much?

She watched the steam rise from the pot and thought of Dragon. His tired body. She still wasn't sure if it was flu or some kind of water contaminant. Jesus Christ, what if it was a Jonathan Blue strategy? A manufactured crisis!

"Think about it," she told Flash later. "Everyone said he prophesized the flu. Maybe he's prophesizing another illness."

"Wait, what?" Flash said, bobbing his head like a spring-headed toy.

"Dragon. Sick. The water. Maybe Blue needs another a plague to prove his power. Maybe Dorn the water guy is manufacturing one for him."

Flash pulled at a few hairs on his chin and thought for a moment. "The CDC prophesized that flu, too, Beatrix. And right now, no one else is sick. Why are you even listening to Blue? You have to drown that shit out."

"Maria del Carmen never turns him off. She's either in rapture, imagining ascending to heaven, or in terror thinking she might be felled by a plague, or by the hoodlums first."

"Blue is good at what he does, I'll give you that. But that doesn't mean you have to cave. Maybe he sent the T-Rize, too?" Flash smirked. "Beatrix, sometimes you push a little too hard."

His words landed in her ears like whip cracks. Pushed too hard? Why were there chickens in the backyard? Why was Halcyon Radio now up and running? Because she'd pushed for them.

Flash loaded up the wagon with empty water bottles and started wheeling it down the walkway. Beatrix followed him, annoyed and confused.

Just ahead, a group of neighbors headed toward the Perimeter, luggage and carts in tow. More? The neighborhood had lost more than half of its residents already. Some to the early round of flu, and others—like Hank and Dolores—to farm country.

Beatrix caught up with the group and asked where they were going. A buck-toothed boy pointed to the sky.

"The Center," the child's mother said. She had short hair and the hearty freckled skin of someone who worked outside.

"What's there?" Beatrix asked.

"Movies," one of the children said.

"We don't know about that," the mother said. "But food, safety. We're out of choices here. I need to protect them." She patted the boy on the head as she said this.

"We will rise," the boy said, repeating Blue's favorite line while standing on his tiptoes.

"Maybe we will," the mother said.

Beatrix tilted her head, skeptical. *Stay here,* she wanted to say. *There's a garden here. There's a community.*

She noticed the boy's chapped lips, his dirty hands, the way his mother's hand rested on his head, the slack look on her face. "Maybe," Beatrix called out as they walked away.

How was it possible that all these people were following Jonathan Blue? Could they not spot a narcissist? *I can show you a new way. I will feed you and clothe you. I, I, I.* Who had that kind of singular power these days?

Blue's seemed such a simple sales pitch. Just show up, be taken care of, and merge with . . . with what, the darkness? What kind of upgrade was he talking about? It sounded so familiar—an easy fix, like a TV dinner or a mechanized car wash. Convenient. Was that the kind of pie-in-the-sky conviction that could fuel a very long walk? How was it that in all her years of organizing, Beatrix had not been able to generate anything even close to that kind of commitment from people?

She helped Flash carry the water home. "This is insane. Everyone is going there."

"No, not everyone," Flash said.

"We need to get *The Red Raven* on the air, like now."

"Agreed."

But could that really keep Maria del Carmen and everyone else from leaving? Was it even possible to do that with a story?

When she asked this of Thelma, Thelma hushed her. Then she pulled out a box set of cassettes—a compilation of old radio stories remastered from the 1930s and '40s. "From my neighbor. His grandfather gave them to him when he was young. He never threw them out."

Beatrix scanned the titles: *The War of the Worlds, The Green Hornet, The Shadow.*

"He also brought this," Thelma said, gesturing to a portable cassette player. "Solar-charged batteries."

She popped one of the tapes into the player. "Research," she said, as Orson Welles's voice came out of the small speaker.

After a while, she stopped the tape. "I'm thinking we need to set it in another realm. Not the everyday. Not even what used to be the everyday. They'll go mad listening to that. Can't have reminders of the comforts we no longer have."

"Right. Or it'll be just like Blue," Beatrix said.

"My dreams keep showing me charred, barren landscapes. Lunar. Lifeless. Except—"

"There's a bird?" Beatrix said.

"A boy."

Rosie stood behind a hedge at the end of the street, where one neighbor's house ended and another began. Technically, she was still in bounds. Still, her heart raced.

Diego put his tongue behind Rosie's ear, then licked her neck. "You taste good," he said, moving toward her mouth. "What's on your lips? I like it."

That morning, she'd given herself a sponge bath and rubbed herself with the lavender sachet that Anita had given her. She'd put on some of the berry lip balm. Effective, she thought now, as Diego breathed her in, moving his hands to her waist and under her shirt, his fingers kneading her skin. Diego took her hand and led her to the park. This was definitely beyond legal land, but Rosie didn't care. They walked through a small village of tents until they came to one that Diego unzipped.

"Whose tent is this?"

"A friend's," Diego said. "He won't mind."

Rosie's heart was jumping out of her chest. She crawled in, and Diego closed the zipper behind them.

The tent was blue, but inside everything looked green—Diego's hand

and her breast beneath it, even her grimy underwear, which he peeled off her body a little too soon. She froze. "Wait."

"Wait for what, mi linda? I thought we were doing this." He looked up at her, his mouth open as if to catch something.

"Yes," she said.

He unbuttoned his jeans. His breath smelled of soap and sinus, and Rosie saw only his eyelashes and the shine of his eyeballs, and then he was pressing his hips onto hers and then, oh, he was taking up all the space down there. She sucked in her breath and held it as his boy body moved up and down, knocking into her, making noises like a dog. After a minute or two, he made a strange high-pitched squeak, and she wondered if that was the coming.

Just then, someone opened the tent zipper. "Who the hell is in here? What the fuck!" The head of a man appeared. His skin also looked green, like theirs, in the light, and his thick eyeglasses distorted his eyes into two oversized saucers. Mortified, Rosie untangled herself from Diego, wriggled back into her clothing, and crawled outside. She rushed from the park, assuming Diego would follow. She was mad, but not that mad, because at least they'd done it, and now they could sneak back to the front porch and he could put his hand on her knee and they'd be forever connected.

But when Rosie got to the edge of the park, Diego was not with her. She turned around and went back to look for him.

Not far from the tent were half a dozen kids on bikes. Rosie's heart dipped deeper into her chest. They were not PBB riders. They carried weapons—a chain, a machete, a knife. They were standing around, leaning on their bikes, waiting. Then she saw Diego. He was holding a stick over the man whose tent they had just vacated.

"Diego!" she called. He looked to her, but at that moment, someone whistled and the kids all took off on their bikes or went running. Diego pulled something from the man's hands, then ran to join the others.

Rosie stood in disbelief, sick to her stomach. Had he been with the

T-Rize all this time? And the sex? What was it for? Had it been some sort of initiation game? Did all the T-Rize kids have to have sex with someone to get in? Her stomach churned.

When she reached the house, she felt the sting of tears. "Please let no one see me," she said under her breath. She snuck to the backyard, crept behind the egg house, and cried.

CHAPTER 10

THE LANDSCAPE WAS a book, and every visual interruption—a cluster of poplar trees, incompetent power lines, dead cars—seemed a silent character. The pages kept coming, and Carson read and walked, read and walked, as Nebraska stretched flat and green all the way to the horizon.

His arm had healed, thanks to the soap and bandages, and the new-to-him boots were working fine. But his feet had swollen in the heat, and his toes burned and itched. He wished for icy drinks and mountains. Springs and water tanks were blessings—signaled by graffiti symbols scratched on surfaces or by moisture in the air and green-leafed trees.

He'd finished the food from the sick woman's pantry—even the cornmeal, which he'd mixed with water and eaten as a sweet and chalky gruel. Now it was back to wild greens and crab apples. He was on the lookout for something elastic so he could make a slingshot. If a dog could catch a bird, why couldn't he?

More and more, he met "Pilgrims" traveling toward the Center. One family reminded him of the group he'd met just outside the tunnel, a lifetime ago it seemed. The men all wore beards, and the women, long skirts, like they'd stepped out of another century. He half expected to find the cherubic little girl who'd given him that cabbage sandwich. But he also came upon modern travelers, in jeans and T-shirts and sneakers—determined and hopeful despite their losses. Within a day, entire tributaries of people were coming from all directions, coursing toward the Center.

"Where we'll finally eat," said a man, maybe late forties, with a grizzled beard, in a Red Sox T-shirt and scuffed hiking boots.

"I'm Randy," he said. His kind, crinkly eyes also reminded Carson of those first Pilgrims: the gaze cast slightly upward, as if following a distant bird or airplane that Carson couldn't see no matter how hard he looked.

"How far have you come?" Carson asked.

"Nearly two hundred miles, I'd say. Kansas City," Randy said. "It was a nightmare there. Nowhere for the shit to go, so it kept piling up. An epidemic just waiting to happen. And we were hungry and out of options." He hooked his thumbs together and held his hands, palms open, in front of his chest.

Carson thought of his students, all their hand signs and signals, and felt like the ignorant administrator he'd once been. For good measure, he put his thumbs together and made the gesture, too. A young woman with stringy hair saw it and gestured back, then scampered off with startling energy, skipping along the track, her well-worn jeans hanging off her thin body. Every few paces, she bent down and gripped the rail lines, lowering her ear to them, as if retrieving some silent message. Then she'd get up again and wave her arms to the sky, relaying whatever she'd heard.

One man, his pink face riddled with acne scars, spoke in staccato sentences strung together into never-ending paragraphs. "I'm alone. I used to sell insurance. I bought stock. I sold stock. I lost everything. The water ran out. I'm not good with my hands. I'm hungry. There are gardens. This could be the upgrade."

It was Blue's term, "a civilization upgrade." Maybe that explained everyone's erratic, energetic behavior—they truly believed they were heading to some sort of advanced Eden.

One woman, with almond-shaped eyes, took Carson's hand and held it as if she'd known him forever. Bundled on her back was a child with the same almond eyes. She leaned in so close to Carson that he smelled her breath—a sweet blend of corn and milk. "We are lucky," she whispered. He hesitated, not quite knowing how to respond. When he finally spoke—what else could he say but "Yes"?—she dropped his hand and dashed ahead to catch her companion, the fabric of her long red skirt swishing as she ran.

Carson quizzed Randy. "So are you going for the food or the"—he hesitated—"family?"

"Look, we're not the ones that have been following him for years. It's a step up from hell. It's gotta be. But I admit, what he says makes a lot of sense. Like maybe this giant unplugging is what we've needed."

Randy was traveling with his wife, Claudia, who cocked her head to the side when listening. The couple had two boys, who looked to be about ten and twelve.

"And there's food," Claudia said.

"A steady supply of it," Randy said. "Truth be told, I've been dreaming about a grilled cheese for two hundred miles."

Carson salivated a little. He'd been craving one, too.

"Power Ninja!" one of the boys said, leaping for his brother.

"We told the boys there would be games. Not video games, exactly, but something better," Randy said, his voice soft and apologetic. "It keeps them walking."

"Everything is possible," Claudia said. "That's what Jonathan Blue says. And I, for one, think he's on to something."

Or on something, Carson thought.

They walked for another hour, then came to a road intersecting the tracks.

"It's northwest from here," Randy said, pointing ahead to where Pilgrims moved in small, dark clumps, like elk.

Carson hesitated. He looked west down the tracks. "Eshu," he murmured, remembering the Yoruba deity of the crossroads. Then he turned to follow the Pilgrims.

They came upon a group resting under a tree, and everyone greeted one another with the hand gesture. "No vans in sight," said a stocky man who seemed like he was used to being in charge.

"The last one we saw drove by yesterday morning," Randy said. "Full."

"What do they run on?" Carson asked.

"Veggie grease," said a woman who was gnawing on something that looked like beef jerky. When she noticed Carson watching her, she held up a piece. "Deer?" she said, her eyes brown and doe-like themselves.

THE CAST OF *The Red Raven* included experienced actors and neighbors chosen for their voices and enthusiasm. They held rehearsals in Thelma's living room, using scripts Thelma and Beatrix had copied by hand.

A violinist slid her bow across the strings, and Thelma cued Flash, who began to read with his narrator voice: "Across a dark, charred landscape, nothing moves but dust and smoke, choking the air. No one lives here. Civilization has been erased. Or so it seems. Into the nothingness, something moves. Above, the silhouette of a bird in flight. Below, a boy walking alone, ragged and searching. He sees something on the ground ahead, something bright. He runs toward it, but the wind carries it away. He chases it and finally catches it. A single red feather. He is standing at the base of large snag, a dead tree, its branches intact. He climbs the tree and finds a large nest. He crawls into the nest and sleeps."

"His voice is absolutely perfect," Thelma whispered to Beatrix.

The sound-effects team readied its voices and props as Flash continued. "In the night, bright flashes of light come to the sky and touch the boy in the nest. When he wakes, he finds himself in a small pool of water.

He drinks. He feels heavier and lighter at the same time. Still clutching the red feather, he climbs down from the tree."

"Pause," Thelma said. "Fantastic, Flash."

She looked to the sound-effects crew. "Just a reminder that you won't be able to clear your throat like that on the air. Does anyone need something to drink?" Thelma gestured to a pitcher of water. She had a way of being in control, kind, and motherly all at once.

"Be careful with that water," Beatrix said. "It's probably poisoned."

"What?" someone said. Everyone looked at Beatrix.

Beatrix explained her theory of Jonathan Blue's deliberate contamination. "Dragon is still sick, after all."

"He does seem to be a bit nutty, that Blue," one of the cast members said. Then: "I'm sorry about your friend."

"No one else is sick, though. So it's probably just a bug," Flash said.

Thelma scribbled on the script she was holding. After a moment, she cleared her throat. "I think perhaps boiling the water from here on out is wise. I do not, however, think it's worth scaring people with stories that are predicated on fear instead of fact."

"It might be true," Beatrix said. "Dragon is sick."

Thelma glared at her. "It is true, or do you just want it to be true?"

Beatrix became aware of her audience. She did not know Thelma well, and she'd certainly never seen her irritated before. No, she didn't want it to be true, but she didn't want the people she loved to leave.

"If you want to make the improbable possible, Beatrix, you do it through fiction. That is why we are all here," Thelma said. "Now, may we continue?"

Beatrix looked down at her feet, her flip-flops staring up at her a little too cheerfully. She felt punished. The conviction she'd held a few moments ago fizzled. Maybe Thelma was right. Maybe Blue was just her own enemy, not everyone else's. Maybe she was being unnecessarily conspiratorial. Maybe this was a fight she could let go of. Dragon is sick. Maria del Carmen and Rosie might leave. Focus on that, she told herself. Let the rest go.

Thelma flipped a page of the script. "Let's fast-forward to present day in the story. We might open here, in the middle of the action. Let's see how it reads."

"Action," someone said.

"There's that trash guy. He's creepy."

"He's not creepy. He's just quiet."

"He's creepy."

"Who's his family? Does he have any kids? A wife?"

"No. They say he just showed up here one day, back when he was a boy."

"Before we were born."

"During the fires."

"That must be why he's so strange."

"He's not strange. Like I said, he's just quiet."

"Let's go talk to him."

"Look at all that stuff he carts around in that wagon."

"Hey, Trash Man, what do you do with all that stuff?"

"Look, he's got bones and branches, an old net and . . . what's that?"

"A plastic comb."

"Cool! Where'd you find that?"

Flash narrated. "Reilly looked at the children in front of him. Then he pointed to a hillside."

"Over that hill? Is there more?"

"Choose whatever you like from here."

"Really?"

"Really."

"Cool. What's your name?"

"Reilly."

Together, the actors animated the story of Reilly Crawford, the man who became the Red Raven as a boy. A shy and awkward man who collects seemingly useless things in a settlement of survivors living in a new world, Reilly shows the children an old landfill. When one of the children goes missing, Reilly transforms with a sudden flash of light into the Red Raven and flies overhead to spot and save the child.

Approximating the sounds of footsteps, wind, and a nearby river, they clicked wood on the table, swished air from their mouths, sloshed water around in a bowl. The violins played, and Flash delivered the refrain: "From the depths of despair and desperation comes the red feather of hope. No more despair, no more fear. The wondrous Red Raven is here. Finding the wings within . . . *The Red Raven*."

"Great job, everyone!" Thelma said. "With just a few rehearsals, you've really made it come alive. Let's be sure we pick up the pace a bit tomorrow, but all in all, wonderful work."

"Yes, everyone, fantastic!" Beatrix said, opening a bar of chocolate and passing it around to celebrate.

"The famous Fair Share chocolate!" said Flash, in his Red Raven voice, and everyone applauded.

"Opening night tomorrow," Beatrix said. "Five o'clock call. We go on the air at six."

"Let's get home, Beatrix. Gotta check on Dragon," Flash said as the cast filed out.

"I'll catch up," she said. She exchanged a few quick ideas with Thelma, then jumped on her bike.

She hadn't gone a block when she heard the sound of another bike behind her. Flash? Glancing back, she saw a young girl riding at her fast, two ponytails flying out from her helmet. The girl swung a chain at Beatrix's leg and hit it. The sting was sharp and sudden, causing Beatrix to lose speed. The girl looped back quickly, jamming something into Beatrix's front wheel. The bike halted, and Beatrix flew over the handlebars and hit the concrete. She pushed herself up as quickly as she could, her hands throbbing from the impact.

She sized up the girl. Scrawny. Beatrix could take her down easily. Her eyes fixed on the loose bike chain dangling from the girl's fist. "Are you planning to use that?" Beatrix said, her own matter-of-fact tone surprising her.

"I did once already," the girl said, pointing to Beatrix's bloodied calf.

She sounded like an elf or a Broadway kid star, her voice high-pitched and forceful. "I'm robbing you," she added, as if it needed explanation.

"You could ask first," Beatrix said. "I'm generous." Not to mention empty-handed. She had nothing on her. She'd even left the script at Thelma's.

The girl glanced at Beatrix's bike.

"Take it," Beatrix said.

"You don't have a bag or purse?"

"No bag, no purse," Beatrix said. "No money. No food."

The girl stepped toward her, pulling the chain tight. "I don't believe you," she said, her lip rising in a sneer.

Beatrix almost wanted to laugh, but the chain was right at eye level, and it didn't look kind. Her heart was battering, and she pressed her hand on her chest as if to stop it. There, in the front pocket of her shirt, was the remaining square of Fair Share chocolate. "Wait," she said. "I do have something."

The girl squinted.

"Put the chain down, and I'll give it to you."

"What is it? Give it to me first."

"Put the chain down." Beatrix reached into the pocket. She pulled the chocolate out of her pocket and held it up. "I'll set it right there." She pointed to the space on the asphalt between them.

The girl dropped her arms to her sides. The chain went slack and hit the asphalt. Beatrix tossed the chocolate toward the girl's feet. The girl lunged for it, and Beatrix backed away, her calf throbbing. She righted her bike, her eyes glued to the girl.

The girl bit into the square of chocolate viciously, chomping like a dog.

Beatrix hobbled onto her bike and pedaled furiously away.

In two days, the group of Pilgrims had nearly tripled. No vans had yet materialized, and Carson suspected they never would. He wondered how many people were really listening to Blue, heeding his call.

He thought about others who had traveled over this landscape, either for need or promise: indigenous tribes following herds of buffalo; pioneers on the Oregon Trail; African Americans moving north for freedom; Okies escaping the dust; Mexicans flowing north for work. Would this, too, go down as one of the great migrations? Or was it just a minor movement of the hungry and hopeless?

Carson walked alongside the couple and their boys, who were taking turns shooting rocks into the sky with a slingshot. Carson wondered what he could trade them for it.

"We lost everything," Claudia told him. "I mean, I still have Randy and my boys. But what kind of life can I give them now? I worked so hard to have enough to give. But now? Now there's nothing."

"And something there will fill you?" he said.

Claudia stopped and faced Carson. She was an attractive woman, he realized—smiling eyes, long eyelashes. She put her fingertips to her chest and tapped. "The Center," she said. "What else is there to try? Where else is there to go?"

Carson waited for her to say more. When she didn't, he tried to imagine her floating up into the air. Jonathan Blue's Ascension. He looked up at the sky and wondered what the trick might be—helium? An IV of uppers?

The boys passed them then, their gangly bodies scuffling along, picking up rocks and stuffing them into their pockets. "Check this out," the younger one shouted. He was loading the slingshot with a golf ball–sized rock. "I'm gonna fling this one so far you're gonna cry." He pulled the slingshot back and let go. The rock shot through the air like a slow, fat bird, then dropped to the ground with a thud.

"Jeez, why all the books on this staircase?" Flash called out, walking into Beatrix's apartment. "What's that smell?" he said.

"Comfrey," Beatrix said. "Maria del Carmen insists I apply it twice a day."

"It looks like spinach," he said, setting down the shoebox and reaching out to touch the goop on Beatrix's calf.

"It's a wonder she gave it to me at all she was so angry about what had happened. She even told me not to go out again," Beatrix said. "And I'm considering following her orders."

"No, you're not," Flash said.

"Right. But damn, this hurts," she said, lifting up her leg.

"What's up with all those books?" Flash said.

"They're for the mobile library," Beatrix said. Before her injury, Beatrix and Rosie had been inventorying library books, and they'd stacked them on each step as a way to organize them. Anita's husband was outfitting a bike trailer with shelves and sitting cushions.

"I have a sinking suspicion I'll be one of the riders hauling that trailer."

Beatrix smiled. "Good deeds, remember?"

"I remember," he said. He reached for the small case of lip balm. "What's this? More goop?"

"For your lips," she said.

Flash smeared some on, then looked at her and smiled.

She handed him one end of a strip of cloth. "Hold this," she said, wrapping the other end around her leg, covering the poultice. "How is Dragon?"

"He's asleep at the moment. The nurse neighbor came by yesterday and said to keep giving him fluids. And he did drink Maria del Carmen's tea earlier, so there's that."

Beatrix circled the bandage around her leg, and when she got to the end of the cloth, Flash reached over to tuck in the last bit. The gesture was so tender and Dragon was still so sick that a lump formed in Beatrix's throat, then quickly dissolved into tears.

"Oh God, did I hurt you?" Flash said, confused.

"No. No, no." The tears continued, and now there was a heaving in her chest. Just months ago, Flash and Dragon had been complete strangers to her. Now, she couldn't imagine not ever knowing them.

Flash had his arm around her now but remained quiet and still. When Beatrix's sobs grew deeper, he said, "It's okay, Beatrix. It's okay."

She looked at him, her face melting. "But what if it's not? What if Dragon doesn't get better?"

Flash scooted closer, and Beatrix let herself fold into him. After a while, she stopped crying and listened to Flash's heartbeat.

Someone knocked, and Flash opened the door to Gary, who was carrying another shoebox.

"More lanterns?" Beatrix said, wiping her eyes.

"I can come back if this a bad time," Gary said.

"No. It's okay," she said.

"I need to go check on Dragon," Flash said, giving Beatrix a wink. They were convinced Gary had a crush on Beatrix. She didn't exactly hate the attention.

"Thanks for those radios," Flash said. "We made some families pretty happy."

"You bet," Gary said. "Are you wearing lipstick?" he said to Beatrix as Flash left.

Beatrix held up the case. "Want some?"

"I'm good," he said. He glanced down at Beatrix's bandage. "How is the leg?"

"Better," she said. "I'm supposed to stay off it for a day or two."

Gary gestured to the sofa and handed her the box. "Not lanterns," he said.

Inside was a bundled-up red-and-black plaid flannel shirt. Beneath that was a small black handgun. Beatrix nearly choked on her own gasp. "Oh God."

Adrenaline rose up in her, and she handed the box back quickly. "Sorry. Nope," she said. "Violence only begets—"

"Beatrix, listen," he said. "You're out there every day, riding your bike all over the place. It's not safe."

"And you think a gun automatically makes me safer?" She thought of the T-Rize girl eating the chocolate. Chain or no chain, was she supposed to pull a gun on a twelve-year-old girl?

"They're not always going to be won over with chocolate. And you really are a valuable part of this neighborhood. You're not one to lock yourself inside. You ought to have some protection."

Gary confused her. He was wrong, but he was also right: she was not one to stay barricaded inside.

"What's wrong with chocolate?" she said. "Maybe I can just stock everyone with it."

It was a stupid thing to say. Beatrix looked at the bandage. The poultice had gone from cool to hot. Her leg was throbbing.

"I admire your idealism, Beatrix."

"But," she said, feeling annoyed.

"Just hold on to it for now," he said, glancing at the gun, then looking back at her, holding his gaze.

"I have no idea how to even use a gun," she said.

"I'll teach you," he said, heading for the door. "By the way, the station's all set for the radio story crew this evening."

Beatrix felt her heart sink a little. "I'm ordered to stay here and heal," she said. "But I'll be listening." And before he closed the door behind him, she called out, "Thank you."

Rosie pulled a skein of yarn out of the basket and searched for a loose end. She wanted to go thank the chicken man—Mr. Green?—who'd given some of his yarn to Beatrix. But how? She still wasn't allowed to go anywhere. She hadn't said a word yet to anyone about Diego and wasn't planning to anytime soon. But after Beatrix's attack, Abuela had her on lockdown.

She held up the yarn—sea blue, the color of her left eye. The color of everything lately. The color of the space inside her heart that Diego had left there. She felt like a prisoner. Inside her own body. A prisoner of silence.

In Rosie's replay of the tent scene, she sometimes edited the ending. In one version, she shouted, "Enough!"—so loud that Diego was flung backward against the tent wall, which tore from the impact, leaving him in a crumple on the grass. In another, she clamped down on the machinery between his legs, forcing a deafening, defeated howl from his mouth. In yet another, she just completely vanished from the scene, dissolved like sugar in water from beneath Diego's body.

To make a God's eye, she wrapped blue yarn around the sticks: under, over, under, over. Diego. What a jerk. They didn't belong together.

The one place Rosie did belong was in the house on Halcyon, with Beatrix, Flash, and Dragon. She stopped weaving for a moment and looked down at the design. This one would be for Dragon, she decided. To help him get better.

But now, Abuela wanted to take her somewhere else, because of what some preacher was promising. It totally sucked. What could she do?

Beatrix was hell-bent on making sure Abuela didn't fall under Blue's spell. That was why she was so crazy about making sure everyone in town had a transistor radio. And now, this Red Raven character was supposed to become Abuela's new guru? What were the chances?

Rosie had her own campaign going: promising to pray, clean the house, fill the tincture bottles, massage Abuela's hands daily. But Abuela was stubborn.

They'd gotten into several arguments about it already. "Why don't you just go? I'll stay here!" Rosie had shouted. Abuela had quietly left the room. Rosie felt horrible. At the end of the day, if Rosie belonged to anyone, she belonged to her grandmother.

Was it possible that things were better at the Center? Maybe what Jonathan Blue said was true. Maybe there were more comforts. Maybe there was power and water that you didn't have to haul from a horse-drawn cart. Maybe there was enough water to get clean for real. Around here, Rosie never felt she got clean enough, which was especially disgusting when she had her period. Her period. Crapola. She prayed it would come this month.

Rosie felt sick as she thought again about what she and Diego had done. He had lied to her and deceived her. And she could not afford a little T-Rize baby. No. No. No.

As the sky outside dimmed, Rosie threaded the blue yarn, over, under, over, under, around and around until she finished the God's eye. She placed it in the basket with the rest of the yarn and pulled out two new sticks. Maybe she'd just sit here in the dark and make God's eyes for the rest of her life.

Her eyes welled with tears. "'Heart, we will forget him,'" she said to no one. She tossed the yarn in the basket, then went to Abuela's altar, where she prayed for a small red miracle.

"Rosie!" Beatrix called from the backyard. "Maria del Carmen! Come outside—the show's about to start."

The show. Rosie had nearly forgotten. Tonight was the first episode of *The Red Raven*.

Gathered at the picnic table outside were Rog and Finn from the garden, along with Anita and her husband from down the block. A fire was going, and the small radio Abuela always listened to sat at the center of the table, like some sort of consecrated object. Abuela took a cup of medicinal tea to Dragon, who huddled in the lawn chair, bundled in a blanket.

"I'm so excited about this," Anita said. "Taking our little Halcyon Radio to a whole new level."

Rog turned the radio dial, and Jonathan Blue's voice came out of the small speaker. *"This is an invitation for expansion. It is not just you and your tiny body, your tiny innards. It is everyone around you, right here and beyond here. This is what it means to join together. We are waiting."*

"Oh Jesus," Beatrix said. "Turn the knob, Rog, hurry."

"The darkness has allowed us to see. You might still want that material thing. But it wasn't ever material."

"Ten-eighty, right? That's where I am, Beatrix. Shit."

"Now, here, you can see it. There is light. Unplugged, you yourself are now the ground. You are the current."

Beatrix gently pushed Rog aside. "Let me try."

"We have created this. This is the future present."

"This is messed-up," Beatrix said, one hand on the dial, the other hand yanking at her hair. "You're kidding! We're right there. Ten-eighty AM. Halcyon Radio. This is where it is on the dial."

"We are continuing to create. We are rising."

"This is bullshit," Anita said, trying the dial. "A little to the right or a little to the left. Either way. Everywhere, it's him."

"You will not need anything. Just come."

Beatrix looked at the others, her eyes wide, her mouth open. "This can't be happening. Where's Halcyon Radio? *The Red Raven*! Where the hell is it?"

Rosie had never seen Beatrix so upset. But she understood. She could feel her fury and sorrow right there, just like her own.

CHAPTER 11

On the seventh day of walking, the Pilgrims crested a small hill and saw before them an illuminated valley. Descending into the glow, they were greeted by a group of six men and three women, all of them armed.

"Welcome," said one of the men in a loud, firm voice. "You've been traveling a long time. You are safe now, but you'll need to leave all of your belongings right here."

As he spoke, the others encircled the group. Some of the Pilgrims murmured fearfully. Carson heard Randy say, "It's okay. They probably do this to everyone."

Right, thought Carson. They couldn't let some rogue terrorist into paradise.

"This is just protocol," said one of the guards, her hand atop the pistol at her hip. "A necessary preamble you'll soon forget."

The Pilgrims dropped their bags and backpacks in a pile and let the greeters pat them down. Carson hesitated. If he wasn't planning on staying, did he really have to give over everything?

"Is there a problem?" said the woman with the pistol.

"No," Carson said. "It's just—" He paused. "Will I get my things back?"

"If you're not suited to stay, yes," she said.

Carson pulled out his notebook, then left his pack with the rest, hoping he hadn't just made a huge mistake.

They were led past rows of canvas tents. A woman leaned out from one of them, her long blond hair draping over her shoulders, and did the strange hand gesture, hands open at her chest. His skepticism rising, Carson had the momentary desire to throw something, a ball, to see if she'd catch it.

A bearded man in a white tunic passed them on the path and bowed his head, whispering, "Welcome." From another tent came the sound of singing. Carson imagined that any minute Jimi Hendrix might strum loudly. But instead, a tidy young man with cropped hair came and spoke with a formal and succinct voice. "Welcome. Good of you to come. We'll go to the meet the greeters."

They continued along a path. Off to the right was a tangle of shrubs and trees, where Carson suspected there might be a riverbank. The air felt damp and fresh. They passed a dirt clearing where five large sculptures stood. They were made from wood scraps, cobbled together and painted white. An arrow pointing upward, an ampersand, an infinity sign, circles bisected by a vertical beam, and a very tall cross that reminded Carson of the sculpture of Jesus Christ he'd seen pictures of in Rio de Janeiro, arms reaching out across the sky like white wings.

They arrived at a cluster of stone buildings. Carson noticed the mortar was solid and intact. A restored old homestead from the 1800s, or new construction? He placed his hand on one of the cold stones, just as a Pilgrim called out, "They're coming."

Half a dozen women in long skirts came, carrying ceramic pitchers from which they poured clear water into small mugs and passed them around. Carson gulped the water down and immediately regretted it. A basket of small, dense cookies arrived in front of him.

"Hockey pucks," Claudia said, leaning in to Carson. "My neighbor used to make stuff like this all the time as part of her Paleo diet. I thought at least they'd have chocolate chips." She sounded disappointed but bit into one anyway.

Carson held the cookie up. It was rock-hard, and full of seeds and grains and yellowish chunks of something. His palms had started sweating. No matter what his intention, there was always the possibility he might not get out of this place. He dropped the hockey puck into his pocket.

Three women in skirts and three bearded men emerged from the building and formed a line, inviting them all to be "received."

"Will they give you a long skirt to wear?" Carson whispered to Claudia.

She shrugged. "Could be worse." She moved with Randy and the boys to the line. Carson followed.

There was a lot of shaking hands, nodding, and gazing, but Carson revised his initial assessment. This place lacked the color of a late '60s hippie fest—everyone seemed too stiff. The last greeter was a woman with dark eyebrows that met above her nose. "Welcome," she said, lifting and lowering the eyebrow quickly.

They were shown to their quarters, men one way, women another. In the regrouping, he lost track of Claudia and Randy. From the twelve beds in the platform tent, Carson chose a bottom bunk and stretched out on it.

A large, muscular man climbed to the bunk above him. "Nothing like paradise," he said as the bunk creaked. "Feels good to finally be here, doesn't it?"

Carson lay in the darkness, wishing he felt that same sense of comfort. He knew a view of the stars would give that to him, and he considered dragging the mattress outside. But he didn't want to draw attention, so he closed his eyes and slept.

EVERY TIME BEATRIX checked AM 1080, Blue's voice droned on. According to the PBB riders who'd gone out to survey, Halcyon Radio had been off the air for at least four days before they'd discovered Blue's intrusion.

"How is this possible?" Beatrix asked Gary.

"On FM stations, it's called encroachment," he said. "It's when one station has more power than another. Doesn't usually apply to AM, but my guess is that Blue has a network of stations and is using something called a translator to repeat his signal farther."

"Whoa! You think Blue actually heard us on the air?" Flash asked, sounding a little too excited. Beatrix shot him an irritated look.

"But how did he get on our frequency?" Beatrix asked. "We had that station. You heard the reports from the PBB. People were tuned in to Halcyon miles away. Before Blue took over." Beatrix shook her head and sighed.

Gary cleared his throat. "I doubt he's intentionally jamming our station."

Beatrix shrugged. "We don't know that."

"Well, no, and we might not ever know. What's more likely is that if our signal didn't carry—because it's not powerful enough—Blue wouldn't have heard us. So he would have thought AM ten-eighty was open. Of course, the FCC would have made all of this impossible. But—"

"There's no FCC," Flash said.

Gary nodded. "The important thing here is getting Halcyon Radio back on the air, right?"

"Obviously," Beatrix said.

"We need to increase the power of our signal. We raise our antenna higher. There are some old stations where we might find something, or we could just build a tower for the existing wire." He looked at Flash. "Want to assemble a team?"

"I'm on it," Flash said. Then: "Dude, you're amazing,"

"Back at you," Gary said.

"You're both amazing," Beatrix said, suddenly feeling more hopeful. "But shame on that rat bastard for talking over our frequency. We'll sock it to him."

Gary laughed, then frowned. "Why do you always think everyone is out to get the little guy? Or more directly, why do you think everyone is out to get you?"

Beatrix blinked, taken aback. "I don't. But this seems pretty possible. Doesn't it?"

"I gave you a perfectly good explanation for what likely happened, but you won't hear it," Gary said. "You just want to believe that Jonathan Blue is threatened by Halcyon Radio."

Beatrix felt her face flush. She tried to think of something to say back.

"Is that because you're measuring your own sense of worth by whether or not the radio works?" Gary said. "Because if that's what you're doing, you should stop it. You are already worthy. You don't need to take down a Goliath to prove it. Or in this case, not even a Goliath, but a weirdo preacher who might not even be telling the truth."

Beatrix bit her lip. She thought she might suddenly cry. Was he right? Was she trying to prove something? And if so, what? And, wait, did he think Blue was a liar, too?

She looked at Gary's hands, remembering that he'd made her candle lanterns and gave her a handgun, which she hadn't asked for but was a gesture of care, nonetheless. On top of that, he had built a radio station, essentially because she'd asked him to.

"Okay," she said. She slowly held up a fist, and he knocked it with his own. "Onward."

• • •

Carson woke early and stepped out to the crisp dawn. A portly gray-haired man walked toward him on the path, hands clasped at his midriff, as if he'd just received Communion. "Good morning," he said.

Carson asked him about speaking with Jonathan Blue, and the man looked surprised. "You will hear him speak soon. He addresses us every few days."

The woman with the unibrow came briskly down the path. "You should be reporting to duties," she said.

The man nodded and continued on, but Carson stood, awaiting instruction. When the woman didn't say anything, he said, "I just got here last night."

"Oh, right," she said, seeming flustered.

"And actually," Carson said, "I'm here to speak with Mr. Blue."

She looked at him quizzically.

"Meaning, I'm not here to stay. I would simply like to speak with him." He held up his notebook. "I'm a historian. I'm writing about what has happened. And he is part of that."

She looked him over and nodded once. "Let me see what can be done." Then she held out her hand. "I'm Marcy. Come with me."

She led him down a path into a meadow of drying grasses. Carson heard the rush of water, and soon they arrived at the edge of a dark creek, about fifteen feet wide. "We are blessed," Marcy said as they watched the water for a moment. Carson wanted desperately to bathe, but Marcy kept moving. He followed her past the large dining tent, already full of Pilgrims eating breakfast. He slowed to peer in, hoping to recognize someone. Marcy led him into the smallest of the stone buildings and gestured for him to sit at an empty table in a dim room. "Wait here," she said.

The room smelled of smoke and fresh soil. Was it a meeting room or an interrogation room? He began to regret telling Marcy why he'd come.

A set of framed photographs hung on the wall. Most prominent was a portrait of a man in his late twenties, with blue eyes and dark hair falling messily over a wide forehead. He wore a white oxford shirt and cutoffs. A skateboard was tucked under his arm. The photo was signed *J. Blue*. Additional photographs showed him: older, again in white, without the skateboard, still with the mop of hair, posing with families, shaking hands with other men, standing in front of a large crowd.

Also on the wall were charts listing group assignments for tasks. Each group had a name: Blue Bird, Blue Jay, Blue Sky, Blue Sea, Blue Fox, Blue Corn.

A teenaged girl wearing a shapeless blue smock over a long skirt came into the room and set a bowl of something resembling cornmeal on the table in front of him. She showed him a jar. "Berries?" she said.

"Please," Carson said, and the girl spooned out some and sprinkled them over the cornmeal. She pulled another jar from her pocket and set it down. "Local honey," she said. "Hyperlocal."

"Thank you," he said as she left the room.

He sat in silence, not knowing what to make of the last eighteen hours. He felt like he'd traveled back in time, to a place where men with rough hands worked the fields, and women did the laundry by hand, and where everyone took turns keeping the fire going at night. He ate the porridge and the berries, and thought about what he would ask Blue. He didn't feel very prepared.

Then the girl came back to retrieve his dishes, and soon after that, Marcy returned and said, "It has been arranged. Come." She led him to a canvas tent surrounded by a dozen women who sat knitting.

"We have sheep," Marcy said.

"Oh," Carson said, surprised. He looked to the women. "And what are they knitting?"

"Socks and blankets, mostly," she said.

Upon seeing him, one woman stood up quickly from her chair, the blue blanket in her lap falling to her feet.

Marcy gestured for the woman to sit down.

It was still too warm for blankets, Carson thought, as another woman came toward him, her eyes beseeching.

Marcy quickly took Carson's elbow and led him away. When Carson looked back, the woman who'd come toward him was still standing frozen, watching him.

Marcy pulled him along. "This way."

Carson stayed quiet for a while, not wanting to jeopardize his meeting.

"How long have you been here?" he finally asked Marcy.

"Since a little before the darkness," she said. "I'd been following Blue already. He had a church—or, rather, a retreat center—in Kansas way before the October Shocks, but he's been preaching for many years."

They arrived at a large clearing contained by a fence. Beyond the fence were grasses, creamy against the morning sky. Small mounds of dirt rose up from ground, and a high-pitched bark sounded. Twenty yards away a rodent perched up on its hind legs, its front legs gathered in front of its chest. The rodent barked again, and three others emerged, surveying the scene. Prairie dogs.

Carson laughed to himself. Did Marcy know they were standing on a prairie dog town?

Marcy's single eyebrow rose up, as if she were lifting a hat. "Oh my," she said, looking at the ground around them. She shrugged. "Well, he says there are no accidents."

AFTER DAYS OF herbal infusions, Dragon was finally able to eat a cooked apple and keep it down. Everyone hailed Maria del Carmen's remedies and her diligence in administering them, but she herself credited Dragon's recovery to God.

Beatrix felt some relief in that—at least she wasn't attributing it to Jonathan Blue.

"What would we have done without you, Abuela? Healing is your superpower!" said Flash.

"Oh, stop," she said. "But make sure he takes it easy. No riding off into the neighborhood."

"I'll take it easy," Dragon said. "It feels good enough just to walk right now."

"Your bike will be ready when you are," Flash said.

There was no herbal remedy for Halcyon Radio, however. They'd started constructing a tower for a new antenna, but it was taking a long time to find the rest of the parts to assemble it. Thelma was happy the cast had more time to rehearse, but Beatrix was champing at the bit. The Red Raven was idling in silence. Maria del Carmen hadn't even met him yet.

In the backyard, Maria del Carmen pinched off golf ball–sized clumps of dough and rolled them into perfect orbs, the first step for making tortillas. Her seasoned hands moved quickly.

Beatrix reached for one of the dough balls. She rolled and stretched it, then began patting it between her palms. But the tortilla came out thick and oblong. "What am I doing wrong?" she said.

Maria del Carmen held out her hands and demonstrated the quick slap back and forth of the dough. "Evenly," she said. "Quicker."

Beatrix tried to do it faster, but the dough still stretched unevenly. "I was going to leave once, too, remember? But I didn't."

"Beatrix, you have faith in many things. I find my faith in Mr. Blue. Leave it to me."

"But what about Rosie?" Beatrix said. "What about her faith?"

"Rosie is a child," Maria del Carmen said. "In my care."

"Fifteen is old enough to make your own decisions about faith. Do you know what Rosie believes?"

Maria del Carmen pulled the last tortilla off the comal and began sorting them into a dozen stacks, her lips moving, counting. When the stacks were ready, Beatrix helped Maria del Carmen wrap them in cloth for pickup, neither of them saying anything more.

• • •

"What do you want?" Rosie said when Diego's friend appeared on Halcyon. She hadn't seen him in months. Charlie, with his big teeth, who liked to play cards. Charlie the sidekick. Charlie, alone.

"I need to tell you something, Rosie."

She glanced at his hands. Was he T-Rize, too? "Oh, I probably already know."

"We stole the bikes, Rosie. From the yard. It was Diego and me."

"What?" Rosie said. But then it started to make sense. "Wait right there," she said. She went inside and returned with Dragon.

"Start talking, kid. Now." Dragon's voice was solid and stern. He hadn't regained all of his strength yet, but he was amped up.

Flash and Beatrix joined them, and Rosie thought maybe together they were going to rough Charlie up.

Dragon leaned in to Charlie's face. "What's the bike-light code? The flashes—tell us what they mean."

Charlie shook his head. "I don't know."

Rosie had never seen Flash or Dragon so angry. She began to feel a little sorry for Charlie. After all, here he was, doing the right thing. Diego was the one they should have been messing with, wherever the hell he was. Bastard. "Tell them, Charlie," she said.

"Five quick flashes are T-Rize. That's how they ID themselves," Charlie said, the words spilling out quickly. Two slow flashes meant a chance to score. Three more quick flashes meant scatter. Yes, they wanted bikes. They had no clear leader, and new rules were made up all the time, but Charlie was never sure who was making them.

"What did you do, specifically?" Dragon asked sternly.

Charlie lowered his head.

"Speak, dammit," Dragon said.

"I helped set some of the fires. I stole bikes."

"Our bikes?"

Charlie nodded.

"Fuck you," Flash said.

"Did you kill anyone?" Dragon asked.

"God, no," he said, looking up at them, his eyes pleading.

"And where's Diego now?" Dragon said.

Rosie's mind flashed back to the tent, the smell of Diego's breath, his weight upon her. She hated him. But she leaned in to hear Charlie's response.

"I don't know," he said. "But I want out. I swear it. I'm done." He turned his palms up and looked at them. "Others want out, too, but they're scared, and most have nowhere to go."

"Which is why they joined in the first place," Beatrix said.

"But how can we trust you?" Flash said.

"I'll do anything," Charlie said.

"Plenty to do around here," Beatrix said. "Stick close then."

Charlie nodded vigorously.

When the others went inside, Rosie stayed with Charlie. She had questions about Diego, but Charlie looked shell-shocked and weary. The whole thing—Diego, the sex, the T-Rize—made her want to puke. "This is the worst time in history to be alive," she said.

"Yeah," Charlie said.

CHAPTER 12

In person, Jonathan Blue was not unlike his image in the photographs. Even in his all-white garb, he looked rugged and hearty, like a longshoreman or a fisherman. His dark hair was cropped, and a thick mustache covered his top lip. His chiseled arms reached nearly to his knees.

Marcy and another woman came and set up folding chairs for the two men and then shuffled away, their long skirts hindering their stride.

"We are so glad you have come," Jonathan Blue said. He smiled as if he'd been expecting Carson and extended a long arm in welcome. "Sit," he said.

Carson sat down and introduced himself. "I'm glad to be here," he said, feeling like a guest on a talk show. It occurred to him that for any of the hundreds (or thousands?) of Pilgrims out there, this encounter would be epic: here he was, face-to-face with the man who'd lured them across the miles on the promise of . . . what exactly?

Blue's eyes twitched a few times before settling onto Carson. "I will tell you that you already know everything you need to know," he said. "You have all the knowledge already inside you."

"I appreciate your time," Carson said.

Something nearby made a chirping sound, loud and continuous. Both men turned to look. A nearby prairie dog was standing on its hind legs, calling out. Its cry was insistent.

"Such marvelous creatures," Blue said, sweeping his hand out across the yard. "They have a lot to teach us."

Another prairie dog popped out of a hole, sniffed the air, and let out a loud cry.

"They have a very complex communication system, you know," Blue said. "Different calls for different predators."

Enough about the prairie dogs, Carson thought. He was eager to get started. "So this is the Center," he said.

Blue smiled, his eyes blinking. "In the material sense, yes, this is what we call the Center. A place of abundance in what has become a bereft world. A place where we can come together. You know, the darkness was a good thing for us."

Carson frowned. "How so?"

"We had become pixelated. Our selves had fragmented across the globe, across an illusory web, the internet. While trying to connect us, it fractured us—we lost our sense of wholeness. How can a body hold all that information? The web sagged and broke. And then came darkness, the answer to a prayer. An invitation to return to the Center. The center of our being. The void." Blue let his gaze rest on Carson. "Close your eyes for a moment, if you will.

"The void," he continued, his voice droning. "You are in the void. You are the center of the void. This is an invitation to call yourself back inside. To the core. The darkness within."

Carson opened his eyes. He wasn't here to fall under a spell.

"It takes practice," Blue said. "It is not comfortable at first. We all want our comforts. That is why many come here, actually. For the comforts. But it will not always be comfortable."

"They seem to trust you," Carson said.

"I am simply a ladder," Blue said. "I give them a boost. I was called to help them," Blue said.

"Called by whom?" Carson asked, noticing that Blue seemed calmer now.

"I don't know how much you know about me, about my past."

"Very little," Carson said.

Blue leaned in. "And what is it that you intend to do with my story?"

"What is it that you want me to do with it?" Carson said, surprised this question hadn't come earlier.

"Tell it as I tell it to you. Without condescension."

Carson nodded. "I can do that."

"I had millions of followers when I was young," Blue said, leaning back in his chair. "I did tricks, filmed them, posted them online. People liked it." He laughed. "It's not really worth talking about, because it was all sort of asinine, but somehow I tapped into something people wanted to look at. We all wanted to look at things to distract us. So I do not fault anyone. I, too, was seeking distraction. Measuring my worth by how many followed me. It was a particular moment in history, was it not?"

"Tricks?" Carson said, caught up in the first part of the story.

Blue shook his head. "I'm absolved of that past now," he said. "I think I'll leave it there."

But Carson wasn't sure. Why was he calling the hordes to him now? Wasn't he still seeking followers?

"I had tapped into the zeitgeist. I was hooked in, connected, making barrels of money, with a captive audience. I had all the things, more things than I knew what to do with." He paused and gestured to Carson's notebook. "You could write that clichéd part of my life story with your eyes closed, and you'd have all of it right. But that's just it—the eyes were closed. All of it became vapid. The screen was just a screen. Inside, I was lost."

Blue's voice sounded different than it did in the broadcasts. Softer and slower, with many pauses.

"But I wasn't *really* lost. I was just plugged into the wrong technology."

"The wrong technology?"

"Yes. We have very ancient technologies that can keep us connected. Technologies of the spirit."

He was entering familiar territory now with concepts Carson had heard on the radio broadcasts.

"The space between the core of the Earth and the ether. This is where we live. But there is so much more than that. We are not just a strip of humanity on the edge of the planet. We are much bigger. We reach into other planets and other universes. And someday soon, we will see how. Because now there is no more interference. The gray technology is gone—the technology that muted us. Someday soon, we will make contact. We need not fear that day. It will be beautiful."

"Make contact?"

"Yes," Blue said, his gaze unwavering. "With the beyond. But first we must make contact within, deep inside of ourselves. This is why I believe the darkness is a gift."

Carson realized he was leaning forward in his seat, as if to catch the words as they fell from Blue's mouth.

"You should stay long enough to hear one of my talks," Blue said. "I think you will enjoy the ideas."

There was so much to ask about making contact. With whom? Where? How? But first, Carson wanted to understand how Blue was reaching so many people. "What about your broadcasts?" he asked.

"The broadcasts are an offering. Sound is remarkable that way. Radio makes the invisible audible. Waves you can hear but can't see. We need no light to listen. In fact, we listen better without it."

Carson looked at Blue's face and tried to imagine his younger self, giddy with gadgets, in pursuit of power and popularity. "You mentioned spiritual technology," he said. "Is radio a form of that?"

"Perhaps," Blue said. "Spiritual technology is what gets us inside ourselves so that we can better expand to others. Supreme consciousness. If you stay here, you will begin to understand more. I do not wish to conceal anything, but it is more complicated than one conversation can clarify. It is a commitment."

"I see," Carson said. He'd expected that kind of response at some point.

"But listening is key. Are you familiar with Teilhard de Chardin, a French philosopher and Jesuit?"

Carson remembered the name. "I believe also a paleontologist."

"Yes. History was important to him, which I'm sure you can appreciate, Carson. But he was a forward thinker. He believed isolation would inhibit evolution. And he believed that one day, we might all find a common God, one that pervades everything. I think he was on to the idea of spiritual technology. 'One day,' he said, 'after mastering the winds, the waves, the tides, and gravity, we shall harness for God the energies of love. And then, for a second time in the history of the world, man will have discovered fire.'"

"That's beautiful," Carson said. He meant it. The words lifted him. The energies of love.

"When everything went dark—as we knew it would—I heard a voice, a very clear voice," Blue said. "So clear, like a songbird." He closed his eyes. "It said, 'Rise. Rise. Rise.'"

Carson scanned his memory for birdcalls he knew. He couldn't think of any that sounded like that.

Blue opened his eyes and said, "An ascension. That was the calling."

The calling. Did everyone hear the calling? Randy and Claudia and their two boys and the woman in the red skirt had heard it. Had he himself? Had he been called to leave his apartment? To walk and record? To arrive, eventually, on the other side?

"We do not like to be alone, do we?" Blue said.

Carson pictured Beatrix's face, the feel of her hand in his, her coarse, curly hair.

Blue swept an arm out. "Cooperation is a kind of technology. Here we work together toward the common goal, whether it is to feed ourselves or call to God. Everyone has his or her task, and they perform it for the whole.

"We started long before the descent, you know. We came here some years ago. Myself and twelve others, my closest allies. Together we laid the foundation. We got the system in order. We prepared for this. This upgrade. I kept doing my work, spreading the good word, sharing my ideas with listeners, letting them know that this was coming. The loss of power was our final invitation. But we had mostly unplugged anyway, in preparation."

In that moment, Carson found it all entirely credible. He felt some envy for Blue, a soul who had found his way.

"Have you seen our farms? We have acres of farmland and greenhouses. It is all nonmechanized labor, to ensure happy humans and happy animals."

Just then a prairie dog scuttled over, as if on cue. Blue bent over, reached out his hand, and scooped it up. The animal perched on Blue's lap with astounding calm, and Blue stroked it like a cat.

Carson felt his skepticism come rushing back. Blue had trained the prairie dogs? Or somehow had built their trust? It was too much.

"Everyone who comes here wants to fulfill his or her deepest desire," Blue said.

"Must they go through you to do that?" Carson asked, hoping to call out Blue's ego. He remembered the strange knitters, how they had stood up and stepped over their blankets when they'd seen him.

"I simply offer guidance," Blue said as the prairie dog dropped from his lap and ran off.

Blue reached both of his arms down and touched the tips of his fingers to the ground. "Root," he said. Then he stood and lifted his arms, pointing his hands straight to the sky, like a football referee calling a touchdown. "To rise." He then opened his arms out into a T and said, "To then disperse."

All this strange gesturing, Carson thought.

Blue smiled opaquely, his eyes as slow and chilled as glaciers. "By that, I mean connect. Make contact."

Carson cleared his throat. "Will you rise, too?"

"I should hope so!" Blue said, sitting down again.

But what did it mean "to rise"? A strange sensation crept from Carson's neck to his tailbone, like tiny hands grabbing each vertebra.

"You seem to be a smart man," Blue said. "I see you are searching for something. I have every reason to believe that you will find it, but, of course, that is not up to me. What I can say is this: I do not know that what you seek is here. If you want information to give to people, you can simply tell them that we are here for them. There is abundance here and redemption for those who wish to have it. I cannot say for sure when we will rise, but I can say with certainty that we will. The darkness has allowed us to turn inward. We root to rise. Everything is possible. Everyone is welcome. They need only come with an open heart and faith."

Carson turned over Blue's statement in his head: *I do not know that what you seek is here.* True enough. Carson had no intention of staying. But he felt a little rebuffed. If anyone could join them, why was he being excluded? And what was it Blue assumed he was seeking?

"Do not perplex yourself," Blue said calmly. "Within darkness, there is light. All we need to do in this life is move toward that which lifts us." He placed his hands on his knees, leaned forward, and pushed himself up to standing. "Take another day or two of rest here, if you like. Before you go, Marcy will give you a tour of the grounds. We have nothing to hide. On the contrary, we hope you will share this beauty with the world."

Wait. That was it? Carson felt ambushed by the sudden end of his interview. What about their power source? How were they broadcasting across the country? How was he feeding everyone? And as more and more people arrived, how would he keep feeding everyone? Dizzy with frustration, he shook Blue's hand, and the preacher held his gaze, his eyes so blue that Carson felt like he'd lost gravity and was spinning in midair.

ENGINEERING WAS NOT a skill in Beatrix's own inventory of assets, but thankfully it was one Gary and a handful other neighbors shared. Over two days, a crew of PBB riders, a horse, and three engineers managed to locate, transport, and assemble parts for a new tower to raise Halcyon Radio's antenna.

It wasn't exactly pretty or sleek—a tangle of metal, wire, and conduit with a pyramid of stanchions reaching to the ground, but Beatrix marveled at it. The final segment of the tower pleased her the most: a fork from Flash's collection of bike parts, its bright-yellow paint visible from the ground.

"I was never gonna find the tires for that baby," Flash said, when he'd handed it over.

"Like a tuning fork," Gary said, after they'd welded it in place.

"A beacon," Beatrix had said.

When Gary gave her the signal, Beatrix went into the recording studio. "This is a test. Halcyon Radio, AM ten-eighty. After some technical difficulties, we're back with you. Are we? This is a test. If you're hearing me now, tune in every evening five to eight for Halcyon Radio."

Then, in case people were listening, Flash announced the upcoming first episode of *The Red Raven* in his signature style: "Finding the wings within . . ."

PBB riders streamed in throughout the afternoon. They'd set up test stations around the neighborhood and beyond. Thumbs-up, all their reports said.

"Back in action," Flash said.

"Where there's a will," Gary said.

"A small miracle," Beatrix said, as she and Flash left Gary's and bicycled home.

"Gary himself is a miracle," Flash said. "Mad skills."

"He's absolving himself of past sins."

"Hey now," Flash said. "He just made different choices than you did. I'm betting no matter his politics, he's always had a kind heart. Besides, he's pretty key to this whole radio operation. Seems a born helper to me."

Beatrix nodded. It was true. "Like you," she said.

"And you," Flash said.

"And the PBB riders, those engineers, Thelma," Beatrix said.

"All true. Everyone plays a part. Kinda like you envisioned, right?" he said. "And *The Red Raven* hasn't even aired yet."

But two days later, it did, on an evening that carried the first faint chill of autumn.

Beatrix went to the station for the live broadcast and watched, full of joy, as the performers brought the story to life. When the violins finished the show, Beatrix looked over at Thelma and saw tears of pride streaming down her face.

"It was well worth the wait," Dragon said afterward. "A boy reborn as a bird. I love it."

Even Maria del Carmen offered praise. "Very enjoyable."

Beatrix felt relieved, as though she'd been waiting for approval from a parent or a mentor. Maybe everything *was* possible.

THE CENTER'S FARMS were not quite the expansive agricultural fields Carson had initially imagined, but garden upon garden, linked with trees and shrubs. "Part of a perfect system," Marcy explained. They walked along winding paths, past natural fences and windbreaks formed by trees, through areas where chickens and rabbits and fish resided in spacious pens and ponds.

Carson was trying to shake off the strange feeling he'd had since his meeting with Jonathan Blue. It was a physical sensation, not horrible, but not necessarily gratifying either—like walking through a cobweb and having the strands of it stick to him. He willed himself to keep his head on straight and looked out over the gleaming zucchini.

"Everything nourishes everything," Marcy said. "We are part of that. The food nourishes us, and we nourish the food. Permaculture. But with spirit." She pulled two biscuit cookies from her apron and gave one to Carson. "Snack?"

He was hungry but not free of suspicion. He declined.

"They're full of good nutrients. Healthy grains but no sugar," Marcy said. "But maybe they take some getting used to."

A dozen or so Pilgrims, now Blue Birds or Blue Corns or Blue Somethings, were at work weeding and harvesting. Marcy gave the Ascensionist wave to all who looked up.

"We hunt as well," she told Carson. "Mostly deer. Sometimes bison. I'm sure they'll send you off with some jerky."

They walked through gardens and ponds and rabbit pens, and Carson wondered if this was what Blue meant by "spiritual technology." He also wondered again if all this was enough for the new arrivals. Or if they would eventually grow too big to sustain themselves, like so many others had before them.

Once they were through the gate, Marcy gently took hold of Carson's arm. It startled him. The feel of her small hand against his biceps made him quiver in an unexpectedly pleasant way. Embarrassed, he coughed.

No one else was on the path, and Marcy tightened her grip. "Listen to me." She looked up at him, her golden-hazel eyes were striking against the thick, dark eyebrows. But in her eyes was worry, and it struck Carson that it was the same look the knitters had given him. "There is more to it," she said.

"What do you mean?" he said.

"He is not who he says he is. Something is happening up the ridge, beyond the farm. I don't know what, exactly, but we are not allowed to go there. I don't want to stay here anymore. Can you take me with you? They are making you leave today. I can go with you. Please, can I go with you?" Her voice climbed with desperation, her brow knit with fear.

"What do you mean?" Carson said, aware again of the cobweb sensation. They were making him leave? Why? Did he know too much? And the knitters—had they wanted to go with him, too?

A man came toward them on the path, almost bouncing. He appeared so quickly and silently, Carson felt like he was suddenly in some sort of odd aviary, bird-men flitting about.

"The chicken manure does wonders for soil," Marcy said, her voice broad and bland. "I was just finishing the tour," she said to the man.

"It is something, isn't it?" the man said. His face was narrow and smooth, with glasses over wide-set eyes. "I'm Russell," he said, holding out his hand to Carson. "I'm one of Mr. Blue's twelve. I was among the first ones to come here to the Center."

Marcy turned to Carson. "It was a pleasure to meet you. I wish you a safe journey." She gave him a little curtsy, then turned to Russell. "I'll be heading back to my post now, if you don't mind." She glanced at Carson. "In the kitchen." She turned away down the path.

"I hope she was good to you," Russell said, his voice suddenly deeper and curt.

"Oh, yes, very thorough," Carson said. "She explained the system perfectly."

"Good," Russell said. "That's something you can share with the world. We have gathered your things for you. We hope you had a good rest and that you got what you came for."

Carson nodded. "Yes, I—"

"As Mr. Blue says," Roger interrupted, "true connection is a commitment."

He guided Carson back along the path, toward the river to a wooden gazebo, where his pack was waiting for him. Carson unzipped the side pocket and found that the gun was still there.

"We would not take anything from you," Russell said. "We are good people, and we are not wanting here."

Carson stared at Russell for a moment. He seemed a competent thirtysomething man. Had he placed his faith in Blue? Was he not troubled by whatever troubled Marcy? Was he somehow, as a man, protected from that? What was really going on here? He felt a twist in his gut.

The teenaged girl who'd served Carson breakfast came and handed him a knit sack. "Vegetables. Some buffalo jerky and honey," she said, flashing her gapped teeth. "Be sure to refill your water bottles at the tank, as well."

"Thank you," he said, looking at her closely, scanning for signs of discontent or doubt. "So this is it?" Carson said.

"It is," Russell said.

Carson put on his pack, hoisted the wonderfully heavy bag of food, and walked with Russell to the road, stopping at the water tank on the way. They passed the large sculptures, and Carson slowed to look at them more closely. The arrow, the infinity sign, the ampersand, the cross. He stopped at the fifth sculpture—two circles with a vertical beam reaching through them, upward. "What symbol is this?" Carson asked.

"It means to turn inward," Russell said, his finger tracing the shape in the air from the top.

"I see," Carson said. He looked again at the shape and, this time, saw that it looked unmistakably like the letter *B*.

Anxiety fluttered through Carson's chest. Blue didn't seem like an evil man. He seemed taken with an idea, but he didn't seem crazy. Still, for all his talk about a spiritual shift, a renunciation of his old ways, his ego was not small.

Carson reached his hand into his pocket and found one of the cookies. Were these Blue's Kool-Aid? Had Jim Jones seemed evil to those who knew him? David Koresh? Marshall Applewhite? Carson blinked his eyes and shook his head. Wits. Keep your wits, he told himself.

"We hope we have given you what you wanted," Russell said. "Please spread the good word. We are here to unify."

"Thank you," Carson said. He paused and then said, "Marcy . . ."

"Marcy?" Russell said.

Carson stuttered. "Uh." What was there to say? Was he offering to rescue her? Did she need to be rescued? Did any of them? Did he want to rescue her? No, he didn't really want to take Marcy with him, but— He looked at his boots. "It's just that . . . she was very kind," he said. "I wanted to make sure to give her credit."

"She will be credited," Russell said. He put his hands together over his heart, the odd Ascensionist wave. "May you be uplifted," he said before turning and walking away.

Carson stood for a long time, staring back at the industrious so-called paradise, wondering if everyone who'd arrived wanted to stay. Did Blue offer the true light in everyone's darkness? An "upgrade," he'd called it. Or was it a trap? Were there others like Marcy, somehow plotting an escape?

Carson walked away uncertain, the weight of the knit bag full of food digging into his fingers.

BEATRIX AND ROSIE stood at the chicken coop, watching the hens scratch and peck.

"So, I have to know," Rosie said. "How did Reilly discover the Settlement? And what happens to his friend Coyote when Reilly leaves the animal community?"

"My lips are zipped. You'll just have to keep listening."

"But," Rosie began.

Beatrix tossed a handful of weeds into the coop. The birds scurried away before realizing what had arrived for them, then circled back. All except for one, who huddled against the door of the egg house.

"Hey, Miss Demeanor, are you okay?" Rosie said to the hen. Against Rog's advice, they'd named each of the hens—Miss Take, Miss Teek, Miss Informed, Miss Nomer, Miss L. Toe, and Miss Demeanor. "She doesn't look so good, Beatrix."

Beatrix crouched down for a better look. Miss Demeanor waddled away slowly, her chest swollen and dragging. "No, she doesn't." She stood up, worried. "Mr. Greeb will know. We'll go talk to him. And ask your grandma."

"Not a chance," Rosie said. She scuffed the toe of her sneaker in the dirt, a slow-motion imitation of a hen. She looked like she was about to cry.

"What it is, Rosie?" Beatrix asked.

"We're leaving tomorrow. Abuela said so. To Jonathan Blue."

"Wait, what? Leaving? No way."

Rosie nodded.

"It's not possible," Beatrix said, the anger rising to her face. "I'll talk to her again."

"It's no use."

"Don't say that."

"You can't be mad at her. It doesn't work," Rosie said. "I've tried it. And besides, everyone has dreams. Isn't that what your aunt Vera said?"

"Oh, Rosie." Beatrix wanted to cry. This kid was so impressionable. She really did listen to everything. "Yes. Yes, of course. Everyone's dreams matter. And so do yours."

Rosie shrugged. Her face was stoic.

Beatrix took a deep breath and put her hand on Rosie's shoulder. "Don't you worry, Rosie. We'll figure this out."

Later, Beatrix went to Maria del Carmen with a bouquet of flowering mustard greens and a little pouch of lavender from Anita. "I've come to beg you," she said, when Maria del Carmen opened the door.

"Such nice gifts, Beatrix." Maria del Carmen sniffed the lavender. "This will be especially good for our journey."

Beatrix's face dropped. "I don't understand. It just isn't safe."

"What *is* safe?" Maria del Carmen asked.

"Not Jonathan Blue!" Beatrix yelled. "How could you possibly leave us, this neighborhood, with everything we have here, to go to some mythical place you've only heard about on the radio? Not to mention the journey itself. If you're too scared to let Rosie walk down the block, how the hell are you going to manage a however-many-week journey on foot, through God knows what kind of danger? Do you even know where you're going?"

Maria del Carmen set the lavender pouch down and looked into the mustard greens. "A group is going together," she said calmly. "They meet at the park tomorrow. And we will go with them."

"I can't believe this." Beatrix fought the urge to swat the greens out of Maria del Carmen's hands. Exasperated, she returned to the angle of doubt. "What if none of it is real, Maria del Carmen? What if Blue is just a voice on a radio recording. What if he's not real?"

Maria del Carmen sighed. "This is why it is called faith, Beatrix."

Beatrix felt her heart collapse. None of her tactics had worked. This is what happened when people gave up. They just followed the shiniest, loudest promise. She thought about the Red Raven, all the work she and Thelma had put in to create him. No illusions there. He wasn't real, but he could inspire people to work together, share, and find their own superpowers, right where they were. A different kind of prophet. But one Maria del Carmen obviously could not hear. Beatrix turned on her heel, furious, and left.

In the morning, Rosie led Beatrix, Flash, and Dragon to the backyard, where God's eyes hung from the plum tree like psychedelic blooms. Each diamond-shaped yarn ornament was marked with a small tag, one for each of them. Beatrix's was a star of red, orange, and yellow yarn. "To match your personality," Rosie said.

"This is so sweet, Rosie," Dragon said.

Trying to lighten the mood, Flash tapped a rhythm on his thighs and started to sing. "Goodbye to Rosie, the queen of Corona . . ."

Rosie laughed but then started to cry.

Beatrix wrapped Rosie in a hug, frustrated with herself for not having averted this. Fighting back tears, she said, "You be strong, okay? You're a fighter, remember?"

Maria del Carmen called Beatrix into the kitchen, where small jars of tinctures lined the counters.

"These are for you," Maria del Carmen said. "For all of you. I wrote most everything down. Dragon has also been helping me lately, so he knows some things now." She placed her hand on a notepad next to the bottles.

Beatrix was moved by the gesture but still felt angry and helpless.

"Come," Maria del Carmen said. She led Beatrix to the altar. She lit a new votive and said, "This is for me and Rosie." She placed it next to a dried bundle of herbs, a small bowl of water, and a string of rosary beads. "To keep us safe and to show you that we are here with you, always." Then she lit a second candle. "This one is for your friend."

"My friend?"

"The friend who you write to. Perhaps he will come to you."

Beatrix opened her mouth to speak, but Maria del Carmen put a finger to her lips. She turned toward the candles and adjusted them slightly. "You keep both lights going, okay? When they burn out, you light new ones, okay? Okay, mi'ja? Sí, mi'ja, sí."

PART THREE

Halcyon

CHAPTER 13

ROSIE AND HER abuela and fifteen others walked away from Halcyon Street and out of the neighborhood toward the highway. The early September sun cut low across the horizon, casting a golden glow and long shadows. Rosie had never walked on a highway before, and for the first half hour she delighted in seeing her sneakers on pavement that had once known only trucks and cars. Now, of course, it knew only bikes and pedestrians, and they'd already seen plenty of each.

By late afternoon, though, Rosie was tired of walking. Her backpack was digging into her shoulders, and her feet were tired. How long were they going to have to walk? She looked at her abuela's face; her eyes were alive, full of hope. Why was she so convinced? What if Jonathan Blue had lied about everything?

Hills reached out like arms sleeved in gold on either side of the highway. Puffs of white clouds hovered above. It was like staring into a photograph. "Fertile," someone said, which made Rosie think first of baby rabbits, and second of her period, which had to be coming any day now. *Please, please, please.* She breathed in the yellow and kept walking.

The first night, they slept in a barn, on beds made of hay. Rosie listened to someone snoring. It was cold, and she pressed herself closer to her abuela. At dawn, dust floated up from the rustling and waking of bodies. Abuela tottered to the barn door, Rosie watching from the lumpy hay. Against the dawn, Abuela's silhouette looked misshapen, like she was not a person, but an animal, awkwardly standing upright.

A man began to sing in Spanish. *"Buenos días, todo el mundo, ya me voy pa' el Centro."* Good morning, everyone. I'm heading for the Center.

The tune was one Rosie recognized, a melodic rhyming song. But sometimes she thought all Mexican songs sounded alike. The old-timey ones, at least.

The singing man folded up his blanket. He looked like someone's grandfather, but sturdy and solid, with graying hair underneath his cowboy hat. *"Me espera la esperanza, espero encontrar el encuentro,"* he sang. Where hope awaits me, if I can find the way to enter.

He held the last note for a long time, and when he finished, everyone clapped. The man lifted his hat and nodded.

Abuela handed Rosie a bottle of tincture. "Three drops under your tongue, please."

Rosie knew the drill. She opened the bottle and wrinkled her nose at the smell.

"No fussing. This is your breakfast."

This is a stupid breakfast, Rosie thought, plugging her nose and dropping the liquid into her mouth.

After two days of walking, Abuela started to speak Spanish. *"Dios mío. Es demasiado."* My God. It's too much. Her feet were swollen, puffing over the edge of her shoes. *"Descanso."* I must rest.

Rosie tapped the shoulder of the singing man. His name was Jesús, he said.

Jesús unlaced Abuela's shoes and knelt down to massage her feet, all the while singing a song about a journey he had made twenty years earlier when he crossed into the United States from Mexico. It was dry and scorching, he sang, and the migrants wanted to stop and rest, but the "coyote" wouldn't let them. He sang about the cacti that jumped off their stems, like little dive-bombers, and landed on their calves and ankles. They looked like teddy bears, but really they were vicious monsters that violently clung to you. They made *chupacabras* seem like angels, Jesús sang. Abuela's exhausted face crinkled into laughter at that.

When Abuela was able to stand and walk again, they went slowly. Some of the group had gone ahead, so now they were only seven. "A good number is seven," Jesús sang. "When they've promised us heaven."

They turned off the highway, walking down a long exit ramp, and followed a smaller road. "Safer," one man said. "Less chance of being robbed."

Not that they had much to steal. Rosie carried just one change of clothes, a toothbrush and her grandmother's homemade toothpaste, the lip balm Anita had made, some sticks and yarn for God's eyes, and her sketchbook.

The fields gave way to trees planted in neat rows, and a narrow church appeared at the edge of the grove. "Orchards for the apples, and a church with a steeple," sang Jesús. And for no other reason than the tune was contagious, Rosie found herself humming along.

"Corridos," Jesús said. "Songs about life, no matter how sad." He looked at her and grinned. His eyes were like little black pebbles, and deep lines fanned out from them like tiny roots. "You try it. You've got the tune down by now."

"No way," Rosie said.

"Try," he said. "It softens the step."

Rosie blushed. She walked in silence, staring at the pavement. But in her head, words came like a train, startling her with their speed. She slowed down to fall behind the group for a while. Then she called out to Jesús, who stopped right away to wait for her.

"Y por donde caminaron, vieron muchas cosas," she sang, her voice shaky and loud enough for only Jesús to hear. And wherever they walked, they saw many things.

He repeated the line, his voice ringing out. Then he looked to her, waiting for the next line.

She covered her face with her hands, embarrassed, but sang the next line a little louder. *"Las montañas muy nevadas, y un árbol con alas hermosas."* Snow-covered mountains and a tree with pretty wings.

"That's it! You've got it." He turned back to look at the tree. "Pretty wings. It does have pretty wings! 'The wings within.'"

"*The Red Raven*!" Rosie said, excited by his reference.

"Your grandmother's feet are better, yes?" he said.

Yes. The swelling had gone, and Abuela was walking just fine. "She's determined," Rosie said.

"Determination is as good as faith," Jesús said.

When they neared the base of the Sierras, they came upon a wagon and pooled their money for a ride. The road wound up through dense woods. Rosie pulled out her only jacket, a too-thin windbreaker, and breathed in the scent of the pines. She leaned on her abuela and tried to sleep. When she woke, they were moving through an alpine town, complete with a saloon and a group of men on horses. One of them waved and tipped his cowboy hat. Eventually, the wagon came to a stop, the road blocked by an overturned semitruck.

Weeds sprouted up through fissures in the broken asphalt, rising up alongside the truck's tires. The cart was too wide to pass by the truck, so the men unhooked the horses, tilted the cart sideways, and wheeled it through. While they worked, Rosie peered into the semi's broken window. On the seat was a pair of sunglasses, some chewing-gum wrappers, and a road map of Nevada. Rosie reached in and grabbed the sunglasses just as her abuela called for her.

BEATRIX AND FLASH made their way through a tangle of dried shrubs and weeds, down the long sidewalk to Mr. Greeb's house. "I think he'll know exactly what to do for Miss Demeanor," Beatrix said.

At the door, a strong odor hit them. "Jesus H, what is that?" Flash said.

"Anyone there?" Beatrix called out. They waited several minutes, but no one came. The door was unlocked, and when Beatrix opened it, the terrible stench flooded out.

"Holy hell," Flash said, his hands over his nose and mouth.

Beatrix pulled her shirt up over her nose and moved slowly into the house, holding her breath. "Mr. Greeb?" she whispered, spying his shape on the recliner chair. "Mr. Greeb?" she said again. He looked tiny, melting into the chair, eyes open but receding, skin collapsing against his skull. She gagged.

Flash put his hand on Beatrix's arm and guided her back out of the house. Flash walked in circles, taking deep breaths, and Beatrix lay back on the brittle grass, stunned. Mr. Greeb was so very dead. Not just-moments-ago dead, but thoroughly and completely dead.

"I should have come sooner," Beatrix said.

"It might not have been the flu," Flash said. "He was pretty old."

"What should we do? We can't just leave him there."

"The mobile clinic?" Flash said. For Halcyon Radio, Beatrix had just interviewed a nurse who had started the clinic, making home visits for checkups and minor treatments.

But of course the nurse said there was nothing she could do. She sent them instead to the undertaker, whose services were still needed no matter how much things had changed.

The undertaker recruited two men from the Perimeter, and they entered Mr. Greeb's house wearing respiratory masks and hospital gloves, and exited carrying Mr. Greeb, still in his chair.

"You know if he has any kin?" the undertaker called out to Beatrix as they lowered the chair to the ground.

"I have no idea," Beatrix said.

"Okay. We'll cremate him."

"Right here?" Beatrix asked.

"You got a better place?" one of the men said.

"No memorial or anything?" Flash said.

"Can't help you there," the undertaker said. "Out of my jurisdiction."

Flash took hold of Beatrix's arm and walked a little closer to Mr. Greeb's body. Flash held his hand over Mr. Greeb's heart and said, "May you rest in peace, old man. Safe passage."

"Kind neighbor," Beatrix said. "Good soul, with so much to share. Thank you for the birds."

The undertaker called to them as they walked away. "You're the ones who do that radio show, right? *The Raven*?"

Beatrix and Flash looked at each other. "*The Red Raven*. You've heard it?" Beatrix said.

"My kids and I have been listening. Great stuff," he said.

"Glad to hear that," Flash said.

"Say, I don't want to meddle," he said. "But I wonder if any future episodes might incorporate something about—" He paused, glancing at Mr. Greeb in his chair.

"Cremation?" Flash said.

"Dying, death," the undertaker said. "It's not an easy thing to explain to my kids."

"It's not an easy thing to explain to anyone," Beatrix said.

"That's right," he said. "Feels closer than before, you know? I mean, for them."

Flash nodded. "It really does." He looked at Beatrix. "We'll see what we can do, right?"

"Absolutely," Beatrix said. "Thank you for requesting it. And thank you for your work here today."

As the man went back to his task, Beatrix said to Flash, "So it might be working."

"I think it is, yes," Flash said.

"We just were too late for Maria del Carmen."

"We were, yeah."

They loaded Mr. Greeb's chickens into boxes and gave their neighbors all but two hens, which they took home to the backyard, along with a majestic rooster with a tail of long black feathers.

IT TOOK FIVE days of travel in the rickety wagon to get Rosie, Abuela, and their fellow Pilgrims to the other side of the Sierras. Somewhere past Reno, they found shelter in a concrete church. They sat in a circle and prayed while the wooden Jesus on the wall watched them. Any minute he might climb down from his post, Rosie thought, loincloth, bloody hands, and all.

She thought of Beatrix, Dragon, and Flash, who were probably finishing up dinner at this hour. What had they eaten? Peaches from a jar? Roasted pigeon? Not tortillas, not anymore.

Flash was maybe singing and playing air guitar, like he always did. Flash said Jonathan Blue was crazy, because there was no such thing as ascending right out of your living body into heaven, or wherever. But Jonathan Blue seemed convinced that you could do that. And it was hard not to believe him. It was like he held a rope and was pulling people toward him, hand over hand. How did someone get that kind of strength?

In the morning, Rosie woke early and found blood in her underwear. Her first feeling was of relief. Then came a fleeting thought of Diego, the asshole. She rummaged through her backpack for the supplies Beatrix had given her, and went outside to wash her underwear at the small tank of water someone had set up.

"Try not to waste, okay?" a scratchy voice said. It was Louise, a woman with blunt gray hair that looked like she'd cut it herself.

Rosie tried to hide the underwear behind her back, but her cold hands fumbled, and the panties plopped to the ground. Mortified, she swept them up and stuffed them quickly into her pocket. "I don't have any soap," she said awkwardly.

"Oh," Louise said, her face softening. She reached her hand toward Rosie, as if trying to touch her. "I do." She brought Rosie the soap. But that wasn't all. For the next five days, Louise kept a thermos of hot water and soap so Rosie could tend to her period without any fuss from anyone.

Every day, Rosie took the tincture drops her abuela gave her. Whatever was in them, they seemed to be keeping her and her abuela healthy. Certainly, it wasn't the watery beans, stale bread, and jerky of unknown origin. She missed tortillas. She missed eggs. She missed milk from the neighbors' goat at the end of the block. She missed plums and oranges.

On occasion, they were offered better things to eat—fresh biscuits, chicken stew, apples. Some people said they'd soon be on their way to the Center, too. Others said they weren't going anywhere, and Rosie wondered if they, too, wanted to ascend, but didn't want to walk for it.

Over the next days, their group went from seven to twelve to fourteen and back to eleven. The Pilgrims came on foot and on mules and horses, and with one wobbly cart, which they loaded up with their meager possessions and took turns pushing. They slept in churches, in backyards, in empty stores, and in camps known as "jungles." Each night, one or two people stayed awake, keeping watch.

They were hopeful and righteous. They quoted Mr. Blue: "You are hungry, we will feed you. You are thirsty, we will quench your thirst. We will restore your connection. We will connect to new technologies, spiritual technologies. We will unite. We will rise, one by one, purified, cleansed, and whole."

Each day, Rosie and Jesús added to their corrido, recording the landmarks, amused by their own rhymes.

Denny's and McDonald's,
all closed up, for business slow.
I sure could use a Big Mac now,
But *adelante* we must go.

Graveyards of automobiles,
Down every street we see,
We can hold our thumbs out all we want,
But none will start for you or me.

"Once we're there, everything will change," said Louise. "There will be fresh food from the gardens, fruits and vegetables, plenty of fresh water. Blue skies." She turned her head upward. Rosie looked at the sky, too, and wished for some kind of interruption—a bird, a rainbow, a bug—but there was only thick gray.

Rosie pulled the lip balm from her pocket and put some on, momentarily cheered by its scent and color. She considered the possibility that Louise was right. That Jonathan Blue had found the Promised Land, and that once they were there, they would eat and eat and feel good. She looked back up at the sky. A raindrop landed in her eye.

Beatrix walked to the end of Halcyon and waited for Penny, the Velocipede cyclist. She held half a dozen letters in her hand, all of them for Carson, except one for her mother and one for Hank and Dolores, letting them know she was okay and staying put for now. She wasn't convinced any of the letters would get there, especially the one for Hank and Dolores, given all she had was the name of the farm and a best guess at the nearest town. And Carson's? It was hard to believe a bike messenger service really could go that far. But whatever—might as well try. Otherwise, they'd keep piling up, useless words that no one would read.

She wished for some conviction, but all she felt was anxiety. Rosie and Maria del Carmen were gone. Miss Demeanor was sick. Mr. Greeb was dead. The T-Rize was multiplying like a cancer.

She remembered Carson's hands, how he'd touched her face, held her hair. How the morning after being with him she had woken and, for the first time in many years, had not wanted to be anywhere else.

She looked at the letters in her hand. *This is why it is called faith,* Maria del Carmen had said.

A bell dinged, and there was Penny, squeaking her brakes as she coasted up to the curb.

"You look happy," Beatrix said.

"I'm on my bike!" Penny said. "And I have a purpose."

"I hope I look like that when I walk out of the radio station."

"Oh my God, yes. Beatrix. *The Red Raven*. It's awesome. That episode when he helps those two neighbors in the field stop arguing? That was funny!"

She and Thelma had landed on the idea during a late-evening writing session: Two neighbors in Reilly's Settlement were clearing a field for a new planting, but their arguing kept holding up their work. In swooped the Red Raven, doing tricks in the sky, then tilling the soil with his feet. In their surprise, the two neighbors stopped fighting and got to work.

"Who'd have thought a big red bird could have such finesse? It's kind of absurd, but it works," Penny said. "And Reilly, that soft-spoken man—he inspires me even when he's not the Red Raven. He doesn't even realize his gifts."

Beatrix smiled. "Most of us don't," she said.

Penny grinned and nodded. "Uh-huh. Totally. That show is gonna do great things for people."

"I hope so," Beatrix said. She spotted a small knife in a sheath on Penny's belt. "So is that how you stay safe?"

Penny patted the sheath. "Well, I guess. I'm fast, too. So I'm lucky that way. This neighborhood is one of the good ones, though. You've got the Perimeter. It really does help."

"Supposedly," Beatrix said. "But . . ." She lifted her pant leg and showed Penny the scab on her leg.

"I heard about that," Penny said. "Glad you're okay. Last week another PBB-er had a confrontation with three kids. One of them had a machete. Pretty bad wound. They're burning houses now, too."

"They're kids," Beatrix said.

"Everyone always says that," Penny said. "But, shit, they're messed-up."

Beatrix nodded. "Yeah." She handed Penny the letters, then unloaded from her backpack a dozen eggs, a jar of marmalade, a stack of tortillas, and a handful of cash—their pre-agreed barter. "Here goes nothing," she said.

"Yeah, well, that's the thing. No guarantees. Since it's regional, we can't really know if all the Cyclicals are functional."

"Cyclicals?"

"That's what the regional operations are called. Think of it like orbiting planets in the solar system, except every now and again the planets touch and, presto, your letters get passed from one rider to the next."

Penny slid the letters into her bag. "I'll do my orbit," she said. She held up a closed fist, which Beatrix matched with her own.

CHAPTER 14

September 8

B.,

Would you believe me if I told you that somewhere in southern Wyoming, I stood near I-80 and saw not one, not two, not three, not four, but five—FIVE!—bald eagles overhead? Although endangered, they do live in this region, so I suppose it wasn't THAT unusual. But I still delighted as if watching the fictional become real.

Many of my tales to you might read like fiction. How is it possible that so many people believe the gospel of a man who once did stupid tricks on the internet? There's much more to him than meets the eye. I'm puzzled. I have no idea how he'll sustain everyone.

But sitting with him, I admit I felt something, too. A sense of promise? A renewed hope? But in what?

Perhaps my own faith falters. I'm not sure what I was thinking in setting out on this trip. I'm not giving up, but it seems unlikely that you'll even be around if and when I get to you. And if you are, well . . . I don't know. I'm afraid I've gone and invented all sorts of things in my head about us.

Have I?

C.

The Magnon Multiplex Cinema was an anachronistic mix of sleek 1960s concrete brutalism and Las Vegas–style bling. A bulky rectangular building fronted by ten arches across the facade, it seemed out of place against the giant blue sky and smooth hills of rural Wyoming. The marquee in the parking lot claimed the place had been retrofitted to show twenty-two high-definition films with surround sound, all at once.

Carson remembered a night, decades ago, when he had trespassed on the ruins of ancient Rome, as a college student in Italy. Drunk on wine, one of his fellow exchange students had proposed a late-night tour, and they ran through the city to the Roman Forum, where they climbed the fence and dropped down into the old, vacant world.

Carson had imagined himself a king or a senator wandering by buildings with melodic names: Comitium, Regia, Basilica Sempronia, Basilica Julia. Julius Caesar walked here, he had thought. Then he wondered: What kind of emperor would I be? What sort of cloak would I wear?

The jasmine was in bloom. The smell caught him in between the structures, an ethereal reminder of what still lived. He heard his name, and there was one of the lovely art students, standing on a bench with her nose up to the flowers.

"Smell," she whispered, pulling the branch down. He breathed in the sweetness of the flower, a trace of the linseed oil from the young woman's clothing, and the wine on her breath. They held hands and ambled down the Via Sacra, the road where chariots had traveled until the Romans had outlawed them—too many, the horse hooves too loud. Centuries later, all was silent.

Now, amidst the silence of the American West, Carson pushed on the front doors of the cinema and was surprised to find them unlocked. The smell of rancid vegetable oil filled the space, and popcorn crumbs littered the dingy red carpet, along with a mosaic of glass from the smashed candy cases. He flicked the dispenser levers on the fountain soda machines, but nothing came. He'd eaten all the food from the Center days ago and now had only a small stash of jerky that a kindhearted ranching family had given him. When he found a lone unopened box of Junior Mints on the floor behind the counter, he held it up like the Holy Grail.

In the quiet wreckage, the idea of twenty-two simultaneous movies seemed preposterous, though Carson could recall a time when it hadn't. Sometimes, he and June would treat themselves to a senseless blockbuster—a dark tale of espionage or an alien robot thriller—just for a Sunday escape. He'd hold June's hand in his the whole time.

Through the glass doors now, he saw the sky darken outside. Fatigued, Carson wandered down the corridor of theaters and entered one, ripe with the smell of mildew. He pulled a tea-light candle from his backpack, lit it, and called out, "Hello?"

Nothing.

"Anyone in here?"

He set the candle on the floor and sat back in one of seats. He pulled the Junior Mints from his pocket and ate them one at a time, savoring.

He thought about Jonathan Blue, how their conversation had unexpectedly lifted him, at least for a few moments. He wondered again about this notion of "calling." Here he was, a man in a theater, his presence unknown to anyone, his purpose self-proclaimed, no one to back him up. An island.

But so many had backed him up to get here—Ayo, Jairo, Fernando the taxi driver. Franklin and Nora in the Jungle camp. The energies of love. Even Daniel and Naomi, despite their oddness, had kept him alive. He felt a rush of gratitude. The archipelago of his recent past. Were they all still alive? Or now only memory?

Marcy's face then appeared in his mind. Those pleading eyes. He felt a cramp in his gut.

He summoned Beatrix's image, her open mouth, her laughter. He rested his head back on the seat. How lucky I am, he thought. Even if I never see her again, how lucky I was to have met her.

When he woke, the candle was out and his body stiff. He dug for the windup flashlight in his pack and lit his way out of the cinema. He made camp on a strip of dried grass at the edge of the parking lot. Stretching out, he felt his body sinking toward the center of the Earth, which in that moment he understood also as the expanse of the whole universe. He was in both places at once, and then there was Blue in between, his arms outstretched like the Jesus statue in Rio. Then Pilgrims came with backpacks and shopping carts, and cats on leashes, and crutches, and when they got to Blue they vanished.

Carson woke and lay still. Above, the darkness was lit with stars, tiny perforations in the void. He delighted in the sight, smiling at the cliché of it—how the night sky could reflect his own smallness and his own immensity in one quick second. How a view of the stars was all he needed to unite history, the present, and the future.

BEATRIX STOOD AT the fence watching Miss Demeanor take slow steps, the hen's chest dragging across the dirt. They'd closed off a section of the coop for the new rooster and other hens, so Miss Demeanor wouldn't be bothered.

It was a good thing Rosie had spotted her. Maybe there was still hope. Rosie. Bless her.

The God's eyes she'd made for them were still hanging in the plum tree, little ornaments too early for Christmas. Beatrix spotted hers—red, orange, and yellow, a tiny fire that produced no heat.

"They just up and left," Beatrix said to Dragon. "You think they'll be okay?"

"I have to hope," he said. "I was always thinking you'd be the one to go—your old MO."

"Not to Jonathan Blue," Beatrix said.

"No, not there," Dragon said. "But this is the longest you've stayed here in years, right? Under normal circumstances, you'd have blitzed back to the equator or to some protest action, to fix up some other neighborhood somewhere else."

Beatrix let his words register. "I felt like I could make a difference."

"Everywhere but here?"

"Yes."

"But now?"

Beatrix sighed. This felt like a therapy session. "I'm practicing what you always tell me: 'Stay with it.' Right?"

"Stay with it," Dragon repeated.

"I'm so glad you're better, Dragon," she said, tossing him a God's eye. "I don't know what I would have done."

"What would the Red Raven do?" he said, smiling.

She looked at the hen, its bald chest still dangling on the ground. "He'd figure out how to save this hen."

"Yes, he would," Dragon said. "And so will we. Here." He read from one of the poultry manuals they'd found in the library collection. "Impacted crop, it looks like. Listen: 'The crop is part of the esophagus, where digestion begins. This muscular pouch is located just below the neck.'" He read in silence, then looked up. "It gets clogged with food and grit. They recommend veterinary assistance."

"Great," Beatrix said, hopelessness settling in.

"But wait," Dragon said. "Check this out: 'With a calm and steady hand, the courageous chicken keeper can do it himself,'" he read.

"Or herself," Beatrix said.

Dragon looked up from the page. "Once the crop is open, you just squeeze and empty it."

Beatrix looked at Miss Demeanor, who stood, teetering and isolated from the other hens. "Well, then."

They set a pot of water on the fire and gathered the necessary supplies—rubbing alcohol, a bowl, and a damp cloth. When the water was boiling, they put a razor blade, a needle, and some thread into the pot to sterilize.

Beatrix fetched Miss Demeanor and propped the hen between her knees, gently stroking her feathers to calm her. Dragon handed Beatrix the razor blade and read the instructions aloud. Beatrix touched the hen's pink flesh at her breast, where the feathers had already worn away. She cleaned the area, then pushed the blade into the flesh. A line of dark blood seeped out, and the bird squirmed. "Easy, missy. Easy," Beatrix said. As she squeezed the crop, the grit came out: nearly a cupful of straw, grass, and rocks.

"Look at all that!" Dragon said.

Beatrix focused on her hands. The bird struggled, gurgling. "Dragon, hold her head up. Make sure she's getting air. Now hand me the needle over there."

Beatrix steadied the bird on her lap and pinched the skin together as she sewed it up. She stroked the hen for a little while before setting her gently to the ground. The bird stood still for a few moments, then slowly moved her head around, looking. After a minute or two, she took a few steps.

"I think you just 'Red Ravened' her," Dragon said.

Beatrix held up a palm, and Dragon high-fived it.

"Here's to library books and courage," Beatrix said.

But the next morning when they went out to the yard, they found Miss Demeanor down, her lifeless body like a crumpled washrag on the dirt.

Rosie and the Pilgrims came to a lake shadowed by pine trees. Someone said they were still in Nevada, but it didn't look anything like the desert they'd just crossed. Ducks scooted across the water and lifted off as the travelers approached. The air was frigid, but they were long overdue to bathe. The women went first, yelping as they touched the cold water.

Rosie held her breath and submerged herself for as long as she could. When she came up, gasping, her skin was numb and it felt like the blood inside her had congealed. She bent her elbows and cocked her head stiffly, like a robot, as she made her way back to the shore. Abuela laughed, and soon all the women were giggling and clapping, exhilarated.

Once dressed, Rosie heard the faint sound of a motor in the distance. The sound grew louder, and soon a dusty white van appeared on the dirt road below.

"They're going to take us to the Center," Abuela said. "It's a miracle!"

They wouldn't have to walk anymore—that was the miracle. On the side of the van, drawn in black, was the outline of a wing and the word ASCEND.

The driver was a bald man with pockmarked skin. Next to him was a woman, possibly his wife, whose wispy hair was combed into a hopeful ponytail. She wore a puffy down jacket over a long denim skirt. She held up her hands, linked her thumbs together, and wiggled her fingers. "Try it," she said. "It's the Ascension wave."

Jesús put his hands together and made the silly bird. Rosie did not.

"We'll get you there in no time," the driver's wife said. A feather slithered down Rosie's throat and tickled it.

The driver and the wispy-haired woman patted everyone down and searched all their belongings.

"Protocol," the driver said. "No weapons allowed."

Rosie thought this was strange, but her abuela was unfazed. "It's fine, Rosie," she said. Abuela, more alive than she'd seemed in days, was the first in the van, nearly hopping up, while Rosie climbed into the back seat with Jesús and slept.

When she woke, they were passing a billboard showing an old couple standing in front of a pool. Their smiles seemed a little too big, almost fake. "That's you," Jesús said, nudging her.

"What—an old white person?" Rosie said.

"No. Desert Rose. That's what it said. The name of the community. Looked like a nice place," he said. "I could have handled retiring there."

"Maybe Jonathan Blue has a pool," Rosie said, poking Jesús with her elbow. "And some old ladies for you."

Jesús laughed out loud, and Rosie leaned her head on his shoulder and went back to sleep.

They drove until dusk, then turned off the highway onto a narrow road that led through a small town where people were huddled around garbage can fires. Rosie pressed her face into the glass and watched a woman transfer potatoes from a sack to a basket. A pack of dogs trotted down the street after the van. The van pulled up to a gate, and the driver spoke to a guard, who let them in.

The houses in the development were large but dark, and they seemed mostly empty. They parked in the driveway of one that looked to Rosie like a wedding cake. A woman in an oversized flannel shirt and a long skirt greeted them at the door with hot tea. The house smelled like baby powder and had six bedrooms. There was a compost toilet outside and a large water tank and a radio, set to Jonathan Blue, whose voice came and circled around the outdoor fire pit. Rosie warmed her hands over the fire and watched her fellow Pilgrims and her abuela nod their heads at his promises. She wished Charlie were there and they could play Crazy Eights.

The weather turned cold again overnight, and in the morning the wispy-haired woman pulled out a bag of winter clothes for the Pilgrims. Rosie picked out a rusty-orange down jacket, and mittens knit with colored yarn, which reminded her of God's eyes. They drove for a while on the interstate, where Rosie and Jesús counted six other cars, then zigzagged along smaller roads for a few hours. Eventually, they turned onto a dirt road that reached all the way to the horizon. Dry brown fields spotted with round bales of hay extended in all directions. They passed groups of Pilgrims who gave the Ascension wave, their faces full of joy. "Not far at all now!" the driver called out.

After several bumpy hours, they arrived at the top of a ridge. "Here we are, heaven on Earth," the driver said. Below, a thin blue river bisected a wide valley. On one side stood a cluster of buildings. Fanning out like sunbeams, all around them, were rows of white tents. On the other side of the river were dry fields, stippled with horses and sheep. Five white sculptures—a cross, an arrow, the "and" sign, and two shapes Rosie couldn't quite make out—rose up from the center of the valley.

"*Dios mío*," Abuela said under her breath looking over the scene. Rosie had never seen her so relaxed, as if the bones in her body had softened and she herself had become a river. The Center was her sea, and she was finally joining it.

Jesús, on the other hand, was scanning the landscape nervously, as if he'd heard a noise and was searching for its source. He pointed to a lone tree on the ridge. "Bet you could climb that if a mountain lion was tailing you. We should put it in the song."

"Not now, Jesús," Rosie said. "We're *here*."

They descended the hill, where two women wearing long skirts greeted them. One of them looked as if she'd been hit in the face: her slightly sunken nose pointed off to the left, and her mouth held a sideways smirk. The other had eyebrows that joined together over her nose.

The air was cold, and Rosie shivered in her jacket as the women led them along the rows of tents. Each tent had a different purpose, the woman with the unibrow explained: eating; food preparation and preservation; sewing and repair; prayer; and reconnaissance.

"Reconnaissance?" Rosie said. She coughed and held her hand over her throat. Even with her mittens on, her hands were freezing.

"Rosie, hush!" her abuela said sharply.

"Is she ill?" asked one of the skirted women.

"No," Abuela said.

The woman with the crooked face took the women to their quarters. Jesús and the men were taken elsewhere. "We separate genders here," the woman said. "Part of the return."

"The return?" Rosie asked.

"Back to the original self," she explained. "Free from the illusions of dark technology, here we finally get to return to our original selves."

What was she talking about?

"Settle in," the woman said. When she smiled, her nose shifted toward the center of her face. "We'll come back in a little while to take you to your God duties. We all do God duties. It's part of serving one another and the greater union." She walked away, her skirt swinging stiffly from side to side.

Inside the tent were four double bunk beds and a woodstove, which made it surprisingly warm. But Rosie wished she were home on Halcyon Street. She could do God duties there: She'd rake the chicken coop every morning. She'd fetch all the water. She'd oil bike chains. She'd weed the garden. She'd even turn the toilet compost. Anything.

"Rosie," her abuela said, patting one of the bunks. "You sleep here, above me."

Rosie climbed up to the bed and rummaged around in her pack. She hung the God's eye from a strip of canvas above her. She put on the sunglasses she'd found in the overturned truck and lay back and watched the God's eye dangle, wondering if with practice she could hypnotize herself. She closed her eyes and imagined a bee hovering above her nose. When she opened them, there was only the God's eye, dim through the sunglasses.

A woman with long, straight black hair came to the tent and placed a stack of clothing on the edge of one of the bunk beds. "These are for you. Warm shirts, wool stockings, and skirts. If you only put one of these items on, make it the skirt."

The woman looked up at Rosie and smiled. She pointed to the God's eye. "I think you'll have to take that down."

"Why?"

"No witchcraft here," she said. "Only the pure light of God."

"This isn't witchcraft," Rosie said, irritated. "It's a *God's* eye."

The woman stood there for a moment, pressing her lips together, then disappeared out of the tent.

Rosie gave the finger to the woman's back, then pulled out her sketchbook and started drawing a tree filled with roosting hens.

Confident in flight, the Red Raven flew beyond the Settlement to the community that had raised him. He found the gap in the trees carved by the river and followed it past the old landfill, over the next mountain range. He scanned the landscape for the granddaughter of the bear that had helped him survive when he was young and alone, and spotted her loping across a scree slope. He continued on, dipping down toward the river to see otters and beavers playing and working. He saw fish in the river, a good sign. He found the ravens—the Conspiracy, they called themselves—and flew with them for some time, catching thermals and showing off.

But when he reached the plateau to look for Coyote, the first friend he'd ever made, he found only his remains. A mountain lion, no doubt. The Red Raven landed, assessed the bones briefly, then stood at his friend's side for a long time and mourned.

When the episode was over, the radio cast made its way into the crisp October night. Beatrix huddled into the hood of her sweatshirt as they came to the park, where people were gathered around a campfire, their bodies dark silhouettes against the light.

"His old friend, dead. That really got me," someone said.

"It's the nature of things. But it still hurts."

It was true, Beatrix thought, listening. That scene had left a few of the cast members in tears as well.

"What I love most is the sound Reilly makes as he's transforming into the Red Raven!" someone else said. "How does he make that sound?"

"Should I just put them out of their misery?" Flash whispered, nearing the fire.

"Please," Beatrix said.

Flash called out the sound perfectly.

"That's it! That's the sound." A tall man in a Greek sailor's cap stood and turned toward them.

"He's so skilled, that Red Raven," said a man Beatrix recognized—the Irishman she'd met at the park months ago. His wife was nearby, the baby now standing at her feet in a tiny winter coat. "We all listen together, here in the park," he said.

A man with thick eyeglasses held up a radio. "Not hi-fi, but it does the trick."

Beatrix smiled and looped her arm around Flash's as they headed home.

When Rosie first saw Jonathan Blue, she was surprised at how normal he looked. Just a tall man with a mustache. He was on the far side of a giant blue tarp, giving instructions to some men about how best to fold it. He wore leather work boots, white pants, and what looked to Rosie like a big white pillowcase as a shirt. But when he held his arms out to the sides, they seemed to reach out forever, the longest arms she'd ever seen! When the clouds shifted, sunlight poured through the tarp, and Jonathan Blue looked like an enormous bird, blue from head to toe.

In the prayer tent, Mr. Blue never really said anything new. It was always all about leaving the old myths behind and moving into the darkness to be reborn. It was like watching a rerun over and over, only in a room full of people whose breath and body odor you could smell. They were allowed to bathe in the river only twice a week, and the soap they were given was chalky with no suds and no scent. Rosie longed for Anita's pouch of lavender.

In the kitchen tent, where she'd been assigned God duties most afternoons, Rosie met a girl named Mary, about her same age, with freckles and gapped teeth. Mary had been there longer and knew a few more things—like about RiverNorth.

That's where Jesús was working. The last time she'd seen him in the dining tent, a good week ago, he'd held out his hands and shown her the blisters that had formed on his fingers. Then he'd leaned in toward her and sang in Spanish: "They handed me a shovel, and sent me up the stream, where I dig and dig and dig, and look for gold that gleams."

"Most of the men go to RiverNorth to dig," Mary explained when Rosie asked about it. "On the north side of the river. Obviously."

"What are they digging?"

"Garden beds, I guess."

"But the ground is hard, almost frozen."

"Yeah. I dunno," Mary said. "Maybe they dig for artifacts. Supposedly, there's old pottery made by Indians in the ground, or something like that."

"How many people are here?" Rosie asked.

"Thousands," Mary said. "I don't know the exact number, but my dad told me, like, ten thousand."

Rosie couldn't tell if Mary was full of shit or not. Her stomach growled. "Is there anything to eat?" she asked.

Mary reached into her coat pocket and pulled out a hard brown cookie, about the size of a matchbox.

"Anything other than a flattened turd, that is," Rosie said.

"Come on. They're not that bad, and they're full of nutritional things. I mean, look at me. I eat a lot of them, and I'm healthy."

Rosie took the dense and grainy biscuit and sniffed it. She took a bite.

Chalky and dry, it tasted like earth, corn, fish, and sugar. She stuck out her tongue. "Not just any turd," she said. "An old, dried turd."

Mary rolled her eyes and held out her hand until Rosie gave the biscuit back.

"What about the ice cream?" Rosie asked.

"It's too cold for that now, though, don't you think?" Mary said.

But it wasn't very cold at all inside the dining tent when all the woodstoves were going. In fact, Mary had just taken off her gray pea coat, complaining that it was too warm. White blotches covered her skirt, stained there since the day she'd been selected to help paint the sculptures.

"Someday you'll get picked, if you're good," Mary said. But Rosie didn't think painting seemed like any big prize.

Mary handed Rosie a stack of cups. They were prepping the tent for dinner, setting places along the long rows of tables. Rosie had tried to count them several times, and once got up to 424, which wasn't even close to halfway. And Mary said there were multiple dinner shifts. All these people wanted to rise into the clouds and be saved? How was that even possible?

Rosie set out the cups, then started with the forks, making her way down the tables. Partway down one row, she looked outside and saw birds tumbling through the air. Thousands of them. She could hear the whirring sound of the bodies as they fell. But when she blinked hard and looked down, there was nothing but scattered forks. Then the first dinner bell rang out, and people began crowding into the tent.

Later, Rosie pulled her abuela close to tell her about the birds.

"It's too cold for birds, Rosie," her abuela said.

The next day, Rosie took a side path past the prayer tent and saw a trail leading into a wooded area. She wondered if maybe this led to the place Jesús had been sent to do his God-duty digging. A cloud passed in front of the sun. Rosie coughed, her throat tickling. She hurried to the kitchen tent.

"I've never seen that trail," Mary said later. She popped a turd biscuit into her mouth. "But my dad said it's best not to poke around. He said Mr. Blue is busy preparing us for when it's time, and we don't want to be interfering with the beautiful plan."

"Time for what?"

"Time to *rise.* Duh," Mary said. "Isn't that why you're here?"

Rosie tilted her head sideways but didn't nod.

"We're lucky," Mary said. "He's *saving* us. Things are only going to get worse out there." She pointed with a stiff finger, as if "out there" were a very specific place. "That's why you're here, isn't it?"

Rosie felt another feather reach into her throat, and she tried to cough it up.

Mary widened her eyes. "We're here to join together," she said. And here she made a circle with her arms and held them out in front of her body. Then she lifted them into the air and opened them to the sky.

When Rosie returned to her tent, the feather was still in her throat. "Abuela," she said, her voice like a little girl. "I want to go home."

Abuela rummaged around under the bed, then stood and held out a bottle of tincture. Did she have an endless supply of the stuff? Rosie didn't know if the drops did any good, but in this moment she found them comforting.

"Take some, mi'ja," Abuela said, motioning for Rosie to open her mouth.

"Beatrix, you've got mail," Dragon said.

Beatrix laughed out loud. "Good one," she said.

"I'm serious," he said, handing her an envelope.

Beatrix recognized the handwriting immediately. She nearly fell to her knees.

"Turn it over," Dragon said. The back of the envelope was covered with thumbprints.

"Each rider leaves their mark," Dragon said. "I counted on your envelope. Thirty-two thumbprints."

Beatrix feverishly inspected the writing again. Uppercase *X*s at the end of her name, the way Carson always wrote them—*BeatriX BanX*.

"Oh, and you'll also be pleased to know that *The Red Raven* is reaching beyond the Sierras," Dragon said. "The rider who delivered your letter told me. It's working, Beatrix. Other stations are rebroadcasting the show."

But Beatrix could barely hear what he was saying. The envelope in her hand weighed more than anything else.

"Who is it from?" Flash asked.

"Hang on," Beatrix said. She went inside, her heart in her throat.

March 25

B.,

I'll keep this one short. Though I have words and words for you, written on pages I haven't known how to send. Now there may be a way. So here's a quick one to shrink our distance. For weeks I've longed for the amenities of the past: little black letters on a white screen, your voice through the phone. Any proof of your presence. The lack of that has been like an amputation.

The power is gone. The trash has piled up. I won't even write about the sewage.

Here is all you need to know now: I am leaving the city. The raiders, whoever they are, are on their way. I hope to be gone before they arrive.

I have a map of sorts and a recommended route. The railroad, if you can believe that, those steel lines of progress. Ayo, my freedom broker, said it's the safest way. Besides, I like the outdoors, and I like walking. There will be history to record. There will be birds to look at.

I don't know when I will arrive. I trust you are still in a safe place.

"Go west, young man," they say. Now I have a reason. Raiders be damned. I simply want to be with you, B.

Love, Carson

Beatrix's whole body grew warm, and inside her chest, her heart took flight. She looked again at the date. March 25. Seven months ago. Where would he be now? *Walking.* She read the letter a second time and then a third. Her hands trembling, she read the last line again and again and again.

CHAPTER 15

On his way to Beatrix, Carson had walked along the tracks, over wooden ties, around cities that no longer sang, past parking lots of dusty cars, past tractors and earthmovers that had been cursed and calcified. Past windmills, crows, and skinny dogs. Past fences, and doors that opened to nowhere. Past piles of leaves, clothes hangers, and sneakers. Past a burned bed and a blue velvet sofa.

He walked through pine forests and dried-out cornfields. He walked through small towns where people bartered for their survival on the sidewalks or barricaded themselves inside or called out to him or let him quiz them, or kept quiet or coughed, forcing him to hurry along. He walked under sagging power lines, over cracks in the asphalt, around cars siphoned of fuel. He walked past oil rigs that no longer sipped and bobbed, streetlights that lit no street, bus depots where no buses came or went. Past gated communities where the houses loomed like lapsed castles, their long driveways deep, empty moats. Past apartment complexes with mucky swimming pools and shriveled lawns.

He walked by a well and looked in, at his reflection in the dark water below. If he'd had a bucket, he would have lowered it. Instead, he picked up a rock and threw it down. The sound satisfied him. So he did it again. And again.

He walked past homes where people flagged him down, asked him about what he'd seen. Moved by his perseverance, they cooked him eggs or spooned out soup.

He passed Pilgrims, travelers, and escapees. Those who had been traveling for a long time knew things. He watched the way they used their eyes, and something other than their eyes. He noticed their hands. He learned.

Others stepped tentatively, glanced over their shoulders, hoarded their food and water. He recognized the fear in their eyes, empathized with their uncertainty. What could he tell them to reassure them? Nothing, really. You learned as you went. There were no magic tricks, no lifesaving secrets. They'd figure it out. Or they wouldn't.

He walked past a saddled horse tied to a tree in the middle of an empty field. He called out for someone, but only the horse answered, with a loud snort. He sat in the field for a long while waiting for someone to claim the horse. Only a crow came. He untied the horse and led it out of the field and down the tracks. He grabbed the saddle and hoisted himself up and over its back. The horse began to walk, then trot. When it got dark, Carson set up his bed on the ground near the horse. I'll travel far with that horse, he told himself. But when he woke, the horse was gone, along with the rope that had tied it.

He walked past shopping malls that looked like prisons, past silos and starving cows. He walked past a graveyard where the gravestones were crude and small, names and dates etched by hand. One had part of his name. CARSON ADAMS, 1852, RIP. He heard his mother's voice. Then his father's. June's. Dozens of voices whispering in a cacophony of hissing and shushing, sentences he could not make out. Finally a unison chorus: *Keep going*, they said.

He walked over bridges and looked to the streams and rivers below. Sometimes, the currents were still and silent, but when the water rushed through, he stopped to bathe and drink. He could follow the stream. He could keep going.

He walked with the memory of June. He could see her eyes, smell her smell, hear her laughter, imagine the place below her earlobe, remember the image of her head on the pillow. The sound of her last breath dissipating. The way his hands trembled as he reached out and cupped her face and kissed it. He still missed her, but the missing was not the same as it had been. Grief lessened but never altogether evaporated.

He sometimes heard trains. The low grumble of the engine, the screech of metal on metal, the hollow horn. Phantoms, all of them, until a chain of train cars appeared on the tracks, rusting and moored. China Shipping. K-Line. Evergreen. Uniglory.

One day in October, he came upon a train yard that was home to half a dozen teenaged girls "freed" from a group home for children with unfit parents. They offered him a solar shower and a caboose to sleep in. He taught them how to kill a chicken and listened to their rules for a new society. A skinny girl with knees like doorknobs poking through holes in her jeans explained the first rule: "Forget the past," she said.

But Carson convinced the girls to let him tell them about the Maya and their fully developed writing system, and about the epic poetic performances of the Greeks. About the Ancestral Pueblo desert people, their fingerprints still visible in the mortar between the rocks. About the riches of Timbuktu, its house of learning. They asked if he'd given a lot of homework as a teacher, and he told them about the Civilization Project, in which his students had twelve weeks to imagine and invent a geography, a culture, an economy, a language, myths, a government, a story of origin. "You should try it," he said. "Make up a society."

"We already are," they said.

In the evening, he pulled out the windup radio, and they gathered around it like a fire. The static gave way to voices—not Jonathan Blue, but other voices. Two young men talking about bicycles. *"Another fix-in this Saturday. Ten a.m., Squat Park. Bring food to share. We'll get you tuned up so you can get your bikes rolling! Want a fix-in near you? Let us know! Leave a note in our comment box, or send us mail via Velocipede."*

The girls took guesses at the meaning of the word "Velocipede." Carson described the old-fashioned bicycles with the giant front wheel and told them about the Pony Express and, now, this new bicycle mail service.

The girls liked the sound of the radio guy, Flash. "He sounds cute," one said.

When Carson gave them the radio, they squealed with delight. He felt absolved.

He left them and continued west. He came to a stand of aspens in the skirts of the mountains and stood amidst their thin, white trunks. He summoned the image of their yellow leaves in autumn, their flicker in a breeze. Inside his boots, he could feel how his skin was rubbed raw. He said a prayer and then kept going.

The tracks sliced through the mountains, and he marveled at the engineering of that. The air became thin and clarifying. Within the damp darkness of tunnel after tunnel, his breath quickened and his mind made convincing arguments about his end. But again and again, he emerged into light.

When the snow came, he wrapped his face in a scarf and kept walking. He bent to touch what had accumulated, a cold white invitation, then began to dig. Into the depression, he deposited the old farmhouse, the lost future, any magical thinking about June's return. He filled the hole again with snow.

As the mountains gave way to desert and the air grew warmer, the steady cadence of his breathing returned. He let the laugh of the woman he walked toward move him like a verb, bold and continuous. More and more, he walked with her name in his hands, in his chest, in his head. Beatrix. He held her name on his tongue.

EVERY MORNING AND every evening at the designated hour, Rosie and her abuela went with their assigned group to the prayer tent. "Rise, rise, rise," everyone would chant. "In the darkness, we find lightness." Sometimes during the chanting, Rosie fell asleep. Sometimes, she fell into daydreams—she was back on Halcyon with Beatrix in the garden, or hanging out at school with a friend, or even wandering a village in Mexico, looking for her mom or dad.

When Mr. Blue came in to preach, everyone got spastic about it. Women would gasp. Whenever Blue held out his arms, the tent itself seemed to quake a little.

One evening, Rosie finally saw Jesús. "Over here!" she said, waving her arms.

"Sit down, Rosie!" her abuela said.

Jesús came, smiling, and gave both Rosie and her abuela a big hug. Dark circles puddled below his eyes, and the creases on his forehead seemed deeper.

"Where've you been?" Rosie asked.

Before he could say anything, the prayer chant started, filling the space with sound. Jesús leaned toward Rosie and said, "Our song is better, *que no*?"

Rosie nodded.

"Keep singing it, Rosie. You've got the voice for it."

Rosie's face warmed with the compliment.

"So much union here," Abuela whispered to Jesús. "We are so lucky, no?"

"Se dicen que el sol brilla como el oro. Yo te digo otra cosa—y busco un farol," Jesús sang softly to Rosie. They say the gold here shines like the sun so high and bright. I say it's fool's gold—go look for another light.

"What do you mean?" Rosie asked.

One of the men in white shirts walked toward them. "Sing to me, Rosie," Jesús said. "Sing to me now. Spanish, *mejor*."

Rosie bit her lip, suddenly self-conscious. She gave him a few lines from the verse she'd composed about the turd biscuits. "Those cookies are so gross, made up of sand and dust. I just want to throw them to the ground, won't eat them out of disgust."

Jesús sang back, in Spanish, "Don't you worry now, my friend, there are other pretty things. And you know how to spot them, and you know how to sing. Have you seen a star shining red, up in the nighttime sky? That glowing star up there can be your new eye."

"I haven't seen any red star," Rosie said.

"Look for it tonight," Jesús said. "It's in the western sky, where we came from, Rosie. Remember that. Whenever you follow it, you are going west."

Rosie nodded. "Did you hear that, Abuela?" But her grandmother's eyes were looking outside, fixed to the large white sculptures.

CHAPTER 16

On Halcyon Street, the autumn days blended into one another. Time became elastic. Birds flew in slow motion. The hours were a repetition of tasks.

Keep paying attention, Beatrix told herself. The particulars of her revolution had shifted. There were no maps to study, no borders to cross. Her country was now only five miles wide. She could bicycle across it without a passport.

Beatrix had kept the flames going on the two candles from Maria del Carmen's altar, and she paused now and then to look at the flickering light. It was something close to prayer, she guessed.

One morning, she did a live interview with Frida from the Gold Mine. They were now offering fresh produce for sale, Frida said, which made it extra worth the trip. That, and she said that a new shipment of auto parts mined from the municipal parking lots had just arrived, with tires and engine parts for reuse.

"And that is why it's called the Gold Mine," Beatrix said, signing off.

After Frida left, Beatrix found Gary outside, measuring one of the back windows of his house. "You putting on storm windows already?" she asked.

"Just making measurements for some weather stripping. Autumn chill is already here." He wiped his hands on his jeans. He nodded to the garage. "Nice interview, by the way," he said. "Always a treasure amidst the trash."

"That's what Reilly Crawford says," Beatrix said. "Oh, get this, after the broadcast, Frida told me they're now starting to use a mobile cart, a way to speed up circulation of recycled and reusable stuff. Kind of like the library."

"Kind of like Reilly Crawford," Gary said.

Beatrix cleared her throat. "Exactly," she said. But inside, she wondered if *The Red Raven* was really making a difference or if they were just fooling themselves.

"What'll he do next?" Gary said.

"Ten-eighty on your AM dial," Beatrix said, then headed down the block to home.

That afternoon, a hard rain came as Beatrix read *Red Raven* scripts. Outside, the thunder boomed as lightning moved closer. One crack made her jump in her chair—way too close. She peered out the window, making sure all the hens had taken cover in the coop.

As the sky cleared, she heard Gary's voice in the hallway, calling her name. He stood at the bottom of the stairs with his hands in his pockets, his face looking pained.

"The transmitter is fried," he said.

The words entered her head, but somehow she could not decipher them. She pictured fried chicken, the crispy crinkles of golden batter.

She scanned her memory of the radio equipment in Gary's garage and remembered the black box, its little white EKG-looking symbol.

"The lightning did it," he said. "It means we can't broadcast tonight. We need to replace the transmitter first."

"Are you kidding me?" Beatrix said. "Are you fucking kidding me?"

Dragon stepped into the hallway, and Gary explained again what had happened.

"But we have to broadcast tonight," Beatrix said. "It's a huge night. They're all waiting for it." The love episode, in which shy, quiet Reilly would muster the courage to ask Wren, a widowed mother of three, out on a date.

"Can't we just replace the transmitter?" Dragon said.

"Sure. Try Best Buy. They're open twenty-four hours," Gary said.

Beatrix sighed. "Surely someone has one."

"I can fix ours," Gary said, "but I'll need to replace some of the parts. Your friend at the Gold Mine mentioned auto parts. If that shipment was from cop cars or fire engines, they'll all have mobile radios. That's what we need."

"There's no harm in trying," Beatrix said. "Let's go."

"Beatrix," Dragon said. "The show is supposed to go live in"—he looked at his wrist, absent a watch—"two hours? No way we can get there and back by then. We'll go first thing in the morning." He looked at Beatrix. "It's okay. It will build suspense."

Beatrix sighed but acquiesced. They were on the same side, after all.

Carson walked into the Basin and Range desert. Utah. Mining territory. The hills morphed into rocky piles of taupe, red, and gray. Golden-leafed aspens stood out from the electric-blue sky. He was weary but felt a surge every time he exhaled into the cold, his breath visible like smoke.

The tracks followed a state highway for a long stretch, and there,

Carson heard a strange but familiar sound, like the whisper of someone from his past whose voice he could no longer place. It trickled into his ear softly at first, then rose into a full motorized growl. He turned around to listen and saw a faded yellow Toyota pickup truck, circa 1983, advancing toward him. Once upon a time, he'd had the same model in red.

"The brakes don't work so good. I suggest you move!" the driver shouted from the window. He wore a black patch over one eye; long gray hair fell to his shoulders.

The truck coasted to a stop. "Where you headed?" the driver said. He was not a young man but seemed fit and strong, at least in the arms.

"West," Carson said.

"Well, you can ride along with Miss Daisy as far as she takes us, if you like."

Carson hesitated for a second, summoning Ayo's smarts. He tried to size up the driver, but it was tough get an accurate read from outside the truck. On the door were monikers penned in black marker: *Grizzly Joe*, *Claybaby*, *Mustard face*, *Beat-(up)-nik*. Other riders, he guessed. He laughed out loud. He'd been waiting two thousand miles for this. He threw his pack in the back, where it joined at least a dozen five-gallon containers—biofuel?—and got in the truck.

Once moving, Carson marveled at the passing landscape. He rolled down the window and leaned out, as if to gulp the transient air. The chug of the engine pleased him like no other sound had pleased him in a long time. He ran his hand over the dashboard and said, "Thank you, thank you."

"I'm Felix," the driver said. "Been on the road for years. Sent off by a lady, you could say. Katrina, that is. August twenty-ninth, 2005. She kissed me a little too hard, knocked me off my feet. Never thought I would leave Louisiana. Glad I did, though. Can't even think of that place without seeing someone in tears. Too many sad ghosts."

Carson listened, remembering the wrath of Katrina, and the racism in her wake. Everything about the Gulf Coast seemed drenched in human error. Thoughts of the flightless birds, coated in oil, still sank his heart.

"So you've been on the road ever since?" Carson asked.

"Except for when I lived on a boat for a blink. I just do my thing and watch what comes at me."

The mountains sped toward them. The sky expanded.

"How'd the boat come at you?" Carson asked.

"I was in Florida. That's when things really started going downhill. Remember all the millionaires with their megayachts? Never paid for. So when the dollar fell, they left them for the repo man. And you know what some crazy motherfuckers did? They just untied their boats. Let them float out to sea. Lucky thing there are dumpster divers, deep sea divers, and crafty squatters, and when we see a good discarded thing float by, we do a little repossession of our own."

Amused, Carson said, "I've been wanting to repossess a horse."

"Well, there you go then. You just send out that prayer, no strings attached, and see what comes galloping up at you."

"This fine truck is what came galloping up," Carson said.

"Loping is more like it. Listen to how she purrs," Felix said, running his hand along the dashboard. He gestured to the back of the truck. "Dunkin' Donuts was a windfall. Cooking oil! I'm just going until I can't go anymore. That's my plan. What about you? You're staying off the highways, I see."

"Railroad," Carson said.

"Smart man. Say, you're not a preacher, are you? You kinda look like a preacher."

"No, definitely not a preacher," Carson said. "I just met one, though. Jonathan Blue. The Center."

"Oh, that guy?" Felix said. "I heard he's not even at the real center. That would be somewhere in Kansas."

"Wyoming," Carson said. "Left of center."

"That's like God's joke right there. I'm surprised you got farther left than that. I heard they don't let you leave once you get there."

Carson laughed. "They let me leave pretty quickly. But maybe not others." He thought of Marcy and chewed his lip.

Felix crinkled his eyebrows together and raised his voice a note. "All the women in long skirts, right?"

"Yes, all the women in long skirts."

"You thought you wanted to 'rise, rise, rise,' then decided hell was better?"

"I went to investigate," Carson said.

"What are you, CIA?"

"No, no. Just a historian, chronicling the times."

He told Felix about the gardens and the system of chores, and about Blue—his convictions, his philosophies. But he kept thinking of Marcy, the look on her face. He shook off the memory.

"Did they have any special Kool-Aid? Or how about that poppy tea I've heard about?"

"Poppy tea?"

"All the rage, supposedly. Like heroin, but just a tea. Any hippie can make it. Ha! No matter what, the people find their drugs, don't they? Anything to get out of pain." Felix took one hand off the wheel to adjust his eye patch.

"I have to admit, it was pretty remarkable," Carson said. "The system, the organization, the way he has attracted so many people there."

"And they'll all rise into the ether one day."

"I didn't quite get that part," Carson said.

"Not on the itinerary?" Felix said.

"I guess not," Carson said, feeling foolish for all the things he'd missed.

The landscape turned to desert. Pale-green sage and black brush reached out across the flats.

"A historian," Felix said, nodding. He let out a whistle. "'The past is never dead. It's not even past.'"

"The past seems pretty past to me," Carson said.

"But not dead. Tell me I'm not the only one who hears it, ringing in my brain loud enough to deafen me at least once every day."

"You're not the only one," Carson said. Different days brought different things—his students, old songs, his former morning routine, people he used to know. "The train comes through a lot. Some days, I swear I hear it coming."

"Like a cell phone," Felix said. "The phantom ring! Remember that? How you'd hear your phone even when it wasn't ringing?"

"Yeah," Carson said.

Outside, the desert blended blue, beige, and green. "Look at this moonscape, would you?" Felix said. "So sparse and beautiful. But you're only good if you've got water. This is bone country. Nothing but skeletons clacking around out here."

After a while, Carson said, "Sometimes, I hear the future more loudly than the past."

"The horizon lures every traveler with a pretty melody," Felix said. "It can paint a pretty picture sometimes."

Carson's mind went to Beatrix—her eyes, her hair, her head. "Damn pretty," he said.

Felix looked over at him. "What are we talking here, pretty-vegetation pretty or pretty-woman pretty?"

Carson smiled again.

"Oh shit. Say it isn't so. Don't tell me you're pulling for some woman out there. Are you? Is that what you're doing?"

"She's almost mythical now," Carson said. "It's like she takes up the whole sky in front of me sometimes."

"Write that down—she'll want to hear that. What'd you say your name was?"

"Carson."

"Well, Carson, I'll get you as close to that myth as I can." He pressed down on the accelerator and sped through the desert.

FLASH RANG THE tambourine at the Gold Mine fence, and a black-and-tan dog wandered out from behind the parked van. "That's not the same dog as before," he said. The dog was scrawny and missing patches of fur. Three more dogs came running behind it, barking.

"Something's not right," Flash said.

Beatrix kicked some stones loose from the dirt. "Here," she said. "Load up your pockets, just in case. Frida?" she called out. Then again. When it was clear she wasn't there, Beatrix said, "I don't think we brought wire cutters."

"I don't think Frida would appreciate you cutting through her fence," Flash said, rubbing his hands together.

"Um, I think Frida would be okay with it if she knew it was for a good cause."

"*The Red Raven*?" Dragon said. "That's your cause?"

Beatrix blinked. "Yes. It is," she said. She wasn't exactly sure when she'd become so fervent a champion of a radio drama, but right now it was all that seemed to matter. "Problem?"

"Nope," Dragon said. "I think it's a good—"

A shout interrupted him, and a figure crested the top of the hill on the other side of the fence. A boy in a black balaclava, holding a machete.

Another kid appeared, and then another, until there were nearly a dozen kids at the top of the hill—many in balaclavas—sticks and chains at their sides. Beatrix wondered what Subcomandante Marcos would say to that. Pilfering idiots, she thought.

"No trespassing!" one of them shouted.

"Where is Frida?" Beatrix called out.

"She's not here anymore," said the kid with the machete, now making his way down the hill, the others following.

"What do you mean, she's not here?" Beatrix said, starting to panic.

The kids stopped some ten to twelve feet away from the fence and held their ground. Their clothes were filthy and torn. One was barefoot. Another wore flip-flops. They looked like inexperienced child soldiers—unyielding, lost, and too young to be holding weapons of any kind.

"She's gone," the leader said. He was scrawny with loose, filthy jeans. Even his fingerless gloves seemed too big. His brown eyes squinted through the holes of the face mask. "No longer with us."

"Oh good God," Beatrix whispered, feeling her knees give out. She scanned the crew in front of her. They were so wretchedly dirty, so young, and so angry.

The leader boy stepped forward. "The Gold Mine is closed for business. Permanently. Now get the hell out of here if you don't want any trouble."

"We need something here," Beatrix said, remembering their mission. "Would you consider selling us something?"

The boy shook his head. "I said, we're closed for business."

"Beatrix, come on," Flash said. "Let's just go."

"We're just going to let them scare us off?" she said. She turned back to the fence. "Shame on you! Big fucking shame on you."

"Easy does it, Beatrix. We're not going to let them get away with it," Flash said, pulling her away from the fence.

"What are we going to do?" Beatrix said, defeated.

"You know exactly what we're going do," Flash said.

"What?"

"We're gonna organize."

Charlie was waiting for them at home on the front porch. His hands were on his forehead, and he looked distressed. "Frida was just here. She said T-Rize took over the Mine. Did you see them?"

"Frida's okay? Thank God," Beatrix said.

"Yes," Charlie said. "She said get a team of PBB riders together. We're going to go reclaim the Gold Mine."

"Good thing we have a secret weapon," Dragon said.

"What's that?" Charlie asked.

"You," Flash said.

Charlie ran his hand through his disheveled hair and grimaced. "Really?"

"Really," Beatrix said. "Because at the moment the Red Raven is tied up."

"Here's where you channel your own superhero," Flash said.

"You got this," Dragon said, patting Charlie on the back.

One night in late October, the tickle lodged itself so stubbornly in Rosie's throat that she could not sleep. In the moments between coughs, she lay staring at the God's eye, which she had left up defiantly. She leaned over the edge of her bunk and peered down at her abuela, who looked angelic, lying still.

She finally slept, waking at dawn to the sound of knocking. A voice from outside called out, "It's time. It's time."

Rosie slid down under the covers.

"Come, Rosie," her abuela said. "Now."

Rosie didn't move for a few moments, but then the cough came and she could not suppress it.

"Rosie, mi hijita, it's time."

The tickle violent in her throat, Rosie grabbed a bottle of tincture and tucked it in her pocket. She and her abuela walked out of the tent and met dozens of others wrapped in coats and blankets already moving along the path.

The air was damp and smelled of wet earth. A team of men in white led them along a narrow trail flanking the river, then through the grasslands, until the sun reached across the landscape, hitting them in the eyes. As they reached a slope of naked trees and began to ascend, some people removed sweaters and jackets, tying them around their waists or simply dropping them to the ground. Rosie kept her layers on, unable to warm up her hands even inside her mittens. She walked slowly and reluctantly.

They reached a small clearing, and Jonathan Blue appeared. His voice was as clear as ever. "This is the morning. It is here. Thank you for your patience. Bless the blue sky. Bless all of you."

Rosie trembled, her hands deep in the pockets of her jacket.

"Today is the day, my friends. Today is the day you become whole. Feel your feet on the ground. Feel that support. Root. And by rooting, we will rise. This is not a renunciation. This is a joining. This is becoming a seed. In darkness, we find the light. Everything is now possible." Jonathan Blue held his arms up to the blue.

Rosie felt a tingling sensation all the way down to her feet. "Abuela," she said, and shook her grandmother's arm.

The men in white passed around something that looked like a Hershey's Kiss, only flatter. She guessed that it didn't taste anything remotely like chocolate. "Partake," one of the men whispered as he held out the tablet to Rosie. She looked around for Jesús and spotted his cowboy hat on the other side of the group.

Her abuela ate the tablet right away, nodding for Rosie to eat, too. Rosie put the not-chocolate in her mouth. It was bitter and waxy, like resin from a tree. She coughed again, but her abuela, so used to the sound, didn't seem to notice. Rosie spit the tablet into her hand.

They were ushered back into the woods and along a thin trail. Rosie wanted to try to catch up with Jesús, but she'd have to get around a man in a white smock. The trail turned rocky and ascended again. She turned around and saw hundreds of people behind her, and still more coming up the path—a slow, dazed herd. Everyone from the tents. All of them.

"Abuela, look." But Abuela, ever determined, was focused only on her feet, on moving them up the hill.

“Abuela,” she said, “we must stop,” but her grandmother didn’t hear her. Rosie pinched her abuela’s arm hard, trying to startle her out of her trance.

“Abuela,” Rosie said again, tears running down her cheeks. But as she turned, Abuela looked weird. She was staring right at Rosie, but her eyes didn’t seem to focus. People staggered past, and her abuela fell into step behind them. Rosie stopped. Her grandmother’s bun disappeared into the ranks of people ahead, one gray knot among the black, the blonde, and the red.

Two men in white stood talking, pointing at Rosie, and she willed her legs to move. Hoisting her skirt, she scrambled off the trail and into the trees. She heard shouts and footsteps behind her, and in her haste, she tripped and fell. She turned around and saw a man in white, and just beyond him another figure, the top of his cowboy hat catching the light.

“Jesús!” she cried.

The man in white stopped and turned around. She had given Jesús away. He waved his arms. *“Rosie, no pares. ¡Vete, vete!”* Rosie, don’t stop. Go, go! *“¡No comas nada de lo que te dan!”* Don’t eat anything they give you!

Rosie started back toward him, but she saw his hat fall to the ground, and then his body. The man in white yanked him up by the arm and pulled him back into the line. “Rosie, go!” Jesús called out.

Rosie ran, and she kept running until she could not run anymore. She stopped to catch her breath, her sides heaving. She listened to the morning, the intermittent *chit-chit* of birdsong. She pressed her hand to her pocket, where the small bottle of her abuela’s tincture was nestled, and felt a small relief.

Into the quiet came Jonathan Blue’s voice, lifting above everything, its deep, clear tone like a red flare in the sky. But the sound was far away, somehow echoing toward her. She crept from the trees to a small outcropping. She flattened herself to a rock and peered down at the edge of another steep ridge, where the crowd was gathering. Far below it, she could make out the shine of the river and, along its banks, mounds of overturned soft brown earth, freshly dug. She remembered Jesús's blisters. RiverNorth, Mary had said. Garden beds? Those were not garden beds. Rosie sucked in her breath.

"Our greatest goal, now realized," Jonathan Blue proclaimed. "What does the spirit want to do? Rise, rise, rise!"

The people in the distance were small, like little birds. So many of them. An ocean of birds. A continent of birds. They fluttered to the rim of the ridge, and then they moved beyond the rim, and then they disappeared. Rosie could not believe what she was seeing. Birds swooping, birds plunging, birds without wings.

Rosie blinked and blinked again, and felt as though all the blood were draining from her body. She looked to the sky to see if maybe some of the people had been chosen and were actually rising. She wanted to see them up there, the bird-people. She wanted everything Jonathan Blue had promised to be true. And maybe it was. Maybe everything he promised was over that ledge, and they found it as the ground gave way beneath them. Maybe they fell into something soft. Like a cloud. Or the sea. But Rosie couldn't see that. All she saw was the dropping of the birds and the blue of the bare sky. A terrible, empty blue.

A sound rose into Rosie's throat where the tickle had been. As she opened her mouth to let it out, one last figure in the distance came into view. It was Jonathan Blue, standing at the edge, his giant wing-like arms reaching out from his sides, as if proclaiming victory.

You cruel beast, Rosie wanted to shout, but no words came out. She put her hands to her throat to coax them. Nothing. She clawed at her neck and pushed so hard her tongue flailed in her silent mouth, and then there was a cry. A shrill whinny that descended into a low cello-like thrum. It emptied from inside her with force and rancor, but it did not seem to reach him. He who stood motionless, arms lifted, head lowered. Rosie kept her eyes on him, seething, until the sound inside her dried up and until, without warning, Blue himself stepped from the ridge and went over.

CHAPTER 17

CARSON WOKE ABRUPTLY as the truck made a sharp swerve, knocking his head against the window. He was fairly certain he'd heard a thud.

"Coyote, dammit," Felix said, slowing to a stop.

The truck seemed unharmed, but the coyote was folded in half. Blood streaked across the side of its head and oozed onto the macadam.

"Shit," Felix said. He got out of the truck and paced, then stopped and whispered something at the sky.

Carson bent over and scooped up the coyote. Its head dangling over his forearm, the limp creature looked like a fur stole. "Dinner?" he said to Felix.

They put the animal in the back and drove on.

They passed a billboard showing smiling retirees in front of gargantuan homes with green lawns. DESERT ROSE, the sign proclaimed. Marking the entrance was a high metal gate decorated with metal roses.

Felix maneuvered past an empty security booth and drove over the sidewalk into the neighborhood, crushing a hedge of dead shrubs on the way.

"The desert roses," Carson said.

"Not anymore," Felix said.

More dead rosebushes along the main road led to a series of cement fountains, dry and bleached white, like bones on the sand. As they coasted down the hill, the fountains gave way to tall palm trees, which cast thin stripes of shade across the pavement.

"This development was never even finished," Felix said as they passed driveways branching off toward empty plots. "But, damn, the houses they did finish are colossal! This must have been a foreclosure jamboree."

"Or a casualty of the energy crisis," Carson said. "How would you have heated or cooled these mansions?"

"Exactly. Looks like everyone flew the coop," Felix said. He looked at Carson. "Where to, sir?"

Carson pointed to a two-story cream-colored house with red trim, a three-car garage, and an expansive lawn of brittle brown grass. "There."

They pulled in and went to the front door. Felix picked the lock with his knife. The house was cavernous and cool, and their footsteps echoed across the white tile floors.

"Built for the wannabe rich and left for the wandering poor," Felix said, waving his hands at the ostentatious details—a glass chandelier overhead, sculpted niches that held art objects, a white marble staircase with an ornate gold-leafed banister. In the center of the wide circular living room was a fireplace surrounded by glossy white bricks.

Carson slid across the floor in his socks and opened the floor-length blinds, which covered a wall of windows and glass doors. The afternoon sun flooded in, nearly blinding them. Outside, an amoeba-shaped swimming pool filled with muddy water took up most of the yard.

"I wouldn't get in there if you paid me," Felix said. "Who knows what kind of disease is lurking in that water. All that bourgeois crud."

Carson remembered Jimmy Weed, the seed collector, how he'd launched himself fearlessly into that similarly murky pool months ago. Where might he be now?

Felix knocked on one of the walls. "Listen to that, would you? Built and bought with paper."

They retrieved the coyote from the truck and laid it out on the front lawn. Carson worked to remove the hide while Felix dug a shallow fire pit with a shovel he had in the back of his truck. They found cardboard and a child's desk in the garage, which they broke down as tinder and piled into the pit. Carson arranged the coyote meat on a screen from the fireplace and set it over the flames.

Cooked, the animal was stringy, lean, and almost sweet. Carson chewed vigorously, feeling virile.

"Not bad," Felix said. "Not so bad at all." He tossed a bone to the lawn. "Happy Halloween, by the way."

Carson had lost track of the days. He held up another piece of meat. "Happy Halloween."

Carson considered his luck. He'd been on the road for over seven months now. And he was still alive. By some miracle of fate, he'd just been catapulted three hundred miles in a single afternoon, thanks to this man and his truck. Could he actually make it all the way to Beatrix? "Sometimes I think I'm just plain nuts," he said. "It's possible she won't even remember me."

They retreated inside. Felix sat on the living room floor, legs straight out in front of him, stretching. Matter-of-factly, he said, "Someone always dies first."

"What?"

"No way around it. Someone dies first. Love equals loss."

Right. Carson knew that as well as anybody.

"There's no such thing as a road without consequence. You can have consequences now or later—it's your choice. But there ain't no getting around loss. And you know what? No one missing thing is any heavier or lighter than any other missing thing. There's no magic scale. We've just gotta be brave."

Gotta be brave, Carson repeated to himself.

"What's she like, this Beatrix?" Felix said. "Is she hot?"

"She's . . ." He paused a moment, thinking. "She's a force. Her mind is always moving. But then she notices something and latches on with a fierce grip. Things the rest of us notice and maybe worry about for a bit but then move past—she digs in. But she's soft, too, a container of compassion."

"Well, then, traveler, you have a lot to be brave for," Felix said. "In Vietnam, whenever I met a guy who didn't have any reason to be brave, I got worried."

"You were in Vietnam? Jesus, Felix, you don't look a day over, what, fifty-five. How old *are* you?"

"Old enough to have been in Vietnam."

"Is that where you lost your eye?"

"No. I gave that away. Someone needed it."

"You gave it away?"

"To a little girl, the daughter of a friend. A dog bit her in the face, and they couldn't repair her eye. Let's just say I wanted to see better what was right in front of me. Don't need stereo vision so much for that. Besides, as we've discussed, the future is problematic."

"And the past is dead," Carson said, smiling.

"Good one," Felix said. "You know what's cool, though? On good days, I don't see just what I see, but what she sees, too." He rolled onto his back and lay flat, his eye open to the ceiling. The bottoms of his feet were calloused and filthy.

"In Vietnam," he said, "there wasn't any time for the past. I met so many guys who were tarnished by their losses, haunted by whatever it was they'd left back home. But there wasn't any room for that over there. You had to pay attention to whatever was right there in front of you. You couldn't let loss get in the way. You just had to be right there, in the middle of all that horror. That's what it took to survive." Felix lifted his head. "That's what it takes to survive anything."

Carson let the words sink in. What had he chosen? The safe thing? Until recently, maybe so. But now?

As SHE WALKED, Rosie kept her eyes focused on the divots in the mud. Dazed and unsure of herself, she took small steps. Above, clouds blanketed the afternoon in gray gloom. If she let her focus wander, she saw piles of feathers, severed wings, tiny bones—small heaps of birds.

She came to the lone tree on the ridge that Jesús had pointed out when they'd arrived at the Center. "A climbing tree," he'd said. She grabbed on to a low branch and pressed her cheek into the bark. She remembered the day they'd stood looking down at the Center, how soft her abuela had seemed, how calm. *Abuela*, she tried to say now, but no sound came out.

She climbed up the tree and looked down into the village—the prayer tent, the kitchen tents, the quarters, the tall white cross, the river snaking its way through the Center. She sat on the limb, holding in a scream.

When everything grew quiet inside her, she climbed down and walked away from the Center, along the dirt road they had driven before arriving. She was grateful for the wool skirt and the down jacket. The midday sun was unobstructed, but the cold stung against her cheeks, and her eyes blurred with tears. *Abuela*, she tried to say again. But there was nothing. Not even a whisper.

She walked for two or three hours. Passing the fields, she could see bodies that looked like elephants, large and stocky. She walked toward one and realized it was a hay bale. She moved deeper into the field and made herself a cocoon of hay. The night was filled with stars, and one of them glinted red. *There it is, Jesús*, she tried to say, but still no sound came.

• • •

FELIX AND CARSON got an early start. "We're gonna risk it?" Felix said, pointing to the Sierras ahead of them.

Carson glanced at the containers in the back of the truck. "Are we low on fuel?"

"Good with fuel. I was thinking snow," Felix said.

Carson looked out at the blue sky. "Not much up there yet, I don't think," he said. "And today's as clear as a bell."

Felix pushed down on the accelerator, and the truck surged forward. As they ascended into the mountains, everything crisped into high-definition—the jagged edges of the peaks, the needles of the pines. Carson felt more hopeful than he had in months.

They drove through a small mountain town where men and women congregated along the sidewalks and boys zigzagged along the streets on BMX bikes. "Look at that cheery train station," Felix said, pointing to the left. "Same yellow as Daisy the truck."

For some reason, the train station made Carson think of June. He felt a warmth in his chest, and he imagined her face, his hand cradling the back of her head.

Within a few miles, however, the warm softness became a cramp in his abdomen. Then came a churning. "Felix, can you pull over?" The cramps intensified, and he darted behind the nearest tree to relieve his bowels.

Maybe the coyote had been a bad idea. He'd never heard of anyone eating coyote meat. Maybe being struck and flattened by a machine on the road somehow harmed the meat, released bad toxins.

Back at the truck, he found the driver's-side door open, but no Felix.

"Over here," Felix called out from the trees on the other side of the road. When he emerged, his hand was on his stomach and he wasn't grinning. "Trick or treat?" he said.

"Trick," Carson said.

They drove another ten minutes, then Felix stopped the truck again. "Can't remember when I had it this bad," he said.

Behind them, the flat desert of Nevada reached out like a memory. A cold wind picked up, and Carson shivered. He pulled out one of his water bottles. "Drink," he said to Felix, who already looked dehydrated, the shape of his skull suddenly more evident behind his features.

Felix bent over and moaned. He stumbled to the back of the truck. "I need to rest for a few," he said, crawling in and curling himself into a ball.

Carson felt his own face, the skin cool, slick with sweat. He turned to look back at the road they'd just traveled: not a soul in sight. Ahead, the trees blurred together into a wobbly mass of green. His intestines cramped again.

Felix shivered in the back of the truck, and Carson covered him with a sleeping bag. He, too, wanted to lie down, but they were vulnerable there in the middle of the road. He climbed into the driver's seat, but as he started the truck, a wave of nausea came. He leaned out the window and dry-heaved. He drove slowly for several miles, following the road upward and higher into the mountains, until he came to a dirt road. He turned onto it and drove until the truck was just out of sight of the highway. Then he lay down on the seat, knees under his chin, and slept.

IN THE BACKYARD on Halcyon, Flash arranged sticks and kindling in the fire circle. As soon as there was a flame, Beatrix held her hands over it to warm them.

"So we just surround them? And then what?" Dragon said. "The T-Rize kids aren't exactly the best diplomats."

"And they have weapons," Frida said.

"We have weapons," Gary said, patting the gun in his holster. He glanced at Beatrix, then stepped toward the fire and stood across from her.

"They're kids," she said.

"Kids are the future," Dragon said. Beatrix couldn't tell if he was being sarcastic or not.

"These are scary kids," Frida said. "They've attacked you and other PBB riders. And now they've taken over a valuable community resource, which also happens to be my home."

Beatrix stared at the gun in Gary's holster. "The T-Rize don't have guns," she said. Did they?

"It's just a matter of time," Gary said.

"So we're just going to throw things off-kilter?" Beatrix said.

"Things are already off-kilter," Frida said.

"It's true," Dragon said. "There is no more equal footing."

Beatrix sat down on the picnic bench, feeling ill. This is what it had come to?

"Look, I'm not going to need to use this," Gary said, putting his hand on his gun. "We just need to surround them and scare them."

"Then capture them," Frida said.

"With what?" Beatrix said. "A big net?"

Flash looked at Gary. "You got a stash of handcuffs or something?"

"Zip ties," Gary said. "Poor man's handcuffs!"

"There are, like, five thousand of them in the garden shed," Flash said. "We can ask Rog and Finn for them."

"And then what?" Beatrix asked.

"We rehabilitate them," Flash said.

Beatrix smirked.

"We'll get the radio parts, Beatrix. Isn't that what you want?"

"Yes," Beatrix said. And she also wanted to cry.

Rosie awoke to darkness, shivering with cold and an ache in her legs. As the sun peered over the horizon, she shook off the hay and started back to the road. Hungry, she pulled out the bottle and took one drop of her abuela's elixir. She wished she'd brought the lip balm, too.

The sound of her sneakers on the pavement offered her a rhythm. She passed two old gas pumps (Gaso and Lina, as Jesús had named them), and inside her head she repeated the corrido they had made up about them, and about the nearby fallow fields the color of her brown eye, and about the cluster of twenty-one mailboxes with no houses nearby.

Rosie walked and walked and gave herself drops of Abuela's tincture. The corrido inside kept playing as the road coursed through woods and then turned and sloped downward. She navigated herself toward the lowering sun, westward.

Before sunset, she heard voices off the road. Following them, she came upon a group of Pilgrims resting in a patch of sun. She stood in the trees watching them, frozen but for the tears streaming down her face.

Eventually, someone noticed her and pointed. A man wearing a long oilcloth coat came to her. "Are you okay?" he asked her. "Are you alone?"

Rosie could barely move. He wrapped his jacket around her and carried her into the clearing. A woman in a red knit hat handed Rosie a bowl filled with something beige. "Chickpeas," the woman said.

Rosie ate, her jaws moving convulsively, like a starving animal's. The woman gave her a round flat disc, like a tortilla, but thicker, along with some kind of dried fruit leather, which was tough but sweet. The man who'd carried her set a jug of water down in front of her.

Rosie drank the water and studied the group. Eight altogether, including two young girls wearing matching sneakers. The girls stared at Rosie expectantly, as if waiting for her to open a book and start reading to them. Rosie watched them turn from little girls into little coyotes, then back into little girls. The adults packed up their belongings, then came to look at Rosie, too.

They were heading toward the Center. Had she been there? What was the road like ahead? Had she seen anyone along the way? How much farther? Rosie understood what they were saying, but she could not make a sound to answer them.

The two little girls were playing a game now, clapping their hands together and reciting a rhyme. One of the girls was missing her front teeth and her words came out with a lisp.

"Mith Mary Mack, Mack, Mack,

All drethed in black, black, black."

Rosie tracked their movements, wanting desperately to join their game. She knew the words and the hand motions, though she hadn't played that game in years.

Rosie closed her eyes and saw only the color blue.

"Tell us," said the woman in the red hat, resting her hand on Rosie's shoulder.

Rosie opened her mouth, and a note came. And then another. Attached to the notes were words, which formed slowly on Rosie's tongue, then unfurled and flew out, one after the other, picking up speed until they became a running rhythm, curling and lifting. She sang of the long unpaved road, the round bales of hay, the climbing tree and the valley below, shining promises, the RiverNorth, God duties, fool's gold and fool's chocolate, the white sculptures and the white wingspan, the voice that never wavered, the deep roots and the digging, the birds and the blue sky. Oh, the birds below the blue that were not birds at all, but her abuela and her friend Jesús and all the others, all of them believers who had believed all the way to their toes, but because their toes were not talons and their arms were not wings and the wind was not right and their bones were not light but heavy, they could not rise.

When she finished singing, Rosie closed her mouth, bowed her head, and cried.

The little girls did not blink. The woman in the red hat cried, too. The man who'd given her water knocked his two fists together, his eyes wide and worried.

Rosie slipped her arms into the coat draped around her. It was too big and dragged along the ground, but it was warm and it would protect her from wind and rain. She picked up the water bottle and walked away from the clearing and away from the travelers toward the next verse of the song. The sound of her voice echoed behind her, but she herself did not look back.

• • •

Carson's hand was numb from the cold and from the tight grip he had on the branch. If he let go, surely he would plummet to his death. He could no longer feel his body suspended below him. He tried to swallow, but his throat felt full of knives. Above, branches fanned open, dense with pine needles. Between the limbs, he could see a lacy shroud of stars. He tried to hold on, but he had nothing left. He closed his eyes and let go.

Nothing happened. He looked up again—same tree, same branches, same stars. Inching his hand down, he felt the cold, hard ground against his body. It was not a branch he'd been clinging to but a root. His mind flashed to the coyote, its limp body on the highway, the streaks of blood on its fur.

A voice spoke. "Everything you need is already right here."

Carson could not see anyone, but he recognized the voice. Jonathan Blue.

"You would like to get up, wouldn't you?"

Carson squinted into the darkness. "Where are you?"

"I am here to help you. From the darkness. All you have to do is listen. Listen and then you can ascend. Simply lift off the ground. You can muscle it, can't you? Just stand up. We'll take care of the rest."

He was hallucinating. "Felix?" he whispered. "Please. I need water."

"Everything you need is right here," Blue said. "You must only get up."

But Carson could not get up. He opened and closed his mouth, like a fish, gasping. "Felix?" he called out weakly. Then, out of desperation, "Blue?"

Silence.

"Hello?" Carson begged.

Fuck Jonathan Blue. What the hell was he doing here anyway? Hadn't they ascended by now? Maybe they were floating above him. Carson imagined it, the skirts of all those women hanging in the sky like stiff silent bells.

•

Some time later, Carson began to crawl. He crawled over the roots and duff and dirt until he came to the road, where he collapsed, panting. "Felix?" he said, staggering to his feet.

In the back of the truck, Felix stirred.

"You okay?" Carson asked.

Felix groaned, and Carson fumbled around in his pack to find another water bottle. The water was so cold he could swallow only a small amount at a time.

"Felix, wake up. You gotta drink."

"Take cover. Take cover here. They're coming."

"Who's coming?"

"My mother said daisies were appropriate flowers. I picked so many daisies for that woman. See, here they all are." Felix moved his hands across the sleeping bag, sifting.

Carson handed him the bottle. "Here, Felix. Please drink." But Felix waved the bottle away.

"I quit drinking twenty years ago, you fool."

"Water, my friend, water." He closed the bottle and set it next to Felix. Then, using all the energy he had left, he pulled out his own sleeping bag and slept in the cab of the truck.

Carson woke damp with sweat. The bottle he'd left for Felix was empty. He searched for another bottle and found it also empty. "Shit," he said. Now they were out of water, and he had no energy to walk or to start the truck and drive. All he could do right then was lie there in the sun. There was nothing left to think or say. He would simply lie there until he rose up into the sky with all the others. Goodbye, Felix. Goodbye, Carson.

After a while, he heard something—a twig snapping, leaves rustling. "Who's there?" If Jonathan Blue had returned, Carson planned to slug him for not helping them. Fucking savior, my ass. He propped himself onto his pack. "Hello?"

A coyote stepped into the light.

"Fuck you," Carson said.

The coyote stood still, staring at him.

"Fuck you," Carson said again. "You're bad news. Felix, our poisoner is here. Thought he'd pay us a visit, see how we were faring."

The animal's fur caught the light, a honey-brown glow. It yawned, then turned away and began to walk. Carson watched it through the front window, prancing along. After about fifty paces, it stopped and looked back at the truck, waiting.

"Well, Jesus Christ, already," Carson mumbled. "I'm coming."

Carson staggered after the coyote, which stopped every few paces as if to wait. Carson moved slowly, focusing on the bushy tail in front of him. Even in his delirium, he knew this was ridiculous. Following a coyote? The coyote turned off the road, hopping over a fallen log. Carson lumbered after it.

It took him a few moments to adjust to the darkness of the dense woods. He reached for the trunk of a ponderosa pine and leaned into it, catching his breath. The familiar bark, patterned like puzzle pieces, was an auburn red, the same as Beatrix's hair. He inhaled. Butterscotch. When he looked up again, the coyote had vanished, but there, just one hundred yards in front of him, was a cabin.

"Sweet Jesus," Carson said, hobbling his way toward the structure. An old forest-ranger station, it had a woodstove, a small table, two wooden chairs, and a cot. The cabinets held two unlabeled cans. There was a two-burner stove and a propane tank, which Carson lifted and guessed to be three-quarters full. An aluminum bucket and a five-gallon plastic container for water sat empty on the floor.

He stepped back outside and mustered a whistle. Where was that coyote? The trees made a curtain of green and brown, making it hard to see anything. He leaned against the porch post and closed his eyes for a moment.

The sound came soft and steady, like wind—a swish, with splashes and gurgles. Water. Carson followed a narrow path behind the cabin. As he descended, the sound grew louder, the air cooler.

The creek was copious and unleashed. It came and came, not stopping for rocks or roots. Carson fell to his knees, gathered it in his hands and drank. He was risking it—there could there be giardia. But his water filter had stopped working miles and miles ago. What did he have to lose? He fetched the bucket from the cabin, filled it, and carried it to the truck.

The day had warmed with the sun, but Felix was still inside his sleeping bag.

"Felix," Carson said, crawling into the back of the truck. "I have water. There's water. There's a cabin. We're gonna be okay, Felix."

Felix did not stir.

"Felix." Carson placed his hand on Felix's shoulder. "Felix?" No response. He pulled, and Felix flopped awkwardly to his back, the patch intact and his good eye closed. His mouth was open, and Carson reached out to feel for his breath. "Oh dear God." He lay his hand on Felix's neck.

Carson's throat tightened, and his saliva turned thin. He'd been gone too long. He'd failed his friend. He leaned over the edge of the truck and vomited up all the water.

CHAPTER 18

FOR DAYS, THE landscape spread out in dry hills of tan, pink, and yellow on either side of the road, and few trees or structures to provide respite from the sun. She had passed through here before on the way to the Center, but everything looked different to Rosie now, bleaker and more blinding. She wished for the sunglasses.

A car was stopped in the middle of the road, and Rosie approached warily, willing to risk it for a ride. A young couple was charging a car battery with a solar panel. The woman was tall, with messy blond hair. She wore glasses that made her look smart. The man had a patchy beard.

The woman looked at Rosie and didn't blink. "Aren't you a sight? Where are you coming from?"

Rosie closed her eyes, silent.

The woman said, "Well, then, where are you going?"

Rosie looked up but couldn't form a sound.

"Honey," the woman said to the man. "Give her some of the venison stew."

The man dished out a bowl and handed it to Rosie, and she sat down in the dust and gulped down the stew.

"Help me untie this thing," the man said, fiddling with something on the roof of the car. The woman reached up and loosened a cable.

"Where do you think she's going?" the man said, loud enough for Rosie to hear.

"I don't know," the woman said, annoyed. "She came from that way, so my guess is she's going our way." As she said this, she made exaggerated arm gestures, pointing east, then west, like a cheerleader.

The corrido was rising inside Rosie, and she needed to let it out, so before they could speculate any more, she stood and opened her mouth and sang for them.

The man squinted at her, as if not believing her words, and the woman's face scrunched up like a raisin. But as Rosie continued, they softened, listening attentively.

"Oh. God," the man said.

"You poor thing," the woman said, but she didn't reach out a hand for Rosie's shoulder or anything. "So it's over? All the radio broadcasts?"

"Jonathan Blue. What a scam artist," the man said.

"Try mass murderer," the woman said. Her words seemed to hang in the air, little three-dimensional objects that Rosie stared at and tried to decipher.

"Do you want something else?" the man asked her.

Rosie shook her head, lying. She felt as if she'd just run for miles and miles from the thing that kept chasing her. She wanted someone's arms around her.

After the battery was charged, the man laid the panel across the roof of the little car and invited Rosie to get in. The interior smelled foul, a mix of sardines and lemon-scented cleaning detergent. It was so strong that Rosie kept her hand cupped over her nose for the first few miles.

The couple carried on a conversation. "Remember that artist friend of yours who made big sculptures out of ice?" the man said. "I wonder what happened to him?"

"Climate change," the woman said.

Rosie sat folded up in the back seat, looking out the window, trying not to inhale the smell. Outside, mounds of rock made chunky caramel-colored mountains, and a river swerved toward the highway, its silver surface shining through the tangled green along its banks. Eventually, she slept.

When she woke, they were at a rest stop, and it was nearly dark. A few hundred yards away were two cement buildings and, between them, a row of vending machines, dark and empty. The couple was setting up a tent. "Not safe to drive through the night," the man said.

"You can sleep in the car," the woman said. "I wouldn't go in the restroom if I were you, though. They're wretched."

Rosie found a place to pee in the dirt.

In the morning, they drove into the sunrise. Mountains appeared in the distance, and Rosie was sure they were the Sierras. Smelly car and all, maybe this couple would drive over them. Please, oh please.

But when landscape turned from desert to defunct gas stations, chiropractic offices, and pallid casinos, the neon hushed and dark, the man slowed down the car and said, "This is as far as we go." He stopped next to a park, where servers were dishing out food to a long line of people who looked as disheveled and desperate as Rosie.

"You can find some help here," the woman said, swiveling around and peering at Rosie from over the top of her glasses. She seemed relieved to be getting rid of her—the sullen teenager in the back.

"They take care of homeless people here," the man said. "They'll even give you a tent."

Before the car pulled away, Rosie caught a glimpse of herself in the car window. The long coat made her look a little Goth, dangerous even. Which seemed like a good thing.

She made her way into the camp and got in the food line behind a woman wearing a tattered red dress. A man in a wool poncho handed Rosie a plate of potatoes, mushy carrots, chicken, and a hard roll.

"Better than Denny's," the woman in red said, then joined a group at the base of a tree, eating.

A cinnamon-colored dog approached Rosie, sniffing. Rosie scooped a few fingerfuls of potato from her plate and plopped it on the ground. The dog lapped them up. The food was bland, but Rosie ate it all and let the dog lick the plate. The dog rested its head in her lap, and Rosie petted it in long strokes. She began to sing quietly, only for the dog to hear.

But the people gathered, too. Looking up, Rosie saw how their mouths fell open when they heard the words. When she was finished, they called out questions, but the woman in the red dress came and gathered Rosie in and shushed them. After a while, the dog got up and trotted away, looking for more food, and then Rosie, too, felt like she needed to walk.

WHEN THE PBB got to the Gold Mine, the dogs were waiting for them. The same hungry, frightened dogs as before, only more of them now—skinny, mangy, barking dogs, baring teeth.

The riders tossed stale bread, bones, and apple cores to the animals as Flash cut an opening in the fence and climbed through. A few stayed on guard at the entrance while Beatrix, Dragon, Gary, and Frida followed Flash in and made their way toward the center of the dump.

As they crested the hill, Beatrix could see the Gold Mine staff quarters at the eastern edge of the dump—homes craftily made from shipping pallets, scrap metal, barrels, and recycled furniture. Bikes were parked there, and a few T-Rize kids wandered in and out of the structures.

"For fuck's sake, they're in my house!" Frida said.

"Not for long," Gary said.

"Where's the stuff we need?" Beatrix asked.

Frida pointed to a slab of concrete several hundred feet away from the residences. "We consolidated everything from the service cars and fire trucks over there," she said.

They watched Charlie make his way to the center. He'd find Diego and he'd say he wanted back in, that it was too boring on the outside. "He'll believe me. Trust me," Charlie had said. He'd taken a set of playing cards with him. "Crazy Eights. They all love to play that."

At the residence area, two boys kicked a soccer ball back and forth. The kids gathered around Charlie, watching him shuffle cards. Once their game was underway, Beatrix, Gary, and Frida headed down the hill. Dragon, Flash, and the others came in from the other side.

The group was young, all under age twelve, it seemed, unarmed and innocent. "These are the babies," Beatrix whispered. "Where are the rest of them?"

When they realized they were surrounded, two bony girls grabbed on to each other, and another boy hid inside an oversized pullover. A boy with a Mohawk let out a loud warning whistle.

"Who are they? What do they want?" asked one of the girls, latching on to Charlie's arm.

Charlie feigned anger at the PBB. "What are you doing here? You're trespassing."

"Wrong," Frida said. "We have come to get our homes back."

"These are our homes now," Charlie said.

Frida held a stoic face. "We're also here for some crates left near the shack last week."

"I don't know what you're talking about," Charlie said. "No one knows anything about any crates, right?"

Oh, for crying out loud, Beatrix thought. Let's just get to it. She slipped off her backpack and pulled out one of the Fair Share chocolate bars. "Hey, kiddos, when was the last time you had something sweet?"

"What is that?" asked the boy in the pullover, his voice high and small.

"That has to be fake," barked the girl in sunglasses, moving closer.

"Not fake," Beatrix said. She tossed a square to Flash, who popped it in his mouth and said, "Mmm!" A dozen pairs of hungry eyes watched him swallow.

"Let me see that," Charlie demanded.

Beatrix lobbed him a square of the chocolate.

"It's real alright," he said, chewing.

"I know where the crates are," said one of the boys.

"I know where they are, too," said another.

"I'm the one who knows," said the girl in sunglasses.

"Give them the chocolate," Charlie said.

Beatrix tossed the bars to the ground, and the kids swarmed to it like pigeons to bread crumbs.

Gary pulled zip ties from his pocket, lunged for Charlie, and pretended to tie his hands together. The children screamed. The girl in sunglasses put her fingers in her mouth and sounded a loud whistle just as Flash got her and tied her arms behind her back.

Beatrix grabbed the boy in the pullover, startled by how thin and delicate his arm was. "I'm sorry," she said, tying his wrists.

"Bitch," the boy said.

"Not that sorry," Beatrix said.

"Let us go!" a skinny girl shouted. She was tied to her friend, so they both fell to the ground. "Ow!"

"If you two just coordinate a little, you'll be fine," Flash said, looking back.

"Hey," one of them called after him. "I recognize your voice. Who are you?"

"No one," Flash said.

"Yes, you are! I know your voice," she said again.

Frida and Dragon pulled out the kids who claimed to know where the crates of car parts were. "Take us there," Frida said. "Now."

A loud cry sounded from the top of the hill, and a dozen or more

T-Rize kids came running toward them—the big kids now, chains and sticks flying behind them like angry snakes.

CARSON LAY IN the cabin on the cot. It smelled of dust and sweat and urine, some of which was his own. Whenever he closed his eyes, he saw Felix's open mouth. *Speak, Felix, speak. Tell me one of your stories. Any story, Felix.* But the mouth never moved.

Outside, a bird squawked. A Steller's jay. Carson remembered now that he'd driven the truck down the dirt road to the cabin. He had tried to move Felix's body but was too weak to lift him. Felix was out there still, his body covered with a sleeping bag. Although Carson felt like this was wrong, he also knew it was how Felix would want it. A traveler, he might prefer to stay above ground. But flies would come, and vultures.

He found matches near the woodstove and lit the propane burner, then set the metal bucket of water on to boil. His stomach had held for a few hours now. He had berries somewhere in his pack. Maybe some rice, too.

He opened the door and looked outside. The day had gone gray and damp. Might it rain? Snow? He had no idea what time of day it was. His heart sank. If it snowed, he was doomed.

He wished with all his heart for the radio. He found the windup flashlight in his pack and set it next to the mattress. The water boiled, and while he waited for it to cool, he slept.

He woke drenched in sweat, his stomach hollow. He stared at the creases where the wood in the wall came together. Above him, a single piece of paper had been tacked into one of the slabs. He got to his feet. On the paper was a xeroxed photograph of a man with a long, wispy beard. John Muir. Below the picture, scrawled by hand: *The world's big and I want to have a good look at it before it gets dark.*

Good advice, Carson thought. He drank some water from the bucket and went outside. The sun twisted the trees into long, serrated shadows. Once, Carson would have welcomed this solitude. But right this moment, the forest seemed wicked. He was stuck here, alone and weak. To make things worse, into this malady had crept a feeling of failure. His destination receded. He felt too weak to go anywhere. He lay back on the cot and slept.

He woke shivering and afraid. What was it Felix had said? You had to pay attention to what was front of you. You just had to face the horror. He looked outside to a cloudy sky. He couldn't hole up here forever. Snow would come.

His stomach growled, a good sign. He rummaged in his pack, found the dried berries, and ate a small handful.

He found his notebook and ripped out a blank page, on which he wrote *S.O.S.* He pulled out the thumbtacks holding John Muir to the wall, then drove the truck down the dirt road to the highway.

At the turnoff, he tacked his sign to a tree. It looked like a puny white square against the immense woods. In the glove box, he found a Sharpie marker—the one Felix's other passengers had used to sign their monikers—and darkened in the letters. He drew a thick arrow pointing toward the cabin. In the truck cab, he found Felix's red-and-white checkered shirt and tied its sleeves around the tree below the sign. It looked like a rigid scarecrow crying for help, but it was something.

The trees in front of him blurred, and he propped a hand against the truck to steady himself. He glanced back at the sign. What if this lured only trouble? He had no strength to fight off bandits now. They'd kill him easily and take the truck. But if no one came and he never got his strength back? Either way, he was as good as gone. It was worth the risk.

Back at the cabin, he drifted in and out of sleep for most of the afternoon. Waking, he would forget where he was until he'd hear the whir of the wind in the trees. Often, he believed there was someone there with him, or nearby in an adjoining room. He would hear a cough, a clink, a shuffle. Sometimes it was Felix. Sometimes June.

A series of high-pitched trills came from outside. Nuthatch, Carson thought. Red-breasted probably. The song amplified the forest into a sprawling wilderness. Yet the bird's immediacy, right there outside, comforted him. He thought of his father, the man who'd taught him how to listen to birds, to pay attention to their calls, to note their markings, to witness their movements to identify them. What did his father know of birds now? Anything? He hoped for his old man's passing, for a quiet slip into the nothing. He hoped the same for himself.

Several minutes later, he realized that someone stood in the doorway, silhouetted against the twilight outside. He recognized the shape, the twisting, turning hair. He sat up, his heart lifted. Beatrix! She was here! How had she found him?

"I'm in the middle of a revolution," Beatrix said. "Everything has changed. How are you faring?"

He wanted to go to her, but his legs were like steel planks. He reached his hand out.

"What are we supposed to do with the bodies?" she asked.

Carson nodded, but didn't know what she was talking about and didn't understand why she wouldn't come to him. He reached for her again.

She did not move from the doorway, and her hand kept moving from her forehead to her neck and back to her forehead, as if she were giving herself a strange blessing. Carson wanted to comfort her, touch her, smell her. But he could not get himself up. What bodies?

June's body? How small it had become after the tea, how hollow. "June?" he had said. But she hadn't answered. It was if she had left the room.

Beatrix was squinting now, cupping her hand over one of her eyes.

"I'm here," Carson said, lifting an arm. He waved. They would work around the bodies, he wanted to say, take care of them, remember them, let them go. The body was temporary. The body was not the life. Surely she knew that, didn't she? No single missing thing was heavier or lighter than any other. There was no magic scale. Felix had said that.

"I'm here," he whispered again. He brought his hand to his right eye. If she couldn't see, he would give her his eye. Like Felix had done. Carson would do that for Beatrix. But when he looked back at the doorway to tell her, she, too, had left the room.

THERE WERE MOMENTS, Beatrix knew, when the only thing to do was accept what was coming at you with resolve. Wit never hurt either. Once, when police fired rubber bullets in her direction at a protest, she'd ducked behind a car: the bullet heading for her belly button had zipped past her ear instead. Another time, when the tear gas came out, she'd quickly pulled from her backpack a mask that Hank had ordered especially for the occasion, and got to work helping others.

She took a deep breath now, planted her feet on the ground, and turned toward the T-Rize children running toward her. They catapulted down the hill, weapons bobbing beside them like awkward extensions of their arms.

"Here comes the future," Flash said.

"So many of them," Beatrix said. "We should have saved some scraps. They are hungry, hungry beasts."

"Hold your ground," Gary said. "Just get them tied up."

"They're armed," Beatrix said, scanning the ground for a stick, a rock, anything. She glanced at Gary's belt, the gun there.

A boy wearing a baseball cap lunged for her. She could smell his sour sweat, his dirty hair. He whipped a chain out. Beatrix dropped to the ground and rolled, and the chain smacked the dirt next to her. The beast had shitty aim. On the third swing, Beatrix felt the anger. She reached out and grasped the chain. The boy yanked, and the chain slid through her grasp, ripping her skin. She switched hands and held tight, trying to ignore the sting.

"I'll drag you," he said. His eyes peered at her from beneath the rim of his cap.

Beatrix recognized him, the dark hair tucked back in a ponytail. "Diego?"

He didn't flinch. The chain stayed taut between them.

A fury pulsed through Beatrix. "You know who I am," she said.

Diego jerked hard on the chain, and Beatrix fell into him. She shoved him hard, knocking him to the ground. He kicked wildly, his boot crashing into her shin.

"You dickhead," someone said. It was Charlie, who'd grabbed hold of the chain. Diego swung and punched Charlie in the chest. Beatrix lunged for Diego as the chain snapped at her head, grazing her hair. She lost her balance and fell, gravel grinding into her hands.

Then there was barking. The dogs had come back.

"Beatrix, get up." Flash was standing above her. She saw muddied blue sneakers running toward her, then lifting off the ground. Flash grabbed the runner, a girl in a jean jacket, and tied her arms.

Where the hell was Gary? Beatrix looked to Flash, who now stood still, looking oddly young and timid. "Help him!" she yelled as Diego lashed Charlie.

Nearby, a dog had clamped on to a PBB rider's pant leg, and a hefty boy was yanking Frida's hair. Beatrix reached for stones on the ground and threw them, hitting the boy in the forehead. He staggered back. Beatrix hurled another rock, this time hitting the dog.

A girl with braids came running and bent over the dog. "Eddie! Oh, Eddie, please be okay."

It was the girl who'd attacked Beatrix on the street a couple of months ago. The girl who'd savored the chocolate.

"Tie her up, Beatrix!" Frida said, tossing zip ties to her, then going to help Charlie.

Beatrix crawled toward the girl, who was whispering into the dog's ear and stroking its coat. The girl looked at Beatrix, then pointed toward the top of the hill, where another group was descending.

Beatrix's heart sank. No. They could not fight off any more kids.

But the people coming were not kids and they were not running. They were adults from the neighborhood, walking briskly, with purpose, their arms full of . . . bags? Trays? Jugs of water?

"Are they bringing food?" the girl asked.

Off to the right, Diego ran toward Flash, something glinting in his hand. Beatrix yelled and picked up a rock from the ground. "He has a knife!" she shouted, just as Diego lunged into Flash.

"No!" Beatrix looked to Gary, who removed the gun from his holster and shot it into the air. And then everything went still and silent.

When sound returned, it came from Flash. A singular high note. He pitched forward, his mouth open, his hands at his abdomen, bleeding. As he fell, the note lowered into a deep, rasping groan.

Beatrix rushed to him, opened his jacket, and pressed her hands into the expanding lake of blood at his belly. "Flash, can you hear me?" She moved Flash's hands to look at the wound, but there was too much blood.

The dog came to Flash, along with the girl with braids, who knelt down and put her hand on Flash's arm. "Find your wings within," she whispered. She looked at Beatrix. "Tell him. It worked for Eddie."

Flash's eyes flickered from the girl to Beatrix, his breath labored and uneven. He shook again, and then a sound came from his throat that was neither cry nor call nor joke nor song. And then there was no sound at all, and something rose up, a wisp of exhale, a thin invisible stream that Beatrix sensed but could not see.

Beatrix felt another hole pierce through her heart.

After a little while, the girl said, "I'm the only one free." She held up her hands. "I'm the only one not tied up."

Beatrix looked around. Indeed, all the other T-Rize kids had been bound with zip ties. Where was Dragon? Frida?

"Is he dead?" the girl asked.

The cavity of darkness expanded in Beatrix's chest. She lowered her head, and the tears fell freely.

Frida and Dragon came across the field, carrying two large crates, which they dropped to the ground when they saw Flash down. "Dear God," Frida said.

"He was from *The Red Raven*, wasn't he?" the girl said, her voice small and strained. "I recognized his voice."

Dragon ran to his fallen friend.

"From the depths of despair and desperation comes the red feather of hope," said the heavy boy, imitating Flash's narrator voice.

"Yeah, that one," the girl said.

"That's not how I pictured him," said the boy.

"Wait, that's the Red Raven?" one of the jean-jacket girls said. "We love the Red Raven."

"Shut up!" said the girl. "Just be quiet, everyone."

Beatrix stood up and walked away from the group, trembling, trying to breathe. She scanned the sky again, longing to see something there. Something moving. A kite. A hawk. Anything besides the white-hot sun.

After a while, one of the neighbors approached her. It was the man with the radio from the park where people gathered to listen. He put his arm beneath her and held her up. "Deep breaths," he said. "Long, steady deep breaths." Then he said, "We went to the station last night to find out what was going on with the show. We came as backup, to support. I'm just sorry we didn't get here sooner."

Two men helped Frida load the cables and wires and radios that had spilled to the ground back into the crates. The rest carried around bottles and baskets and offered water and food—breads and apples and jerky and hard-boiled eggs. And because the children were zip-tied, the adults peeled the eggs and tore bits of the bread and bit off bite-sized pieces of apple, and fed them.

• • •

Rosie walked through a neighborhood that reminded her of her own. Bicyclists moved down carless streets. People stood in line with buckets and bottles at a bicycle-drawn water truck. A group of children bowled with a ball and plastic soda bottles.

On a corner, a small crowd gathered around a man shouting into a bullhorn about "the casinos, empty vessels, liabilities." Nearby, she saw a bicycle with a PBB decal locked to a lamppost. Her stomach jumped. PBB? Here? Someone she knew? She sat down on the sidewalk next to the bike to wait.

A young man wearing a hooded sweatshirt and a red backpack came to unlock the bike. Rosie stood up, her heart quickening.

"Hey," he said, pushing the hood off his head.

Rosie stared at him in silence.

"You got something to say?" he said, wrapping the chain around the seat stem. "What? We gotta play charades?" His eyes bulged, and he stuck out his tongue. She thought of Flash. She smiled.

"Whoa, you have cool eyes. One blue and one brown. Never seen that before."

She looked at him and blinked.

"How about this, then?" he said, pulling a notebook and pen out of his messenger bag and handing it to her.

I need to get over, she wrote, and pointed at the mountains.

"Oh!" he said. "Well, that's not gonna be that easy. Where did you come from?"

She pointed to the mountains.

"How did you get here?"

Foot. Wagon. Van. Car.

"A car? Lucky you. Where you coming from?"

The Center. Rosie dropped the pencil then, her hand trembling.

"No shit. Seriously?"

Rosie clamped her eyes shut, and on the other side of her eyelids, it all played out again—Jesús's hat, Abuela's bun, the chocolate tablet, the men in white, Jonathan Blue's eyes and arms, the bodies falling. All those bodies.

When she opened her eyes, she could not see the young man in front of her as anyone other than Flash, and because she did not know what else to do, she began to cry. Deep, wrenching sobs she hadn't ever heard from herself before. The boy reached out and patted Rosie's back, woodenly but sweetly.

His name was Ralph. He walked her a few blocks to a yellow house with a dried yellow lawn. "My sister, Clare, lives here," he said. "It's kind of"—he opened the front door—"temporary."

The front hallway was padded with dingy carpeting and smelled like old bananas. A tie-dyed tapestry was pinned loosely on the wall. Ralph led Rosie into the living room, where a stick-thin woman lay on the sofa, her stringy blond hair waterfalling over its edge.

"Clare, hi. This is—" He turned to Rosie. "What's your name?"

Rosie paused, then wrote *Rose* on the notebook. A new name to try on.

"This is Rose," Ralph said.

Clare lifted her head and looked out through heavy eyelids.

"Poppy tea," Ralph said. "She's addicted. If she offers you any, don't take it. Shit is evil."

Clare's eyes fluttered back in her head, and her hand flopped against the table. She looked like someone who was once pretty, Rosie thought.

Water bottles lined the floor along one wall. Ralph picked one up and handed it to Rosie. He took her long coat and hung it over a chair in the dining room. He led her to the backyard, where there was a fire pit, and a swimming pool half filled with slimy green water. Three bicycles were stacked against the wall of the house.

Ralph opened up a metal trunk and pulled out some dried apples and a biscuit, which he handed to Rosie. "Supposed to get some meat later tonight," he said.

A man with thick arms and muscular thighs came into the yard.

"Rose, this is Bobby, my sister's boyfriend. Bobby, this is Rose. I'm gonna try to help her find a way to get west, over the mountains, back to her family. Right, Rose?"

Bobby looked kind of like a movie star, maybe from Greece or somewhere, with dark eyes and bushy eyebrows. "You going that far away?" he said.

Rosie nodded and took another bite of apple.

"So I'm gonna go check on some things," Ralph said, standing up and brushing his hands on his pants. "First, I'll see if my friends can help you get where you need to go. Can you ride a bike?"

Rosie nodded.

"Can you hang here till I get back? Bobby, don't give her any of that tea, you hear me?"

Bobby pulled something long, green, and stringy from the pool and slapped it onto the concrete. "I hear you."

Rosie wanted to lie down somewhere and sleep, but she didn't want to go back into the living room with Clare. She hoped Ralph wouldn't be long. She sat down on a plastic chair and stretched her legs out.

She felt Bobby's eyes on her and pulled up her legs, crossing them and folding her arms over them. Bobby looked away and fiddled with a radio. "Let's see what we can get here," he said.

Rosie recoiled from the radio like it might bite her. She covered her ears and wrapped her feet around the legs of the chair.

The initial static gave way to voices. "Have you heard this show?" he said. "It's pretty cool."

Rosie lifted her hands from her ears.

"Hey, Reilly, can you give a hand? We need help with this shelter."

"Sure thing."

"We're doing it the Amish way. Everyone helps everyone raise the roof."

"Happy to help."

"This here's a roof for Wren. Do you know her? Over there. The woman in the blue coat."

Rosie put her hand to her mouth, incredulous. How had they broadcast this far?

"It's about this, the darkness, only things are worse than they are here. Except for this raven. A super-raven," Bobby said, his eyes again moving over her body. "And when he's not a raven, he's just a dude. It's a good show."

I know, thought Rosie. I know all about it. She pulled off her worn sneakers and socks and placed her feet in the pool. The water was cold, but it felt like medicine for her bones. She put her hand to her mouth again, this time to cover up a smile, as Flash's voice said: *"From the depths of despair and desperation comes the red feather of hope. No more despair, no more fear. The wondrous Red Raven is here. Finding the wings within . . .* The Red Raven."

"Girl, you need some new shoes," Bobby said, pointing to Rosie's sneakers, which were nearly worn through at the soles. "Maybe Clare has something to fit you. Wanna go check?"

Rosie hesitated but then followed him inside. She did need better shoes. In the living room, Clare was staring into the flame of a candle. "Check this out, Bobby," she said. "It's like an enchanted forest."

Bobby moved to her quickly and blew the candle out. "Be careful, baby! You're gonna set your hair on fire."

Rosie felt a tickle start in her throat as Bobby led her down the hallway to a bedroom with a big walk-in closet. Shoes covered the carpeting—pumps, knee-high leather boots, Birkenstocks, wedge sandals, and several pairs of sneakers. "Look at these," Bobby said, stepping deeper into the closet.

Rosie reached for a black sneaker with neon-orange laces.

"Come here," Bobby said, suddenly grabbing her arm. He pulled her closer and shoved his lips onto hers.

Rosie pushed him forcefully, kneeing him in the groin. He fell into a shelf of sweaters, and she ran out of the room, down the hallway. She grabbed her coat, a water jug, and a backpack from the table, then hurried out of the house.

She jogged to the end of the block, then stopped. She opened up the backpack and found a solar bike light, a jar of peaches, and a ziplock baggie filled with half a dozen letters. This was the backpack Ralph had been wearing, she realized, wondering why he'd left it behind. She pulled out one of the letters. Addressed to *Grandma B. Neddle*, in a child's handwriting.

Rosie smelled the scent of her own abuela—a blend of cinnamon, wheat flour, and vinegar. The scent was pleasant, but it dizzied her. She put her hands on her cheeks, as if to hold her head steady.

So Ralph was part of the mail service—what was it called?—and these were his letters to deliver. She had to take them back.

She went back to the house and opened the front door quietly. Strange noises came from the living room: grunting and breaths and moans. She tiptoed down the hallway. Bobby was on the sofa now, naked, the muscles in his back flexing as he moved up and down. Clare was underneath him, one of her long legs dangling. Rosie flinched at the sight of them, remembering Diego on top of her in the same way. She scooted quietly along the wall to the dining room and left the letters on the table.

She silently slid open the glass door to the pool and went outside to the bikes. She pulled the first one off the stack. The gate leading outside was padlocked, so she had no choice but to go back through the house.

Only Clare was in the living room now, sprawled out on the sofa, eyes closed. Shit. Where was Bobby? Rosie's heart raced as she wheeled the bike down the hallway to the front door. When she opened it, Bobby was there in only his boxer shorts.

"Where you off to?" he said, as if nothing had happened.

Rosie jumped on the bike and rode down the walkway and down the steps. She sped down the block into the evening dusk.

She rode to the homeless park and rested there for a while. The cinnamon-colored dog found her again and together they curled up beneath Rosie's long coat.

At dawn, Rosie woke, bid farewell to the dog, and rode out of the park, following signs for the interstate. She passed a wagon and a slow-moving car, both traveling east. She came to the on-ramp, inhaled into the cold, and headed toward the mountains.

CHAPTER 19

BEATRIX STRAINED TO remember the feel of Carson's hands on her. Even with the arrival of his letter, he had become blurry. If she didn't see him in person soon, she knew he would dissolve completely.

For now, Flash remained perfectly vivid, outlined in movement. Beatrix saw him plainly: Strumming the guitar. Standing up on his bicycle, pedaling tight figure eights. She could hear his voice, too, its singsong clarity, a long-lingering adolescent trill. *Awesome blossom!*

Rosie was still vivid, too. Her two-toned eyes. Her giggle and sass.

Sitting on the front porch, Beatrix closed her eyes and listened to her own breath. She let the blackness fill her. When she opened her eyes, Gary was coming up the walkway.

"May I join you?" he said.

Beatrix nodded and scooted over.

"The new transmitter is up and running," he said. "All set for tonight's broadcast, the one everyone's been waiting for."

"Bless you," Beatrix said, her eyes welling with tears.

They sat quietly together on the step.

"I'm so sorry," Gary said.

Beatrix put her hand on his. "Flash liked you a lot," she said. "He helped me see you."

"And me, you," Gary said.

At the end of the block, a fleet of bicycles passed, at least five or six of them, gliding fast down the pavement. Beatrix cursed. But then she remembered: most of the T-Rize had disappeared after the Gold Mine.

"Let the rehabilitation begin," Gary said.

"Let's hope," Beatrix said.

"In the meantime, we stay vigilant," Gary said.

Beatrix nodded. The tears came then, and she let them fall. Gary put his arms around her.

After a while, Beatrix said, "It's a different world."

Gary tilted his head to the side. "In many ways, yes. But in some ways, no."

She remembered that he'd seen things she'd never seen, knew things she didn't know. "I was naive," she said.

"No," Gary said. He clasped his fingers around hers. "Just fiercely hopeful. Please don't give up now." He added, "It's going to be a good show tonight."

"It is," Beatrix said, smiling. "Thank you. Thank you so much for believing in it."

"Are you kidding?" he said, getting up to leave. "I love Reilly Crawford. I'd do anything for that guy."

Gary walked away, and another flurry of cyclists swirled by at the end of the block. They moved like insects, tiny and quick, as if skimming across water. Beatrix multiplied them into a parade in her head, a procession of riders against the sky, a moving horizon.

At dusk, Beatrix and Dragon sat together on a bench in the park to listen to the broadcast. "It's what Flash would have wanted," Dragon said.

Beatrix recognized other neighbors—the Irishman and his wife, a woman wearing earmuffs and her grinning partner. A pair of young girls, sisters, held sticks into the fire, with their father looking anxiously on. They commented back and forth about the Red Raven, making the others laugh.

"If I had wings, I'd save everyone here from meanness," one said.

"If I had wings, I'd fly all the way across the ocean," said the other.

Dragon put his arm around Beatrix.

Anita and her husband came then, along with Rog and Finn. "We haven't missed anything yet, right?" Finn said.

As the prologue began, Beatrix thought of the cast huddled in Gary's garage. She squeezed Dragon's hand tightly as the new narrator spoke. One of the T-Rize kids, the one with the voice they'd all heard that day at the Gold Mine. Thelma had made him a deal: he could have Flash's part if he left the gang.

"He's good," Dragon said.

Beatrix nodded. He was good.

They listened as Reilly Crawford the trash collector transformed into the Red Raven superhero and helped the Council of Elders address the issue of the disgruntled teenagers, who'd been sneaking out of the Settlement to illegally trap animals. They listened as the youths formed their own council, a way to have their grievances heard. They listened as the Red Raven took flight for a full view of the Settlement, his red wings dark against the sky. They listened as Reilly Crawford reemerged, awkward but endearing, from his alter ego's triumph. They listened as he nervously approached the confident Wren, and finally mustered the courage to ask her to dine with him. They listened as Wren said yes.

And they listened to the deep, warm song of the violins as the narrator described the first kiss, at the edge of the boneyard, beneath the circling vultures.

"Nothing like a good romance," Finn said when the episode ended.

"A romance with backbone," said a woman.

"And courage," Finn said. "He always seems to know how to do the right thing."

"But, you'll notice, he rarely acts alone," the Irishman said.

"I want to be a raven," one of the young girls said.

Beatrix leaned her head on her dear friend Dragon's shoulder, feeling gratitude amidst the grief.

As THE ROAD inclined, Rosie stood up on the pedals for more power. Sweating through her clothing, she removed the long coat and wound it around the outside of the backpack she'd taken from Ralph. She used trees in the distance as motivating goals. Just get to that one, she told herself. Now that one.

A gray-green river mirrored the road like a steady hissing serpent. Rosie stopped to refill her water bottle. Maybe it was dirty and unsafe, but what other option did she have?

She came to a town tucked into the high slopes, and she remembered having passed through it. Tourist shops no longer open for business, shingled homes with their painted white porches. A handful of people walked the sidewalks. She rode past the yellow train station, where Jesús had imitated a train whistle.

She stopped in front of what once had been a coffee shop and leaned her bike against the window. Two kids rode by on small BMX bikes, then stopped and circled back around. Rosie stiffened.

"Are you one of those riders?" called one of them. He couldn't have been older than twelve. "Are you delivering mail?" he said when she didn't answer.

Rosie shook her head no, and they rode on.

She pressed her forehead into the window of the former coffee shop. On the floor were a dozen or more heads of cabbage, five or six unmarked cans, and clear plastic bags filled with something red. She pushed on the door, and it opened. She entered quietly and grabbed two cabbages and three cans. As she was stuffing them into her backpack, the boys on the bikes appeared again.

"Hey! You're stealing!" one of them said.

Rosie hopped on the bike and pedaled away fast, relieved that they did not come after her. She pushed past the fatigue in her legs with a mixture of remorse and resolve. Yes, she was stealing. And now it occurred to her that she had nothing to open the cans with.

As the sun lowered, the temperature dropped, and Rosie stopped and fished out Ralph's gloves and hat from the backpack. She thought of the night ahead. If she were cold now, she'd be even colder in a few hours. Just a little bit more and she'd stop. She had yet to come to the overturned semitruck, the one the horse cart had had to squeeze around on the way. If it was still there, maybe she could sleep inside it.

Ahead, a figure stood at the side of the road, leaning against a tree. She stiffened. A hitchhiker?

She approached, and the figure remained still. It was not a person, but a tree, with something tied around it. A red-and-white checkered shirt. A dirt road turned off to the right. The wind picked up a loose paper on the ground, held it aloft for a moment, then scuttled it gently toward Rosie's feet. *S.O.S.*

Carson felt as if his bones had melted and his lungs had dissolved, as if the air he breathed could no longer sustain him. If he stood, his body would fold like cloth. His cupped hands could hold neither liquid nor dust. He was a sieve, lying in a cabin in the woods. If he could make it outside, surely the wind would whistle through him. But why should he get up? Everyone he loved was gone, and not a soul in the world knew where he was. Even the crafty coyote had abandoned him.

He was not feeling sorry for himself. He was simply staring truth in the face. There was no need to pretend anymore. No need to walk anymore. He could surrender his body. He was not his body anyway. His body was a ruined container. The man, Carson Waller, would become history, a story no one would tell. A silent history, he thought, closing his eyes. He imagined himself floating in midair or warm water, weightless and untethered. It was not a bad feeling. He did not feel afraid.

He heard a sound outside, leaves shifting. The coyote? Then he heard footsteps on the wooden planks of the porch, and a silhouette appeared in the doorway, a woman in a dress with tousled hair. Not Beatrix.

She moved slowly into the room, covering her mouth and nose. He had probably shat or pissed or vomited, or all three, there in that room, and now someone was finding him, shameful stink pool that he was.

"Hello," he whispered.

The woman jumped and turned back toward the door. The light revealed her to be more girl than woman. Her dress was actually a long coat, and she wore fingerless black gloves. She looked like a character from a bad film about the end times.

"You probably have a rifle inside that coat," Carson muttered.

Because she did not answer him, he was not sure if he had spoken the words aloud or just imagined them. He wanted to tell her to put the metal bucket of water on the stove to boil. Fetching it had nearly killed him this time. But he couldn't muster the words.

She leaned toward him, and as the light reached her face, he saw her eyes. One was blue and one was brown, just like June's old dog. "Roxy," he said, remembering.

Rosie froze, startled. Had he said her name? It sounded like he had, but how would he have known? She must have imagined it.

She covered her mouth and looked down at him. His eyes were open wide, but his body was like a crumpled piece of paper.

The man whispered something, and Rosie bent down to hear him.

"Did you see my sign?" he whispered.

Rosie nodded. And now what was she supposed to do? He was not well, and maybe even contagious. She shuddered and went to the window. The sky was a smoky gray. A wind tilted the trees and brought a spattering of raindrops. The bicycle leaned against the porch where she'd left it, and as much as she wished now she had not turned off the main road, she was grateful not to be riding anymore.

She'd followed the dirt road and seen the truck, and in it, the body that hadn't moved. Of course it hadn't moved. She'd seen the death on him, his eyes sunken, his body siphoned of air. She had assumed he'd been the one who'd made the sign and that she'd been too late.

The rain came down harder now, and Rosie shivered inside her coat. The man on the cot shifted, the sleeping bag swishing. What if she hadn't stopped? He would die. He might still.

Flash had said that you had to do your own good in the world. At this moment, Rosie was quite sure she had not yet done *any* good in the world. For one thing, she was now a thief. Worse, she had abandoned her abuela there on the ridge at her final hour. How could she have done that? Tears spilled from her eyes.

After a while, she heard the man breathing heavy, asleep. She looked at him, the hump of his thin body. He will probably die, she thought, slipping off her backpack.

She brought in an armload of wood from outside and piled more on the porch to keep dry. She arranged the wood in the stove, found some matches, and lit a handful of twigs as kindling. When the flames threatened to die out, she looked for fuel and found a notebook on the table. She tore out some blank sheets, crinkled them up, and added them to the fire.

She rummaged around in the man's pack and found a can opener along with a bag of rice. She put a few handfuls of the rice in a pot of water and set it to boil.

She opened a window. Despite the damp and cold, the place needed some air. In the light, she could see dust and dirt on the floors, along with a drying pool of vomit not far from the man's bed. She summoned her abuela's strength and found a broom in the closet. She swept the floors, shoving the dirt out the door, then found a rag under the sink, wiped up the vomit, and splashed the whole floor with water from a metal bucket.

When she was finished cleaning, she pulled a chair up to the table and sat down. There was a candle there, and she lit it. She stared at the flame as the sky outside went dark. The man stayed asleep, his breath slow and constant. The rain thickened into sleet. She slid the notebook into the small puddle of candlelight and flipped it open to a page of handwriting. It was a letter, addressed to *Beatrix*. Rosie felt something leap inside her chest. Beatrix? She looked at the man lying on the mattress, his arm thrown over his forehead, his skin glossy in the dim light. Beatrix? She began to read.

THE CABIN WAS warm, like a womb, when Carson woke again. The girl had her head down on the table, and her hair was tossed over one of her arms, catching the glimmer of a single candle. He rolled onto his side and saw a small cup of water near him. Had he put it there? Had she? Hearing him stir, the girl lifted her head and came to refill the cup from the bucket. She brought a small glass bottle from the table, opened it, and demonstrated, squeezing a few drops from a dropper in her mouth. She motioned for him to open his mouth. Without saying a word, she blinked. One blue eye, one brown, closing, opening. He opened his mouth, the bitter liquid pooled under his tongue, and he swallowed it. Then she brought him a small bowl and fed him some rice.

AS SOON AS it was light enough to see inside the cabin, Rosie put on her coat and went outside. She had been holding her bladder all night, afraid to go because of the body that lay in the truck nearby. It was stupid. He was dead. But death was sly and crafty—who knew when it might reach for her? She hobbled into the woods, the muscles in her legs stiff and stinging from the miles of pedaling.

"Good morning," the man said when she returned. He was sitting up on the cot.

Rosie gave him a nod, then rubbed her hands together and pressed them into her cheeks.

"Cold out there?" he said.

She nodded.

"What's your name?" he said.

Rosie looked at him, his matted hair, his beard, his warm eyes, his broad forehead. She reached for the notebook, wrote her name at the top of a blank page, and handed it to him.

"Rosie," he said with a small smile. "I'm Carson."

I know, she said inside.

He stood up slowly, the filthy sleeping bag falling to the floor like a sigh. He wore only a thin T-shirt and pale-blue boxer shorts, both crusty and discolored with stains. She flinched and turned away.

"Outhouse," he said.

When he returned, she gave him more drops of the tincture and some more rice. With his can opener she broke into a can of green beans. She also opened the jar she'd found in Ralph's backpack and poured one peach into his bowl and one into hers. They ate, and she smiled at the sweetness.

By MIDMORNING, CARSON felt a little stronger. As though the blood had returned to his veins after a long absence, his bones and muscles could function again, and his mind could think more clearly.

When he asked Rosie about the drops, she wrote: *My grandmother made them from plants.*

"A magic potion," he said. "I feel so much better. Thank you for feeding me."

Rosie nodded.

"You saw my sign?" he asked again.

She nodded.

"Coming from the east or west?"

East, she wrote.

"On a bicycle?"

She nodded.

"And where are you going?"

Home.

He wanted to know more, but he knew to be patient. Girls her age were reserved, particularly with men old enough to be their fathers. Trust had to be earned. His students, the brightest at least, had always withheld at first. He'd be consistent and kind and deliberate, and then, in time, they'd come forth. Whoever she was, this girl was resilient and bright. She was entitled to her privacy. She had followed the road and found the cabin, she had cleaned the floor, she had given him medicine.

Rosie made the trip to the creek with the bucket. The air was cold, but the sun came through a clearing above, and she took off her coat and leaned up against a large boulder, letting the warmth soak into her skin. There was enough rice in Carson's sack for another pot, which could feed them both for a day or two more, along with the other two cans and the cabbages. But Rosie had a journey ahead of her. She did not know what Carson had planned, but she doubted his truck had any fuel. She had only the bike, and it would be mostly downhill from there. She did not owe him anything.

She returned to the cabin and put the rice on to boil.

That afternoon, Carson steeled himself to deal with Felix's body. There was no shovel to dig a hole with, and he did not have the strength anyway. He gathered rocks and began to arrange them. A circle was what he wanted, something to hold in the body, at least symbolically.

It would have been nice if he could have done this sooner, he thought. Before the girl had come. She'd seen Felix, of course. Maybe she thought he had killed him. Maybe he had.

What was she doing here anyway? A teenaged girl on her own in the mountains? Was she alone? Was she even real? He turned away from the grave and looked back at the cabin. Rosie stood at the window, watching him.

He moved slowly, his body still weak.

WHEN SHE SAW what he was doing, Rosie felt glad. She did not like the idea of a dead body in a truck. After a while she went outside, gathered more stones, and brought them to him.

"I only knew Felix for a few days, though it seemed like we'd been friends for years," Carson said. "He was smart, quick, adventurous. Not naive. Confident."

Rosie stacked large rocks side by side, then placed small stones into crevices. She liked the puzzle-like nature of the work, the pausing, the finding, the filling. Without realizing it, she began to hum the corrido.

THE SOUND SURPRISED Carson. It had been weeks since he had heard any woman's voice at all. Hers was deeper than he'd imagined it would be, and lovely. The melody was bouncy and repetitive but also held notes that were solemn.

When they finished with the grave, Carson looked down at his own body: thin, filthy, and ravaged, but alive. "I need to bathe," he said.

At the creek, he removed his clothes and stepped into the water, so cold it bit him. He splashed himself, and in the splashing, he heard laughter. He whirled around, but the girl was not there. The laugh came again. Beatrix. It was her laugh. His heart lifted, buoyant. He moved to deeper water, dipped himself under, and remained submerged, his head freezing. He would live to hear that laugh again. Whatever it took, he would hear it again.

He went to a large rock and lay down upon it. The sun pierced the trees and poured over his body. *Every day another blessing*, Ayo used to say. He was probably darting through the streets right this moment, greeting people, laughing, holding up just fine.

CARSON RETURNED TO the cabin and suggested Rosie bathe while the sun was still warm. "Go. It's a whole new life. I'll stay here."

Rosie walked downstream a bit, then stripped off her clothing. Gasping, she quickly dunked herself into the stinging cold. She remembered the lake where she and her abuela had bathed on their way to the Center, how her abuela had reached for her on the way into the water, how warm her abuela's hand had been.

AT THE CABIN, Carson was lying on the porch, napping. Rosie stood over him and began her song again, this time with words.

Carson woke and listened to her sing about the women in skirts, and the man with long arms, and the chocolate that wasn't chocolate, and the birds that were not birds. A sharpness coursed throughout his body. Cold? Heat? He couldn't tell. He remembered Marcy, the look in her eyes when she'd asked him to take her with him. He leaned forward onto his knees to steady himself.

WHEN SHE FINISHED singing, Rosie felt empty and numb from the cold and the story. She stood stiffly, her eyes red and frightened.

CARSON REACHED FOR her and held her as the light changed and made the trees grow thicker and dark. He remembered the way Jonathan Blue's eyes had squinted into thin blue lines. He remembered the prairie dog on Blue's lap. He remembered how he'd felt put off and comforted by the preacher all at once. Blue. This complicated man and his "civilization upgrade." And now Rosie's account. The preacher had done himself in. Or had he ascended, after all?

He held Rosie a little longer, and then it seemed like the thing to do was to walk, to put themselves in gentle, steady motion and let the losses inside them shift and move and find a bearable placement. They went to the dirt road, past the truck, their steps slow and synchronized. The breeze hummed through the pines, and every now and then, branches knocked and creaked. They walked the length of the dirt road to the highway, where Felix's shirt still hung.

In the distance, they could see a large, bruise-like cloud. Carson felt a shiver up his legs. As great as Felix's truck, Daisy, was, she did not have four-wheel drive to navigate slippery roads, even if it was all downhill from here. A breeze picked up, lifting Rosie's hair and fanning Felix's shirt against the tree. Carson gestured to the cloud. "When it comes, that will be snow. We need to go soon. We'll put your bike in the truck, okay?"

Rosie nodded.

Once they were inside the truck and moving west down the mountain, Carson told Rosie where he was going and how he'd gotten that far. He told her about Ayo and the railroad and the jungles, and about his trying to capture history right while it was happening so that people could learn from it, so that maybe someday he could teach it. He told her about the people who'd helped him, all that kindness and luck, and about the close calls, and how his time in the cabin was the closest of them all.

They came to an overturned semitruck in the road, and Rosie pointed to a narrow passage. Carson turned off the road, and they bumped through the brush past the semi.

Carson told Rosie he was finally going to see his friend Beatrix, and when he said her name out loud, he felt warmth all over his body. Beatrix was an amazing woman, he told Rosie. She was feisty and intense, not unlike a coyote. He told Rosie that Beatrix's hair was the color of the trunk of the ponderosa pine, and that many times along his journey he'd imagined holding it in his hands again. She was the one who had brought him back to life the first time and had kept him alive over all these miles. "You have that in common with her," he said. "You both saved my life."

He looked over at Rosie and saw that tears were streaming down her face. Oh dear. He'd been so careful with his words. He hadn't told her about his trip to the Center, knowing it might be too much for her. But still had he said something wrong?

Rosie made a small sound. Laughter. Yes. She was laughing. Then she took his notebook and turned to a blank page and wrote the words that told him who she was.

A NEW KIND of world required a new kind of funeral. Word got out easily, thanks to the radio and the PBB riders, many of whom had found a friend in Flash. On the day of the event, they came cycling across the highway, a migration of wheels moving north to the park. They'd built a bicycle out of cardboard and scrap wood, as a memorial. They stood it in the center of the park on a small knoll.

Some of the T-Rize kids were there, too, accompanied by adults. After that day at the Gold Mine, the T-Rize had surrendered. Some of the older kids, Diego among them, had scattered and disappeared. Many more, shaken by Flash's death, had turned in their weapons.

"They need food and clothes," Rog said. "And homes." He and Finn had taken in two kids. A few other neighbors had as well, and together they were encouraging more to do the same.

Anita had invented a way for kids wanting to leave the T-Rize to identify houses where they could stay safely, provided they agreed to some rules. She'd made signs with a Red Raven symbol for people to hang on their front doors.

Now there was talk about starting up a school again, at the library. The tenacious school principal had already rounded up a handful of teachers.

"Flash was a dedicated pedaler," Dragon said, addressing the crowd.

"One of the fastest riders in our Cyclical, he was not only a speedster, but also an excellent mechanic and a true teacher, full of grace and patience. He taught anyone how to ride and how to change a tire, no matter if you were six or sixty-six. Flash was an idea man."

As night fell, Dragon and the other PBB riders lit scraps of paper and kindling underneath the handcrafted memorial bike, and flames engulfed the effigy, smoke rising high into the sky.

"Goodbye, Flash," Beatrix said. "Goodbye, friend."

CHAPTER 20

Rosie and Carson drove into a landscape of rolling hills covered with drying grasses. The day was nearly over, and the sun made the hills look like the flesh of a breathing body. The yellow truck coughed and surged before coming to a halt. Carson tried to start it again, but the engine chugged and quit. "That's it," he said. "End of the road for Miss Daisy."

Rosie recognized the road that snaked off the highway, the sign posted alongside it with a painted picture of a black-and-white cow.

"There's a barn down that road," she said. She paused for a moment, surprised by the sound of her voice, but then continued. "We slept there."

Carson stared at her for a moment, then nodded and began to gather their things. With the black marker from the glove box, he drew his moniker on the side of the truck. He handed the marker to Rosie. "Everyone leaves their signature on Daisy," he said.

Rosie wrote her name, dotting the *i* with flower petals.

Carson took the bike out of the truck, and they wheeled it past the cow sign down a thin road to the barn. He turned back once to look at Daisy, half expecting to see Felix in the driver's seat, pulling away.

In the morning, they woke to a dull drizzle. Carson was grateful for the wool jacket he'd scavenged from a jungle camp. He dug his hands deep into the pockets to warm them, and found seeds in the pocket seams. Apple seeds, probably. He tossed them to the ground, scratching them into the soil with his boot. His friend Jimmy Weed would be proud.

Pushing the bike, they walked west across a wide, empty valley, once a vast array of irrigated agriculture but now a wasteland at the mercy of the rains. Sticky mud crept onto the edges of the road.

They came to a small square of emerald green, where crops rose up from the ground. Carson called out, "Hello," and a farmer wearing a rain jacket and rubber boots walked toward them and sized them up.

"We mean no harm," Carson said. "Just passing through."

The man's hand was large and rough, and when Carson shook it, his own felt weak and inferior. "This is the greenest patch for miles," Carson said.

"We're resurrecting the land by hand," the man said, his beard damp with moisture. "No more mechanization. Cuba did it. We can, too. Started some years back, of course. Oxen don't learn that overnight." He pointed to the other side of the road, where a pair of hefty oxen pulled a plow. A woman in a poncho walked behind them, clucking encouragement.

"With good snowpack, we can divert stream water all spring and summer. Store some there," he said, pointing to three large water tanks at the edge of the field. Then he pointed to a strip of leafy greens. "Beets," he said. "Corn and beans there.

"But it's not for the faint of heart," the farmer said, pointing to a scar on his face. "Marauders," he said. "When they want what you have, they'll try to take it. They'll hurt you for it. Watch yourselves."

Carson nodded. He had been watching himself for months and miles. He was sure Rosie had, too.

The farmer pulled something resembling a white brain out of his wheelbarrow and handed it to Rosie. "You're not a marauder. Have some cauliflower."

"Thank you," Carson said.

"You're almost there, son," the farmer said.

Almost there? They hadn't said where they were going. And "son"? Carson felt more like a father now than a son.

They continued on. When the day warmed up, they pulled apart the cauliflower and ate it—a sweet and crunchy lunch.

"Look," Carson said, pointing to the mountains from where they had come.

Rosie's face lit up. "Snow!"

"I wish you could hear it," Carson said. "It has a quiet hiss and makes everything seem soft."

Watching Rosie's delight, Carson felt something he had not felt for a long time: Joy?

He could summon sorrow easily, could feel its weight inside him. He'd lost the past, his wife, his work, his home, the city, a friend. A world had died. But not everything had gone with it. Wasn't this the nature of grief? That within its darkness lay the strange shape of possibility? That somehow a slant light could come through the open windows of absence and clarify the most important and beautiful things?

He considered the miles he'd traveled. Persistence was indeed a kind of faith, he thought. He remembered the Pilgrims, picturing the cliff-side in Rosie's song. Had they been given the chance to discover that faith?

He put his hands to his face and thought again of Beatrix. She did not know this beard. She did not know his gaunt ribs, the now-visible knobs of his spine. But she knew Rosie. And now he knew Rosie, too, and if there was ever a sign from the universe or God or fate, or whoever dealt the cards or threw the chips to signal that he was on the right path, Rosie was it.

Late in the day, they came into a residential neighborhood. Carson knew they were close, because Rosie began to show signs of anticipation, nodding and bouncing. His heart quickened, and he clenched his hands into fists to calm his nerves. A bicyclist passed them. And then another. Rosie peered at each of them, as if searching for someone she knew.

The streets and houses were as he imagined them, tree-lined, sunny—though tired and altered, as everywhere. Now and then, windows were broken or boarded-up. Overgrown weeds swallowed walkways and porch steps. Trash flittered down the street gutter. But there, a door was open, and a man inside stood on a ladder, hammering. A woman stacked jars in the back of a bike trailer. There, four young girls played jump rope, their rhymes familiar and new all at once. There, a garden growing: broccoli, chard, carrots. Here were houses that were still homes, warm and operative and inviting.

Small signs had been posted on porch columns or in the front windows of some of the homes—sky-blue squares with something red in the center.

"Ravens," Rosie said, smiling. "They're red ravens!"

Carson turned up one walkway to look more closely.

An older man wearing suspenders opened the front door. "Can I help you?" He glanced at Rosie. "Does she need help?"

"We're fine," Carson said. "What is that?"

"The Red Raven," the man said emphatically, as if Carson should have known. "It means help is here for the kids."

"From the show?" Rosie said.

"Yes," the man said.

Rosie turned to Carson and said, "It's a radio show that Beatrix and my other friends started."

Carson smiled and nodded.

Rosie moved on, pushing the bike. Above, a flock of pigeons lifted off from a telephone wire. The birds spiraled into the air and flew together, making a loop in the sky before landing again.

"Rosie, watch," Carson said. The pigeons rose up again, this time flying in a different direction, but still together, their wings pulsing quickly as they circled and landed on the wire. Carson loved this circle dance that pigeons did. It cost them to fly that way; they had to flap their wings much faster to keep together. But they were safer as a group, and maybe, too, it helped them navigate. Or maybe, it was some kind of love. That's what Beatrix had meant, wasn't it? That day in the gallery so long ago, when they were looking at photos. That's what she'd seen in that cluster of birds, blurry in flight.

They turned onto Halcyon Street.

From Alcyone, the Greek myth of the kingfisher, the bird that nested on the sea during a respite of calm from the storm. Carson took a deep breath. May this street offer me my own respite, he thought.

Rosie felt as though she had a strand of yarn inside her body—one end pulling her down, the other end tugging upward. The downward pull was sorrow: She was coming home without her abuela. They had walked this street together and had slept in the parked car that had been their home, and she would never be on this street, or anywhere, with her abuela again. When she closed her eyes, Rosie could still see the birds falling.

But as they neared the house, she felt the upward tug. She was returning to what remained of her family—Beatrix and Dragon and Flash and Anita and Rog and Finn and everyone else in the neighborhood. Her feet did a little skip on the sidewalk when she imagined seeing Beatrix, who now felt to her like a sister or an aunt, or maybe like a mother. She skipped again and thought that maybe what was happening was the validation of a dream.

Carson kept up with Rosie's stride, feeling feral and full of purpose. Like a coyote. And yet no coyote had as many thoughts as he did. Was Beatrix really here? Would she recognize him? Welcome him? He was no longer the Carson she knew. He was changed. Everything was changed. There was no such thing as going back.

But the past wasn't past at all. He could hear Felix's voice clearly. He could instantly summon June's small, smooth hands. He had been hearing Ayo's advice for thousands of miles. Nothing was dead so long as there was memory, the only kind of history there was.

Beatrix. Her name came to his tongue again, and his stomach jittered. He looked down at the sidewalk, where someone had written in chalk, *Halcyon Radio. It will change your life.* It looked like her handwriting. Everything here looked like Beatrix had touched it.

The house was as she had described it—two stories, a front porch, fading green paint. He looked up to the second-floor windows, his heart ready to jump from his rib cage.

Rosie leaned the bike against the porch and leapt up the stairs just as a woman opened the door and stepped out—unmistakably Beatrix. Carson smiled as he stood absorbing her, his body awakening. He thought for a moment he might be hallucinating, but he glanced down and saw his boots, dusted with dried mud. He moved his toes around, rocked back on his heels. His feet were his reckoning. He was here. She was real.

When she saw Rosie, Beatrix made a funny squeal, which made Rosie laugh out loud. Beatrix hugged her and began to cry, but she was also laughing.

"You came back! You came home!" Beatrix said, her face flushing. She put her hands on Rosie's face, then hugged her. "You came home."

Beatrix saw that Rosie's face had been changed by wherever she had been. She wanted to know everything: Where was Maria del Carmen? Where had they gone? Soon she would have to tell Rosie about Flash, and his death would break her heart, as it had her own. But she didn't want to explain that right now. So she was relieved to see someone else there: a tall, thin man with a beard and a backpack, a stranger who nonetheless kept coming until he got to the bottom step, where he stopped and held out his hands to her.

Rosie was looking at the man and smiling, and then looking at Beatrix, still smiling. The man looked like he needed something. What did he want? Why were his hands empty?

"Beatrix," he said, his voice choked, but with a clear pronunciation of the *x*.

As soon as he spoke, she knew who he was. She knew from the shape of his forehead, from his hands below his jacket sleeves, from his eyes, drinking her in. Light came through the holes in her heart, filling them. "You're here."

CARSON STARTED UP the stairs, but Beatrix came to him instead, erasing the distance that remained between them in three swift steps. Inhaling, he smelled her: soil, sweat, sweetness, as if someone had just peeled an orange. *Every day is a blessing.* He reached for the quarter around her neck, then pressed his palm over her sternum, letting her heart beat into his hand.

All of history, it seemed, had conspired to bring him right here, to this place.

BEATRIX LEANED INTO him, into this moment, this once-impossible moment. She had no idea what came next in this undone world. The future wasn't here yet, but Carson was, and it felt like morning. She slid her hand over his, nodding. Yes and yes and yes and yes.

ACKNOWLEDGMENTS

WRITING THIS NOVEL was the equivalent of a coast-to-coast journey on foot (or maybe several). So many people gave me directions and resources, offered new trajectories, fed and sheltered me, or cheered me on.

Among them were friends who offered encouragement, useful conversation, or both: Lori Adkison, Maribel Alvarez, Jeff Banister, Lisa Bowden, Vicki Brown, Greg Colburn, Hannah Ensor, Katherine Ferrier, Annie Guthrie, Amanda Hamp, Jen Hoefle, Ben Johnson, Yarrow King, Sarge Levy, Jill Lorenzini, Leia Maahs, Michelle Marks, Amanda Morse, Rosie Perera, Paul Reimer, Robin Reineke, Eve Rifkin, Bob Rodriguez, Shuchi Saraswat, Josh Schachter, Barbara Seyda, Aisha Sloan, Kierán Suckling, Kephart Taiz, Suzanne Tershak, TC Tolbert, Lori VanBuggenum, and Robert Woolsey. And friends who read drafts, offered insight, and said, "Keep going": Charlotte Adams, Darcy Alexandra, Beth Alvarado, James Bronzan, Nancy Hand, Laura Markowitz, Mary Martha Miles, Teena Jo

Neal, Kristen Nelson, Ian Johnson, Claudine LoMonaco, Spring Ulmer, Kara Waite, Laura Wexler, and the BAABs book club women. Special gratitude to writer friends Charlie Buck, Shannon Cain, and Frankie Rollins, who helped shape the book into a novel, with both skill and love. Thank you also to Adam Jackaway, for consistent support and for teaching me the true meaning of perseverance.

Thank you to the young people I mentored at Voices, Inc. and in schools throughout Southern Arizona; the neighbors and friends who model how a neighborhood can become both refuge and micro-society, especially Brad Lancaster, Janet K. Miller, Shannon Scott, and David Walker; community organizers I met in coastal Ecuador so many years ago; and dedicated school teachers and principals everywhere, especially Tim Glick, who left us too early. You all are the real-life Rosies and Beatrixes and Carsons.

While purely a work of fiction, this book leaned on what was possible and plausible. I'm grateful to those who answered research questions that helped my characters and plot to develop: Stefano Bloch, Chris Bushman, Carrie Brennan, David Forbes, Simone Gers, Samuel Kolawole, and the wonderfully responsive folks at Prometheus Radio—Jeremy Lansman, Pete Tridish, and Paul Bame. Thank you to the editors and contributors to the November/December 2004 issue of *Adbusters*, which sowed the first seeds of this story. French artist Sophie Calle's "Exquisite Pain" exhibit gave me the notion of icons of grief. Krista Tippet's *On Being* interview with Kevin Kelly on spiritual technologies and Teilhard de Chardin helped me shape some of Jonathan Blue's teachings. Thank you.

Artist residencies gave me generous time, space, beauty, and validation. Thank you to Mesa Refuge, Blue Mountain Center, Djerassi, and the Island Institute / Rasmuson Artist Residency Program in Sitka, Alaska. Thank you to the Tucson Pima Arts Council (now the Arts Foundation of Tucson and Southern Arizona) and the Arizona Commission on the Arts for financial support.

I'm forever grateful to Dara Hyde, who took the book without a real pitch and edited with so much care and faith (and to then intern Hanna Bahedry, who urged her to keep reading). To my editor, Kathy Pories, for saying yes and for polishing all that was there and stripping away all that wasn't needed. To copyeditor Elizabeth Johnson, designer Pete Garceau, and the whole team at Algonquin Books. You all made the process of ushering a book into the world a delight.

My deepest love and gratitude for Eddie Bear, Lalo, and Jazzmin, the most loyal canine companions a writer could ask for. To Julius Martinez, whose superb edits and well-placed tears helped me along the final stretch. To my parents, Fred and Tura, whose bottomless support and steady love meant I never stopped believing the journey was possible. Thank you thank you thank you.

Lastly, thank you to the activists of the world, for following your convictions, showing up, revealing the interconnections, and speaking out for equity, justice, and inclusion—again and again. May the flawed and beautiful experiment of America be re-imagined by your love.